Stroke of
LOVE

The Remingtons, Book Two

Love in Bloom Series

Melissa Foster

ISBN-13: 978-0-9910468-6-7
ISBN-10: 0991046862

STROKE OF LOVE

Cover Design: Natasha Brown

WORLD LITERARY PRESS
PRINTED IN THE UNITED STATES OF AMERICA

A Note to Readers

I come from a family of several artists, so I was really excited to write Sage's story. He's got a heart bigger than the moon, and when he finds Kate, a woman who is equally driven to help others, it's a match made in heaven. Their story has taken us on a romantic journey to Belize, and I hope you enjoy the getaway.

Stroke of Love is the second book of The Remingtons and the eleventh book in the Love in Bloom series. While it may be read as a stand-alone novel, for even more enjoyment, you may want to read the rest of the Love in Bloom novels.

Melissa Foster

To those who reach out and touch the lives of others in a positive, meaningful way

PRAISE FOR MELISSA FOSTER

"Contemporary romance at its hottest. Each Braden sibling left me craving the next. Sensual, sexy, and satisfying, the Braden series is a captivating blend of the dance between lust, love, and life."
—*Bestselling author Keri Nola, LMHC*
(on The Bradens)

"[LOVERS AT HEART] Foster's tale of stubborn yet persistent love takes us on a heartbreaking and soul-searing journey."
—*Reader's Favorite*

"Smart, uplifting, and beautifully layered. I couldn't put it down!"
—*National bestselling author Jane Porter*
(on SISTERS IN LOVE*)*

"Steamy love scenes, emotionally charged drama, and a family-driven story make this the perfect story for any romance reader."
—*Midwest Book Review (on* SISTERS IN BLOOM*)*

"HAVE NO SHAME is a powerful testimony to love and the progressive, logical evolution of social consciousness, with an outcome that readers will find engrossing, unexpected, and ultimately eye-opening."
—*Midwest Book Review*

Chapter One

THICK BRANCHES SCRAPED the sides of the all-wheel-drive passenger van as it ambled along the narrow dirt road that divided the dense, unforgiving jungle. Sage Remington startled as a mass of giant leaves slapped against the grit-covered window. Plumes of dust billowed in their wake, swallowing the road, and Sage wondered if they were really heading toward civilization or away from it. The van keeled to the left, sending Sage and the other passengers flying across their seats until the bus rocked back to center and found its balance. Sage had never experienced anything like the trek to the remote village of Punta Palacia, and as he listened to the other passengers bitch and moan, he turned a deaf ear—and focused his artist's eyes on the verdant jungle boasting some of the most vibrant and interesting hues he'd ever set his eyes on. He'd been living in the concrete jungle of New York City for the past five years and rarely had a chance to venture beyond the streets, offices, and subways. When he'd heard about Artists for International Aid (AIA), a nonprofit organization that brought educational, medical, and environmental programs to newly developing nations, he'd immediately volunteered to be a part of one of their two-week projects.

"This is such bullshit. Belize, my agent said to me." Actress Penelope Price gathered her long blond hair in her hand and pulled it over her shoulder, fanning her face with an exhausted sigh. "Think beautiful beaches and sunshine, she said." After some fancy twisting and poking of a long, gold needlelike thing, she looked as if she was ready for the red carpet—or at least her hair was. The rest of her body—and her legs, which were long enough to wrap around any man's waist twice—glistened with sweat. "My Chanel is ruined!"

Sage shook his head at her Oscar-worthy performance. AIA worked with artists and celebrity volunteers, and as he listened to Penelope bitch, he wondered why she'd even volunteered for the project. He pulled a bandana from the pocket of his cargo shorts and wiped his forehead, which had long ago stopped beading with sweat and succumbed to the drenching wetness caused by the heat and humidity of southern Belize. Despite the sweat-soaked tank top clinging to his body like a second skin and the bitchy prima donnas he was traveling with, he didn't regret his decision.

"Stop your bitching," Clayton Ray snapped. Clayton was a country music star and—from what Sage had witnessed at the airport and during the long flight over—an asshole extraordinaire. "You'll have air-conditioning when we get there."

Sage hid his laugh behind a cough. *AC, my ass.* At least he knew what he was getting into. Apparently, the others hadn't been clued in to the realities of Punta Palacia. Sage was looking forward to the simplistic lifestyle, braving the heat and humidity of the jungle, and maybe, just maybe, figuring out why the hell a man who had enough money to buy half of New York and a career doing what he loved most felt so damn empty inside.

"All I can say is that if there's no air-conditioning, I'm heading back to Belize City. Pronto." Cassidy Bay, a B-list actress, dabbed at her streaked eyeliner. "I can't sleep in this weather, and without sleep, my eyes will be puffy."

Penelope whipped her head around to commiserate. "We can do that? Then why didn't we just stay there?"

Sage had been distracted and rushed when they'd boarded the van at the landing strip, and he had caught only a glimpse of Kate Paletto, the program director for AIA. He was six four and guessed she was about five two and weighed a buck ten soaking wet. He hadn't gotten a good look at her face, but as she led them through to the van, he couldn't help but notice her slim hips and sleek, feminine arms. From his seat in the second row, he could make out her long, silky dark hair, and he had a clear shot of her hand as it gripped the armrest so tightly her knuckles turned white. He wondered if it was from the banter or the bumpy ride.

"No, Penelope. We talked about this, remember?" Luce Palmer, Penelope's public relations specialist, sat in the back of the van. She was known in entertainment circles for being a hard-nosed negotiator and, most notably, for being able to turn around any celebrity's bad reputation. "You're here to rectify the damage you caused to your image. This is two weeks of...hardship to show you care about people other than yourself."

Hardship? Hell, Sage would relish being away from the stress and distraction of New York City. He worked late into most nights on his artwork and rarely even heard the phone when it rang. Maybe being away would help him to pay attention to other, more important things, too, and help him to not get so lost in his work. Spending two weeks in Punta Palacia seemed like the opposite of a hardship to him.

Kate turned in her seat, flashing her vibrant blue eyes. She had dark lashes and the softest-looking skin he'd ever seen. *The face of an angel. Jesus, where did that cliché come from?*

"I still don't see why I couldn't have gone on a vacation someplace else and gotten the same publicity," Penelope said to Luce.

"Because you're here for humanitarian purposes, not a vacation." Kate spoke with the confidence of a seasoned drill sergeant. Her harsh tone contrasted sharply with her soft features, giving her a good-girl, bad-girl vibe that she appeared to be completely oblivious to—and that Sage could not ignore.

Sage had come to Belize with a plan. His artwork commanded six figures, earning him a fine living and drowning him in feelings of unease. He'd always felt a desire to give back to the community, but no matter how much money he gave to charities, or how many hours he volunteered in New York City, he still felt hollow, as if, in the grand scheme of life, nothing he did made a difference. He hoped that experiencing a different type of giving back, in a country that wasn't so gluttonous, might spark a deeper level of fulfillment. And now that he'd smelled the humid jungle air and drank in the passing beauty of the jungle, an idea was coming to him—and a woman wasn't part of the plan. Not even a woman as beautiful and as intriguing as Kate.

A whisper of a thought floated to the forefront of his mind while the others bitched and plotted about their *predicament.* Instead of just donating money, he could paint the local landscape and the people and send those paintings back to New York to be sold. The profits could come back to Punta Palacia. Surely they could use the money, and he couldn't imagine anything being more fulfilling than doing what he loved for a bigger purpose. A few pieces each year could bring significant funds for areas that needed it much more than he did. His pulse kicked up as the idea took hold.

"Well, this is *not* what I signed up for, so we'll just see about this," Penelope snapped.

Cassidy made a *tsk* sound and turned away.

The vehicle was taller and wider than a typical passenger van with a narrow aisle dividing two rows of seats. Kate rose to her feet, clutching a clipboard against her small but perfect breasts. "This is exactly what you signed up for," she said to Penelope.

Clayton's leg stretched across the aisle like he owned it, and he made no attempt to mask his leering. His eyes took a slow, hungry stroll down Kate's body. Sage's muscles twitched. The guy was the epitome of the status-driven celebrities Sage sorely disliked— entitled. Motivated by money and fame, he used people like pawns and stepped on anyone who got in his way with no regard for their feelings.

Kate narrowed her eyes in his direction. "Problem, Mr. Ray?"

Sage was drawn to her confidence, the way she wasn't afraid to challenge Clayton, and he was powerless to turn away. And her sexy little cutoffs weren't helping him any. With his artist's eye, he did a quick sweep of her features, hiding his glance behind his hand as he wiped his brow again. Her deep-set, slightly upturned, smoky blue eyes stopped him cold.

"You too, Mr. Remington?" Kate arched a brow.

Shit. Now he looked as bad as Clayton. *Am I?* He opened his mouth to explain—*I was just checking you out from an artistic standpoint. One quick glance. Jesus, you have the sexiest eyes I've ever seen. Fuck. Never*

5

mind. Luckily, before he could put his foot in his mouth, she spoke.

"Let's get one thing straight. I'm sure this is very different from the harem-filled exotic resorts you're used to, but here at Punta Palacia we have one goal. To help the community. And that does not include any sort of sexual action from me or any other AIA volunteer." She eyed Penelope, whose gaze was burning a path directly to Sage, and Cassidy, who was sizing up Clayton. "What you do among yourselves is your business, but we expect you to carry out your humanitarian efforts with respect for our staff and the community. Got it?"

The silence was deafening. Kate's lips held tight in a don't-mess-with-me line.

"Got it." The words were out of Sage's mouth before he had time to think.

She gave a curt nod.

"Alrighty, then. We'll see where we end up," Clayton said with a heavy Southern drawl.

Kate exchanged a half smile with Luce, as if they were sharing an inside joke. "When we get to the compound, you'll be assigned a cabin. Once situated, we'll meet at the community rec area. The path behind the cabins will lead you to the rec area. Please try to be there within thirty minutes so we can get everyone up to speed as quickly as possible." Kate turned and lowered herself into her seat as the bus took a bumpy turn to the right and came to an abrupt stop.

Despite himself, Sage wondered what Kate would be like if she weren't wrangling self-centered celebrities. As he stole a peek at her profile, he realized that she'd lumped him in with Clayton, and he cringed. They hadn't even arrived yet and already he was on some celebrity shit list in her mind. Or on that damn clipboard.

KATE WAITED IMPATIENTLY while the prima donnas made their way down the dusty steps of the van. She'd been with AIA for almost five years and this was her second assignment out of the country. Each assignment lasted for two years, with an additional three months of training. In a few short weeks it would be over and she'd be flying back home to see her parents. She had misgivings about this assignment coming to an end. Punta Palacia had been her home for just over two years. She'd become close with the children at the school and the community, and she'd been lobbying for the installation of a well in the village. Just thinking about leaving everyone, especially before the decision on the well was made, caused her chest to constrict. Kate was good at a lot of things, but saying goodbye was not one of them.

She held Clayton's stare as he exited the bus. She'd learned early on that holding her ground with entitled celebrities was the only way to keep them in line. They were all the same: cocky, surly when she turned down their sexual advances, and goddamn needy. It would take less than five minutes after they checked out their small cabins for them to stomp back with a demand to leave. Kate had never given too much thought to what it must be like going from a world of having everything at their fingertips to a developing nation such as Belize. She'd grown up traveling with her parents on Peace Corps missions and had been surrounded by families who worked with the Peace Corps her whole life. Once she'd graduated college, she couldn't wait to leave the United States and get on with helping people who really needed it. Lately, though, she'd also longed for something more, although she hadn't been able to put her finger on just what that *more* might be.

"Where to, darlin'?" Clayton flashed his perfectly

capped teeth with a wide smile.

"You're in cabin one. The first cabin you come to." She pointed to the cabin, and when his smile widened, she knew she was in for trouble.

Sweat dripped from beneath Clayton's Stetson. He swiped at it with his forearm. "You don't need to worry about us. We're harmless." He took a step closer.

Kate was hyperaware of Sage standing behind him, his dark eyes narrowed, his jaw clenching.

"Unless, of course, you'd like to try ridin' a stallion." Clayton's smile morphed into a smirk, the left side of his mouth tilting up.

Kate had been propositioned by celebrities before, but that didn't stop her hand from fisting around her pen as she pulled her clipboard to her chest like a shield. As she opened her mouth to tell him what he could do with his offer, Sage stepped from the bus in his sweaty tank top and cargo shorts and cleared his throat loudly.

"Cabin one, Ray." It was clearly a command.

His tattooed arms were solid muscle and so well defined that she had the urge to let her fingers travel their hard ridges. He was built for power, a protector, or...*No.* She wasn't going there. She'd seen too many temporary romances during these assignments to allow herself to be drawn in only to be forgotten after the guy went back home.

Clayton walked away with a swagger, turning back once and tilting his hat at Kate.

She groaned.

"Listen, I'm really sorry for the way I looked at you on the bus."

The command in Sage's voice was gone, replaced with sweet richness, as smooth as melted butter. Kate felt her cheeks flush. *Damn it. What is wrong with me?* She lowered her eyes, steeling herself against the warmth that had found her belly and was slowly traveling lower. She dared a glance at his handsome face. He had a strong chin, and his eyes hovered somewhere between gunmetal blue and indigo. *Shit. Really?* At least he wasn't perfectly manicured like the others. His eyebrows were a little bushy, a peppering of whiskers covered his cheeks, and his clothes looked like they came right off the rack at anyplace *but* a high-end store. Unfortunately, that only made him more appealing.

Focus.

Kate drew in a deep breath and ran her finger down her clipboard. Now she was stuck trying to figure out if he was just playing her—standing up to Clayton and apologizing like he was her savior—or if he was really a nice guy. She decided to ignore the conundrum altogether and focus on her job instead. Focusing on her job didn't require evaluating the motives of celebrities. Her job was safe.

"Remington. Let's see...You're in cabin three." She pointed to a small cabin at the end of the complex.

He nodded silently and walked away with a dejected look on his way-too-handsome face.

Luce stood on the steps of the bus with her arms crossed. "Well, look at you, staring after him like he's a piece of meat. Maybe I'll start calling you Clayton." She stepped from the bus. This was Luce's third trip to Belize. Kate couldn't keep track of all of the celebs she handled PR for, but she was always glad to see her friend.

Kate realized she was not only staring at Sage as he walked away, but more specifically, staring at his perfect ass. She spun around. "What? Just making sure he figured out which cabin was his. They all look the same." *No. They sure as hell don't all look the same.* And she wasn't thinking about the cabins.

"Uh-huh. You stickin' with that story?" Luce's blond hair was clipped at the base of her neck in a low ponytail, and she reeked of bug spray. Luce was always prepared. It was one of the things Kate admired most about her.

Kate smacked Luce's arm with the clipboard. "Why didn't you warn me about those women? You said they were a little highbrow; that's different from—"

"No. No, no, no." Penelope traipsed across the yard, waving her arms and lifting her legs high to avoid the thick grass and the flourish of dust that clung to her legs. "Luce, there is no way I'm staying in that bug-infested sauna." She crossed her lanky arms, rolled her eyes, and huffed a sigh.

Luce glanced at Kate and lifted her palms to the sky. "Sorry, Pen. This is what we've got. It's only two weeks, and—"

"Did you see the screened-in sleeping area?" Kate mustered a peppy voice even though what she really wanted to say was, *The cabins are fine. There are people who have real needs and you're here to help them. Suck it up and let's get going.* "The screen will allow the air in and it'll keep you cooler at night," Kate suggested. "There's a nice shower and bathroom that's all yours. I know it's not what you're used to, but remember, this was once a mahogany logging camp, so think of it like you're reliving a time in history."

"And that's supposed to make me feel better? The bathroom is awful." Penelope let out a loud breath.

Luce put her arm around Penelope and guided her back to the cabin, saying something Kate couldn't hear. Kate checked her watch. In another twenty minutes she'd hold orientation and then hand out the assignments. She'd been looking forward to working with Sage the most. She loved his artwork and she knew how much the children loved art as well, but whatever the hell was going on in her lady parts when he was around had her on high alert. She'd have to build a little higher fence than she was used to.

Who was she kidding? She needed ten feet of barbed wire—to keep herself in.

Chapter Two

SAGE GRABBED A bottle of water from the mini refrigerator in his cozy cabin, which couldn't be more than two hundred square feet including the bathroom and the screened-in sleeping porch. Despite the low ceiling, it was perfect.

He applied bug repellant and left the heavy wooden door open when he went to find the others, leaving just the screen door to keep the bugs out. Coming from the forest, there was a loud sound that resembled a dentist's drill or an electric saw of some sort—high-pitched and constant, and he wondered what it was. He stopped to listen to birds squawking and chirping, the drilling sound, and varying pitches of other indistinguishable jungle sounds. *Can't get that in the Big Apple.*

Each cabin was similar to the next, constructed of wood and concrete with thickly thatched roofs. He took a moment to breathe deeply before finding the path Kate had spoken of. His body had already begun to adjust to the humidity. Back in New York his days were consumed with deadlines, moving as fast as he was able from one thing to the next. Even buying groceries was a lesson in efficiency and crowd maneuverability. He went to bed thinking of his next project, the next gallery opening, the next article he had to prepare for, and he woke up feeling like none of it mattered but not knowing how to break from the life he'd created. It had been way too long since he'd had any time to enjoy being outdoors with nothing but grass and trees as far as the eye could see.

He walked down the narrow path, bordered by fronds and foliage so shiny and brightly colored that they could have been fake. Giant green leaves arced over the path, and smaller stalks and bushes pressed into it. Sage moved them carefully aside, making his way through to the clearing.

Kate stood before the others with her clipboard and a large bottle of water, looking comfortable in her AIA V-neck T-shirt and sneakers, but in her eyes Sage saw a shadow of stress. Penelope and Cassidy had changed into tank tops and shorts, and Clayton wore the same T-shirt and jeans he'd had on earlier. *Hot* was all Sage could think, and not the sexy kind. Jeans, jungles, and humidity didn't make for a comfortable afternoon. Sage had never given much thought to the clothes he wore, choosing comfort over style. Watching Clayton squirm uncomfortably in his thick jeans and Penelope and Cassidy making futile attempts to brush the dirt from their designer shorts, he was glad he'd never drank the haute couture Kool-Aid that was common among people of his economic status.

Kate lifted her chin in his direction. "I was just telling the group what you can expect while you're here. First and foremost, keep the bug repellant handy. We left some in your cabins. After you get your assignments, you'll have a brief meeting with your mentor, and then you can enjoy the town, relax, or grab

14

some food in the mess hall." Kate pointed to a building similar in style to the cabins at the far end of the clearing. "We offer three meals each day, but many of our celebrity guests like to eat at one of the cafés in town. The town is right down that road." She pointed behind her to a stretch of road defined by two dirt ruts with a grassy mound in the center. "The town's quite small but friendly. Besides two small cafés, you'll find an Internet café for those of you who need to be tied to the outside world, and there's a local watering hole, fresh-fruit stand, and other basics. I wouldn't advise drinking too much alcohol in this heat. You can dehydrate fast." Kate pointed to the surrounding jungle. "The jungle is...well, it's a jungle. It can be dangerous and it's easy to lose your way, so I urge you not to venture out alone."

"Should we worry about being stalked by a jaguar or something out here?" Sage asked.

"You have a better chance of seeing a peccary or maybe a tapir," Kate answered without glancing his way. "Oh, and most of the residents speak English when they're talking with us, but you'll notice that they speak Belizean Creole when they speak among themselves. Creole is similar to English. Some people say it sounds like an island or a Jamaican accent. They tend to speak very fast when speaking Creole, and though the words are similar to ours, the meanings are not always the same."

From his seat on the wooden bench, Sage listened to Kate and cataloged her features. He was careful not to look into her eyes. Something in them rendered his mind almost useless, so he slid his gaze lower, hovering at the most adorable dimple in her chin. It wasn't significantly deep, just evident enough to warrant a second glance to be sure of it. His eyes slid down her deliciously lean and feminine arms, to her slim hips and perfectly sculpted legs. *Christ, she's beautiful.* Sage's eyes traveled back up, soaking in her long, dark hair and following it to her thick bangs. He had an urge to brush them aside. As an artist he knew that the most beautiful faces needed nothing at all to camouflage them—not hair, makeup, or sunglasses. Kate had one of those faces.

Sage realized that Kate was looking at the others as she spoke, but her eyes had yet to move in his direction. Had he seemed like that much of a heel when she'd caught him looking at her on the bus? He watched her glance at Clayton, who had practically visually devoured her on the bus. Surely he didn't seem like more of a sleaze than Clayton.

A bug climbed up his leg, pulling him from his thoughts. He swatted at the pest and brought his attention back to Kate as she spoke of the local culture and then went on to advise them of their assignments. She spoke confidently. Her eyes conveyed strength and surety, a don't-mess-with-me quality that could not be misconstrued.

"Penelope and Cassidy, you've been assigned to the community outreach division. Clayton, you're in the elderly outreach project."

"I thought I was here to sing a little, mingle a little. You know," Clayton said as he wiped his face with his arm.

"You can sing and mingle all you want. The idea is that you spend time getting to know the people of Punta Palacia. Music therapy is a good thing for the elderly. I think you'll enjoy your post. Okay, you three will be meeting with Caleb Forman, who will walk you through the duties and expectations of your jobs while you're here."

A tall, thin, twentysomething guy with stringy brown hair and skin far too pale for living in Belize came to Kate's side out of nowhere. Sage realized he must have been standing nearby the whole time, but he'd been so wrapped up in Kate that he hadn't noticed.

"Sage, you'll be working with the local kids on art mentoring."

Sage ran a hand through his sweaty hair, slicking it away from his face. "Will I be working with a teacher? In a school? How does this work?"

For a moment Kate didn't respond. Her eyes slipped his way for a breath, then dropped to her clipboard. She sighed. "You'll be working with me, at the school."

Unable to determine if that was an *aw, shit* sigh or a mildly interested sigh, Sage nodded and tried to quell the stirrings in his stomach. *Great. This is all I need.* To follow around a beautiful woman he could not read. The beautiful part was great, but the inability to read her spelled trouble.

Sage watched the others follow Caleb toward town. Kate was flipping through her clipboard as he approached.

"Why don't you use the calendar on your phone for your schedules?" He nodded at the clipboard, but she never saw it. Her eyes remained trained on her clipboard.

"I need visual stimuli. I tried a smartphone, but I kept forgetting things."

Visual stimuli. Damn, you're about the best visual stimuli I've ever seen. The intensity of his attraction to her was vastly different from how he normally reacted to women. He couldn't remember the last time he'd thought about a woman so much after knowing her for such a short period of time.

"So, it's you and me," he said easily, noticing that up close she was even more petite than she first appeared.

"And about thirty kids." She brushed her hair from her shoulder and finally lifted her eyes to his.

And sucked him right in.

Christ.

Sage cleared his throat, trying to ignore the searing heat that had just gripped him below the waist. "Thirty kids. Great."

"We focus more on education and literacy than art. You know, give them as much of the important stuff as we can before we lose them."

"Lose them?" Sage followed her toward the road.

She nodded and tucked a wayward strand of hair behind her ear. Sage wondered what her silky hair would feel like slipping through his fingers. Then, just as quickly, he reprimanded himself for going there. He was only in Belize for two weeks, and he sure as hell didn't need to feel like more of a heel during that time.

"The kids don't always make it to school or stay in school for the whole day when they do show up. Some are needed at home to help with cooking and other chores, or they work with their fathers in the fields. Even the younger kids have to work for their families to survive. They're up before dawn hauling water from the river and gathering sticks for fires so the women can cook."

She ran her eyes over his face, sending another shudder through him, which he hoped to hell he was able to mask.

"It's nothing like you're used to. These families are lucky to have enough food and water to survive." She upped her pace as they turned down another dirt road, and a long concrete building came into view.

Sage was surprised at her sharp response. "I know things are very different here, Kate. That's why I volunteered, to learn about the culture and try to help as much as I can." He kept his eyes trained on the one-story building, feeling the ping-ponging of her eyes as they bounced from him to the building and back.

She let out a loud, dismissive sigh.

Sage stopped walking. "What is that sigh supposed to mean?"

She didn't slow her stride or glance in his direction. With her eyes locked on the building, she continued walking at a fast clip.

He caught up to her, annoyed with her attitude. "Look, I don't know why you're treating me like this, or who you think I am, but..."

"I know who you are. You're an incredibly talented artist, and we're lucky to have you here to help us." Her tone was friendly, but her determined steps spoke of suppressed frustration.

"Actually," Sage began, "I think I'm the lucky one."

They walked in silence for another minute as they neared the building, and Sage was surprised to realize that the noises that he'd stopped to listen to outside his cabin were present everywhere.

"What's that drilling noise?" he asked.

"Cicadas. You'll hear howler monkeys, cicadas, birds, all sorts of animal noises during the day; then at night the amphibians come out. You'll get used to it."

She reached for the door of the school, but Sage beat her to it and held the heavy wooden door open for her. Kate hesitated, giving him a long, hard stare. Then she walked inside. The air in the small classroom was heavier than outdoors. Three lines of neatly aligned desks filled the small room, and colorful pictures hung on the walls. A dark-skinned man walked into the room, and Kate's face lit up.

"Oscar. What are you still doing here?"

"Just doing a final sweep up for tomorrow. Might be rain on the way." He spoke kindly with a thick Creole accent and nodded at Sage.

Sage felt Kate's eyes on him, and he knew she was watching to see if he was having difficulty understanding Oscar. He smiled in her direction to let her know he was fine.

"This is Sage Remington. He's an artist from the States, here to work with the kids for a couple of weeks." Kate turned to Sage. "Sage, this is Oscar. He's our savior for all things that need fixing."

Sage shook his hand and sized him up. *Strong handshake, late twenties or early thirties, friendly smile.* "Nice to meet you, Oscar."

"You too." His bright white smile reached his eyes. "I've just finished. I'll see you tomorrow?"

"Yes. We'll be here." Kate waited until he left, then continued. "This is one of our classrooms. We have three. We divide the kids up by age: elementary school, middle school, and high school." She spoke in a short, clipped tone. "Some days we have only a few students in each class, and other times we have full classrooms."

Irritation gnawed on Sage's nerves. He wasn't used to being treated as though he were anything other than a nice guy. Kate was definitely treating him as though she needed to be wary of him. He also wasn't used to feeling a rush of heat from nothing more than a woman glancing his way, regardless of how unfriendly she was.

KATE WALKED OUT of the classroom at a quick pace. She had to get away from the electricity that radiated from that fine specimen of a man. *Shit.* She'd made it two years without falling into the arms of any of the men who were just passing through, and now, just weeks away from leaving, her hormones decided to wake up? What was up with that? His tattoos gave him a bad-boy quality that she normally stayed far away from, but she found them way too tempting on him. It was his eyes, though—*Jesus, those gorgeous, contemplative eyes*—that had nearly knocked the wind from her lungs when he'd confronted her. Then, when he'd said he was the lucky one to be there, the sincerity in his eyes *and* his voice had thrown her for a loop. Kate was used to actors who could feign just about anything, from being in the throes of passion to sadness, but an artist? Would he be adept at such manipulations? And the way his voice cracked a little when he'd asked what her sigh meant? No way he faked that. She'd have to cinch that barbed-wire fence a little tighter, because the last thing she needed was to fawn over some guy who would soon be gone. She was too smart to be left pining after what might have been. *Nope. I am not going there.* She'd just have to ignore the masculine, earthy smell that radiated from him, the midnight-blue eyes, and the sexiest smile she'd ever seen.

She showed him the other two classrooms and the small room the staff used for the administrative work. She picked up a drawing from the desk and looked it over, then held it to her chest and smiled.

"Someone special?" he asked.

"Javier. He wants to be an artist." She hung the picture on a corkboard by the desk and they headed out of the building. The less conversation the better.

Sage held the door open for her again.

"Thanks," she said.

He turned and stared at the building.

"I know it's dank and dirty, but with only the rain to clean it off..." She shrugged.

"Actually, I was just thinking about how we could breathe new life into it by painting a mural on this wall. You'd be surprised how color can perk up morale." He rubbed his chin and moved closer, studying the rough texture of the concrete. "We could involve the kids. This could be their project."

Kate tucked her clipboard under her arm and took a sip from her water bottle. "We don't really have funding for that. We barely have enough supplies to carry out—"

"I can take care of it."

She shook her head. *Of course. You're just like all the others.* "That's not always the answer, throwing money at problems."

Sage moved closer to her. "Kate, I'm not throwing money at a problem. I'm offering to lift the spirits of the kids, to allow them to let their creativity flow on a canvas that matters to them."

"I don't know. We have very specific programs that we try to run for them." The sun crawled behind the trees, leaving them in a dusky haze, made darker by the surrounding forest.

"I'm sure you do, but..." He ran his hand through his hair again.

God, you look sexy when you do that. She cringed. She had to stop thinking about him like that.

"Listen, I was thinking as we drove in this afternoon...Another way that I can help bring resources here is to paint the local scenery, capture the spirit of the community, and sell them back in New York; then the funds can be given back to the community, less the cost of shipping the artwork back to the States, of course."

She rolled her eyes. "And less your commission, no doubt. We should start heading back." She turned toward the road, and Sage reached out and touched her arm. Her muscles tensed beneath his fingers. She stared at his big, strong hand. Even after he moved it from her arm, warmth lingered where it had been.

"I'd never take a commission." He stalked off ahead of her.

Kate caught up to him and they walked in silence,

broken only by the sounds of birds chirping, Sage's breathing, and their footsteps on the dry ground. The clearing fell away behind them, and the compound was still too far away to see. They were encased beneath the umbrella of the jungle as it arched over the road. Kate had conflicting messages playing in her head. *He's just like the rest of them, a celebrity to the core. Maybe not. He claimed not to want a commission, and he was thinking of the kids.* She wondered what it might be like to be in his arms, to tether that brooding energy and kiss him. To touch that incredibly muscled chest of his. A flutter snaked its way through Kate's stomach. *Stop it.*

"I'm not sure I follow your thinking about the mural."

His voice brought her back to reality. She cleared her throat. "What do you mean?"

"You're here to help these people, right?"

"Of course."

"Well, I'm offering to help. Why does it matter if I have supplies flown in or if I donate a few thousand dollars and go through a different channel to get it done? There's more red tape if I have to go the donation route. Hell, you know how that works. There's even a chance you'd never see the materials. The funds could be appropriated elsewhere." Sage paused to take a drink of water, and Kate stopped beside him.

"Because a few thousand dollars can do incredible things for them medically, and if it were used for food? Well, you can buy a whole lot of staples for that money." She watched his Adam's apple bob up and down as he drank. He lowered the bottle and licked his lips with an *ahh* that had her stupid stomach fluttering again.

"Then I'll donate twice as much," he said softly.

"That way they have the money they need for medical supplies and food, and I can do a little art project with the children."

"And paint other things so you can send them home and make a living." She tilted her head. *See? I've got your number.*

He laughed, which completely threw her off balance.

"You're laughing at me?"

"Kate." He shook his head. "If I never worked another day in my life, I'd be fine. I don't need to make a living. Besides, everything in life isn't about money. *That's* the problem." He capped his water bottle and walked off in the direction of the compound, leaving Kate staring after him.

She reached the compound as the door to Sage's cabin smacked closed behind him, and Penelope, Cassidy, and Clayton came around the side of Penelope's cabin.

"We're heading into town," Penelope said, with the others in tow.

Boy, are you in for a surprise. She didn't know what they were expecting, but by the actresses short skirts and high heels, she knew it was a far cry from a night out in the tiny town of Punta Palacia, where dressing up meant wearing a skirt once between washes down at the river instead of three times.

"Okay, but please stay together. It's really easy to get lost in the dark. Do you have flashlights?" The women carried tiny purses. There was no way flashlights would fit in them, but she knew better than to push a celebrity to do anything. That would be grounds for a *How dare you try to tell me what to do* diatribe.

"No, but Clayton will protect us." Cassidy looped her arm into Clayton's. Her dark hair had frizzed in the humidity and curled around her face in tight ringlets.

"Well, then, have fun." Still fuming from her conversation with Sage, Kate was in no mood to discuss their stupidity. She stomped to Luce's cabin and knocked on the door.

Luce pulled the door open with a wide smile. "I counted down the minutes after hearing sexy Sage's door slam. It takes a lot to rile that guy."

Kate pushed past her and flopped onto her bed. "What do you mean? Do you know him? I mean, before coming here, did you know him?"

Luce sat beside her. "I live in New York. How can I not know him? The guy's an icon in the art industry, and I happen to love art. I go to all of his gallery showings. He's like Mr. Chill."

"Mr. Chill," Kate repeated. "Great. What does that say about me?"

"Depends. What did you do?" Luce leaned back against the wall and stretched her feet out across the mattress.

The evening air felt ten degrees cooler than the afternoon had, and sitting beside Luce, Kate felt the muscles in her neck relax a little. She missed having a friend to talk to. She and Caleb were the only AIA volunteers in the small community. And Caleb was not very social. She was always glad when Luce came with her clients. They'd met a year and a half ago and had instantly hit it off. They remained in touch with email. Kate felt comfortable with Luce, and she trusted her, which made it easy for Kate to be honest with her.

She rubbed her thumb over the ridges on her water bottle. "I don't know. I'm used to the Clayton Rays of the celeb world, you know? So I just assumed that he was like them. He wants to paint a mural on the school building."

"Of course he does. He's an artist. That would be

phenomenal." Luce's eyes widened, then narrowed. "Wouldn't it?"

"Yes." Kate smiled, then drew her brows together and hit her thigh with her water bottle. "Maybe. I don't know. He'd have to fly in supplies, which is really expensive."

"He can afford it."

"I know he can, but you know I hate that these guys come out here just for the publicity, and having him fly this stuff in is probably just a way for him to get more publicity. It's gotta be about the kids, and I mean, how often do we see anyone really connect with them?" She took another drink of water, and they sat in silence for a beat or two.

"Some do."

Kate shot her a look.

"Okay, not many, but some do. Believe it or not, there are some people who do things for the same reasons you do." Luce touched her hand. "You can't judge him until you know him."

"Sometimes I hate you." Kate turned toward an unfamiliar noise. "What is that?"

"Grunting?" Luce went to the screened porch and peered out. She covered her mouth and waved Kate over. "Hurry," she whispered.

Sage was lying prone on the ground, lifted up by his toes and his fingertips as he grunted out push-up after push-up. In the light of the moon, every muscle glistened with sweat. His massive biceps flexed and his hamstrings jumped with each exertion.

"Would you look at that yummy beast? Jesus, Kate, whatever you did, take it back. That's a prime specimen right there."

Kate flushed, mesmerized by the power in his body. It had been a very long time since she'd seen masculinity of that caliber...so close...so hot...so...*Shit.*

What am I doing? She tried to turn away but was drawn to him like metal to magnet. His tattoos twitched and stretched across his broad back as it lifted and fell, gracefully tapering to his trim waist and that perfect ass.

"God, just one night with that. That's all I ask for."

Kate smacked Luce's arm.

"What?" Luce whispered. "If you're not going to take a stab at him, why shouldn't I?"

Kate couldn't think of one reason Luce shouldn't. Except that she could. The slamming of her heart against her chest told her that maybe, just maybe, she didn't want to write him off completely. Not if he really wasn't like the other celebs. Not if he held any sort of promise for...*Oh hell, what am I thinking?* He was a man, and he looked like *that*. There was no way he was the kind of man she hoped to one day end up with—a man who cared more about others than himself. A man who didn't put money ahead of time spent helping others. A man she could count on.

"Go for it," she said halfheartedly to Luce and dragged herself away from the most spectacular scenery she'd seen in five years.

"What on earth is wrong with you? Have you gone nun on me?"

"No. Yes. I don't know." Kate rubbed her hands over her face. "He's not going to be the man for me in the long run, so why bother?"

"Why bother? Oh, honey, you've been here too long. Don't you miss the feel of an orgasm ripping through your body like nobody's business? Tying all of your nerves into a knot, then exploding and stealing your last breath? The feel of a man's arms around you, holding you so tight you can barely breathe and begging him to hold you tighter?" Luce let out a dreamy breath.

Kate stared at her, jaw agape.

"What?"

Kate blinked in rapid succession and shook her head. "I don't know. I guess...No. I mean, yeah, I would miss that if I'd ever had it." She felt her cheeks flush again. *Could sex really be like that?* She wasn't a virgin, but never had any sexual experience even come close to the feeling Luce described.

Luce lifted her hair from her neck and fanned her face. "You're serious?"

She nodded.

"Not once?"

She shook her head, wishing she could disappear. Then, in the next breath, Kate wondered what it might be like to experience what Luce described just once *before* she disappeared.

Chapter Three

SAGE STOOD UNDER the showerhead, dripping with sweat and praying the water pressure would kick in. He soaped himself up, then maneuvered his body in the two-foot-square shower until the impotent stream of water cleared the froth. Not quite as refreshing as he'd hoped, but about a thousand times more refreshing than knowing he'd walk out his front door in the concrete jungle and into the masses of self-centered people, too busy to say hello or walk around someone instead of barging into them as they stared at their phones. He dried himself off, thinking about Kate and wondering why she was so dead set against him using his own funds and resources to paint the school—and why she was so jaded to think that he'd want a commission from his paintings.

The heat had stolen his hunger, and he was too agitated to sit still. If he'd been at home, he would go up to his studio and paint or work his frustrations out with his hands, sculpting clay or heating and reforming metal until he lost his mind in it. Hell, if he were in New York, he could call his younger brother, Dex, or his older brother Jack and go out for a drink, or he could go for a run. It was too hot to run, and he had no interest in heading into town, but he wouldn't mind taking a walk.

With a flashlight, a drawing pad, and a bottle of water in hand, Sage headed for the path that led to the community area. There was a plethora of noise coming from the forest, and it grew louder as he entered the path. He'd have to remember to ask Kate about these new and different noises. He couldn't single out a sound. They all ran together in waves and pulses of odd noises. Once he reached the other end of the path, he headed toward the concrete, rectangular building. Most people probably saw a mess hall, but to Sage it was another blank canvas, just like the school. *Maybe I was drawn to AIA and Punta Palacia for a bigger reason.* Sage believed in fate and in most things intangible that others scoffed at, like following his gut instincts. He always had. He walked around the building, sizing it up, conjuring ideas. He'd need to spend some time in town, taking in the culture, feeling the energy of the people, the spirit of the community. He envisioned painting colorful fruits and vegetables, a woman dancing, a man playing a guitar, another playing drums, his hands suspended in midbeat, a child with a tambourine. The thought of it made his heart race, and just as quickly, the excitement dissipated. Kate had already nixed the idea of a mural at the school. There was no way he'd be allowed to touch this building.

Inside, he found Luce and Kate sitting at a table near the door, with a bottle of beer each and a bowl of biscuits between them. *Now, that looks appetizing. The beer and Kate.* Sage saw them exchange a glance, and a pink glow crawled up Kate's cheeks.

Hmm. "Hi, Kate. Luce." He purposely shifted his eyes away from Kate's. He had no idea how his body would react to her after the heat that had seared through him earlier.

"Hi," they said in unison.

"Care to join us?" Luce waved at a chair.

Sage couldn't miss the tension that pulled Kate's shoulders up toward her ears. "Kate? Do you mind? I'd be happy to buy each of you a beer—even if I have to pay double." He smiled, hoping his levity about "buying" the drinks might ease Kate's tension. The look she slid him in response was anything but relaxed.

Luce kicked her under the table and tossed a biscuit toward him. "Sit, please, and have a Johnnycake."

Sage wondered what that kick meant. He noticed the glare Kate gave Luce and the arching of the brow Luce shot back and tried not to read too much into it. But how could he not with Kate working so hard to keep from looking at him?

"Was all that noise outside from the animals you mentioned?" he asked Kate.

"Mm-hmm. Amphibians." Kate took a swig of her beer.

He picked up the biscuit and took a bite. "That's really good. Cornmeal?"

"They're delicious. And addicting. They're cornmeal cakes, a local fave." Luce rose to her feet. "I'll grab you a beer from Kate's secret stash."

"You have a secret stash?" he whispered to Kate.

The edges of her lips curved up. Their eyes met, and he felt a zing of attraction all the way to his toes, causing his pulse to speed up. It was all Sage could do not to either lower his eyes and break the connection or lean across the table and kiss her. *What the hell am I thinking?* Thankfully, Luce returned with a cold beer. It was damn good timing. Sage had a feeling that if she had taken a moment longer, he might have chanced

31

that kiss and probably would have ended up with a black eye followed by a miserable two weeks of groveling apologies. What the hell was happening to him? Sage was a handsome man, and women flirted with him everywhere he went, but he didn't date often, and he rarely paid attention to the women who came onto him. He certainly had never felt anything like the attraction he felt toward Kate—which was weird given that he clearly rubbed her in all the wrong ways.

"Thank you, Luce. Kate, I'll reciprocate. Show me where to buy them tomorrow, and I'll pick up a few." The condensation soaked his hands as he brought the cold bottle to his lips. The salty ale quenched his thirst, and he suppressed the urge to suck down the bottle in one long drink. Sage wasn't typically a big drinker, but after the heat and frustration of the day, and with the remaining confusion surrounding the beautiful woman before him, he'd welcome a little deadening of the senses.

"She knows all the best places to buy everything. She'll hook you up," Luce said.

Kate sucked down her beer in one unladylike gulp. "Excuse me." She pushed from the table and rose to her feet.

Sage watched her slim hips sway as she made her way to the kitchen. Jesus, something about her had a hold on him in all the right places. He shook it off and focused on Luce.

"Not anything like the Big Apple, huh?" Luce lifted her bottle.

"Thank goodness for that." Sage couldn't help but watch Kate as she bent over a freezer in the kitchen, then struggled with the twist-off cap to another beer. She shook her hand and pressed it against her hip, scrunching her face in a frustrated scowl. A soft laugh escaped Sage's lips.

Luce turned and followed his gaze. "She really is a sweet girl."

"Sweet?" Sage took another drink of his beer. "I see flashes of that, but she's a tough nut to crack."

"She has to be. Look at where she is. She's almost twenty-seven, single, in a developing nation with all sorts of dangers and no one to lean on." Luce spoke in a hushed tone, her eyes serious, her perfectly manicured, barely there brows knitted together.

Sage nodded an acknowledgment as Kate approached the table. She set her still-capped beer on the table with a *clunk*.

"I swear you need a leather glove to open these damn things." She stared at the bottle.

Luce looked at Sage. "Let's see your alpha brawn in action."

Sage grunted like a Neanderthal. Then he picked up the bottle and covered it with his enormous hand, cupping the cap with his palm. With a single twist, the hiss of sweet relief cut through the air.

"M'lady." He motioned as if he were bowing and handed the bottle to Kate. She wrapped her fingers around its neck, brushing his hand with hers. Like a schoolboy going through puberty, he felt another jolt of heat to his groin.

"Thanks," she said. "I can usually do it myself."

Stubborn.

Luce stifled a laugh.

"I'm sure you can. Tell me about your assignment, Kate. How long have you been here? What changes have you seen?" If he was going to work with her over the next two weeks, he had to try to break through the icy barrier they were struggling against.

"Changes? I'm lobbying for a well for the village, but I'm not sure if we'll get it. The clinic that Caleb runs is really efficient and it's made a world of difference for the elderly." She took a drink of her beer. "I've been here for almost twenty-five months. We're tasked for twenty-four months, but they add three months of training before the assignment begins, even though most of the training takes place at a central location, so the assignment is really twenty-seven months."

"Where will you go next?" Sage asked.

"I don't know. We usually request a location and then we have to wait a few months before we find out. I'm going to have a difficult time leaving here. I've come to love so many of the people, and starting over is exciting, but really hard. I know I'll lose sleep over leaving the kids and the families."

"What do you miss most from home?" Sage asked.

Luce and Sage watched Kate mull over the question.

"Probably my favorite writing journals. I can't get them here, and if I order them, shipping is a fortune." Kate sighed. "The Stardust leather journal with artist paper. They always make me happy. Stupid, I know." She swatted the air.

"You and your journals," Luce teased. "She writes in them every day. God, I'd miss real restaurants and spending time with my friends. You're so alone here."

"I'm not alone. There are plenty of people around. And I can't even tell you the last time I went to a real restaurant." Kate finished her beer and looked expectantly at Luce.

"I think it's my turn to snag another round." Sage headed for the kitchen and came back with three bottles. "So this is what aid workers in Belize do. I always wondered what went on at night."

"There's a place in town where you can dance," Luce said.

"Oh God, Luce," Kate said.

"Note to self. Kate does *not* like to dance." Sage

34

opened each of the bottles and handed them out.

"Thanks, Sage." Luce lifted her beer with a nod. "She loves to dance."

Kate glared at Luce and Luce glared right back. "She just doesn't like anyone to see her."

"Well, not to worry, Kate," Sage said. "I'm not exactly racing to the dance floor myself."

"God, you guys are boring." Luce took a swig of her beer. "Two fuddy-duddies. Maybe I should have gone with Penelope and the others."

"Oh, please. You'd last half a minute with them before smacking Penelope silly with her neediness and *I'm-too-good-for-this* attitude."

Luce touched Kate's arm and said softly, "No, hon. That's you. I live and breathe these people. Their stuff doesn't bother me one bit."

Sage listened intently, gleaning what he could from the impromptu lesson on all things Kate and Luce. An hour and two beers later, they were all spilling secrets.

"So tell us, Sage." Kate's voice lingered on his name. "Why are you really here? Did you sleep with someone's wife and now you're on damage control? Sprinkle a little humanitarian effort in the press and push all that naughty stuff aside?"

Sage didn't know what he was expecting her to ask him, but that was certainly not anywhere near the realm of possibilities. He shot a look at Luce, who shrugged. Clearly she was just as surprised as he was.

"You do jump to the worst with people, don't you?" He smiled at Kate, doing his best to conceal the sting of her question. "Well, ladies, this has been fun, but I was advised not to get too drunk by my fetching mentor." Sage finished his beer and rose to his feet.

Kate stood and swayed.

Sage reached across the table and grabbed her arm gently, steadying her. "Whoa. You okay?"

"Yeah. I'm good." Kate reached for Luce's hand. "Luce?"

"Steady as a rock." Luce took her hand.

"If you're leaving, too, I think I'll walk with you. Put my alpha brawn protectiveness to good use." He winked at Luce.

"We don't need a bodyguard," Kate said.

"Think of me as a tagalong. What kind of man would leave two women to walk home alone in the jungle?" He walked beside Kate, fighting the urge to wrap his arm around her waist, just to ensure she was really okay. *Or maybe just because I want to.* She'd held her beer well until that last one, which did her in. He'd seen the spark simmering in her eyes, but who was he to tell a self-sufficient woman like Kate that she should stop drinking?

Luce led them along the narrow path, with Kate in the middle and Sage taking up the rear. He kept one finger loosely linked in a belt loop on the back of Kate's shorts. He wasn't going to take a chance of her tumbling into the thick brush. Luce seemed more stable on her feet, and she had a good ten pounds on Kate to soak up the alcohol.

When they reached the end of the path, Luce led the way to the middle cabin. "My place is right here. Thanks, Sage." Luce wrapped her arms around Kate and whispered something in her ear that Sage couldn't make out. *Probably telling her to steer clear of me.*

"Where's your cabin, Kate?" Sage asked, his finger still locked in her belt loop, surprised she didn't try to pull away.

Luce pointed to a path just beyond Sage's cabin.

"I'm fine." Kate pushed at his hand. "G'night, Luce. Breakfast tomorrow?"

Luce waved over her head as she walked inside. "Sounds good."

"Okay, let's get you home safe and sound," he said to Kate.

"I'm fine. Really. I don't need you to walk me—" She stumbled forward.

Sage pulled her upright by her belt loop and settled his hands on her hips. God, she felt good. Too good. She grabbed his arms, leaning against him for stability, and looked up at him. *Christ.* He had been with plenty of women, mainly models and artists, and Kate seemed so *normal* compared to them. Never had he felt drawn to anyone the way he was drawn to her. He had no fucking idea why, but he had the strange desire to know all of her secrets. *What the hell is that all about?* And with her breasts pressed against his chest, her thumbs pressing the sensitive area just inside his pockets, and those goddamn alluring eyes looking right through him, it took all his restraint not to lower his mouth to hers.

Her lips parted and her tongue ran slowly over them, leaving them slick. Inviting.

He reluctantly tore his eyes from her lips. Sage had never been the kind of guy who took advantage of an inebriated woman, and he sure as hell wasn't going to start now. *Not with you.* He pried her fingers from his hips. "Let's get you home."

She swallowed hard. "Um...Right. Okay." He kept his arm placed lightly around her waist, telling himself he was doing it to keep her steady, but damn if he didn't love the feel of her pressed against him. She was so tough and so delicate at the same time. Sage slipped behind her on the narrow path—a path he hadn't even noticed in the daylight. They broke free of the forest about fifty feet later, and Sage did a quick visual sweep of the dark area surrounding Kate's cabin, which wasn't a cabin at all. It could be described only as a hut built on stilts, like a tree house. It was made of wood with a thatched roof. Brush had been cleared in a circle around the wooden stilts, giving Kate a yard of about twenty feet. It was the most romantic setting he'd ever laid eyes on.

"Don't you get scared out here by yourself?" He glanced down at Kate, and she had one finger looped into his waistband.

"Nope." She moved toward the steps, and Sage walked alongside her. Normally, he'd stop at the bottom of the stairs and give her space so she didn't feel that he was pressuring her for something he wasn't. But Sage had just arrived in the jungle, and he wasn't quite as sure as Kate was that there wasn't someone lurking, waiting to touch this pretty little lady when she was all alone and unsuspecting. He followed her up the steps and inside. The room was slightly bigger than his. Her bed had a colorful comforter, which brightened the dark wooden interior. Scarves hung in front of the windows, and Sage could think of several things to use them for that had absolutely nothing to do with curtains...or sleeping. Sticky notes clung to the table, the walls, and her clipboard, scrawled with reminders. There were three spiral notebooks on the table beside a handful of pens. He read one of the sticky notes. *Meds to Olivia. Javier, pad/crayons for Xmas?*

"See? Safe and sound." She spun in a circle. As she began to take a dizzy fall toward the floor, he wrapped a strong arm around her waist. "Whew, that was close." She hung on to him.

Bad idea. Very bad idea.

His heart hammered against his ribs. He wanted to kiss her, to taste her. Just once.

Do not do it.

She put her hand on his stomach, and Sage felt a warm sensation lower, in someplace much more sensitive, which seemed to be happening a lot when he was near her. He took her hand in his and brought it to his lips. He pressed a soft kiss to the back of it, then lowered her until she was sitting on the bed. She grabbed his shirt as he drew back. For a moment they were inches apart. Her warm breath stroked his cheeks, the sweet-and-sour smell of alcohol mixed with the fresh smell of Kate drawing him in. She closed her eyes, and Sage took her hand in his, this time pulling it from its purchase on his shirt and placing it in her lap.

"Thanks for a fun night, Kate."

Her eyes flew open, and she stared in disbelief. Then her lips closed, and her cheeks flushed. She pushed to her feet, seemingly more aware of her footing. "Um...right. Thanks."

"If you need me, you know where I live." Sage turned to leave.

"Sage?"

Do not kiss her.

"Yeah?" he asked with one hand on the door handle.

"I'm sorry I asked about...well, why you were here."

He turned to look at her, and the sincerity in her eyes reeled him in again. "No worries. You don't really know me yet. One day you'll realize that's not who I am."

Chapter Four

SAGE SPENT MOST of the evening sketching what he'd really like to be painting—on canvas, the school building, anywhere he could. He had to do something to keep his mind off of *not* kissing Kate, but sketching into the wee hours of the morning hadn't done anything more than make him tired. Rain had come on strong during the night, easing the odd cadence of the amphibians, and offering a nice break to the humidity. Eventually, it had lulled him to sleep.

He awoke to the smell of fresh rain, the singing of the birds—and the humidity—all of which he relished. It was a far cry from waking up to the sounds of horns and cars in New York. He showered and dressed and headed over to the mess hall for coffee and breakfast. Sage saw the beauty through the oppressive heat. The grass was slick, and the dirt had turned to mud. The colorful forest shined brightly against the sun's sharp rays, and Sage had the burgeoning need to create. It pressed against his chest and ached like a sore. To sculpt something that would mirror the beauty of Punta Palacia would be incredible, but it would be impossible to get his sculpting supplies and equipment to Belize. He'd have to make due with painting—and he'd have to convince Kate that it was the right thing to do.

A middle-aged Belizean woman wearing a bright yellow skirt and blouse and a friendly smile greeted Sage at the kitchen. Her dark, shoulder-length hair was tucked beneath a wide-brimmed hat.

"Good morning," she said with a thick island accent. She had kind, dark eyes. She held a large wooden spoon in one hand and waved the other at the stove. "What is your pleasure today?"

"Good morning," Sage said. He held out a hand. "I'm Sage."

She smiled and squeezed his hand gently, but she did not shake it. Instead, she nodded. "Sylvia." She motioned to two other women behind her, their hands covered with flour, kneading dough on the counter beside the fridge. "Mila and Luisa." They smiled shyly.

Sage waved and smiled. "I'll have eggs and one of those wonderful Johnnycakes, thank you."

"Ah. You like the Johnnycakes. Good man. They'll give you energy. You are here to work with the children?" she asked.

"Yes. Kate told you?"

Sylvia nodded. "My nephew Javier is very excited about art lessons. Thank you for volunteering."

Javier. Sage remembered the picture Kate had found in the school office. "I'm looking forward to meeting him, and all of the children." Sage filled a mug with coffee and went to join Luce, the public relations rep for the other volunteers, in the mess hall.

Luce had a hot cup of coffee and her nose buried in a novel.

"Mind if I crash your party?" Sage set his food down and sat across from her.

She lowered the book. "Of course not. Good morning."

"It's quiet today." Sage felt his stomach growl. Skipping dinner hadn't been the best idea in the world. He wolfed down his eggs in a few fast bites.

"You're kidding, right? Penelope, Cassidy, and Clayton won't even wake up until noon, and Kate's at the school." She looked up at the ceiling. "The rain really did her in. She and Oscar have to mop up before the students arrive."

"Mop up?"

"The roof leaks. She didn't tell you?"

Sage shook his head.

"She's so used to it, she probably didn't even think of it. They've fixed the roof like a hundred times, but they can't stop it from leaking." She sipped her coffee.

Sage rose to his feet. "I'll go see if I can help."

"If you can mop, you can help."

Sage would do one better than that. In college, he'd spent one summer helping a buddy with his father's construction business, and he happened to have a knack for roofing. He grabbed a second cup of coffee for Kate before leaving and then headed over to the school.

WHAT WAS I thinking, drinking so much last night? Kate's head was pounding. Her arms were already fatigued from mopping, and when Sage came into the school, embarrassment rushed in. He handed her a warm cup of coffee, eyeing the water on the floor, the desks pushed to the outskirts of the room. She tried not to stare at his powerful arms or the tattoo snaking up the back of his neck, but damn it, how could she not? She remembered the feel of his hard body—and it was hard—against her when he'd caught her after she'd lost her footing last night. *Shit. Stop thinking of him like that.*

"That's a hell of a leak," he said.

"The bucket caught the water this time, but I kicked it over by accident." She sipped the coffee. "Mm. Thank you for this."

"You okay this morning? Sleep okay?" He walked around the room, looking up at the exposed beams in the wooden ceiling. The wood was drenched right through in certain spots, with nails poking through. "Is Oscar around?"

"Yes. Right here." Oscar entered the room with a mop in hand.

"Morning, Oscar. Can I get up on the roof?"

"Wait, Sage. That's not your job. Oscar knows what he's doing." Kate set her coffee down and leaned on her mop.

"I'm sure he does. I have a little experience in this area, too. Do you mind? One quick look?"

Kids would be arriving shortly, and she had more pressing worries than him poking around on the leaky roof. "Be my guest. Just don't fall off."

A few minutes later, she heard their heavy footsteps overhead. Kate was just happy that he hadn't made any mention of how drunk she'd been the evening before. She hardly ever had more than one beer, and four—or was it five? She couldn't remember—whatever it was, it was over her limit. She hadn't even known she had a limit until last night. *Of all the nights to find out.* She sighed, remembering the heat of his breath as it brushed her lips. The way she'd wanted to touch the sprinkling of whiskers along his jaw and the way he smelled when he'd settled her on the bed. Masculine. Virile. So damn sexy.

Holy cow. What am I doing?

A loud metallic sound rang out above, followed by a muffled dragging sound, startling Kate. She listened to the men shout and then the sound of...digging? In wood? Scraping? Heavy footsteps crossed the roof. Kate closed her eyes. The last thing she wanted to do was question Sage after she'd embarrassed herself the night before, but with kids coming in for classes, she had to know what was going on and if the noise would continue after the kids arrived. She went outside and looked up at the two men bending over the aluminum sheathing on the roof with heavy tools in their hands, looking very macho. She shielded her eyes from the sun to get a better view, and oh, what a view it was! Sage had stripped off his tank top. His broad, muscular chest and narrow waist glistened in the sun. She couldn't help but follow the line of his abs to the waist of his cargo shorts, which had slipped dangerously low.

Focus, focus, focus. "How's...how's it going up there?"

Oscar waved. "He has found the problem. He is very good with his hands."

I bet he is. Two minutes on a roof and he can fix the problem that we've been dealing with for two years? "Really?"

Sage glanced over, wiped his brow with his arm, and nodded. "Give us an hour. We'll get it fixed, good as new."

Kate could think of a bunch of things she'd happily give him an hour to do, none of which included a roof. Or tools.

A little over an hour later, Kate had just finished cleaning up the classroom and rearranging the desks when Sage and Oscar appeared in the doorway. Sage had put his shirt back on, and it clung to his glistening muscles.

"How'd it go?" she asked hopefully.

"You should be good to go. There were nails that had been hammered through the wood. At some point the roof must have been replaced, and..." Sage shrugged. "I guess they never replaced the wood beneath. They just covered over it. The nails were encased in dirt and muck, so there's no way Oscar would have known to even look for them." He slung an arm around Oscar's shoulder. "You did a great job, Oscar. Thanks for letting me help you."

"*You* taught *me*. I am grateful." Oscar had fashioned a rope into a tool belt, twisting the rope around the head of the hammer, which hung from his hip.

Kate watched the two men bond and felt the walls around her heart loosen just a little. "Sage, thank you. We've been dealing with that forever. So you think we won't need the buckets?"

He had such an easy, sincere smile. It reeled her right in.

"Hopefully not, we'll see." He wiped a hand on the bottom of his tank top, lifting it just enough to flash a strip of ripped muscle.

Kat couldn't look away. How long had it been since she'd seen anything so wickedly sexy? *Shit. Never.* She forced herself to turn away.

"So, what's next? When do the kids arrive? What should I do?" Sage asked.

"I'll be on my way. The store in town had a leak, too. Okay?" Oscar waited for Kate to respond.

"Oh, yes, of course. Thank you, Oscar." She watched him leave, then reminded herself that Sage was just like any other six-foot-four mass of gorgeous muscle who had ever volunteered with AIA. *Yeah, right. Tell me another lie.* She began moving the desks back into position to avoid staring at him again.

"The kids will be here any minute. Their teacher is in the office, so she'll handle their lessons, and your art classes will take place around one."

"Great, so we have a few hours?"

"Mm-hmm." She put the mop in a closet in the back of the room.

"I need to go into town. Want to come along?"

How can you be so casual when all of my womanly hot buttons are going off?

He softened his gaze. "Please? I need to go to the Internet café, and I want to refill your secret stash. Waddaya say?"

"Um...sure?" *What am I doing?*

During the half-mile walk into town, Kate felt oddly rigid beside Sage, who was excruciatingly relaxed.

"There's something about being here that's so much more...I don't know...real, than New York." Sage breathed in deeply.

Kate tried not to notice the muscles in his chest expanding, or the way his biceps twitched when he drew his arms out in a stretch. She had to get her mind off his body.

"How did you hear about AIA?" she asked.

"I was talking to a friend about wanting to do something more than give money to charities and he mentioned AIA. He said he'd read an article about it, so I looked it up, and here I am."

She listened for a hitch in his voice, a hesitation, something that didn't follow his story from yesterday about wanting to find a way to pay his good fortune forward. He had to be putting up a front. She couldn't remember the last time she'd met a volunteer at Punta Palacia who was there for reasons other than their own reputations.

"Is it what you expected? What did you think it would be like?" *A vacation?*

He shrugged. "I didn't really think about it. He said AIA brought artists into developing nations to work with the communities, and I figured anything they needed me to do, I would be happy to."

Damn if every word didn't seem sincere. The celebrities and artists who had volunteered would never have climbed on a roof—even if she'd asked them to. He hadn't thought twice. He'd even insisted after she'd tried to deter him. Sage was definitely different.

"Do you like living in New York?"

"Everyone thinks living in New York is glamorous and exciting, and I think for many people it is. But for me, it's just the place that made the most sense to settle down. I grew up about an hour outside the city, and the galleries and clientele I work with are there, so moving there seemed like the right thing to do. But now, after five years, I feel like a caged tiger." He looked away. "Not that I'm complaining, because I know how fortunate I am. Anyway, thanks for coming with me. How's your head?"

"*Ugh*. A few Tylenol and a Motrin helped. I don't usually drink like that. I'm not sure why I did."

He narrowed his eyes, but his lips curled up in a smile. He knocked his elbow softly against hers. "We both know why you did."

Gulp. "We do?"

"Sure. You help others all day long, and then you have to deal with the...personalities of all of us. Luce is here, and she's obviously a friend. You were just having fun. By the way, I had a really nice time last night. Thanks for letting me crash your reunion."

Okay. Sure. I'll go with that reasoning. "I don't mind the personalities."

He narrowed his eyes.

"Okay, maybe some of them. But it is nice to have Luce here." *And you*. The silent acknowledgment rang true and brought a smile to her lips.

The road widened, and the jungle to their right

gave way to a clearing of grass, which led to a small town where a strip of low concrete buildings lined the dirt road.

"So this is Punta Palacia?" There was a fruit stand in front of the first store, bursting with bananas, oranges, papayas, mangos, noni, and pineapple. There were only a few people on the street.

Kate waved to a woman in a colorful dress. "Hi, Maria."

The woman waved back. "Good morning. Glad for the rain."

"Yes. We needed it. How is Lorena?" Kate asked.

Maria nodded. "Better. Thank you."

Kate turned her attention back to Sage. "Lorena is her mother. She was sick for a few days last week. I'm glad she's better. Anyway, this is our little town, population of a few hundred." She knew that to someone from New York, there was nothing particularly impressive about the small town, or the people, but Kate took pride in the area. She'd come to love the close-knit community and the ease of their lifestyle. "See beyond the strip of stores?" She pointed farther down the road. "If you follow the road, you'll come to a small group of homes at the base of the mountains, and that's where most of our students live."

"I'd like to see that sometime."

"Sure." She couldn't find one thing to dislike about Sage so far, but Kate was still wary. "Let's go to the Internet café first. The Internet's not always great, so don't be surprised if it's spotty."

"That's okay. I have an international phone plan, so I can always call, but my mother wants to see my face and know I'm alive."

Kate looked at him out of the corner of her eye. "Your mother? How old are you?"

He laughed. "I know. I know. Twenty-eight. But

hey, it's better than her not caring, right? Besides, she's the one with the artistic talent in the family. She was kind enough to pass her talent down to me. I think I owe her the peace of mind of knowing that I'm okay. My older brother Rush is visiting them for a few days, so I'd like to see him, too."

"You have a brother?"

"Actually, I have four brothers and a sister. Rush is a competitive skier, and he's the second oldest. How about you? Any siblings?"

Kate shook her head. "Nope. Just me and my parents."

He nodded. "That must be nice. All that attention."

She felt a smile press forth. "Yeah. My parents are great. Although, I have to admit, I've often wondered what it would be like to know there was someone out there that I could call and they'd know exactly what I was feeling before I said a word. I hear it's like that with siblings."

"It can be. They can also be a pain in the ass. But I swear my mother knows things about each of us no matter where we are. She has some motherly sixth sense or something."

Two plump, short women waved to Kate.

"Hi. Good to see you." She leaned closer to Sage and whispered, "Adela and Indira. Mother and daughter. They speak Belizean Creole, but with a much thicker accent than Oscar does." Both women wore cotton shirts, skirts that hung below their knees, and identical expressions that were common to the area: a permanent squint to ward off the sun and a ready smile. Adela's face was heavily wrinkled, giving her a much older appearance than her fiftysomething years, much different from Indira's smooth, soft-looking skin.

Indira touched Kate's arm as she passed and glanced up at Sage. Kate had an easy six inches on each of the women. She squeezed Indira's hand and said, "Sage Remington. He's an artist from the States. Here to work with the children."

Indira looked up with her beady, yet friendly, dark eyes and nodded. "Thank you," she said just above a whisper.

"Thank you for sharing your beautiful country with me," Sage responded.

Kate felt her skepticism of Sage chipping away.

They entered the Internet café, and Kate waved at a tall, slim man sitting behind the counter. "Hello, Makei. Sage is a new volunteer and he needs to use the Internet."

Makei pushed himself up from the cushioned stool with great care and walked across the concrete floor one careful step at a time, moving as slowly as a sloth. Sage looked at Kate, and she knew he wondered if Makei moved like he did for a medical reason. She'd wondered the same thing when she'd met him, but she'd quickly learned that this was simply Makei's normal pace.

"You're not in New York anymore. We move a little slower around here," she said to Sage.

"Actually, I like the pace around here."

Once again, he surprised her with his answer. She could practically hear the pieces of her steely resolve hitting the floor as they fell away.

"Sit." Makei motioned to two stools by the counter.

"I only have U.S. currency." Sage slid worried eyes to Kate.

"That's okay. They take it here," she assured him.

Sage paid him, and Makei pulled a computer monitor from beneath the counter and set it up on the thick wooden counter. Then he set a keyboard down in front of Sage and nodded. "Go ahead."

"That's it?" Sage asked.

"Yeah. Easy. But don't expect too much. Like I said, coverage is spotty at best." She looked around the small café. "Do you want me to wait over there? I don't mean to hover." She rose from her stool, and Sage touched her arm, sending a goddamn shiver down her back.

"No need. Stay. Makei, can I buy Kate a cold drink?"

Makei smiled, his dark eyes slanting to near closed. "Yes, my friend."

"Oh, you don't have to." *But thank you.*

"You bought last night," he reminded her.

Makei held up a finger. "Banana papaya. Kate's favorite."

"Ah, you have a favorite." Sage smiled as he looked around the empty café.

Behind the counter, cups, plates, bowls, and napkins were stacked on wooden shelves. The concrete walls appeared textured, though Kate knew the uneven finish was due to poor workmanship or lack of proper tools rather than created by design.

Sage checked his email as Makei put the ingredients in a large plastic cup, then turned a larger cup upside down on top of it and shook the contraption for a minute or two. Then he poured them each a full cup.

Sage took a big drink of the deliciously cold, fresh-fruit smoothie. "This is incredible."

"Thank you, Sage. You didn't have to buy them."

"They're your favorite. Now I know."

Stop being so damned perfect. She watched him click on Skype and then hover the mouse over the connection link.

"My mother is lovely, but my brother Rush can be snarky." He looked away, as if he was picturing him. "Well, you'll see, and if it gets annoying, go do your thing and I'll catch up with you when I'm done."

"My thing?" she asked, intrigued about his mother and brother. There was no way she was leaving the seat she had to this show. She was dying to see from his family whether he was as authentic as he seemed.

"I just don't want you to feel trapped with me." Sage swung his stool around, and his hand hovered over her thigh, then quickly grabbed the table, as if he had suddenly realized he was going to touch her.

Kate's stomach fluttered again. She felt like a schoolgirl with a crush-gone-wild.

He clicked the link, and it took several tries before he was able to connect. The other line rang three times before quieting. They watched the circle on the screen spin. Then stop. Then spin again. Eventually, the page came to life.

"Hi, Mom," Sage said loudly.

The smile that graced his gorgeous lips reached his eyes, and Kate could feel happiness emitting from him, very different from the scorching, sexual blaze she'd felt last night—the one she hoped hadn't been just a figment of her drunken imagination.

"Sage," his mother said in a loving voice. "Oh, honey, I'm so glad you could call. Look at you." She had the prettiest blue eyes, long gray hair, and a pleasant, friendly face.

He nodded. "I'm here and I'm fine. What's happening there? How're you? Dad?"

"Hey, asshole." A male voice came from the computer.

Sage turned to Kate. "That'd be Rush. Four years older, handsome, and cocky as hell."

She saw a look pass through his eyes and wasn't sure what it meant.

"Lemme see you, Rush," Sage said.

Rush popped his head over his mother's shoulder. "Sorry, to invade your space, Mom."

His hair was a shade lighter than Sage's, his eyes as bright blue as his mother's. He had the same chiseled features, though he was clean shaven and his face was more animated. He was strikingly handsome—and Kate felt absolutely nothing. Not a single butterfly in her stomach, not even a hint of attraction. And then she looked at Sage, and those damned butterflies let her know they were still there.

"Dude, what's up? How're things in Belize? Meet any hot babes?" Rush's voice was deeper than Sage's, and he spoke fast, teasingly.

Kate felt the question like a punch to the stomach, killing the flutters as quickly as they'd appeared. She watched Sage's jaw clench.

"You're an idiot," Sage said to Rush.

"Rush, please. We don't know how long Sage has to talk," their mother said.

Sage glanced at Kate. "He's an idiot."

No, I'm the idiot for thinking you might be different.

The screen pixilated, blocking out half of his mother's face.

"Sage, honey, who are you talking to?" his mother asked.

"Oh, um. Kate Paletto. She runs the show for AIA here." He leaned toward her and whispered, "Would you mind saying hello?"

Don't do it. Do not do it. Get up and leave. He's exactly like the rest of them. Before she could answer, he wrapped his arm around her shoulder and pulled her in front of the monitor. Cheek to cheek with him, and damn did he smell good.

"Mom, this is Kate. Kate, Joanie Remington." His mother's image became clear again.

She forced her teeth to unclench. "Hello, Mrs. Remington."

Rush pushed his face back into the frame. "Hi, Kate.

I'm Rush."

She felt Sage's hand go rigid on the back of her shoulder. "I'll let you guys talk. Nice to meet you." Kate tried to pull from his grasp, but he held on tight.

"Nice to meet you, too, Kate," his mother said.

Sage didn't move his arm from her shoulder when she sat up, and the heat of it was making her body awaken in places she wished would stop reacting to him. She wasn't about to become one of the string of women he probably had God knows where waiting for him. Brothers talked. She knew that. She wondered what he would have said if she weren't there with him. Would he have mentioned Penelope? Cassidy? *Me?*

"Honey, tell me about the culture. What's it like there? What have you done?" his mother asked.

"I'll fill you in on that after he's off the computer," Rush said with a laugh.

Oh my God, really? What an ass.

"Hush up, Rush. You'd think you were fifteen again. Please," his mother chided him.

"Today I fixed a roof at the school, and I think we're working with the kids later. The town is small, a few hundred people. I haven't seen many of the locals yet, but, Mom, it's so beautiful here. I wish I had all my supplies. I'm working on Kate to let me paint a mural with the kids on the side of the school."

"Oh, honey, that's a marvelous idea. So good for the children," his mother said.

Kate's ears perked up at the mention of the mural.

"I'm working on it. It's one reason I'm calling. Mom, if Kate agrees..." He slid his hand from around her shoulder and held up a finger, indicating for her to hear him out. "Can you arrange for the supplies? I want to donate as much to the charity as it takes to fly the stuff here. Equal amounts."

"Yes, honey, of course. What does Kate think about

the idea?"

"Ask her." Sage pulled Kate in front of the monitor again.

She tried to wiggle out from his grasp, but again, he held on too tight. She shot him a hot stare and tried to keep her anger from her voice. "Well, I'm not really against the idea. I just...It will cost a lot of money, and that's money that could pay for medical supplies, food, and other, more necessary things." *Jesus, now your family will hate me.* She tried to lean out of his grasp, but she was stuck. And mad.

"Oh, honey, in some aspects, I suppose you're right," his mother said. "Well, I'm sure you two will figure it out."

She breathed a sigh of relief to be off the topic and she thought of Javier, his big, dark eyes and mop of pitch-black hair. The way his face lit up when he told her of the paintings he was going to create when he was older. She felt her resolve soften, even if she wasn't ready to admit it yet.

Kate talked with his mother about how long she'd been in Belize and how excited she was for Sage to work with the children, and then she left them alone to chat while she sat at the counter, nursing her smoothie and thinking about Sage.

After Sage ended the Skype call, he and Kate sat in silence for a few minutes, listening to the sounds of the birds outside the window.

"You know, I know just where you're coming from about the mural." Sage ran his finger through the condensation of his glass. "The money is important for all of the necessities in life. But for the children who are living with so few material things and seem to really feel the joy of giving and receiving..." His eyes lit up. "Think of the picture you found in the office yesterday. You were so happy to find it, and I'm sure Javier was thrilled to draw it for you."

Do you have to sound so damn sincere?

"You know these kids better than I ever will, but I can only imagine that taking part in a community art project will allow them to give back to you and their teachers, to do something they can be really proud of. It's something they'll see every morning and every afternoon and think, *We made that beautiful mural.*"

Well, hell. Who could deny that logic? She looked at Sage, his eyes filled with such hope that it rendered her mute.

"Everyone needs something to be proud of. Not that I'm trying to pressure you or anything," Sage said, lifting the right side of his mouth into a crooked smile. "And I'll donate the same amount of funds for medical or other purposes. Would that be so bad?"

She sighed, though it was all for show. Her anger had given way to reluctant acceptance. No way could she deny the children what he'd just described. "Fine. Okay. You've convinced me."

Sage wrapped her in his arms and kissed her cheek with his soft lips.

"Thank you," he whispered.

The rough scratch of his whiskers sent a full-body shudder through her. When he drew back, his gratitude-filled gaze pinned her heart to the barbed-wire fence, and she swore it sprouted legs and tried to climb over.

Chapter Five

"DO YOU THINK it was a setup?" Kate said to Luce. They were eating lunch on a bench in the community rec area, and she'd just finished explaining to her what had transpired at the Internet café.

"Calling his family?" Luce asked.

"It's stupid. I know. But you know how the more you see someone with their family, the warmer you feel inside. Maybe it made me a softie."

"A conspiracy. Now I get it." Luce shook her head. "You're losing your mind, and by the way, I want details on last night."

"Ugh." She'd been groaning a lot lately.

"No way. That bad?"

"I'm a little fuzzy, but I'm pretty sure I tried to kiss him."

Luce threw her hands up in the air and said, "Hallelujah."

"And he didn't kiss me. He left."

She tucked her hair behind her ear and spoke with a serious tone. "Oh, Kate. Are you sure you don't just think you tried to kiss him?"

"Trust me. I've been over this a hundred times. All night long, in fact. I closed my eyes like a schoolgirl, puckered my lips, and...waited."

Luce laughed. "Sorry." She cleared her throat. "What did he do?"

"I don't know. He said something about me not knowing him, or it not being who he was. I don't know." She sighed. "Maybe I would have regretted it in the morning anyway. I don't know, and I can't remember exactly what happened. I was too busy being mortified. Then he showed up this morning and fixed the damn roof like it's what he does every day. Mr. Millionaire Artist *and* roofer." She buried her face in her hands.

"I guess he's not just like the others," Luce pointed out.

"Shut up. It's a farce. I know it is. Oh, and his brother Rush...He definitely said stuff that made it seem like Sage isn't as good as he seems."

"You can't trust anything a brother says. Mine would have all sorts of shit to say about me that isn't true."

"I guess. Whatever." Kate looked around. "Where are the others? Have you checked on them to be sure they're not dead?"

"They went into Belize City. Don't worry. I spoke to Caleb already and let him know they wouldn't be there today. It sounded like this happens all the time."

Kate rolled her eyes. "It does. Poor Caleb. He's always left without any volunteers, and he never complains. He does his job and then disappears until the next morning."

"He doesn't disappear. He reads and he writes."

"Whatever. He's like a ghost. I tried to get to know him when he first showed up, but he made it very clear that he wasn't here to socialize."

"Do you still go down to our beach?" Luce whispered.

Luce and Kate had happened upon a remote, and seemingly undiscovered, white sandy beach at the end of a red clay path one afternoon when they were hiking in the jungle. It had been so hot that they'd taken their clothes off and jumped right into the water, and that had become their *thing*. Skinny-dipping at the beach they now called Undiscovered.

"Yes."

Luce scooted closer to her on the bench, as if there was anyone else around to hear her. "Wanna go?"

Goose bumps chased excitement up Kate's limbs. Did she want to go? *Hell yes.* "It's Sage's first day with the kids, but we can go after we're done." *Sage. I'd like to see him skinny-dipping.*

"Of course. But what's that hesitation I'm hearing?" Luce ran her eyes over Kate's face.

"Nothing."

"Right, and I'm a virgin."

"You are?" Kate feigned surprise. "Sage has just thrown me a little off-kilter."

SAGE AND OSCAR set up tables outside the school for the art class. He snuck glimpses of Kate as she placed pencils by each of the seats, and his mind drifted to the morning. He hadn't expected to introduce Kate to his mother, much less Rush.

After Rush's comment, he'd expected Kate to stalk off. Her body had gone completely rigid, and she'd clenched her teeth so tightly that he could hear them grinding together. He was pleasantly surprised when she'd stuck around—even if forced to do so by his arm around her shoulder. But then, when he'd kissed her cheek...Oh, when he'd kissed that soft skin and smelled the sweet fragrance that could only be described as

61

tenderness personified, he hadn't wanted to stop.

"I think we're all set." Kate's voice pulled him from his thoughts. "The kids are excited."

"Awesome. Hey, Kate, listen. I'm sorry about my family. Rush isn't really a jerk. He's a good guy, but he's my older brother, so you got to hear how brothers treat each other. If you felt pressured, we don't have to move forward with the mural."

"No. We'll do it. You can contact your mother later and have her arrange for the supplies. I think you are right. What you said finally got through to me." She locked her eyes on his. "So did Rush. Loud and clear."

He narrowed his gaze. "What is that supposed to mean?"

"Nothing I care to discuss."

She turned away, and he caught her by the arm. He'd been doing that a lot lately, and it never failed to surprise him how simply touching her set his nerves ablaze.

"You don't really believe that shit, do you?" His voice was a heated whisper.

She yanked her arm away. "Why do you care what I think?"

Christ. Goddamn it, Rush. "How did we go from being friends to this?"

She looked away, but not before Sage saw a flash of hurt in her eyes.

"Kate, maybe I misread the signals between us. God knows I'm not the best with women. But even if I did, you gotta know that I'm not anything like what Rush said."

She didn't respond. He was beginning to see why Rush always said that women were a big pain in the ass and he needed a woman in his life like he needed a hole in his fucking head. He was so damn confused. Why did she look hurt? It was him who should be hurt by her implication. And how the hell had he completely misread her? It was the beer. It had to be the beer. Without it, she had no interest in him, obviously. Why was he so damn attracted to a woman who was so frustrating and judgmental? If he wanted that type of person in his life, he could date any number of women back home.

He didn't want any of the women back home.

"Forget it." He nodded toward the kids gathering around the tables. "Let's just get through this. Then I'll go to town and arrange for the art supplies for the mural. The next two weeks will feel like they're over before they even have a chance to get started."

Before we even have a chance to get started.

Chapter Six

THE CHILDREN PORED over their drawings, their faces intent, pencils clutched tightly in their eager fingers as the afternoon sun pulled sweat from their limbs. Kate watched Sage crouching between two middle school boys. He showed one of them how to grip his pencil properly, then laughed when the boy put it in his left hand and mimicked the grasp perfectly. He came up on his feet and reached around the other boy, holding his hand as he guided it along his drawing. The boy turned thankful and excited eyes up toward him. Sage was so easy with them, as if he'd been teaching children all his life, which made Kate wonder about his past. He had five siblings. Did he have nieces or nephews? Had he spent time with children somewhere, or was he just naturally kind?

Or naturally a womanizer?

She watched him cross the yard toward her, and her stomach tightened. He flashed a smile as he came to her side.

"Wow, they're incredible. What a rush this is." He ran his hand through his hair. His face and arms had already begun to tan.

"I know. This is what makes me the happiest, watching them enjoy something this much." *And watching you, but I blew that one big-time.*

His voice grew serious, as if he'd just remembered that he was supposed to be mad at her. "Yeah, well I can see why." He made another sweep of the tables, helping a teenage girl and two more elementary-school-age boys.

"Miss Kate?" Javier looked up at Kate with wide eyes.

She crouched down to speak to him. At seven, Javier looked just like his father, with thick wavy hair and eyes as black as night. But it was his sweet demeanor that stole Kate's heart. He handed her a picture he'd drawn.

"Javier, this is beautiful." She looked at the drawing of his family.

"Mr. Sage showed me how to draw the eyes better. Bigger. He said they show more feelings that way." He used his pencil-thin index finger to point to the eyes of the woman. "That's my mother. See her happy eyes? That's how I remember her." It had been almost a year since his mother died, and from what Kate could glean from the psychologist she'd spoken with about Javier, the fact that he remembered what she looked like at all was a blessing. His mother's sisters, Sylvia and Louisa, now shared caring for Javier and his siblings, as their father spent many hours working in the fields. From what Kate had seen, Javier had adjusted well to the difficult situation.

"I think your mother would be very proud of you, Javier." She patted his shoulder, and he wrapped his arms around her neck.

"I will draw you next time."

"I would love that. And I think your aunts would

like to be in a picture, too."

"Mr. Sage says we're gonna paint the school pretty colors. He said we can help."

Sealing the deal through the children. Very sneaky.

"Yes, we're very excited to begin the project."

Javier flashed a bright smile and then ran to Sage. He held up the picture, and although Kate couldn't hear what they were saying, when Javier wrapped his arms around Sage's legs and stared up at him, her knees weakened.

LATER THAT AFTERNOON, Sage Skyped his mother and arranged for the art supplies to be flown in. As an artist, his mother would know exactly what he needed, and as a mother, she'd ensure that he didn't miss anything that the children would need as well, like smaller brushes. He asked her to pick up a few other items, avoided her questions about Kate, and he shut her down when she'd apologized for Rush's behavior. It wasn't her job to clear the air for Rush, and he knew that Rush hadn't meant any harm. He was just doing what they'd always done to each other. No harm, no foul. Only, the call had harmed Kate. *What's done is done.* Fame had taught Sage a valuable lesson. He wasn't in control of what others believed. He could only be the best man he knew how to be and hope it was enough. And that's exactly what he intended to do.

While in town, Sage replenished Kate's secret stash of beer as well as picked up a few for himself. He was carrying them to the kitchen when Caleb came from around the side of the cabins and caught up to him.

"Sage Remington, right?" Caleb was soft-spoken, his stringy bangs hung in front of his eyes, and he fidgeted nervously with the edge of his T-shirt.

"Yes. Caleb, right?" Sage held the beer toward him. "Want a cold one?"

"No, thank you."

"Do you mind talking while we walk? These will boil if I don't get them in the fridge soon."

"Sure." They walked into the mess hall. "Heard you're going to paint the school."

"Wow, word travels fast. That's what we hope to do, anyway. So you run the elderly and community outreach programs?" Sage asked.

"Yeah. We distribute medication and food and visit community members to see what other needs we can meet." He helped Sage load the beer into the refrigerator. "Your brother is Kurt Remington, the novelist, right?"

Sage wiped the condensation from his hands and smiled. "Yeah, that's right. You familiar with his books?"

Caleb's thin lips curved into a smile. "He's the best. I've read all of his books."

"Yeah? I'll have to connect you with him. He'd love to hear that." They headed back out of the building.

"Really? You'd do that?" He brushed his bangs from his forehead. "That's really cool of you. Thank you. I'm a big fan. I'm actually writing while I'm here. That's why you don't see me around much. I'm sure it's not very good, but..."

"Hey, don't say that. If you don't believe in yourself, who will?" Sage heard a car rumbling down the road.

"That would be the celebs," Caleb said.

"The celebs. That's what you call the volunteers?" Sage slid him a look. Part of him hoped to see Kate as they headed back to the cabins, and another part of him was still annoyed that she'd given credence to Rush's comments.

"Well...yeah. I mean, in a day or two the photographers will show up and take their pictures with some of the residents. They'll get all the media they want, and then they'll go back to the States and never think of the people here again."

Sage's muscles tensed. "Okay, fair enough. I can see that. But don't lump me in as a *celeb*, please. I'm an artist, not a celebrity, and I'm here because I want to be here. I don't have a PR person with me, and I don't have press that'll cover the trip. This is just me being me."

"Cool. You can be the *non*. As in non-celeb."

Clayton, Penelope, and Cassidy stumbled out of the car in fits of laughter. Caleb nodded toward them. "See? They haven't done one thing for the elderly or the community, but when those cameras are rolling? Whole different story."

"Hey, Sage!" Penelope yelled.

Sage narrowed his eyes. "They've gotta be plastered. She hasn't said two words to me since we arrived." He raised a hand in greeting, then turned his attention back to Caleb. "Hey, you wanna grab some dinner in town?"

Caleb shrugged. "Sure."

As they turned back toward the road, thundering feet stopped them in their tracks. Penelope and Cassidy chased after them in their skimpy skirts and barely there tops. They wore flat designer sandals. Behind them, Clayton jogged to catch up in his cowboy boots and jeans. Clayton was a hair taller than Sage, and while he was a stocky, muscular guy, probably two thirty or so, Sage's chest was broader and his muscles more pronounced.

"Wait!" Penelope yelled.

"Aw, shit," Sage mumbled.

"Dude, you should have gone into town. This place is dead, but the city? Man, it's a wild place," Clayton said. "It was kick-ass."

Sage noticed how none of the three of them had even acknowledged Caleb, and he wasn't going to allow them to ignore him. "You guys remember Caleb."

"Hey, bud. How's it hanging?" Clayton slapped Caleb on the back.

"Hi, Caleb," Penelope and Cassidy said in unison. Penelope linked arms with Sage.

He tried to pull away, but she wrapped her other hand around his arm as well, and short of yanking her arm off and causing a scene, Sage was trapped. She stood just a few inches shorter than him, which made him think of how petite Kate was—and how much better he felt beside her.

"We're going to get dinner. You guys eat already?" Stupid question. There was no way Penelope or Cassidy had eaten. Sage was sure they existed on air.

"Nope. We'll come along." Clayton slung an arm around Cassidy's shoulder. "There's a café in town that has dancing, too. We were there last night."

"Doubt I'll be dancing," Sage said under his breath.

They walked down the middle of the road, Clayton and Cassidy talking loudly. Caleb shoved his hands in his pockets, and Sage could see in his darting eyes that he was thinking of escaping.

He leaned in close and whispered, "I'm glad you're coming along. Thanks."

Caleb nodded, his eyes finally focusing on the road ahead.

Sage tried to keep a modicum of distance between himself and Penelope and took a step to the side. She tightened her grip on his arm. *Damn.* Shuffling in the bushes drew his attention away from Penelope and to the sound of laughter and fast footsteps. If he hadn't heard the laughter he would have wondered if the sound of the foliage shuffling was from a peccary or some other animal.

Kate and Luce burst through the forest and ran into the middle of the road, laughing so hard they had tears coming from their eyes. Sage was struck by the sound of Kate's laughter, her eyes full of happiness, her wet hair clinging to her T-shirt. His eyes locked on the two wet patches covering Kate's breasts, her nipples standing at attention.

Before he could tear his eyes away, Penelope put her cheek against his and whispered, "That what you like? I'll show you better, later."

Sage shook his head at the idea. *Hell no.* He looked up and saw Kate crossing her arms over her chest, staring at his and Penelope's intertwined arms.

Luce stifled her laughter.

"We goin' or what?" Clayton asked, pulling Cassidy forward.

Penelope dragged Sage past Kate. Sage locked eyes with Kate as he passed, seeing shadows of hurt and anger in them. The edges of her lips drew down, her jaw tightly clenched. He couldn't look away. He couldn't say anything, not with Penelope's tentacles wrapped around his arm. He drew his brows together. *It's not what it looks like.* He hoped Kate could read the discontent in his eyes, but she never had the chance. She'd already stomped away.

Clayton sidled up to Sage and grabbed his other arm; then, remarkably, Cassidy looped her arm into Caleb's, and they headed into the town. *The celebs and the nons.* Sage took one last glance behind him and decided to *man up*, as his father would say. Kate had her own beliefs about the type of person Sage was, and just thinking about her made his gut twist. *The hell with it.* A few drinks might ease the pain.

Chapter Seven

"KATE. KATE!" LUCE caught up to her as she blazed through the path to her cabin. "Jesus, woman, slow down."

"Slow down? Slow down! Did you not see what just happened? Why was I even considering that he *wasn't* that guy?" She spun around, and Luce ran right into her chest. "*Ugh.* You know, watching him with Javier and the other kids today, I just about believed that he was this nice guy. I had even disregarded the comments from his brother after what you said about siblings. But come on, Luce." She spun around, batting the plants out of her way. "What kind of guy hooks up with...with...her?"

"Penelope? She's not that bad. A little spoiled, but come—"

"Luce! Not helping!"

"Sorry. Well, if you want him to know you're interested, then you gotta do something besides making him feel like he's a bad guy who wants to do all the wrong things. I mean, even I know that, and I'm not very aggressive when it comes to dating." Luce followed her up the stairs and inside. "Wow. I love what you've done with the scarves. The last time I was here, the windows were bare."

"I needed color," she snapped.

"Well, your sticky notes add that."

Kate paced the small room, three steps one way, turned on her heel, then continued with three steps the other way. "I don't want him. I just don't want her to have him."

"Liar."

Kate crossed her arms and huffed.

"Just sayin'."

"Where are they even going? The town is an inch long." Kate flopped onto the bed, then popped right back up and paced again.

"You're making me nervous." Luce moved to the side of the room so Kate had a clear path to pace. "I've never seen you like this. What's got your panties in a bunch?"

Kate pressed her lips into a tight, angry line and stared at Luce as understanding dawned on her.

"Oh...that's what it is. *He* has your panties in a bunch. Or rather...Oh, never mind. Well, that's quite a problem, then, isn't it?"

"No. It's not a problem because he's just some guy. He'll be gone soon, and I'll move on to another location." She looked down at her shirt, which was nearly dry, the outline of her breasts still visible, and she remembered the way Sage had looked at her, like she was the hottest girl on the planet. She never felt hot, and in that one second, she'd never felt hotter. *Or angrier, or maybe hurt. Ugh.* She didn't know what she felt. She flopped on the bed again and blew out a breath. "That was fun this afternoon. I miss doing things like that."

"I bet. There aren't many girls to have girl time

with around here, are there?"

"Wanna go get a drink?" *Or twelve?*

Luce reached for her hand and pulled her off the bed. "Brave girl after last night."

"Shut up. I need to chill."

Luce followed her back toward the mess hall. "I'm not walking you home tonight, just so you know. I hate that creepy path."

"You brave New York City every day and you can't walk through a little jungle path?" Kate tried to sound carefree, but inside, her stomach was one big, angry, and hurt bundle of knots. *Do I have to be model pretty for him to notice me?* Granted, she had sent him mixed signals. Maybe Luce was right. *Maybe I do need to step up my game. Shit, who am I kidding? I have no game.*

Two hours later, she and Luce were two sheets to the wind...again. And she felt damn good. All that festering confusion was cast aside and replaced with a lighter, freer feeling. She put her arm around Luce's shoulder as they stepped from the empty mess hall into the darkness. "Did you buy that beer?"

"No. I think your alpha hunk did."

"Really? Hm..." *My alpha hunk. I like the sound of that. Oh God. What is wrong with me? No, I can't like the sound of it...but I do.* They hadn't stopped to get beer after his Skype call. He must have gotten it when he Skyped his mother to get the art supplies. *His mother. What kind of man Skypes his mother the day after he arrives?* Maybe he was secretly a wimp. A loser. *Yeah, right. A big, sexy, talented loser.* She felt like a yo-yo. Her mind was right back to wondering if she'd judged him too harshly. "Wanna go dancing?"

"Girlfriend, I wanna find my bunk and hunker down for a room-spinning night of reading romance and pretending I have a man." Luce laughed. "No. Seriously. That's what I'm gonna do, minus the reading.

But you can't go into town this late by yourself."

Kate sat down on one of the wooden benches. "I'm not. I'm just gonna sit here and stargaze. I'm not ready to go home. I feel too good."

"You sure you're okay? I can stay with you."

Kate waved her hand. "I'm cool. Really. I do live here without you ninety-eight percent of the time, or something like that."

SAGE PRIED PENELOPE'S hand from his thigh for the millionth time that evening. She was like superglue. No matter how many times he disengaged from her, she found her way back. When she wasn't hanging on his arm, she was plastering herself around his body. He and Caleb had been exchanging eye rolls all evening, but unlike one of his brothers, Caleb had no idea how to diffuse the situation. Any one of his brothers would have taken a hit for him—thrown themselves at her as if she were a land mine—and given him a chance to escape.

Penelope and Cassidy excused themselves to use the ladies' room, and Sage debated taking off while the coast was clear, but that would have been rude.

Clayton leaned in close. "Dude, she's primed and ready after a few beers, and she's a maniac in the bedroom."

Sage's muscles twitched. "Cassidy?"

"Penelope. I was with her last night."

So, basically you're a dick. He clenched his jaw to keep from letting the words slip out.

"Two for one." Clayton raised his brows in quick succession. "But, hell, if you're not gonna do her, send her my way. I bet I can convince Cassidy to do a three-way."

Sage bit back the bile that rose in his throat as the women returned to the table. Clayton's reputation preceded him. Sage had taken the rumors with a grain of salt, but now, hearing firsthand what a pig he was, it took all of his restraint not to throw the asshole against the wall and knock some respect into him.

Sage rose to his feet, and Penelope grabbed the pocket of his shorts.

"Dance with me," she pleaded.

Despite her beautiful green eyes, silky blond hair, and the alluring package of perfect breasts and sensual looks that was Penelope Price, Sage saw the real Penelope. His artist's eye had the ability to see, not just external beauty, but the sincerity, generosity, and ulterior motives people kept hidden deep inside. In Penelope he saw loneliness and an ill-advised heart seeking comfort in all the wrong ways. Unfortunately, while for some that might inspire empathy, it didn't make him want to cross an intimate line with her. Sage had learned some things growing up: There was always a willing woman to sleep with, and while meaningless sex was a great stress reliever and ego boost, it didn't solve loneliness. He'd sown those wild oats, and he no longer needed the ego boost. Now he craved something more. Very similar to the way his fame and monetary success made him realize that what would fulfill him would never be found in either one.

He unfurled her fingers from his pocket, forced a smile—because his mother had taught him manners, after all—and excused himself to use the men's room.

Once free of Penelope's grasp and her pushy stare, he splashed water on his face and stared long and hard in the mirror. He'd been forcing himself not to think of Kate, but every goddamn time he turned around, it was her face he saw. The hurt that had flashed in her eyes, the smile she wore when she was with the children at the school, and the way she looked at him like a hungry tigress in one breath and as if he were the enemy in the next made him crazy. As complicated as she was, when he was with Kate, his whole world felt different. She'd snuck into his brain when he wasn't looking and weaseled her way into the crevices of his heart.

How the hell did that happen?

Back at the table, Cassidy and Clayton were wrapped around each other, whispering something Sage couldn't hear. He set his eyes on Caleb, hoping Penelope would opt to stay there and have another drink with the others.

"Buddy, I'm gonna take off." He threw seventy bucks on the table, knowing it would cover far more than the four beers he'd drank, and ran his hand through his hair with a sigh.

Penelope stood and wrapped her arm in his.

Sage didn't miss the laugh in Caleb's eyes as he rose to join them on the walk back. With a reluctant sigh, he wondered how in the hell he was going to get out of the web Penelope was so carefully weaving around him.

Chapter Eight

THERE WAS SOMETHING about Belize at night that calmed Kate from the inside out. She breathed in the dense, jungle-scented air and, feeling far less of a buzz than she had an hour earlier, she lay down on the wooden bench. When she'd first arrived in Punta Palacia, she'd been careful not to go out alone at night, and she'd taken extra care while in town to always watch her back. She'd heard so many reports about the dangers of Belize City that she'd assumed Punta Palacia would be privy to the same types of trouble, but she'd quickly learned that the hazards of Punta Palacia were nothing like the trouble that Belize City was known for. Nights in Punta Palacia had a way of sucking her into a vortex of serenity and hope. Serenity wasn't dangerous, but hope could be. She'd lain awake too many nights to count, hoping she would gain approval for a well for the village, but knowing how remote the chances were. The village of Punta Palacia was small compared to the larger villages, and the government deemed their needs insignificant in comparison.

Voices broke the silence of the night, and Kate

turned in their direction. It was too dark to make out anything more than figures and a flashlight beam. As they came closer, she recognized the sheer volume of space Sage's body took up compared to the other lithe figures that all seemed to meld together. Kate held her breath.

Should I say hello? Pretend I'm not here? She went with hoping to remain invisible.

They cut across the grass toward the path. Kate saw the closeness of Sage and Penelope's bodies as the others trailed behind them. She felt their intimacy as if every step shot prickly thorns in her direction—piercing her heart.

He's with her.

Push her away, damn it. That should be me on your arm! Me pressed against you! Jealousy tore through her like a stampede, and she turned away, nearly falling off the bench. She caught herself with one palm on the ground and sucked in a breath, hoping they didn't hear her.

How can you not know how I feel?

Another realization brought a lump to her throat.

Because I acted like a judgmental bitch.

She lay under the cover of the night, listening more intently now and wanting to shut them out at the same time, existing in a painful middle place of self-loathing and the need to know how far he'd go. She knew it was ridiculous for her to feel jealous of Penelope. Sage wasn't hers. He was a free agent. A man for any woman to entice. *Damn it. Damn it. Damn it.* For the first night in two years, Punta Palacia didn't feel quite so serene, and hope was out the door altogether.

She listened to their voices fade, and though she hated doing so, she counted the sounds of the doors as they knocked against their frames. *One. Two.* Two? What the hell did that mean? It didn't take more than a second for her to realize that Sage and Penelope had coupled off. She lay on her back, staring at the stars. *Why had she acted the way she had?* She arced her arm over her eyes and groaned aloud.

I'm an idiot.

A fucking fool.

If you'd be with her, then I wouldn't want you anyway.

Kate felt more than heard Sage standing beside her. Her pulse sped up, and that sinking feeling in the pit of her stomach now burned with anticipation. She wouldn't dare lower her arm. *Please think I'm sleeping.*

She felt him sit on the bench beside her. His hips pressed against her side. She lay perfectly still, breathing shallowly. *Go away. Stay. Oh God!* His big hand was shockingly cool against her wrist as he gently lifted her arm from her eyes. She clenched her eyes shut. His fingers brushed her bangs from her forehead. She could barely breathe. His touch was so light, almost nonexistent, yet so intimate it stole her ability to think. Then his cheek was against hers, his whiskers sharp and titillating. His warm breath on her ear stirred her desire, her need for him. He didn't speak. He didn't need to. He was there with her. Not with Penelope, not angry at her bitchiness. Not anything but...here.

SAGE'S HAND TREMBLED as he sat beside Kate. He'd felt her sadness when he'd walked by earlier. He swore the energy had changed when they'd neared the path. Then he'd heard it. A gasp. A hurt, painful gasp, and he'd known it was Kate. He'd felt it reverberate through his body. Now she lay in her shorts and T-shirt, her eyes tightly closed, and he drank in the scent of her, the feel of her silky skin against his cheek. Sage wasn't driven by a need to sleep with her, although every fiber of his being craved her. No, it wasn't testosterone that drove him there. It was something deeper, something he hadn't felt before but embraced with curiosity and desire. She was so little, but the bench was thin, barely deep enough for her body and his hip. Still, he didn't let his mind overcome his intuitive nature. He'd make himself fit. Sage stretched out beside Kate, wrapping his arm around her shoulder and drawing her to him: chest to chest, cheek to cheek, heartbeat to heartbeat. Her breathing sped up as her arm gracefully settled over him, and her leg nestled in between his, like they'd been lying together forever. Sage stroked her back, his fingers tangling in the silky threads of her hair. *Damn, you feel good.*

"You're here," she whispered.

"I'm here."

"But—"

"Shh. I told you that I'm not who you think I am." He brushed his lips over the corner of her mouth, testing, tasting. Her arms gripped him tighter; her hips pressed against his. She tilted her head, her lips parting, welcoming his as he settled his mouth over them, and he relished the first luscious stroke of her tongue against his. *Sweet, delicious Kate.* Sage's heart swelled. He felt himself getting hard, but it wasn't those sexual urges that drew his hand to cup the back of her head and tilt her head, giving him better access to deepen the kiss. *Christ.* Kissing Kate was a thousand times better than any fantasy he'd conjured up over the past few days. He drew back, needing to look in her eyes.

"Kate?" He searched her eyes, looking for a sign, something to tell him she wanted this as badly as he did.

Her eyes fluttered open, filled with the sleepy haze of desire. She opened her mouth to speak, but no words came out.

Sage pressed his cheek to hers again.

"Kiss me again," she whispered.

He slid his cheek against hers and then took her in a hungry, deep kiss, capturing her sweet moan of pleasure and spurring his body into a frenzy of need. His hand slipped beneath her shirt, caressing her warm back; then, despite knowing they should take things slow, he cupped her breast, her nipple already taut beneath her silky bra. He kissed the dimple in her chin, then dragged his lips lower to the sensitive spot at the base of her neck, feeling her quickened pulse against his tongue. His lips lingered there, weighing his throbbing desire against his worry about what she thought of him.

"Sage," she said in one drawn-out breath.

He closed his eyes, fighting the urge to take her right there on the bench, just pull down her shorts and drive into her, the night air at their backs. *No, not with Kate.* He tasted alcohol on her breath, and he wasn't taking any chances that she'd wake up tomorrow regretting what they'd done tonight. He reluctantly pulled back, drew her hair away from her face, and kissed her forehead.

"I really like you, Kate," he said, feeling like a teenager admitting a crush, but in reality, the emotions that were gripping him felt a hell of a lot deeper, as if they'd slipped clear through to his soul.

"Me too," she said.

He closed his eyes for a beat, soaking in her words and unable to believe what he was about to do. When he opened them, the desire in Kate's eyes drew him into another kiss, pressing his hips to hers, feeling her body against his hard length. Christ, he wanted to make love to her. He dropped his hand and cupped her firm ass. *Sweet Jesus.*

She moaned against his lips, pressing her breasts

against him. He nearly caved. She was finally there, in his arms, and...he forced himself to draw back again.

"Kate." He breathed heavily. "I...we...I can't do this. Not like this."

Confusion filled her eyes. "I don't understand."

He rested his forehead against hers. "If I make love to you now, you'll wake up tomorrow and think it was because I didn't do it with Penelope and needed to satisfy an urge, or it was because I drank, or...Hell I don't know." He pressed a kiss to her lips again. "I only know that I don't want to chance it."

She breathed heavily against his lips, her eyes searching for more answers. Sage's heart ached. He pushed himself up to a sitting position and leaned his elbows on his knees, then rested his forehead in his palm. *I'm doing the right thing.* Kate drew herself up next to him, worry coming off of her in waves. He wrapped his arm around her and pulled her close.

"You okay?" he asked.

"Mm-hm."

Bullshit. He drew her chin toward him, pinning her with his gaze. "This is the hardest thing I've ever done, Kate. I want to take you into your cabin and make love to you until you forget your name. Hell, until I forget my name, which if those kisses were any indication, wouldn't take very long at all, but I'm not willing to chance you thinking anything bad about me."

"Okay." Her voice was a shaky thread.

"If we were in New York, I'd want to take you out, get to know you. Here..." He looked around. "I don't know. You're so..." He drew his eyebrows together, feeling completely inept at stringing words together. "I have a feeling you're anything but a fling, Kate, and I want you to know that. To feel it. But here? How do I show you that?"

Her eyes searched his, and Sage read the

disappointment in them and in her body language as she pulled away.

"It's not you. Jesus, you're gorgeous, and your kisses are like heaven. You're..." He smiled, unable to lie. "You're frustrating and strong, and soft and feminine and, Kate, I might be making the biggest mistake of my life by stopping us here. Now. You might wake up tomorrow and want nothing more to do with me, but I have to do what feels right. I'm willing to chance it."

She turned to face him, her knees brushing his legs, causing his chest to constrict. She placed her palm on his cheek and closed her eyes, a sigh slipping from her lips. When she opened her eyes, the worry was gone.

"I've been wanting to do that," she whispered. "Not just the kiss, but to touch your cheek."

He covered her hand with his and pressed it to his cheek, unable to find a single word to fill the silence. They sat together for a long time, her body tucked beneath his arm, her head on his shoulder, and Sage was in no rush to break their connection. Eventually they made their way to Kate's hut. When they reached the door, Sage forced himself not to go inside.

Kate opened the screen door and stood inside her room with the door open, their hands still clasped, the threshold of the door a barrier between them. "You can come in."

He was rooted to the porch. If he took one step inside, he knew he wouldn't leave. He brought her hand to his lips and kissed it, then did the safe thing and pulled her to him. On the porch. Cheek to cheek, chest to chest.

He kissed her deeply, feeling his resolve chipping away with each stroke of her tongue. She pressed her hips to his. It would be so easy. Three steps and they'd be across the floor. Two more and they'd have reached her bed. Then he could touch her, fall into her warmth, and love her until they were both too exhausted to think. She made a sexy little moan, and it brought him back to his senses.

He pulled back again. "Kate." He kissed her again. "I can't." *Jesus. What guy would turn her away like this?*

She bit her lower lip and looked up at him through her thick lashes.

"Jesus, I want to carry you to that bed and make love to you right now. This second. But damn it, Kate. I want you to know what kind of person I am before we come together. I can't be close to you knowing that you think I'm someone I'm not." He kissed her dimple. God, he'd wanted to do that since he first saw her.

She nodded. "Okay." Her voice was barely a whisper.

"Okay." He kissed her again, then opened the screen door for her and closed it after she was inside. She pressed her hand against the screen and he did the same. If he didn't go now, he was going to walk right through that door. He blew her a kiss and turned away.

With each step as he walked away, he told himself he was doing the right thing. He turned back at the bottom of the steps. Kate stood inside, her hand still pressed to the screen. He blew her another kiss, then took his leave, feeling like he had just found the person he never wanted to be without and knowing just how crazy of a thought that was.

Chapter Nine

KATE AWOKE THE next morning filled with adrenaline. Despite the drinking. Despite the fact that Sage had turned her down. *Again.* Everything he had said and done the night before had waylaid any worries she'd had about him. She danced to the radio as she showered and dressed, feeling as if new life had been breathed into her lungs. She touched her lips, remembering the feel of his, the sensuous way he'd kissed her and the way she'd lain in bed craving his touch for hours after he'd gone.

She turned off the radio and met Luce at the mess hall for breakfast.

"Press comes in today." Luce took a long sip of her coffee.

"Mm-hmm." Kate's heart slammed against her chest as she eyed the door. Nervous and excited about seeing Sage again. She had no idea how she was supposed to act around him.

"You okay?" Luce asked.

"What?" Kate twisted the ends of her hair.

"What is going on with you? You're off in la-la land.

Am I missing something?"

"What? No." She sighed, wishing Sage would come through the door. "I heard you. Press comes in today. The celebs might even be up before noon."

"They have strict orders to be up and ready by nine. Camera and makeup crew should be here by ten." Luce touched Kate's hand across the table. "A watched pot never boils."

She drew her eyes from the doorway. "I know. I know." *Oh shit.* "You know?"

"Now I do." She arched a brow. "Spill."

"Nothing happened." She leaned across the table and whispered, "Again."

"Nothing?"

"Well, we kissed. Oh my God, did we kiss, but not...you know. He got all chivalrous on me. He's so...He just wants to do the right thing, I guess. I'm so freaking nervous. I mean, *ugh.* How am I supposed to act? You know what I mean?"

"Yeah, I know, and you're about to find out." Luce nodded toward Sage as he walked into the mess hall with Clayton. Clayton's eyes were puffy, his walk sluggish—evidence of a night spent awake—in stark contrast to the serious look on Sage's face as he scanned the room and headed directly over to Kate and Luce. Penelope and Cassidy were right behind them.

Sage leaned down and kissed Kate's cheek. "Good morning."

Momentarily stunned by his openness, Kate stammered, "Um...uh...hi." She felt her cheeks flush, and when he rested his hand on her shoulder, her eyes shifted to Penelope, catching the virtual daggers being tossed her way. *Great.*

"Do you mind if I join you after I get coffee?" he asked.

"We've got a seat right there with your name on it."

Luce pointed to the chair beside Kate's.

He squeezed her shoulder. "Be right back. Can I get you anything?"

Still unable to speak, Kate slid a pleading look to Luce.

"We're good. Thanks," Luce said. She watched Sage walk away and then snapped her attention back to Kate. "Jesus, I've never seen you like this."

"I know," she said in a harsh whisper. "It's like he sucks my brain cells away. I'm so embarrassed."

"Well, get your shit together before he comes back. Seriously, Kate, and, by the way, you are the cat's meow right now, causing man-envy from the pretties over there." She lifted her chin toward the celebs.

"Great, so they think I'm an easy lay." *Just what I need, a reputation I can't even live up to.*

"Do you really care? You know the truth, and that handsome man knows the truth. Besides me, who else matters?"

Kate glanced at the celebs, feeling a sliver of pleasure tingle her nerves at being the woman Sage chose to be with. With that thought, she pulled her shoulders back and let out a long breath.

Sage sat beside her and draped his arm over the back of her chair, sending another shiver through Kate's body. His biceps stretched the sleeves of his T-shirt to the shredding point, the outline of his pecs and abs evident beneath the thin cotton. Kate wanted to reach out and touch his chest. She wanted to feel the beat of her heart against his again.

"What's on our Punta Palacia plate today, mentor?" He sipped his coffee and smiled at Kate.

She hadn't experienced a racing pulse or fluttering belly from a guy since she was in college and her sophomore crush asked her out. Her crush had been exterminated in the first twenty minutes of their date, when he'd cornered her in the elevator on their way downstairs and groped her. She didn't know what she'd expected, but something more than being groped before they'd even had a conversation, that was for sure. Now, with Sage, she had a hard time pushing the desires that she'd been suppressing from coming forward. She *wanted* to be groped. Hell, she wanted so much more. She couldn't look at his lips without remembering the taste of them or the feel of them against her neck.

She forced herself to speak like a normal, not lust-driven, person. "Press arrives today, so there'll be a bit of mania around them, of course."

"Press. Hm." Sage took a drink of his coffee. "Any chance I can avoid that?"

"Don't you want to be in the papers? You're doing the most work of all of them here. It would be really good publicity for you," Luce added.

"I didn't even let my PR rep know I was coming here, Luce. The last thing I want is to be pressured into taking trips for press purposes. That's when people become jaded. Doing things because they have to rather than because they want to." He slid his hand from the back of Kate's chair to her shoulder and gently rubbed his hand across her back. "I would really like to avoid ever becoming that person."

Luce tucked a strand of her hair behind her ear and glanced at Kate. Kate knew Luce's heart was melting as quickly as her own was. The feel of his fingers against her back was comforting and electrifying at the same time.

"Sure, um. When I have their schedule, I'll let you know, and you can sort of maneuver around where they're gonna be." Kate nearly sighed aloud when his entire hand rounded her shoulder and pulled her close. When his lips touched her temple, the sigh broke free.

"Thank you," he said softly.

THE TOWN HADN'T felt quite so small before the press moved in. Sage did his best to avoid them, but it seemed that they were everywhere. They filtered through the town and invaded the school and the compound. He needed a break. Between the heat and the stress of their presence, he wished there was a cave he could hide in. And as he watched the craziness come to life, he realized that while he loved the idea of helping developing nations and villages like Punta Palacia, he wanted to do so without the hype or the recognition.

He returned to the mess hall a few hours after lunch, figuring he'd missed the worst of the press, and grabbed two bottles of cold water. Sylvia was in the kitchen making corn tortillas.

"Hi, Sylvia. Are you getting any peace?"

She shook her head. Her apron was covered with powder, and her large, capable hands worked the dough with practiced skill. "It happens every time," she said. "They think they own the place." She shook her head again.

"Yeah. I'm sorry you have to go through this. They'll be gone soon."

He turned to leave and ran smack into Penelope's chest. *Damn it.* Last night she hadn't taken his refusal to come into her room very well. She'd been downright pissed, and she hadn't tried to hide the fact, calling him a coward and accusing him of being less than a man.

He steeled himself for her wrath. "Sorry, Penelope. I didn't realize you were there."

The clicking of cameras sounded from the doorway.

"For Christ's sake." He masked his anger and plastered a fake smile on his lips as he made his way

91

out the door. He wasn't on their list of celebrities to photograph or interview, and as they followed him, snapping picture after picture, he grew angrier by the second.

"Mr. Remington," someone called after him. "Care to give us a statement?"

Sage stopped and turned back around. "Yes, actually. I'd love to, but only if you will then keep me off your radar. I'm not here for the press, and I'd like to make it through the day without having to dodge cameras." He knew they'd take the bait. Everyone wanted what they couldn't have, and because Sage kept his press contact to a minimum, he was their van Gogh.

"You've got it." A short, red-haired man held a microphone at the ready. Two other men and a woman had pen and paper in hand.

Sage pulled his shoulders back and looked into one of the cameras with a serious stare. "The people of Punta Palacia have been gracious enough to invite and accept us into their community. We're fortunate to have the honor of being here, under the generous tutelage of people like Kate Paletto and Caleb Forman, who have given years of their lives to help the community without the promise of anything more than a place to rest their bodies at night. Those are the people who deserve to be recognized for their efforts." He turned on his heel and stalked away.

Luce caught up to him at the edge of the road—not that he had any idea where he was going, but he had to get away from the story-hungry leeches behind him.

"You know you're going to have a shit storm to deal with one way or another, right?"

"Why? For telling the truth?" He walked at a quick pace.

"You never give impromptu interviews. You're a million miles from home without your PR rep guiding

Stroke of Love

you on what to say, and you just gave them what you thought was a simple, honest statement." Luce shook her head. "They'll either clip it and post it with a picture of you scowling and make it appear that you don't appreciate being here, or they'll slap a photo of you and Penelope on the front page with the headline *Sage and Penny, the New Humanitarian Couple!*"

Sage shot her an angry look. When they reached the town, he kept going. "Don't you have to handle your people or something?"

Luce laughed. "They have enough handlers today. Besides, I gave them my spiel earlier this morning and advised the makeup and clothing teams of what was appropriate. Penelope can fuck this up all on her own, and I'm not Clayton or Cassidy's rep, so whatever they do, they can deal with. I'll deal with Penelope's mess once I see what hits the fan." She hurried to keep up with him. "Where are you heading, anyway?"

"I'm sorry, Luce. I don't mean to come across gruff. I'm not really sure where I'm going. Away from there; that's all I know."

"You really don't like that attention, do you?"

"You could say that." Everything about the press rubbed Sage the wrong way. It wasn't that he was against public relations in general. He was against public relations when it wasn't deserved. Sage followed the road through town, passing the Internet café and the little bar where they'd gone for drinks, and wound down the path Kate had told him about that led into the village. The town fell away behind them, and the mountains flourished before them. Sage breathed a little easier and slowed his pace.

"Have you been into the village before?" Luce wiped her brow.

"No. Look how beautiful it is. I mean, when you're in the city, do you ever think about places like this?"

93

Sage had spent his whole life wishing he could spend more time surrounded by nature. When he was a boy, he used to spend hours in the woods with his eldest brother, Jack. Jack was a born outdoorsman. Burly, confident, and ready to take on the world, he reminded Sage of a lumberjack, while Sage thought of himself as more of a nature lover with a softer touch. Sure, he was as masculine as the next guy, but his love of nature stemmed from the serenity of it, the joy of being surrounded by the living organisms and the natural paths of life that fed civilization in so many ways.

"I think more about places like Maui and the white sandy beach resorts of Belize than I do the villages and towns," Luce admitted.

He let out a long sigh. "Yeah, most people do."

"But not Kate. She thinks about helping others, no matter where she is."

Sage had wondered if Luce was going to try to pry him for information about Kate. He glanced at Luce, with her hair clipped efficiently at the base of her neck, and her tan shorts and her sleeveless, white button-down shirt. She looked as if she'd walked off the pages of a tourist brochure. She'd dressed the part of public relations rep today. Sage supposed she'd had to. He liked Luce. He'd known of her before coming to Belize, and since spending time with her, he liked her feisty and forthright nature. He could tell she didn't put up with any bullshit, and it was obvious that she cared for Kate. That alone endeared her to him.

"So what you're saying is that Kate has a generous soul." He already knew the answer, but this was the easiest way of diverting the conversation away from his growing emotions for her.

"The most generous, or so I thought until I heard your speech back there. Did you say that because of Kate?"

Kate. Sage hadn't been able to stop thinking about her since he said good night at the foot of the stairs to her cabin last night. If he hadn't forced himself to leave, the stairs wouldn't have been all he was mounting.

"I would have said it about anyone who work like Kate and Caleb do. They're selfless in their pursuit of helping others in a way that is genuine and deserves a hell of a lot more recognition than those clowns back there." A group of small homes came into view. "I'm sorry, Luce. I know your clients are important to you, and I'm sure some are genuine in their efforts. It's just one of those days." *Pent-up sexual desires and heat don't mix well.*

"That's okay. Well, I'm not trying to pry...or maybe I am. I've known Kate a few years now, and I know how she comes across sort of hot and cold. She's skeptical, but look at what she deals with day in and day out. She's my friend, and I care about her. Just give her time."

Sage thought of how right she'd felt in his arms. "I've got nothing but time."

The first home they came to was built from wide-planked boards, with the same thatched roof as the cabins where they were staying. There were two sections to the home. Sage slowed to take in the smoke rising from the back section of the hut.

"Why two sections?" He craned his neck to peer inside. Two women stood before a cooking area, stirring the contents of two large metal pots, smoke billowing around them. One of the women lifted a woven fan and fanned the smoke away. The other said something, causing them both to laugh.

"One's a cooking house. The other is a sleeping area."

"Do they have running water? Electricity?"

Luce shook her head. "Not yet. They get their water

from the river. They're really an amazing group of people. If you think people in the States work hard, then you're in for an eye-opening realization. The families here rise before dawn. The children gather wood for the fires and go down to the river to fetch water for cooking. Then the women prepare breakfast. The men leave for the fields before the sun rises. Sometimes the older boys go with their fathers, if their help is needed. The men return right before sunset for dinner with the family. Then they bathe in the river at night."

"But we have water just up the road." Sage was beginning to feel like fate had brought him to Punta Palacia for a much bigger reason than meeting Kate. His mind was wrapping itself around an idea that at the moment seemed a little far-fetched, but as Luce continued, the pieces began to fall together.

"You're right. Wells are as close as the town and the cabins, but they'd need a separate well here because they're too far to use the same one. That's one of the issues Kate's been working on, getting a well for the village. But funding for such a small community is hard to come by." She nodded at two women in the cooking house, seemingly oblivious to the sweltering heat. "I could never do what they do."

The basic necessities that he took for granted began to take on a whole new perspective. Sage glanced at the women in the cooking house and listened to them talking. Their Creole accents were so thick that he couldn't make out what they were saying. Then he thought about Penelope and Cassidy bitching about their accommodations—which had running water and electricity—and it struck him how spoiled they were and how oblivious they were to the things in life that really mattered. *People. Love. Spending time together.*

"We have so much, and at the same time, we have so little." His mind traveled down a fast and furious path. With Sage's connections, and the connections of his family, he was sure he'd be able to pull together enough resources for wells for the village. But he couldn't fund every community, and surely there were thousands in need of the same resources. Sage realized that his idea of creating artwork that reflected the area to sell in the States toward donations for Punta Palacia was small potatoes. He needed to think globally. The idea seeded on their way back to the compound, and by the time the cabins came into sight, the idea had bloomed to a full-blown concept.

Sage was relieved that the press had already left when they reached the compound and he headed into the mess hall for more water with Luce.

"Hey, Sage," Clayton called from the path.

"Go on in. I'll be right behind you," Sage said to Luce. *What the hell do you want?*

Clayton sidled up to him and put his arm around Sage. Sage cringed.

"Dude, thanks for last night."

"Excuse me?" *What the hell?*

"Dude, you primed Penelope. She was livid with you, so of course she went to Cassidy's place to commiserate, and...well...let's just say three's definitely *not* a crowd."

Sage's hands fisted. He shrugged out from under Clayton's arm and stomped off toward the building. Clayton, apparently as thick-headed as he was horny, caught up to him again.

"So, if you wanna do the same with that hot little volunteer, Kate, I'll gladly take your throwbacks."

The heat of the afternoon and his annoyance at Clayton, Penelope, and the press exploded in a rush of adrenaline. In the next breath, Sage had Clayton by the collar. He lifted him off the ground and slammed his back against a tree, seething between clenched teeth. "If I ever hear you mention her name again in that way, I will tear you apart."

"Dude." The veins in Clayton's neck bulged. He held his arms up in surrender, holding Sage's stare.

Every muscle tense, every nerve tight and hot, Sage lowered his voice and pressed his face an inch away from Clayton's. "Shut up. Not one word, you hear me? Stay the fuck away from me, and stay the fuck away from Kate, or I promise you this: I will ensure that not only can you never touch another woman, but you'll be lucky if you can walk. Got it?"

Clayton swallowed hard. "G-got it. Okay. Dude, I'm sorry. I didn't realize it was serious."

Sage dropped him to his feet, and Clayton stumbled away, cursing under his breath. Sage spun around, blinded by rage. His chest swelled with each heavy breath, his veins protruded from his arms—and his eyes caught on Kate and Luce standing at the entrance to the mess hall, looking at him as though he'd lost his mind.

Perfect. Just fucking perfect.

Chapter Ten

"SAGE!" KATE'S EYES locked on him. His shoulders were pulled back, every muscle ripe with anger. His jaw was set tough and tight, his eyes dark and angry. She took a step in his direction and Luce held her back.

"You might want to give him a sec."

Give him a sec? What the hell was going on? He looked like he was going to kill Clayton. She pulled her arm free, took a last look at Luce, then ran to Sage as he stalked off.

"Sage, what happened?"

He shot a look at her that clearly said, *Back off,* and stomped through the path toward the cabins.

She pushed the foliage out of her way and kept after him. "Sage, if it's something I should know about, please, tell me."

He stopped walking. Kate held her breath, desperate for him to turn around. She had to talk to him, to see his eyes. To know what could have possibly caused the even-tempered Mr. Chill to react so violently.

He finally turned to face her. His massive arms

were tense, ready to finish the fight. He closed the gap between them and stared down at her, his nostrils flaring. Kate held her breath. Heat and anger coalesced in his eyes and rolled off his body. *You're a way-too-sexy badass.* She watched his dark eyes narrow, his lips part, and in the next moment she was in his arms, his lips were on hers, and his tongue—*oh, that glorious, talented tongue*—was stroking away her brain cells again. It was a rough kiss, driven by passion or anger. She didn't know—or care—which. Every nerve in her body was on fire, and when he put his enormous hands beneath her arms and lifted her up to his height, she didn't need a single brain cell to wrap her legs around his waist and soak up his heat.

One strong arm slid beneath her, holding her against him. His other hand moved up her back and cupped the base of her head. And oh, the sensations that sent between her legs, where his abs pressed against her most sensitive parts...He pressed her closer to him, deepening the kiss. His glorious cheeks scratched against hers. She didn't care about whisker burn. Loved it, in fact. When he finally drew back, they were both breathless, panting, wanting more. *So much more.*

"I really fucking like you."

It was an accusation, with his piercing stare and his angry tone, but it was more. It was a statement of fact *and* an accusation. He really did fucking like her, and holy hell, what did that mean? How the hell was she supposed to respond to that?

Honestly.

"I really fucking like you, too." *Why am I whispering?*

He kissed her again, rough at first, then softer, more meaningful, more lovingly.

"What the hell are we gonna do?" His voice still

held a thread of anger.

He searched her eyes, and the answer was too obvious. Wasn't it? What did all adults do when they wanted each other? Maybe the anger had stolen *his* brain cells.

"Um." She panted. "Go to my cabin?" *Now. This second.*

He rested his forehead against her. "I don't want you anywhere near that asshole. I know it's your job, and I have no business telling you what to do or with whom, but the thought of you and him kills me."

He was still holding her, and she could barely comprehend what he was saying. His body was too close, too hard. Damn hard.

"Me and Clayton?" was all she could manage.

His nostrils flared, as if she'd said, *Oh yeah. Me and Clayton—we're gonna fuck like bunnies.*

"I can't tell you what to do," he said again.

Shit. His brain isn't working. "No, no. Not me and Clayton. I meant—"

He set her down, and she missed the feel of him against her. She hooked her finger in the waist of his jeans and settled her other hand on his hip.

"I know what you meant." He ran his hand through his hair and looked away for a beat, then trained his eyes on hers again. "I don't have any claim on you, so you can do what you want. But I want you to know that I really like you. Way more than I probably should."

His eyes raked over her body, and Kate felt it as if he'd caressed every inch of her with his hands. She shuddered, opened her mouth to speak, and he settled his finger over her lips.

"Just hear me out." He backed her up against the thick, prickly bark of a tree, giant leaves engulfing them both.

Kate swallowed hard against the thrum of

excitement his touch sent through her.

"Kate. I'm trying to do the right thing by giving you time, but that doesn't mean I don't want to lay you down and take you right here. I just want you to know who I am and how I really feel about you."

Kate was stuck on the idea of him taking her right there. In the path. In the heat of the afternoon. *Yes. God, yes.*

"I...um." *Gulp.*

"I'm not the person you think I am, but I'm not a fucking saint, either." His breath still came hard and fast, but his eyes softened.

"I...know."

"No. You don't, but you will."

Jesus, my heart is beating so loud you have to hear it. "Okay." *Okay? What the hell does that even mean?* "I don't want a saint." *Better.*

His eyes darkened, and when he lowered his face toward hers, she closed her eyes, ready for another incredible kiss.

"Good," he whispered in her ear; then he settled his mouth over her neck and pressed soft strokes with his tongue as he sucked just strong enough to harden her nipples...and make her damp down below.

She moaned, or mewed. She had no idea which. Whatever she did, it drew him back with intense pleasure in his eyes.

"I'm not playing, Kate," he said in a serious tone.

"Me neither," she managed. She pressed her hips to his. *Nope. Not playing.* Though he could be. The man was as hard as a baseball bat.

He ran his thumb along her jaw and softly kissed her lips. "I gotta work off this anger and apologize to Penelope."

"What? Penelope? Why?" *Zap!* Just like that, her brain kicked into high gear.

He looked away. "I brushed her off last night, and she slept with Clayton." He met her gaze again. "And Cassidy."

"But...Wow. Wait. How is that your fault?"

"Because women have all kinds of crazy shit in their hea—" He must have caught her glare, because he corrected himself immediately. "Because the last thing she needs is to feel less about herself. She's weak, insecure. I don't want to feed into that." He cupped her cheek. "Don't worry. I only have eyes for you, but I won't sleep well until I tell her I didn't turn her down because she wasn't attractive. She's not, to me. I mean she's not my type, but...Oh hell, Kate. I'm trying to do the right thing. I'm gonna tell her it was because I really like you. Period. Okay?"

She nodded, caught between feeling like he was the sweetest man on earth and the most naive.

"Can I see you later?" he asked.

She nodded again, unable to speak. If she opened her mouth again, she'd likely tell him what she thought. *Penelope made her own choice. She is an adult, and nothing you say will change what she did.* Shit, she'd probably do it again in a heartbeat. But that wasn't what she wanted to say to him.

"You're a good man, Sage. Too good," she admitted. Her feelings for him felt like tiny beads of hope sending chills right through her.

"Not *too* good. Trust me on that." He winked and it set fire to her belly.

Oh my. She watched her alpha badass walk away and swore she saw a little piece of her heart in his back pocket.

Chapter Eleven

AFTER A HUNDRED push-ups and a hundred sit-ups, Sage stepped beneath the pathetic stream of water that passed for a shower and finally let out the frustrated breath that had been festering within him. He set his palms against the shower wall and let the water bead the tension from his shoulders. When that didn't work, he let his mind do it for him. *Goddamn Clayton. He's slime, the lowest of the low. Pathetic.* Feeling mildly better, he soaped himself clean, his thoughts drifting to Kate and to the feel of her in his arms, her legs wrapped around him. Just the thought was enough to arouse him. He debated his situation, eyed the impotent drip of the water and his definitely *not* impotent body part. *Well, hell.* He rinsed off and tried to think of anything other than Kate. Fat chance at that.

Twenty minutes later, with his anger under wraps and his desire for Kate simmering, he left his cabin in search of Penelope. He cursed his mother for instilling manners into his thick head. Why couldn't he be like most men and turn his back on whatever drove Penelope into bed with Clayton and Cassidy? He knew damn well why. Ever since his sister was born, he'd been protective of her. Siena was one of New York's top models. And still he worried about her. He'd known enough models and actresses to know that beneath the confident, beautiful exterior, there often lurked a weak, insecure individual. He hadn't ever seen any indication of that from Siena, but he knew how hard his parents had pushed her to believe in herself. Siena was bullheaded and strong in every sense of the word, despite her willowy exterior. *Sort of like Kate.* Still, his mother's words from the time he was a small boy resonated in his mind. They'd usually come on the heels of him calling Siena a stupid girl. *It's not your job to tear your sister down. It's your job to build her up. The rest of the world does enough damage to women's egos. Don't be part of that effort, Sage.* Swap *Sage* for any of his brothers' names. It didn't matter. His mother's message was loud and clear, no matter who it was directed to. Respect women and help them respect themselves.

He blew out a breath before knocking on the door of Penelope's cabin. She opened the door holding a battery-driven fan in front of her face.

"You change your mind?" She flashed a seductive smile and arched a brow.

No chance in hell. He had no idea why women like Penelope turned him off so vehemently, but he felt like he was standing in front of a lioness about to pounce. Oh wait, yeah, he knew why he felt that way. Another one of his mother's life lessons. *A girl who respects herself will always respect you. Leave those who don't for the men who have no respect for themselves either.*

"Actually, I came to apologize."

She opened the door and moved aside to let him by.

Sage hesitated, then nodded and took a step inside,

wanting to get this over with as quickly as possible. The minute he did, she closed the door, and the walls pressed in on him. She stepped closer, and he took a step backward, slamming into the rough wall.

"Penelope, please." He held a palm up between them. "I'm not here for..."

"No?" She narrowed her blue eyes, then ran them down his body, settling just below his waist, and drew them back up slowly to meet his gaze. "What, then?"

Sage felt cheap, dirty, as if he were on display, and vowed never to do *that* to a woman again. He slid out around her so he was clear of the wall. "I came to apologize. I'm sorry if I made you feel bad the other night. The truth is—"

"Bad? Is that what you think?" She turned off the fan and tossed it on the bed, then crossed her arms and jutted out her right hip. "You don't have the power to make me feel bad." She lifted her chin insistently.

"Fair enough." *The hell with this.* "Then I'll be on my way." He turned and reached for the door.

"Besides, Clayton is more of a man than you are any day."

Ouch. Fuck. His neck muscles and jaw clenched. Unwilling to stoop to her level, he turned and said with as gracious of a feigned smile as he could muster, "I'm sure he is." Then he walked out the door and headed straight for Kate's cabin.

Chapter Twelve

SAGE'S PULSE KICKED up as he ascended the stairs to Kate's cabin, a handful of freshly picked flowers in his hand. He had no idea what they were, but the reds and oranges were too vibrant to pass up. The wooden door to her room was open, the screen door closed, giving him a clear view inside—of the colorful scarves that had his mind running down a dangerously sexual path. He wasn't sure if it was the thought of Kate or of everything that had gone on that afternoon, but he felt like a teenager about to go on his first date. Even his damn stomach was fluttering. What the hell was up with that? A seductively fresh, floral scent traveled through the screen, amping up his nervousness.

He heard Kate humming before he saw her pass in front of the screened door wearing only a towel, her wet hair clinging to her shoulders. She bent over to pull on her thong, lifting one leg and then the other and flashing Sage an eyeful of her beautiful ass. He needed to turn around, or let her know he was there, but his legs were rooted to the ground, his voice stuck beneath a big tangle of lust. His desire flared, making him hungry for her and hard as a rock. *Christ.*

She dropped the towel, revealing the most exquisite back he'd ever laid eyes on and the most delicious-looking dimples at the base of her spine. Dimples he'd like to run his tongue over. She shimmied into a tank top. Just knowing she didn't have a bra on beneath the sheer material almost made him lose it. He forced himself to turn away. His feet shuffled, causing Kate to spin around.

"Sage?"

He closed his eyes. *Fuck.* He was caught. Luck was not on his side tonight. Without turning around, he said, "I'm sorry, Kate. I didn't mean to see...Really, I tried to turn away, but—"

"But my beauty was too much?"

Her sarcasm caught him off guard and sent him spinning on his heel to face her.

"Yes." *Holy shit.* Her wet hair covered her shoulders and fell over her breasts in tangled strands. Her tank top barely covered her hips. Sage realized he was looking at her body the same way Penelope had leered at his. *Shit.* "Jesus Christ, Kate." Out of respect, he turned his face away. "You're so damn beautiful."

She opened the screen door, and he turned back toward her. She was nibbling on her lower lip, her cheeks flushed pink. Each time he saw her, he was more drawn to her. She could be wearing a paper bag and she'd turn him on. It was more than her physical beauty that reeled him in. It was the million different ways she looked at him, the way her insecurities lay beneath her thick, confident exterior, too deep for most to recognize and too close to the surface for him to miss. He stepped inside, and his hand fell naturally to her waist as he leaned down to kiss her cheek. She turned in to the kiss, and hell if he wasn't going to kiss her back. Deeply. Passionately. In a way he wasn't sure he could stop. She tasted fresh, minty, deliciously sensual. Each stroke of her tongue brought his body closer to hers. His hand slipped over the thin line of her thong, lingering at the curve of her hip, and it wasn't enough. Despite his desire to go slow and share a walk, a meal, something more than their bodies, he had to have more of her. *So much more.* He grabbed her ass and pulled her against him. Holy hell. With only a thong between them, she might as well have been completely naked. She moaned against his lips, a sexy, aching sound that cried, *Yes. More. Please.* Sage kicked the wooden door closed without breaking their kiss, then swooped her into his arms and laid her gently on the bed, hovering above her, their bodies so close he could feel her legs trembling.

The desire in her beautiful eyes left no room for misinterpretation. He brushed her wet hair from her face. "I wanted to wine and dine you."

She bit her lower lip. "Not necessary."

"But this isn't just sex. You have to know that."

She placed her palm over his racing heart. "I feel it."

He settled his mouth over hers again, sliding his hand up her shirt to her rib cage. His thumb brushed over her nipple. She gasped a breath, and he pulled back from the kiss, rested his forehead on hers, and closed his eyes, giving them both a moment to catch their breath.

"You feel so good, Kate." He listened to the sound of her rapid breathing, felt her fingers traveling to his back, running sexily along his ribs and spurring him on to take more. His lips found her cheek, her neck, the spot beneath her earlobe that made her shoulders rise. "Let me love you," he whispered.

"Yes. Like your shirt says."

Sage pulled back with a smile. "What?"

She bit her lower lip again. Goddamn, she was cute.

"Your shirt. *Artists do it one stroke at a time.* Love me one stroke at a time."

He laughed softly, having completely forgotten what his T-shirt said. It had been a gag gift from his brother Kurt, the writer.

"Absolutely," he said, then lowered his lips to hers again and kissed her lightly. He pushed her shirt up over her breasts, and for a moment the artist in him was stunned into submission as he drank in her flawless skin and her lovely, gentle curves. He had to close his eyes as he lowered his lips between the perfect mounds of her breasts and pressed a soft kiss to her warm skin before moving his hand to touch her breast and his lips to her nipple. She gasped another breath—the seductive sound stoking the fire he felt for her. He moved to her other breast, and she tangled her hands in his hair.

"Sage," she whispered, then whimpered when he took her in his mouth while at the same time lowering his hand and grasping her hip.

He ached to be inside her. It took all his concentration to slow his pace and focus on her pleasure. He hooked a finger in her thong and drew it down slowly, feeling the rise of her hips, as she allowed him to slip it off and toss it aside. Jesus, her skin was silky. He kissed his way down her belly to the softness beside her belly button, where he licked a path, then ran his thumb over the wetness and pressed it to the perfect indentation beside her hip. She moaned again, and he loved knowing he was bringing her such pleasure. Her knees fell open, her hands met his shoulders, urging him lower, but Sage was a patient man, and when he wanted to be, he could be a patient lover. At that moment, having the entire night ahead of them, he wanted nothing more than to love every inch of her. He was in no rush to have this extraordinary pleasure over with, no matter how tempting it was to ease his own need.

He ran his hand up her right thigh, brushing his thumb along her damp center. Her wetness sent a shock of need through him, which he restrained in pursuit of her pleasure. She writhed beneath him as he teased her with his thumb, grazing her inner thigh with his whiskers. He dragged his tongue along her thigh, feeling her quiver beneath his touch, which made him want to draw out her pleasure even more. She arched her hips, urging him on.

"Sage," she whispered again. "Please."

He lowered his mouth to her, stroking her with his tongue, tasting her sweetness and feeling the sheets beside them pull into her fisted hands. He used his finger to stroke the sensitive nub that caused her thighs to tense and her hips to rise. His free hand rose to her breast, rubbing her nipple between his index finger and thumb and bringing her up over the edge. Her heels dug into the mattress, and her inner muscles pulsated as he slid his fingers inside her, eagerly stroking her with his tongue as his name fell from her lips, time and time again in long, breathless cries. She came down slowly, panting, arcing one arm over her eyes. Knowing she would be overly sensitive, he used his thumb to caress her again.

She gasped. "Oh, Sage. Oh...Oh."

He slid up her body and took her breast in his mouth, continuing to drive her up toward the edge of another orgasm with his hand. She arched her chest and raised her hips. Her hands clenched the sheets, then found purchase on his back. The pain of her nails was exquisite as she peaked again, her entire body quivering as her hips lifted with each pulsation.

KATE COULDN'T BREATHE. She was going to die right there on the bed beneath the most talented lover she'd ever had. Not that she'd had many, but three counted as some experience, right? Holy shit, they hadn't even had intercourse yet and she'd already come twice. *This is what Luce was talking about.* Their bodies were slick with sweat. Kate panted beneath Sage, who was not breathing terribly hard and showed no signs of wanting to move on to reaping his own reward. She felt his hard length against her leg. He was ready. She was ready. *Come on!* He was busy driving her out of her ever-loving mind. His tongue ran circles around her nipple, sending erotic little shocks signaling her brain and body to come again. She pulled at his powerful arms.

"Sage."

He gave her nipple one last, long suck, then released it, lifted his eyes to hers, his tongue sliding across the sensitive skin. *Oh God, really?* How could she ask him to stop what he was doing when it was bringing her right back to the edge of another glorious release?

She closed her eyes and pressed his head back to her breast. He slid his finger inside her again and caressed a spot she didn't even know existed, spiraling her into another mind-blowing climax. A thousand lights exploded behind her closed lids. Her hips rose from the bed. She was powerless to stop them, powerless to make heads or tails of anything at the moment, lost in a sensation she hoped would never end. When he lifted his mouth from her breast, she whimpered and opened her eyes.

He smiled down at her. "You're exquisite when you come."

She flushed all over and turned away. He took his fingers from inside her, and she drew her eyes back to him just as he brought them to his mouth, then drew them out slowly and licked his lips.

Holy shit. She'd never seen a man do that before—everything inside of her went white-hot, and suddenly she couldn't get enough of him. She pulled him into a kiss. Needing him, wanting to have every inch of him inside of her. She clawed at his back, pulling his hips toward her, forgetting he was completely clothed. He kissed her—hard. Deep. With an intensity that made her feel animalistic. When he groaned against her lips, it heightened her excitement. She pulled at his shorts and he caught her wrist in his hand.

"Not yet."

She let out a breath. "Seriously?" She panted, every inch of her shaking with need. "Sage, come on."

He looked at her like she was ruining all his fun, his eyes sad, a pout on his luscious lips. There was more? What could he possibly have in mind? "Please," she begged. *Begged! Oh my God, I'm begging for sex.* She felt her cheeks flush.

He kissed the edges of her cheekbones. "You're so sexy, Kate. I can hardly stand it."

"Then make love to me."

He pulled one of her hands over her head and then drew her other one up, holding them both in one of his large hands. He looked down at her with hunger in his eyes and held her gaze. "You okay?"

She nodded, feeling a tightening between her thighs at the erotic position he held her in. He ran his tongue up the underside of her arm. Goose bumps rose when the warm air hit the slick line. He ran his other hand up her side, over her ribs, then cupped her breast and brought his mouth to it once again. The tension of his hands against her wrists and the sensation of his tongue on her nipple brought her close to the edge again, and when he lowered his hand from her breast to her center and teased her ever so lightly, she moaned for more. She arched her hips, but he settled his body over hers, rendering her still beneath him.

"Oh...God...Sage." She rocked her head from side to side, fighting the impending orgasm that pulled at her nerves.

He took her in another deep kiss, his legs trapping hers beneath him, his chest pinning her to the mattress, his fingers teasing her until she was about to...*Oh God*. He kissed her harder, breathing air into her lungs, capturing her cries as her body exploded with the power of a thousand needles upon her skin.

He released her hands and kissed her softly as she lay with her eyes closed, trying to resume some semblance of normal breathing, though at the moment she couldn't even remember what that might feel like. She opened her eyes as he reached behind his back and drew his shirt over his head, then helped her take off her tank top, which she'd forgotten she even had on. Then he pulled a condom from his back pocket and drew his shorts down, kicking them to the floor.

She felt her eyes widen at the site of his erection. He was enormous. Massive. *Holy shit.* He ripped the condom open with his teeth and rolled it on. She was on the pill, but she couldn't manage to speak. She bit her lower lip, trying to settle her nerves as he lowered himself beside her.

"You okay?" he asked.

She nodded, still breathing hard. "Nervous." What they'd just done was so incredible that she couldn't imagine what it would feel like to be even closer to Sage.

He brushed her hair to the side. "Me too."

She rolled her eyes. "Right."

"Kate, I told you I'm not who you think I am. I've only been with a handful of women."

She rolled her eyes again. "Right."

"I can count them on my fingers, not counting my thumbs."

She arched a brow.

"Yes." He kissed her forehead. "Really."

"Hmm." She believed him, but even if she didn't, it would have been a very thoughtful fib.

"Sure you're okay?"

She nodded. "Still nervous."

"Want to go slow, or want to wait?"

She drew her eyebrows together. "You just made me come harder than I ever thought imaginable, and you'd be willing to wait for your own...pleasure?"

"Yes. If that's what you want."

She lowered her eyes to his erection. "*That's* what I want."

He laughed softly. "You're so damn adorable. You sure? No pressure. I'm happy knowing you're happy."

She swatted him. "Stop being so damn nice and get up here."

He perched above her hips, looking deeply into her eyes. She nodded—approval and desire—and Sage lowered his hips and pushed in slowly, until he was buried deep. They both gasped a breath at their first moment of coming together. He moved with a gentle pace and then in a slow, circular motion, every move stroking that spot he'd lit with fire earlier. She bit her lip and moaned, and he nuzzled against her neck, kissing and licking as he brought her to the precipice again. He hovered there until she thought she might explode, and then finally—*Oh God, mercifully*—he thrust into her to the hilt and carried her over the edge again.

"Oh God. Oh God." She grabbed at his hips, urging him to remain deep, and he slowed his pace again.

With gritted teeth and tense muscles, he quickened

his thrusts again, one after a glorious other, each one a little faster, a little harder, until she was—impossibly—gasping for breath again and again. He looked into her eyes and pinned her to the mattress with the passion she saw there. Then his cheek was against hers as he grunted through his own powerful release, shifting her up on the mattress with each thrust. She wrapped her legs around him to keep him buried deep. He placed his hand beneath her hip, holding her in place as each tiny pulsation of hers stroked him through the last seconds of his orgasm. Kate held on to his muscular shoulders, never wanting to let go. They lay together until their breathing eased and their muscles no longer held any tension.

Sage reached for her hand and squeezed it gently. "Feel that?"

Kate closed her eyes, still basking in the glorious feeling of being so close to him, how much of a gentleman he was, how caring and attentive he'd been toward her.

"What?" she managed.

"The nervousness. It's all gone. I feel like I'm exactly where I'm supposed to be. "

She snuggled in beside him, wondering how they could experience such similar feelings at exactly the same time.

AS DAWN CREPT in, Sage lay awake, listening to the sounds of the birds in the forest, trying to distinguish one high-pitched chirp from the next and thinking about how right he felt with Kate curled up against him. He'd been so nervous to make love to her, and once they were together, they'd moved in perfect sync.

"Good morning," she said in a sleepy voice. Her hand slid along his stomach; then she rested her head on his side and hugged him close.

"Morning." He kissed the top of her head.

"Thinking about painting?"

"No. I was thinking about you, actually, and how nice it was to wake up beside you. I could get used to this."

She came up on her elbow, and he saw a content smile on her lips; the shadow of worry in her eyes was gone. "I've heard of people saying they felt this way that fast, but I've never believed it. Until now. Kinda weird how fast it happened, isn't it?"

He brushed a strand of hair from her cheek. "Yeah, but who am I to question it?"

She rested her cheek on his chest and sighed.

He knew she was going through one of her lists in her head, organizing her day, and he was probably taking up the time she had allotted for something or other. He stroked her hair for a minute or two, soaking the feel of her in, before letting her off the hook.

"We should probably get moving. We need to plan out the mural, and I'm sure you have a list of things to do this morning." He pulled her into a hug, then sat up, reluctantly relinquishing the most comfortable spot he'd slept in for years—the spot beside Kate.

Sage went home to shower and change, giving Kate space for whatever morning rituals she might have. By the time he met her outside her cabin to have coffee, the sun was high in the sky and the birds were drowned out by the cicadas. Kate had a clipboard tucked under one arm.

Kate breathed in deeply when he kissed her. "My room smells like you now."

He took her hand in his and squeezed it lightly. "Wow, that sounds bad. I'll be sure to bring air freshener next time."

She laughed. "I don't mean it like that. It smells good, like your body wash, or cologne, or whatever it is that makes you smell so fresh and earthy."

He cocked his head. "I sound like an evergreen tree."

"A very masculine tree, and it's nothing like evergreen. It's...I don't know. You just smell so good, and I'm glad my room smells like you. I love it, so don't change a thing."

Sage pulled her closer, making a mental note not to change his cologne. They walked over to the mess hall hand in hand.

Sylvia eyed their hands and smiled. "Good morning," she said with a hint of excitement in her voice.

Sage felt Kate's hand tense in his. He opened his hand, giving Kate the opportunity to put some space between them if she wanted to. She tightened her grip, and he smiled down at her. "It's a beautiful morning, that's for sure." That moment of acknowledgment was worth the roller coaster of emotions they'd encountered on the way into each other's arms.

After eating breakfast, they sat at a table in the mess hall and began conceptualizing the mural for the school. Sage was having a hard time concentrating. Now that he'd been intimate with Kate, he saw everything she did through new eyes. She jotted notes as they spoke, numbering some, underlining others. He wondered what it must be like to live in such an organized mind. He was such a spur-of-the-moment, go-with-his-gut guy that he couldn't fathom living any differently, but he loved the way her mind worked. And he was in awe of her ability to manage so many things at once without ever losing her cool. In that regard she was so different from him. When he worked, he was totally focused. Once he started painting or sculpting, he became oblivious to anything and everything around him. It was one of the things he hoped being away from New York might help him to change. He'd done it for as long as he could remember, and while it allowed him to concentrate on his art, which he believed led to a higher quality of work with more emotion and passion in each piece, he also knew that it was a disruptive habit. He'd missed meetings, important phone calls, and God only knew how many women he'd pissed off by forgetting to pick them up or by showing up late. Now that he was with Kate, he had an even bigger reason to try to squelch that habit.

Kate tapped the pen on the clipboard. "Okay, so you're thinking that the mural will center on a large, full tree, representing life and hope."

"Yeah, with a wild jungle on one side with birds and snakes for the children to paint."

"Oh, and how about bright fruits, tall grasses, and some smaller trees, too?" She scribbled something on the paper.

"Perfect. I was also thinking that the roots of the big tree could fade off to the right, into a sandy beach, and then there could be a hint of water at the edge of the building."

She touched his hand. "That sounds so perfect. I'm sure the kids and the community will love it."

With Kate's hand on his arm and the sun at his back, Sage began to wish he'd signed up to volunteer for six months. Two weeks with Kate would never be enough.

Chapter Thirteen

THE NEXT FEW days passed quickly, with Sage outlining the mural and Kate making the afternoon rounds with Caleb to pick up the slack of the other volunteers, then she and Sage coming together again in the evenings. Each morning they awoke in each other's arms brought them closer together. Kate stood beneath the tree in the schoolyard watching Sage put the final touches on the outline of the mural as the children gathered around him. They pointed and whispered, and Kate realized that there were too many children to have them all painting at once. She began jotting down a schedule for them on her trusty clipboard.

Javier came to Kate's side and leaned against her leg. He pointed and whispered, "Look, Miss Kate. We're going to paint that."

She dropped her hand to his shoulder, knowing she'd made the right decision and feeling mildly guilty for initially turning Sage down. The air crackled with enthusiasm, and as she watched Sage draw each line with practiced precision, she became mesmerized by his movements. The muscles on his back flexed as his arm rose above his head. She could almost feel their strength against her palms, as she had earlier that morning when they'd made love.

Oscar came out of the school and joined Kate in admiring Sage's talent. He nodded appreciatively.

"The children are happy. Yes?"

"It was the right thing to do." Kate smiled at him.

"I'm going back to the village to get ready for the meeting about the wells. See you soon?"

Kate had scheduled a meeting with the community to discuss what else they might do besides sending emails to the Ministry of Rural Development to lobby for a community well.

"Yes. See you soon," she said.

Even outlined, she could see how the mural would breathe life into the dingy building, and she was glad she'd been a part of it. Sage had worked night and day on getting the mural ready for the children to paint— first on paper, then on the building—and Kate was surprised by the way he became so lost in his work. The Sage she'd gotten to know seemed very far away when he was creating. Now, as he completed the outline of two children at the water's edge, one of whom looked an awfully lot like Javier, he was in what Kate had begun to think of as his trancelike state. It was as if he were painting in a bubble and the rest of the world fell away.

She went to him then, needing to be closer. "You do realize that these kids don't really know how to paint within the lines, right?" Kate stood behind him, and when he didn't answer, she placed her hand on his shoulder. The warmth of his sun-kissed skin sent a shiver through her. She'd never felt so close to another person. He seemed to read her mind—not just sexually, but emotionally, as well. He was patient, caring, and attentive.

"Sage?"

He shook his head as if he'd just realized she was there. "Yeah?" He didn't turn to look at her or stop drawing.

"Will it bother you that the kids don't stay within the lines you've drawn? Because they're kids, not artists. I just don't want you to be disappointed."

"The beauty of art is that it's different for everyone. They could paint blobs and those blobs would represent something to them. That's what matters." He turned to face her, his eyes serious, brooding. "Kate, I've been wanting to talk to you about an idea I have. I've been thinking about how artists can *really* help the community, and I've come up with an idea I think can work."

"What do you mean?"

Sage set his pen down and rose to his feet. "I'm thinking about using my connections in the art world to raise money for places like this, negating the need for celebrities being here altogether—unless they were coming solely to help and not for publicity. I'm thinking of something with almost no onsite publicity. Auctioning off the art to get funding for projects."

"Auctioning...I'm not sure I follow." Kate checked her watch. Caleb and the others should be back from the clinic by now. She had to get ready for her meeting, and she needed to touch base with Caleb before she left for the village. She had just enough time to get there if she left now. "I have to get ready for my meeting. Can we talk about this a little later?"

"Yeah. Sure." He turned his attention back to the mural, settling his left palm on the wall as he drew with his right.

"I want to hear about your idea. I just don't want to be late."

He smiled over his shoulder. "I know. Good luck."

He blew her a kiss.

As she headed back toward the compound, Kate wondered what he had in mind. Auctioning art? A few minutes later, she came around the side of the cabins, and Penelope's angry voice caught her attention.

"I'm leaving tomorrow, and that's nonnegotiable. I've already called and made arrangements." Penelope stood before Luce, arms crossed, lips pinched tight, nose in the air.

Oh God. What now?

"That's not the deal, Penelope, and you know it." Luce gave Penelope a death stare, dark eyes narrowed to slits, shoulders back. "Two weeks of working with the community. You only have a few days left. You're here for damage control, and cutting your humanitarian effort short in order to run back into the arms of your married lover is not going to help your cause. In fact, it will negate your efforts here completely. You'll be a laughingstock."

Luce had filled Kate in about Penelope's indiscretions before they'd arrived in Belize, and she'd assured Kate that she wasn't wasting the volunteer spot on someone who would cut and run. Kate had handled enough celebrity volunteers to know that most of them ended up trying to leave early. She wondered how they got along being so self-centered.

"I'm not sure how you'll get to the airport, Penelope." Luce crossed her arms and flipped her chin, sending her hair over her shoulder. "Transportation isn't scheduled to report back until the end of your scheduled stay."

Penelope ran her eyes over Kate's AIA T-shirt and jeans shorts and sighed. "I've already taken care of that. They'll be here to pick me up."

Kate shot a look at Luce. "You're leaving, too?"

"Not me. She is. I'm staying through the end of the

scheduled trip."

Thank God. She liked finally having a friend to talk to. And she knew she shouldn't care if Penelope left or not. Penelope had shown up to help Caleb on their assignments only a handful of times, and from what Caleb had told her, she'd been less than interested in interacting with the locals. But her leaving would reflect poorly on AIA. There was already a stigma hovering over her site because their volunteers were celebrities, while other sites had the joy of working with real volunteers. Volunteers like Kate and Caleb, and maybe even Sage, who were there for the *right* reasons.

"Yes, I'm leaving. I've done what I needed to do," Penelope said emphatically.

"You've done nothing but gained a little publicity," Kate said. She saw Clayton approaching from his cabin and she shot a look at Luce. "Penelope, it's really not good for the morale of the people here if you leave. They know you're supposed to be here for two weeks."

Penelope rolled her eyes.

The hell with the stigma. She was probably the only one who felt it anyway. "Let her go, Luce. It's her reputation, not ours." She spun on her heel and walked away, pretty sure she was leaving a trail of steam in her wake.

AFTER MEETING WITH the community, Kate stopped in town and put a Skype call through to her boss, Raymond. It was time she put her foot down about celebrity volunteers. Even if she was being sent to another location after her mission there was done, the next program director shouldn't have to deal with the same crap she did. She could use the satellite phone, but it was cheaper to Skype and she needed to see his face to get her point across.

She stared at the pixelated image of Raymond, catching only every other word he said. *Damn Internet.*

"Kate, calm down...know how they are. They give a lot of money...Lucky to have funding."

"Raymond, we have a community here who needs help. If we could just bring in more *regular* volunteers, then I know we could get more involved with the housing, the wells, and get more programs for the elderly that actually focus on the people rather than the publicity." She thought about what Sage had said about his idea that would negate the need to have celebrities in the community at all. She longed to be rid of celebrities like Penelope Price altogether.

Raymond's image disappeared and then reappeared just as pixelated. The pixels made his black mustache spotty, as if it were constantly moving. His voice cut in and out.

"...funding cuts for next...You'll be at another locat...pull out of Punta Pal..."

"What?" Kate's pulse sped up. She pushed her face closer to the monitor, as if that would help the reception. "What? We're pulling out of Punta Palacia? Raymond. No. We have done so much and there's more to do."

"Kate? Kate, I can't..." Raymond's image disappeared.

"No." Kate tapped on the mouse, watching with desperation as the circle spun endlessly on the dark screen, then froze. She pushed back from the counter. "Damn it." She glanced up and saw Makei wiping a small round table with a wet cloth a few feet from her, looking at her with raised brows. He shook his head and went back to cleaning the table. His cotton pants and shirt hung from his body two sizes too big.

"I'm sorry." She sighed and turned away from the computer. "Sorry, Makei. Thank you."

Pulling out of Punta Palacia? How could they do that? What would happen to the people without their help? Kate had known she'd be sent somewhere else, but the idea of leaving the community on their own seemed unreasonable. They were getting medical supplies that they would not otherwise have. The government was finally taking notice of the village and was open to discussing wells and a better route for medical supplies. Kate knew that another aid resource might come in and fill their shoes, and the residents would probably find a way to get what they needed. But what if they didn't?

As she sat in front in the quiet café and debated calling her parents to get their take on the whole thing, she thought of Javier and his family, and her heart sank. She leaned her elbows on the counter and rubbed her temples. She needed to call her parents. Maybe they'd have some ideas of how she could turn this around.

Chapter Fourteen

SAGE SAT ON a bench in front of the mess hall, his back pocket filled with permanent markers. With the outline of the mural complete and the supplies his mother had arranged to have delivered arriving the next day, he was buzzing with adrenaline. He was guzzling a bottle of water when the sound of tires on dirt broke through the peaceful afternoon. He headed through the path to the cabins, where Penelope was loading her luggage into a dented and dust-covered car.

Luce stood with her arms folded, watching her.

"What's up?"

"She's leaving. Can you believe this shit?" Luce said angrily. "I come all the way out here to help Penelope turn her reputation around, and here she's going back early to be with that asshole whose marriage she fucked up. When the media gets ahold of this—and you know they will—they'll use it to slam her again. Sometimes I feel like all of my efforts are for naught."

"Sorry, Luce. See? That's why I don't drag my PR rep through any of this. I'm sure I'd only piss him off." Sage smiled, hoping to lighten her mood.

"Your PR rep has other issues."

"Mine? Why?" Sage had no idea what she could be talking about. He was a pretty low-key guy. He showed up at the galleries when he was supposed to, he handled interviews tactfully, and he dated so infrequently that his PR rep was never put on damage-control missions. He'd purposely kept his PR rep away from the trip. In Sage's eyes, he was a PR rep's dream client. He paid his monthly bill and did as he was told.

"You're just as bad as they are, only in the opposite direction. You're like a PR rep's nightmare." Luce started for the road toward town.

Sage caught up to her and walked with her toward town. "What do you mean?"

"You won't let them do anything to get you publicity. You're doing that wonderful mural and you're doing it for all the right reasons. Why not let the world know about it?" Luce walked with angry, determined steps.

"Luce, wouldn't getting publicity just contradict my efforts to do something because I want to? I don't need the PR."

"No, you don't, but this place does."

"What are you talking about? I'm not fundraising. I'm painting. The rest of the world will think it's cool, but they won't send money this way, which is really what they need most." A toucan squawked to their right and then flew into the jungle. "I swear those are the prettiest birds I've ever seen."

Luce stopped walking and put her hand on her hip. "Sage, I get that you're all about doing the right thing, and you love the beauty of Belize, yada yada, but you've been in the game long enough to know that all publicity is good publicity. This place needs to be taken seriously so that they can draw more people like you and less people like..." She turned back toward the way they'd

132

come. "Them."

"Well, I want no part of it. Can't you whip up some press for the other programs here? For the elderly, the medical assistance, the food programs?"

Luce began walking again. "If only it were that easy. People love to give to the arts, and sharing the kids' smiles with the world, instead of dragging sad and hungry children's faces through the media, would bring a whole new level of donations. Anyway, none of it matters. It's not like you're going to change. I'll do what I can to help Kate and pitch in where Caleb will fall short because of Penelope leaving."

"Listen, if I offend you in some way because of my lack of PR, then I'm sorry, but I gotta do what feels right. And having a camera crew follow me around so I can look good while painting feels very wrong." The more Sage thought about his idea, the more real it became.

They arrived at the Internet café and Sage tried to lighten the mood. "I have an idea I want to talk to you about. Let me buy you a smoothie."

"How about tequila instead?" Luce grinned.

"A little early, but whatever. Sure."

They found Kate inside the café on a fuzzy Skype call. Sage and Luce sat at the bar, and Luce opted for a smoothie instead. Sage smiled when Kate looked over, but her blue eyes were shadowed with worry and her slim shoulders were rounded forward.

"Do you know who she's talking to?" he asked Luce.

"Sounds like her parents, but from the monitor it looks more like two aliens."

Sage tried not to eavesdrop, but it was difficult in such a small area, and he hated the idea of Kate being unhappy.

"How did you stand it?" Kate pleaded. "All those

years, and in the end you know it comes down to politics and dollars and cents, even when the work you did wasn't driven by that."

"Kate, our work was meaningful. Your work is meaningful. Don't let the politics take away from that," her mother said. "Things in life happen for a reason. There are other places where you're needed. You've put structure into Punta Palacia. You've created a system that their people can now follow. You should be proud of that."

"And if they don't? And what if the government drops the ball with regard to the wells?"

The wells. That was Kate's biggest concern, and he began to wonder how much the wells would cost. How long did installation take? What kinds of red tape would they have to go through to get them approved with outside funding? Sage needed more information.

"Katie, honey, you can't control what happens next. You can only hope that what you have done will continue to help," her father said. "You've been through this before. Why is this hitting you so hard?"

Kate shook her head. "I don't know."

Sage restrained himself from going over and taking her in his arms to soothe the frustration that had her shaking her head and covering her eyes. He turned back to Luce.

"She's having a really hard time with this. Any idea what's really going on?" he asked.

"I know she goes to a new location in a few weeks. Maybe it's about that move?"

Sage and Kate had been so focused on the mural during the day and getting lost in each other's arms at night that he realized they had yet to discuss much other than their immediate situations.

When Kate finished her call, she let out a long sigh before joining them.

Sage pulled her into his arms and kissed her cheek. "You okay?"

"Yeah." She looked at Luce, who rolled her eyes. "Okay, fine. No, I'm not."

"Wanna talk about it?" Sage asked.

"Nope. I wanna go for a swim."

"Wait a minute. There's a place to swim and you haven't told me about it? It's like a hundred and fifty degrees out here." Sage's eyes jetted between Kate and Luce.

Kate touched his arm. "It's kind of a secret."

Sage lifted his eyebrows. "I love secrets."

"Oh my God." Luce finished her smoothie and rose to her feet. "I don't even want to know about the secrets you two have. Kate, I'm gonna go back to my cabin and wallow in PR angst. I need to make some arrangements for Penelope's backslide. I'll catch up with you guys later."

"You sure?" Kate asked.

"Oh yeah." Luce pointed at Sage. "Think about what we talked about."

After seeing Kate's distress, it was all he *could* think about.

KATE HELD SAGE'S hand as they made their way through the thick forest toward the beach. Sage hadn't pressed her for information about her conversation with her parents, and by the time they reached the red clay path that led to Undiscovered, she was a little annoyed that he hadn't even asked about what was going on.

"What is that noise?" Sage asked.

"Howler monkeys."

"Really? It sounds like strong wind blowing through a tunnel." Sage looked up at the trees.

"You can hear them a mile away, so you probably

won't spot any." She hated how snappy she sounded, but she couldn't rein it in.

"So, there's really a beach nearby? You've been holding out on me," Sage teased.

"A girl's gotta keep a few secrets," she snapped again, and swatted at a leaf that was in their way.

"I thought I picked up on something. What's wrong?"

"Nothing." She stomped over a leafy bush.

"Kate, you told Luce you didn't want to talk about whatever was going on, so if you're mad because I haven't asked about what's bothering you, that's why I haven't."

She turned to face him. "That *is* why I'm upset. You should have asked me anyway." *God, I'm so whiny.*

"I'm sorry, Kate. I was just trying to do the right thing. But you may have to tweak my boyfriend skills when it comes to reading you in that way. I try, but..."

"No, you're great. I'm sorry. I'll be fine after we swim and relax a little." She pushed through a plant with giant green leaves, and a perfect stretch of white sandy beach came into view.

He threw his arms open and drew in a deep breath. Kate couldn't help but notice his broad chest expand and his biceps twitch.

"You've brought me to paradise?"

"Undiscovered."

"Paradise undiscovered?"

"No. Luce and I found this place when she first came out, and we call it Undiscovered. I think we're the only ones who use it."

Kate slipped off her shoes and Sage did the same. Then pulled her into his arms.

"I want to know what's wrong. Hell, Kate, I hate seeing you upset."

She pressed her cheek to his chest, soothed by the

steady beat of his heart. He leaned down and kissed her, and for a few blessed seconds she was able to forget everything else and think only of how good she felt right there in his arms, his lips on hers, his hard body pressed against her. His kisses had the remarkable power to chase away her worries. When he drew back and looked down at her with his gorgeous dark-blue eyes, she wanted to pretend her worries didn't exist at all.

"Want to talk about it?"

She shook her head and stood on her tiptoes to kiss him again. When he lowered his mouth to hers, Kate pressed her hips in to his. *I've become a sex maniac with you.* Only with you. *Forever with you.* The thought took her by surprise, and she drew back from him, searching his face. Wondering if he felt the same thing. It was a crazy thought, and she took a step back to distance herself from it.

Kate had seen too many volunteers hook up while they were there. She knew that what happened in Belize stayed in Belize. What she and Sage had together had taken her by surprise. That had to be why she was hoping for more. Maybe it was the sex. *God, the sex is amazing.* She didn't want to be a hookup. Not with Sage.

Now was not the time to turn into a blundering idiot, and he was looking at her with a question in his eyes. He was so freaking good-looking, and so damn good to her, that she wanted to crawl into his arms and disappear.

She had real issues to worry about. Talking would take her mind off of being intimate with him right then—and daydreaming about forever.

"Yeah, let's talk," she finally managed.

They sat side by side beneath the shade of a large tree. Kate drew in a deep breath of the salty sea air. She loved the way it felt lighter than the air of the jungle. More refreshing.

"I Skyped my boss, Raymond, after going to the village for the meeting, and he said some stuff that really bothered me, so I Skyped my parents," she began. "I was hoping they'd help me figure some things out."

"Luce told me that was them. I could tell they really care about you."

She picked up a twig and began breaking it into tiny pieces. "I know. They've been involved with the Peace Corps forever. I grew up traveling with them, and when we weren't traveling, we hung around with people who had also been involved with the Corps. Some people are military brats." She looked up at him and smiled. "I'm a Peace Corps brat."

"Well, I think it served you well. Look at the wonderful things you're doing now." Sage reached out and held her hand. "Is there anything I can help you figure out? I want to be here for you, Kate. More than just sexually. I want to be here for whatever you need. I'm a good listener."

You're so much more than a good listener. She sighed. "I think they're closing the volunteer station here."

"What? Why?"

"I'm not sure if they are or not. The Internet was spotty. But I worry, you know? Will the people here get the wells they need? How will they get the medical supplies we bring in for them now, and will they have people to pitch in when the teachers are sick?"

"And what happens to you and Caleb if they close it? I mean, how long were you supposed to be here?"

"I'm supposed to leave the week after your group leaves, and Caleb would be reassigned, I guess, but it's not me I'm worried about."

He pulled her close and kissed the top of her head. "I know you're worried about the people here. I just realized that I have no idea how long you're here, or what your plan is after this."

She leaned in to him. She'd been wondering about that as well. The idea of not being with Sage made her pulse race—almost as much as being with him did. *Stop it. Be realistic. This is a fling to him.* She wasn't sure if she was trying to convince herself of that or if she really believed it, but the thought came to her and she couldn't ignore it.

"I was supposed to be placed someplace else when I left here, but now..." She shrugged. "I feel like everything we do here is just temporary. I never used to feel that way. I was so proud of my parents for everything they did, but I guess I just never saw the other parts of social aid. My parents said they went through this a bunch of times, but they must have shielded me from it. Or they just grew immune to the worry, so I never saw it. I don't know."

Sage was quiet for a long time, and Kate wondered if he was thinking that she'd just become too complicated for him.

"What do you want to happen?" he asked.

"Want? I guess for them to continue the effort. I want to know that the elderly will get the medication and food they need. I want to know that the people of Punta Palacia will have wells that work, so they can have better access to water. I want to have a lasting impact on the community. I want what we do to make a long-term difference. Is that too much to hope for?" She looked up at him and immediately worried that she sounded whiny again.

He took her chin in his hand and looked deeply into her eyes. "No. It's a beautiful thing to hope for."

He kissed her softly, and in that moment it was

treacherously hard for Kate not to want more with him—more time, more of a relationship. She pulled back from him in order to save herself from emotional hell in a few days when he was gone. At least at night they had hours together, learning every curve of each other's body, kissing and tasting, touching and teasing, until they were both satiated. At night it seemed like morning would never come. But in the light of day, with the stress of the future of Punta Palacia and AIA pressing in on her, fear riddled her heart.

"I do have an idea that I think will help. AIA used this place like a media playground. I think we can earn the funding without the craziness of celebrity PR."

"So, you're thinking about donating?" She was having a hard time concentrating. Between the heat, wanting to be close to Sage, and her conversation with Raymond, she really just wanted to forget it all for a few minutes.

"No. Auctioning off art, the proceeds going to a company, and running that organization with the total focus on helping places like Punta Palacia. It seems like wells are one of the most vital issues, so maybe a nonprofit that focuses primarily on well installation." He took her hand in his. "Kate, I've been looking for a way to give back, to give more than just money. I don't know if I'm using the right terminology for something like this, but...running a cause like this would allow me to do some good with my income and connections, and being right there, working with the communities while the wells are being installed, would allow, I don't know, a month at a time in each community. Maybe four times a year."

Running a cause? "I don't understand. Running a cause? Do you mean starting a nonprofit? A whole company?" She swallowed hard. *Who the hell are you?* Who made big decisions like that based on a few days?

Or based on one village's need for a well?

"Yes. I think so. I need to get more information, but it's something I'm contemplating."

Holy shit. She knew exactly what kind of person made life-altering decisions for the good of others, and he was staring at her with the sweetest eyes and the most sincere smile she'd ever seen. She needed to clear her head.

"This is a lot to think about. Can we...Do you want to take a swim?" She stood and reached for the zipper on her shorts.

"Skinny-dipping?" Sage took off his tank top and tossed it on the sand. "You're standing there taking off your clothes and asking if I'd rather skinny-dip with you or talk about wells? Seriously?"

Oh dear Lord, I want you.

Sage put his hands on her hips and brushed his lips over the curve of her shoulder. "I think I like it here even more than before," he whispered.

How could she think that swimming with Sage would do anything other than make her want him more? He lifted her shirt over her head and unhooked her bra, then tossed it on the warm sand. Her nipples instantly tightened. His hands skimmed her waist, settling on the button of her shorts.

"Swim, remember?" she said, only half teasing.

"Right." He stepped from his shorts and stood before her naked. And aroused.

Kate laughed as she took off her shorts, feeling her cheeks flush hot.

He glanced down. "Swimming? Really?" He reached for her waist again.

"Uh-uh." She took a step backward, suddenly feeling playful, less worried about wanting more of him. *Jesus.* He really had stolen her brain cells. She turned and strolled leisurely toward the water, feeling the heat of his stare and knowing she was torturing him as much as herself. She swayed her hips a little more than usual and cast what she hoped was a seductive glance behind her, tossing her hair over her shoulder as she turned back toward the water. By the time she recognized the approaching sound as Sage running, she was in his arms being carried into the water. He covered her mouth with his and kissed her passionately.

She melted against him.

"Swimming?" he asked, breathing hard.

She opened her mouth to say yes, but nothing came out. She nodded.

Sage shook his head. "Okay." He swung her in his arms.

"Sage, don't you da—"

He threw her toward the deep water. "Sage!" flew from her lips as she sailed through the air. She sank beneath the water and paddled her way to the top. He was already reaching for her. She wrapped her arms around his neck and laughed.

"Are you gonna kiss me or what?" he asked.

Oh, hell yes. She wrapped her legs around his waist and felt his legs pedaling hard to keep them up. He held her with one arm and used the other to push them backward toward the shore until his feet touched the bottom; then he folded her in his arms again and deepened the kiss. She felt the tip of his arousal pressing against her, and she wiggled her body lower, trying to maneuver him inside of her.

"No condom," he said between kisses.

"I'm on the pill," she said in one long breath.

Sage held her tightly against him and tilted his head.

"What?" she asked.

"STDs. Any?"

She pulled back with a gasp.

"What? You're an attractive woman. I can't assume..."

She didn't know if she should be offended or take it as a compliment, but he felt so damn good pressed against her, and she felt so much more for him than she ever knew was possible, that she didn't want to overanalyze it.

"Never. You?" she finally answered.

He shook his head. "Never." He loosened his grip, and she slid down his body and took him in. All of him. He sucked in a breath.

"Jesus, Kate. You feel so good."

His desirous, sexy voice sent a thrum of excitement through her. Knowing she was making him feel as good as she felt excited her even more. She buried her face in his neck and kissed the muscles that bulged there as he moved her body in tune to his own powerful thrusts. He was so big, so strong. She loved how feminine she felt when she was with him and was taken by surprise each time they made love by how uninhibited she felt. Now, with the sun beating on her back and him buried deep, she wondered how she could be so consumed with worry one minute and overtaken by desire the next. She looked into his eyes and felt her heart swell with emotion.

She pulled his mouth to hers and kissed him again, closing her eyes to revel in the feel of him. He held her hips still, then pressed her hard upon him again and moved in the same circular motion he had the night before. Kate's eyes flew open with the sensation. She gripped his shoulders and closed her eyes.

"Look at me," he said.

She opened her eyes, but she was on the brink of falling apart, and it was too much. "Can't." she said and closed her eyes. Her head fell back and his mouth found the curve of her shoulder. His tongue caressed her as he sucked and kissed her right up over the edge.

"Kate," he said in a deep, throaty voice. He gripped her hips tighter as he followed her over the edge, both of them breathing hard, clinging to each other as if their lives depended on the strength from the other.

Half an hour later, their bodies dry from the warmth of the sun, they dressed and sprawled out on the sand. Sage took a pen from his pocket and lifted Kate's shirt above her rib cage.

"Signing me?" she teased.

He shrugged. "I had the urge to draw, and I can't think of a better canvas." He ran his hand over her belly. Kate tried to block the sensual urges from her mind as she watched the muscles jump beneath his tattoos.

"How much does it hurt to get a tattoo?" she asked as he began to draw. She held her breath against the tickle of the pen.

"More than this does." He kissed her stomach.

Kate ran her hand through his thick hair.

"Tell me about where you go from here, Kate. If they continue to help this community, do you stay? Do you leave? When do you go home? Where do you even call home?"

She stifled a laugh as the tip of the pen traveled over her ribs. "Even if AIA doesn't pull out, I'm slated to go to another location a few months after I leave here. I'll have a few weeks, maybe two or three months in between assignments. When you work for a company like AIA, you really don't maintain a home, unless you own it outright. You have to prove to AIA that you have no debt that you could default on while you're on an assignment, so..."

He met her gaze. "That makes sense. So when you go *home,* what does that mean? Do you stay with your parents?"

"Yeah, I stay with them. They live just outside of DC. I haven't seen them in person in almost two years. They were going to come visit, but it's so expensive."

"You must miss them."

She was too distracted by the tickling of the pen on her skin to answer. She tried to see what he was drawing, but he shielded it with his hands.

"Don't peek." He kissed her stomach again. "I promise I'm not drawing something inappropriate."

"I've never had anyone draw on me before."

He smiled up at her. "Then I'm honored to be your first."

He spoke with a sexual undertone, as if he'd said, *I'm honored to have been your first lover.*

He went back to drawing and said matter-of-factly, "But I'm awfully tempted to lift this shirt up the rest of the way."

"Not much up there." She'd always been self-conscious of her small breasts, and the words came out of habit. With Sage, she realized that she didn't feel that way. He looked at her like she was the most beautiful creature on earth.

"You're kidding, right?" He propped himself up on his elbow. "You're perfectly proportioned. Everything about you is lovely. Feminine. Sexy as hell." He kissed her, then slithered back down her body and went back to drawing. "Do you miss your parents?"

"I know it sounds a little silly, but I do miss them."

"Why is that silly? I miss my family and I've only been here for a short time. What about friends?"

That was a more difficult question. Most of Kate's friends from college kept in touch via email, but she almost never saw them, and she didn't really have close friends, except for Luce, whom she saw sporadically. Kate's career didn't allow for very close friendships.

"I guess I don't need many people. I'm pretty content with the people and the life I have here. I don't really *miss* the friends I have." *Or at least I thought I was content, but when I'm not with you, I find myself missing you.* She sighed. *Stop it.*

"Hm."

"What does that mean?"

"Nothing. I was just curious."

He stopped asking questions, and Kate wondered if he thought she was weird. She knew that not having a lot of friends might appear odd to some people, but with her lifestyle, it was just what it was. Sage finished drawing in silence. As the sun began to sink from the sky, he looked at what he'd drawn with serious eyes.

"Can I see it now?" she asked.

"Sure."

"Can I touch it?"

He sat up beside her and rested his arms on his knees, staring solemnly at the water. "Sure."

Kate ran her fingers over the fine details of a perfect replica of a globe, atop of which she and Sage were sitting side by side, hand in hand, their legs dangling off the edge of Central America. In the center of the Gulf of Mexico, deep in the water, which looked so real Kate wanted to dive in, it read, *Sage + Kate.*

"I love this." *I could love you.* She touched his arm, expecting him to lean over and kiss her. When he didn't move—not even so much as a smile—she realized something was wrong. Terribly wrong. Only she had no idea what it was. "Sage?"

"Yeah?" Again, he didn't even look at her.

"What's wrong?"

Sage pushed to his feet. "Nothing." He reached for her hand and helped her up. "We should probably go back before the sun goes down."

This was just what Kate needed. A moody artist on one of the most difficult nights of her life.

Chapter Fifteen

THE MORE SAGE got to know Kate, the more of a connection he felt toward her. He'd always felt like a bit of a fraud living in the heart of New York in an enormous townhouse that cost far too much money. He would be much more comfortable in a small cabin in the woods, using a rustic barn as a studio. He'd thought about making changes in his life often over the last year or two, and the thought excited him, but then the excitement was quickly chased away by his father's voice pushing him to *be more. Do more.* Make more money. Be the best he could be. The days he'd spent with Kate had reignited his love of the outdoors and a more comfortable, relaxed lifestyle. The work he was doing there felt like the missing piece he'd been searching for. Now he wondered if he was really being *the best he could be* by not doing more.

He reached for Kate's hand on the way back to the cabins, chewing on what she'd said about not needing many people in her life. He felt closer to Kate than he did to anyone else, but he'd begun to worry that perhaps he was feeling something she wasn't. And he might just be setting himself up to be hurt. *Will you miss me when I leave?* The thought of leaving—and the lingering question of how Kate might answer the unasked question—made the pit of his stomach ache.

"You didn't mention your meeting with the people in the village. How did it go?" he asked.

"Great. But if we pull out of here, who will advocate for them? We've been trying to get this through for the last year and a half, and we're so close." She sighed. "I just hope that Friday's meeting will make a difference."

"Friday?"

"Yeah. There's so much to all of this, and I'm not an engineer or anything, so my voice is just one among many, but I think it's important that I help. On Friday the Ministry of Rural Development is sending an engineer out to review the area and meet with the residents. I can at least speak my mind and hope it makes a difference."

"It's government. They're all about dollars and cents." *Which is why a nonprofit focusing on wells makes so much sense.*

Kate sighed again and shook her head, like he totally didn't understand. Which was accurate, because he didn't understand how a volunteer could make that big of a difference where politics were involved. Greasing a palm maybe, but good intentions rarely got things moving in government.

"Is there some way I can help? I know you don't like me to throw money at problems, but this is a prime example of how if you'd agree to let me create a few pieces and sell them for charitable proceeds, the money could benefit the community."

"I just..." She blew out a breath as they came to the cabins. "Yes, this is about funding. But the government has the money. They're just diverting it to larger communities, like the small ones don't matter. Like if there are fewer people, they don't need the same resources."

Listening to the passion in her voice, and knowing how hard she worked for the community in all regards, not just for the well, made Sage feel even more for her. He brushed her damp hair from her shoulders. "I'm proud of you, for all you do and how much you care. You're amazing, and you should be proud of yourself, too." He felt protective toward Kate, and that feeling had only grown since their first kiss.

She blinked several times, as if she couldn't believe what he'd said. "Thank you."

He pulled her close and kissed her cheek. He knew it was dangerous to allow his heart to embrace her, given the distance between where he lived and where she might be in a few months, but he was unable to stop himself from being drawn into everything about her. "I want to help, and if you won't let me help monetarily, then please let me help in some other way."

"I guess you could come to the meeting. That would help. The more supporters the better."

"Okay. I'll be there."

"Really? It's Friday at three in the village."

"Absolutely."

"What about the mural? The kids?" Her eyes held a mixture of hope and worry, and Sage wanted to satisfy both.

"I'll talk to the teachers and see if they can accommodate the painting before the lessons. Then I'll meet you there."

"I don't want you to mess up your schedule, but this is really important to me. It would mean the world to me if you went."

"And you're important to me. I'll be there."

Her lips curved into a smile, and when it reached her eyes, the worry seemed to disappear. "Thank you."

Every nerve in Sage's body ached to discuss where they were headed—and if there was any chance of seeing each other after he left. But he worried that Kate would slide him back into the pushy artist or celebrity category. He would wait it out. Kate hadn't indicated any interest in seeing each other beyond their time together in Belize. In fact, she might have been telling him otherwise just a few minutes earlier. *I guess I don't need many people. I'm pretty content with the people and the life I have here.*

Sage would take all the time he could get.

LATER THAT EVENING, Kate and Luce stopped by Sage's cabin on their way into town. They found him sketching in the screened-in sleeping area, wearing nothing but a pair of gym shorts, sweat dripping from his skin. Kate stood on the outside of the screen looking in, thinking about how his wet body had felt against hers earlier in the afternoon.

"You do have a shower, you know," Luce teased.

Sage didn't lift his eyes from the sketchpad. "Yeah. I'll get to it."

"What are you drawing?" Kate stood on her tiptoes, trying to see what he'd drawn. Her hand dropped to her stomach where he'd drawn them sitting on top of the world. When she'd showered earlier she'd been careful not to scrub the image away.

"I want to remember everything here so I can capture it when I return home. In the jungle, right by the end of the path near the beach, I saw the most beautiful red flowers. That's what I'm drawing." His eyes remained intent on the drawing.

Kate felt a spear of guilt. She hadn't been close enough to any artists to understand what they must feel when they're inspired. Now, watching Sage so engrossed in capturing what he'd seen, she wondered if she'd made a mistake and stifled that inspiration by not allowing his canvases to be shipped in for paintings he'd send back to the States.

"We're heading into town for dinner. Want to come?" Kate asked, but she could tell by the fact that his eyes did not once waver from his drawing that he was in some sort of artist's zone again.

"No thanks. You guys have fun. I'm gonna finish this and then work out."

Kate waited for him to add, *Can I see you later?* or *I'll catch up with you afterward,* or *Let me kiss you goodbye,* and when he didn't, it pierced like a needle to her heart.

Luce tucked her arm into Kate's. "Ready, girlie? Fajitas are calling me."

"Um, yeah." She glanced at Sage again. "Okay, well..."

His eyes darted to her and her hopes soared—for a brief second they connected—and then he dropped them to the drawing again. "Have fun." With his eyes locked on the drawing, he added, "I'll come by later."

Once out of earshot, Luce said, "You have quite the moody artist there, don't you?"

"Who knew?" She tried to make light of Sage being completely absorbed by the drawing instead of her, but she heard the hurt in her own voice and knew Luce would too.

"Hey, you okay? He's just doing his own thing."

"Yeah, I guess. I just...You picked up on that, right? I mean...he wasn't even a little excited to see me." *God, I sound like a needy brat.*

"Look at you! All jealous over a drawing. Is this the same Kate who hasn't needed a man in forever? The Kate who runs an entire program in a developing nation far away from everyone she knows, without any help? Suddenly you're lost without Sage? What's up with that?" Luce started with a teasing voice, but her tone grew serious.

Kate stewed on the way into town. She didn't even know what this thing with Sage was. A fling? A relationship? How could she know? They hadn't defined it. She'd just gone along with her feelings—for once—and it felt good. But it also felt confusing as hell.

"Luce, I shouldn't feel hurt that he wanted to draw instead of being with me, right? I mean, if I had to make a choice between seeing him and attending a meeting for the well, I'd still go to the meeting. It's the same thing, right?"

"He's just doing what artists do, Kate."

Kate sighed. "Well, then, it's probably a good thing I find out now rather than later. It's also probably a good thing that I didn't give in and let him make paintings to sell back in New York, or I'd never see him."

"You know I love you, right?" Luce said as they walked into the cozy café. The interior walls were painted bright yellow, and there were several small tables. Three older men sat at a table near the back, three bottles of beer on the table and two empty plates. Their leathery skin was heavily wrinkled from the sun, and bags of fatigue hung heavily beneath their eyes. Luce chose a table off to the side.

"But?"

"This whole thing is kind of ridiculous. He should be painting and selling what he makes in New York to fund the community here. Who cares what it does for his career? I'm not saying he'd do it for his career, because he's *definitely* not like that."

They ordered drinks and dinner from a middle-aged woman in a dark skirt and blouse whom Kate recognized from the village, but she could not recall her name. She wore her long hair loose, and when she smiled, her yellow teeth contrasted sharply against her dark skin.

"So you think I'm being ridiculous? After all the crap you've seen that goes on here with celebrities showing up just to increase their own exposure?" She took a long drink. A margarita had never tasted so good.

"I just think that you should take whatever you can get." Luce lifted her drink. "I mean, funding-wise and Sage-wise." She winked.

On one level, Kate knew Luce was right, but on another level, allowing things that only furthered celebs public relations went against everything Kate stood for. She looked at her friend, her straight blond hair pulled back in a tight ponytail, no makeup on her face, her tank top hanging off her shoulder, and her eyes locked on Kate. Luce looked nothing like a New York public relations specialist, but at the moment, Kate hated that she sounded exactly like one. She'd been brought up to do the right thing by others, and when it came to the people of Punta Palacia, she felt a protectiveness that she took seriously. *And then there's how I feel about Sage.*

"You know I hate that we don't have real volunteers out here, so how can you say all that?" She finished her margarita and ordered a second.

"I don't know, Kate. You're here." She shrugged. "Why not make the most of whatever can help the people here? Even if some of it is a little...greasy. Does everything have to be squeaky clean?"

"In my world it kinda does. I feel like if I give in, I'm condoning that behavior."

Luce narrowed her eyes and locked on Kate's with a serious stare. "Listen, hon, whether you want to admit it or not, just being here and running a program that serves celebs condones that behavior."

"Really? Oh God. That's a horrible thought." *Am I condoning their behavior?* Kate sighed. It was all overwhelming. "Do you think I'm hurting his career, too, or just not allowing him to make the most of it?" She covered her face with her hands. "Listen to me. *Just not allowing him to make the most of it?* Oh my God. Who am I to *allow* him to do anything? What has happened to me? Somehow I've become so attached to what I'm doing here that...that..."

"That you've forgotten how the real world works?" Luce asked.

"No. I'm just realizing that maybe you're right. Maybe I shouldn't be here in the first place. I'm compromising my own beliefs by catering to celebrities." It hit her like a kick to the gut.

I allow the system to work the way it does. I assist it. I make it happen. What the hell am I doing?

Chapter Sixteen

SAGE GOT UP at the crack of dawn and went to Kate's cabin. After she and Luce had gone into town last night, he'd tracked down Clayton and Cassidy and told them in no uncertain terms exactly how the rest of their trip was going to go down. *No more talking shit about Kate. No more shirking your responsibilities. You need to pitch in now that Penelope is gone. The people here deserve that much. Kate and Caleb deserve that much.* And by the grace of God, they had acted almost human and agreed. Sage had gone back to his drawing feeling more at ease, and he'd gotten so engrossed that by the time he'd set it down, it was well past two o'clock in the morning. He'd gone to Kate's cabin, but she was already asleep, and he didn't have the heart to wake her. Even if he'd like nothing more than to sleep with her in his arms.

As he ascended the steps to Kate's, he inhaled deeply. This walk toward an apology was nothing new to Sage. He'd gotten lost in his art enough times to know exactly what type of an asshole he was. He'd been told off by dozens of women for missing dates or showing up late. Hell, even his own mother had given him grief for missing family dinners, and she understood what it was like to be in the zone. He hated knowing Kate was now added to the list of women who'd felt scorned because of his art.

He saw Kate through the screen door, sitting on the edge of her bed in a pair of shorts and a black tank top and scribbling in a notebook.

"Hey," he said softly. "How mad are you?"

She turned to face him, and the look in her puffy eyes drew him into the room. She set the notebook on the mattress. He knelt beside her, strangled by guilt. "Kate, I'm really sorry. I get caught up in my work. I can't help it. It just happens." He used to make up excuses, but Sage knew that excuses were worthless, and Kate, looking hurt and exhausted, deserved the truth. *This is who I am.* He was the guy who got lost in his art. He always had been, and she needed to understand that.

"I'm not mad." She touched his cheek and her gaze softened.

"You're not? Why not?"

She shrugged. "I just have a lot going on, that's all." She pushed to her feet. "You aren't tied to me. You were doing your own thing. That's fine, Sage. Really."

"No. It's not fine, and I'm really sorry." He leaned down to kiss her. She kissed him quickly, pulling away well before he was ready.

"Kate?" Her eyes were burdened, shadowed, and he knew it was his fault. "I get caught up in my work, and I know it's wrong and it's hurtful."

"Sage, it's okay. I get caught up in my work, too. Or at least I used to." She let out a breath and headed for the door. "Your supplies come in this morning."

"Kate, wait. Can we talk?" *Don't all women like to talk things through?*

"Let's talk on the way. I want to get coffee and be there when the truck pulls up."

He bristled against the iciness in her voice and the distance between them as she hurried ahead of him. "Kate?"

She turned toward him and flashed a tense smile.

Shit. He reached for her hand. "I'm really sorry, but don't just brush me off. Please."

"I'm not brushing you off. I just have a lot on my mind."

That's when he saw it, a fissure in her steely resolve that bubbled up and dampened her eyes. He closed the gap between them and drew her to his chest, feeling his own heart shatter when her arms remained hanging limply by her sides.

"Kate, I never meant to hurt you."

She shook her head against his chest and finally lifted her hands to his waist. "I know."

"You got to see the other side of me. The nonartist side, but when I'm in artist mode, it's like my mind has tunnel vision. Everything else falls away, but that doesn't mean I don't care about you. It's not like that at all."

"Sage."

"It's like nothing can penetrate the zone my mind goes into."

"Sage?"

"I'll understand if you want to ease up on seeing me." *But I'll fucking hate it.* "I know my flaws."

She pushed away from him. "Sage." She was breathing heavily, her brows knitted together, and her tone was definitely angry.

"Yeah?"

"I'm not mad, okay?" she snapped and shook her head. "I just realized that there's a bunch of other stuff I need to get worked out. I understand that you get into the zone, or whatever it is that artists do. There is more to me than just you, you know. I have a life here, and work, and responsibilities."

"I know all of that."

"Well, I have things to deal with that are bigger than if you show up for a booty call or not." She pushed past him and stomped toward the path that led to the mess hall.

"A what?" Sage caught up to her and grabbed her arm. He lowered his voice, his chest tight with anger. "A booty call? Is that what you think this is?" *What the hell happened between last night and this morning?*

"I don't know what I think, Sage." She turned to walk away.

"Hell no, Kate. You're not getting off that easy." They stood in the narrow path with giant green leaves surrounding them, streaks of the rising sun's warmth sneaking through the tall foliage. At any other time it would feel romantic. Now it felt claustrophobic.

"What do you want from me, Sage? I'm in the midst of life-changing things here, and somehow I'm supposed to make all the right decisions for everyone, and...and..." Tears sprang from her eyes. "And it doesn't really matter what I do, because AIA might pull out anyway, and then the people here will be left with nothing. And I'm screwing up your career by not allowing you to paint, or sculpt, or whatever it is you want to do and sell in New York."

He reached up and brushed the tears from her cheek with the pad of his thumb. The pieces of her broken heart were falling into a more understandable puzzle. "You're overwhelmed. I was just the icing on the cake."

"I am not," she huffed, crossing her arms over her chest.

Goddamn, she was cute, but Sage knew better to

say *that* aloud. That's when he remembered his mother's advice. *Telling a woman to calm down, or that she's overwhelmed, or that a few pounds don't matter are all cause for a fight or an emotional meltdown. Don't go there, Sage.* Too late.

"I've handled more than this." She glared at him.

Afraid of saying the wrong thing and knowing Kate could handle anything she was dealt, he simply wrapped his arms around her and held her. She struggled against him, but he didn't relent. Even angry and overwhelmed, she needed love. She turned in to him, her body rigid. He scooped her up into his arms and guided her legs around his waist.

"Don't get any dirty ideas. I just want to hug you." He flashed a flirtatious smile.

She laughed under her breath, allowing him to hold her. His cheek found hers, and with one hand beneath her and the other wrapped tightly around her back, he whispered, "You were never a booty call."

Only then did the rigidity leave her body.

"I'm sorry, Kate. I'll make more of an effort to be in tune to what you're going through. But please don't shut me out."

Kate pressed her cheek to his and placed her hand on the back of his neck. "I'm sorry," she said softly.

"Don't be sorry. Just be you. I lo—like all of you. Mad. Sad. Happy. I'll take my knocks for letting you down. I deserve them. Hell, I'll even take the brunt of you feeling angry at everyone else, but just remember who I am after you come out of your anger, and I'll try to do the same."

Sage knew that promising and doing were two entirely different things. He had faith in himself to try to not fall into oblivion when he was working on his artwork, but he didn't have faith that trying would lead to success. He'd tried before and failed.

He set her back down on the ground. "Tell me what I can do to help with what you're dealing with."

"Just…" She let out a loud breath and looked away. "I don't want to be one of those needy women, but can you just try to let me know if you *think* you're not going to see me when you say you are?"

Sure, but I'd be lying. I never know when I'll fall into the zone. When he looked into her eyes, he knew he wanted to be the man she needed him to be. He didn't know how to get from here to there, but he wanted to try.

She met his gaze, and he placed his hands on her cheeks. "I don't ever want to hurt you, and I'll try my best to be more thoughtful, but I need a safety net."

She smiled. "A safety net?"

He leaned down and pressed a kiss to her lips. "Yeah. I know myself, Kate. It's not like I enjoy letting people down, or coming across self-centered when I'm in my own little world. I need to know that if I fail, you won't walk away. You'll help me through."

They began walking down the path.

"So let me get this straight. When you forget to show up, I'm supposed to…what? Come get you and remind you that you forgot about me?"

He smiled down at her. "That would be great."

She smacked his arm.

"What? Not good?"

"Not even fair," she said.

"Okay, then *if* I forget, you can be as angry as you want, but just don't give up on me."

She was quiet for a long time. When they took a seat at the table by the door in the mess hall, he said, "I'm worth it."

She cranked her mouth to the side and flipped her hair over her shoulder. "Oh, really?"

"Yeah. I'm kinda cute, I'm pretty talented, and best

of all"—he took her hand in his and kissed the back of it—"I'll try to anticipate your needs."

"You are cute, and you're wicked talented, but the other thing? You had no clue what I was upset about this morning, so I don't think so. Nice try, though." She leaned across the table and kissed him. "Okay. I'll help you through it, but I expect you to be worth it." She raised her eyebrows in rapid succession.

"Don't you dare treat me like a booty call," he teased. As relieved as he was by their conversation, Sage had a sinking feeling in the pit of his stomach. *How the hell am I going to change something I've done forever?*

Chapter Seventeen

KATE'S STOMACH HAD been fisted all morning. She felt like such a fool falling apart in front of Sage. What was she thinking? That was the problem. She hadn't been thinking. Ever since Luce had made it perfectly clear to her that everything she'd been doing for the past two years went completely against the very principles she believed in, she'd been confused, angry, and tied in one giant knot. When Sage hadn't come by to see her the evening before, it drove the point home. No matter how much she liked him, he was a celebrity. He was— at least a little—self-centered. How could he *not* be? Weren't they all? But then he'd held her, and when she was in his arms, all of that fell away. Her principles didn't matter like they had when her feet were firmly planted on the ground. *Maybe I'm losing my mind altogether.*

Kate watched Sage and Oscar carrying the supplies from the delivery truck to the school. She pressed her clipboard to her chest, wondering how she could feel so much for Sage and be so confused by him all at once. She agreed to help him through forgetting about her?

What the hell was she thinking? *Sure, forget me and it's okay?* But the way he'd asked for help, and...Damn it. Everything about him threw her for a loop. She believed that he didn't mean to forget to come see her, and she believed that he wanted help to stop doing it in the future. Was she being naive? Was she catering to another self-centered celebrity? *Ugh!* She pushed the thought away as Sage and Oscar headed back toward the truck. Sage waved to someone behind Kate. She spun around and saw Clayton and Cassidy walking toward them. *Great.*

"You guys are with Caleb today," she said abruptly. Sage had told her what Clayton had said about her, and it was all she could do not to call him out on it.

"Sage asked me to help him unload the truck." Clayton flexed his biceps. "Put my muscles to work."

Kate rolled her eyes. "Go right ahead." She nodded at the truck and watched Clayton strut toward it, wondering how Sage went from slamming the guy against a tree to asking for his help.

"He's the sexiest thing, isn't he?" Cassidy ogled Clayton with a sensual smile on her painted lips.

"He's something," Kate said flatly. She watched Clayton and Sage working side by side. Both men had sculpted arms, strong backs, and powerful legs. Any other woman would probably be thrilled watching them as they hefted enormous boxes onto their shoulders, their muscles straining beneath the weight, sweat dripping off their hard bodies. Kate's eyes shifted from Clayton to Sage, and in that moment she saw the difference between the two as clear as day. Clayton moved in a practiced fashion. Each step carefully placed, as if he knew he was being watched. When he returned to the truck, his eyes shifted to Cassidy, then to Kate—which made her stomach clench. Sage moved with purpose, each determined step a movement toward a goal— delivering the box, retrieving the next. His eyes focused on the next box as he settled his grip and hoisted it up. Then his dark eyes shifted to the path across the grass to the building. His eyes didn't drift to Kate, and while someone else might feel a little put off by this, she found it reassuring. He was focused, determined. He wasn't going through the actions looking for a pat on the back, and she felt her resolve soften toward him once again.

When all the supplies had been delivered, Sage went through them to ensure they'd been received free of damage. She watched him as he signed off on the paperwork and thanked the driver, and then he knelt beside a large box and withdrew a number of tools. Hammers, a crowbar, an electric drill. *What the hell?* He then withdrew a thick leather tool belt from its plastic wrapping and gathered it all back into the box and brought it to Oscar.

Oscar looked in the box, set it on the ground, and then embraced Sage. She couldn't hear what he said, but she saw the look of gratitude in his eyes. By the way he held Sage a beat or two longer than a typical welcome or goodbye embrace, she realized that when Sage had asked his mother to send the supplies for the mural, he'd also asked her to send tools for Oscar. Her reluctant heart opened a little more.

Sage's body glistened with sweat; beneath his tight, sweat-soaked shirt, his muscles twitched from the hard work. He ran his hand through his hair as he approached Kate, training his eyes on her with a serious, dark stare.

So damn hot.

"What?" she said, probably too harshly.

"Hold on a sec." He turned to Clayton as he walked by. "Thanks, man. I appreciate the help."

Clayton shifted his gaze to Kate. Kate bristled. Then

he looked at Sage again. "No problem. We'll go find Caleb now."

Kate watched them walk away. "So you're buddies now?"

"Hardly." Sage turned his attention to her. "I had a little talk with him and Cassidy. Let's just say that we shouldn't have any more trouble with him, and I think they will pull their weight and help Caleb out from now on."

"Really?"

"Yeah."

He stood close, his body radiating heat. She had the urge to touch him. *To stroke those steamy, sexy muscles, and...Shit. Stop it.* She cleared her throat and locked her eyes on her clipboard. "I...I saw the tools you got for Oscar. That was really nice of you."

"Yeah. He needed a few things. The poor guy didn't even have a solid tool belt. Anyway, listen. We have a little problem." Sage wiped his brow with the crook of his arm.

"I thought all the supplies came."

"They did, but there are a few things here that I didn't order."

She let out a breath. "Well, we can send them back. Why didn't you say something before the delivery truck left?"

"Because I think my mother sent them for me. I didn't say I didn't want them. I said I didn't order them."

"I don't understand."

He took her hand and brought her to the side of the school, where he tore open two large boxes, revealing two large canvases. "She's an artist. I'm sure she just assumed..."

"Really, Sage? I'm supposed to believe that you didn't order these?" *Why does the sun suddenly feel a zillion degrees hotter?*

"Well, I didn't, so yeah." He crossed his arms. "Listen, Kate. I know you're going through a lot of shit right now, but haven't you learned anything about me since we've been together? Namely that I don't lie?"

"Yeah, but—"

"You know what? I'm hot. The kids are waiting to paint, and I have a lot of prep work to do. You can believe whatever you want to believe. To be honest, I'm glad she sent them. I'm dying to get my hands on a brush and work through some of my own frustrations, outside of the school."

Shit. Say something. A lump had formed in Kate's throat, so thick and solid that she could barely breathe.

"There's too much real shit to worry about to sit and argue over whether or not I lied to you. I told you before. I'm not who you think I am." He turned to walk away and hesitated. "You know what? I thought we'd moved beyond this shit."

For the second time in less than three hours, Kate felt her world spiraling out of control, and for the first time in her life she felt like she was unable to rein it back in.

Chapter Eighteen

SAGE STEWED ALL afternoon about Kate as he and the children worked on the mural. He had been in the wrong when he didn't go see her when he'd said he would, but he sure as hell hadn't lied to her. Sure, maybe he'd overreacted. He was hotter than hell, and he knew the minute he'd told her about the canvases she'd suspect that he'd gone against her wishes. It was times like these when Sage wished he *were* a practiced liar. He could have worked on the canvases without Kate knowing and probably even had them shipped back to the States with her never the wiser. But damn it, that's not how he was raised, and he'd be damned if he was going to sink to that level now. *Fuck.* He came to Belize to clear his head, and now it was so full of Kate that he could barely think past her.

After the kids each had a turn painting and he'd cleaned up and put the supplies away, he surveyed the mural. Bright greens and reds, streaks of browns and oranges, popped from the side of the building. It was too early for the images to take shape, and he could manipulate the edges to be a little more refined if need be, but it warmed his heart to know the children were pouring their energy into the mural.

As he turned away from the school, his body sweaty, his mouth dry, he was torn between ridding himself of the frustration with Kate by getting started on a canvas and trying to clear the air with her. His affection for Kate drew him back to the cabins. He'd skipped lunch, and now that it was nearing dinnertime, his stomach was rumbling. He went to Kate's cabin and, finding it empty, he headed over to the mess hall. As the sun began to descend, the heat of the afternoon eased, but the temperature inside the building was oppressive. Sage grabbed a bottle of water and two bean and rice fajitas and took them outside, rehashing his earlier conversation with Kate in his mind, trying to recall if she'd mentioned where she was going.

"Still mad at me?"

Sage turned at the sound of Luce's voice. "I was never mad at you. Hey, have you seen Kate?"

"Okay, mad was the wrong word. Still disagree with my thoughts about PR? Kate went over to the village earlier, but I haven't seen her since she left."

Sage guzzled the water. "It's gonna be dark soon. Think I should look for her?"

"Uh…" Luce looked over Sage's shoulder. "I'm not sure that's gonna be necessary. What the hell?"

Sage turned to see Kate, Cassidy, and Clayton walking down the center of the dirt road. *What the hell?* Cassidy held Clayton's hand, and on his other side, Kate walked at a leisurely pace, a notebook tucked under her arm, her full attention on Cassidy. Clayton looked over and waved.

"Holy crap. I never thought I'd see the day," Luce said, waving at Clayton.

"You're telling me?"

Kate turned in their direction. Her mouth lifted

into a tentative smile, her eyes shifting from Luce to Sage, where they held just long enough—he hoped—to read the narrowing of his eyes. Sage went to greet them. "How's it going?" He reached an arm around Kate and kissed her cheek, as much to claim her in front of Clayton as to try to bridge the gap between them. As upset as he was, he was still unable to deny his feelings for her. "You okay?" he whispered.

"Yeah. Fine."

"Kate was telling us about the whole well situation and the meeting that's coming up next week. We thought we'd show up," Clayton explained. "Luce, we know you're Penelope's PR rep, but can we pay you to set up some visibility for us?"

"Um." Luce shot a glance at Kate, who shrugged. "I can't act as your rep, but I'm sure we can work with your PR guys to coordinate something."

"Kate, you're okay with this?" Sage asked.

"I'm just thankful for the support." She sidestepped out from beneath Sage's protective arm.

"That's great." Sage eyed Clayton, trying to determine if he had something else up his sleeve.

Clayton flashed his winning smile and smacked the thigh of his jeans. "Well, we're gonna grab showers. Luce, catch up with you later to discuss the details?"

"Sure." Luce watched them walk away; then she sidled up to Kate. "What the hell's up with that?"

Kate began walking toward her cabin with Luce and Sage in tow. "What? They offered to go. You're the one who said I needed to maximize the exposure to help the community."

"Yeah. I did, didn't I?" She arched a brow at Sage. "I was just gonna read for a while. I'll catch you guys later."

"I thought you hated publicity." *And Clayton.*

"I do."

"So, why the change of heart?" They walked along the path toward her cabin.

She stared straight ahead. "Luce said that I might be shortsighted on that, so I'm giving it a try." Her voice was cold, distant, forced.

When they reached the stairs to her cabin, Sage lowered himself to the bottom step. "Wanna talk a minute?"

Kate sat beside him, fidgeting with the edge of her tank top. He wanted to pull her against him, to kiss her sweet lips, but so much had transpired over the course of the day that he felt like they were on opposite sides of a ravine and he had no idea how to bridge the gap.

"Was your day okay?"

"Yeah. I went to the clinic, then checked email in town."

He could feel her pulling away, and all he wanted to do was grab hold and not let her go. "Did you hear anything more about AIA and if they'll pull out of here?"

"No. I won't know anything until I talk to Raymond again."

Goddamn, this is hard. Sage was a patient guy, but the stress of Kate thinking he'd lied to her had been brewing all day, festering in the heat, and his patience had worn thin. "Kate…"

She met his gaze. *Christ.* One look in her blue eyes and he realized that the last thing he wanted to do was argue with her. He was head over heels for her, and that emotion won out. "Hell, Kate," he said just above a whisper. "I hate this."

"Me too."

"Do you?" He knew he must sound pathetic, his voice full of hope, hanging on to every word she said, but he didn't care. When he looked at Kate, he felt full of hope. And goddamn it, he liked it. He just needed to clear the air. "But if you don't trust me, then we..." He ran his hand between the two of them. "This. Us. We won't work."

"I know." She glanced down at her hands, then settled a hand on top of his.

Sage breathed a relieved sigh that he hadn't realized he'd been holding in. He closed his eyes for a second; then he pulled her close and kissed her temple.

"I believe you about the canvases. And I'm sorry I said I didn't earlier. I've been under a lot of pressure, and..." She looked up through her thick lashes, her brows knitted together. "I'm sorry, Sage."

"I don't know how we got so sidetracked, but I'm sure my not showing last night kicked it off." She held his gaze, and his love for her grew. "Kate, I can't lie to you. I'm gonna fuck up. I know I am. My brain works in weird ways when I'm in my creative zone. I'm gonna try my hardest to be there every single time I say I will, but..."

"I know."

That was all she said. It was all she needed to. When their lips met again, the warmth and closeness returned. Sage lifted her onto his lap and deepened the kiss, feeling like a starving man satiated for the first time in weeks. Kate filled parts of him that he hadn't realized were empty.

When they drew apart, the tension was gone from Kate's eyes. "Sage, I was really overwhelmed today. I didn't sleep last night, and Luce said some things that really hit home with me. I wanted to talk them out with you last night, but then you didn't show up, and then today...." She sighed. "I think with the news from Raymond, and not knowing what I'm doing a few weeks from now, it was all too much."

A few weeks from now.

Sage caressed her back. The sound of Clayton's

guitar filtered through the darkness. "I'm sorry that I added stress to what was already on your plate. Maybe we can figure some of this out together. What did Luce say that was so bothersome?"

Kate sighed. "She didn't really say anything wrong. She just said that I shouldn't be so against PR and..."

"And?"

"And that by running this program, I'm condoning the behavior of the people who come here only for publicity."

The pain in her voice was palpable. Before he could respond, Kate continued.

"She's right, you know," Kate said. "I thought about it, and of course she's right. I mean, Caleb and I are doing what we need to in order for the programs to run well, and sometimes volunteers are really here to help, like you are. But in general, I'm running a babysitting program for celebrities like Penelope Price to repair their reputations or jump-start their ailing careers. It's kind of pathetic."

"Babe, that's not completely true." Sage slapped a bug from his leg.

"Let's go inside and talk." Kate took his hand and led him inside.

Sage grabbed a blanket and Kate's pillows and laid them on the floor in the screened-in area at the rear of the cabin. Kate sat on the blanket and Sage lay back with his head on the pillow, looking out the screen at the darkening sky. "There aren't many stars tonight."

"I think they're hiding. Afraid I'll bitch them out."

"Come here." He pulled her down, and Kate rested her head on his chest.

"You run important programs, Kate, and even though some people come here with different intentions than you hope, they're still putting income into the community, and that's important. So don't get too down on yourself for what you do."

Kate placed her palm over his heart, and Sage closed his eyes, reveling in her touch.

"You have a kinder heart than anyone I know, Kate. You're here, giving your life to help others. You can't fault yourself for what others choose to do with their lives."

"Maybe." Her voice was soft, tender. "But I could be doing so much more someplace else. Someplace where volunteers are lining up to help. *Really* help the community."

Someplace else. "Will you do this forever?"

"What?"

"Work with groups like AIA? Travel the world. Help communities? Give back?" He listened to the solemn pace of her breathing against the night sounds of the jungle. She didn't answer right away. "You okay?"

"Yeah. I'm just thinking. I always thought I'd do this forever, like my parents did. You know, travel and help wherever there's a need, but now..." She wrapped her arm over his stomach and cuddled in close.

"Now you're not sure?"

"I don't know. I just have a lot to think about. I can't even imagine the people here not having the aid we provide, but then I know there are a million other places that also need help. I'm one person, you know? And I wonder sometimes if I want to get into the real world for a while just to try it out."

He looked down at her. "I think you're more in the real world than I am in New York."

Kate shimmied up his body until her chest pressed against his and they were eye to eye. She kissed him softly. "You surprise me."

"How so?"

"Everything. Even the way you got lost in your work was surprising to me. You're so attentive and...present when you're not working. You're aware of everything around you. You listen to what I say all the time, not like most men who only half listen."

"Don't make me into something I'm not. You've seen me drawing. I zone out completely."

"Yeah, you do. But when you're not working, you're right here with me."

"That's where I'd always rather be. Except when you're calling me a liar."

Kate's body went rigid.

"I didn't mean that," he said, though he kind of did.

"Yeah, you did. And it's fair. I'm really sorry about that. I shouldn't have judged you unfairly. I'm not used to people being honest all the time."

"My father drilled honesty into our brains since we could comprehend speech. And my mother? She'd knock me on my ass if she thought I lied or mistreated a woman."

"She would not." She laughed.

"No, she would never hurt a fly. But she'd give me this look." Sage narrowed his eyes and pressed his lips together. "And I'm sure she'd say something like, *Sage William Remington, have you gotten so big in those britches of yours that you've forgotten what it means to be a gentleman?*"

"I think I like your mom already." Kate ran her finger over the tattoo on his right arm. "Does she mind that you have tattoos?"

"My mom? Nah. She wasn't crazy about it when I got my first one, but all of us except Jack and Siena have them. Rush, Kurt, Dex, and I each have quite a few."

"Sage." Seriousness crept into her tone, then settled in her eyes.

"Yeah?"

"Would it be way too pushy for me to ask if I could

visit you in New York after you leave?"

In one swift move, Sage flipped her onto her back beneath him and trapped her between his forearms. His smile pressed at his cheeks.

"Seriously?" He kissed her.

"Does that mean it would be okay?" She laughed. "I mean, I know we haven't talked about seeing each other beyond when we're here, but I'm going crazy waiting for you to bring it up, and—"

"Waiting for me? I wasn't sure if you'd want to see me after I went back home."

She reached up and ran her fingers through his hair. "Really? Because you think I'm the kind of girl who has her way with hot, sexy artists in Belize and then casually tosses them aside and makes room for the new crop?"

"Something like that, you little minx, you," he teased.

"As long as we're clear, then," she whispered. "This amazing sex we have, it's just a time filler."

Her fingers slid down his cheek, and he leaned in to her palm. Her touch was sensual and loving, and his body responded with a surge of desire.

"A time filler," he repeated. "You make me want to fill time over and over again. I never realized I had so much downtime to be filled." He nuzzled against her neck. "Kate," he whispered. "You're so much more than a time filler. It scares the shit out of me."

Chapter Nineteen

THE NEXT FEW days passed quickly. Sage and Kate had found their groove as a couple. While Sage worked on the mural, Kate and Luce helped Caleb. Clayton and Cassidy had helped at the clinic, and on most afternoons, Clayton could be heard playing his guitar and singing. Sage worked on the mural late into the evenings, adding finite detail to the children's hard work, while Kate read or wrote in one of her notebooks. Then Sage would walk Kate back to her cabin, and he'd return to his cabin to exercise or shower or whatever it was that men did to prepare to see a woman. All Kate knew was that by the time he came back each night, she felt like he'd been gone for days, and he smelled like—and felt like—sheer masculinity: earthy, rough, and oh so good.

Tonight she was thinking of the canvases his mother had sent as he carried the last of the paints inside, then returned to her side and held out a hand to help her up from the ground.

"What will you do with the canvases?" she asked.

He shrugged. "I guess I'll see when I'm done with

the mural."

"But you're leaving on Sunday. You can't possibly get more than the mural done, can you?"

He shrugged, and they walked hand in hand back to her cabin. The night air was comfortable. Ribbons of pinks and grays surrounded the moon. Sage's hand was warm and sure in hers. The thought of him leaving made her stomach twist. Even knowing she'd visit him in New York didn't quell the longing that had already begun to settle in. She was used to Sage now. She counted on him. The bed felt empty without his body wrapped around hers on the entirely too-small twin mattress. How had she ever slept without him beside her? How would she sleep when he was gone? She tried to push the thoughts away. *Now* was what mattered. Now he was right there with her, one hand on her lower back as he climbed the stairs behind her, the other— *Oh my. A*t the top of the stairs, Sage pressed his body against hers. He gathered her hair over one shoulder, then lowered his mouth to her bared skin. His low, sexy growl sent a shudder of heat through her.

She reached behind her. God, she loved the feel of his coarse whiskers against her skin, the way he dragged his tongue along the back of her neck. He gripped her hips and turned her around. She pressed her palms to his chest, feeling his heart beating fast and hard, then slid her hands beneath his shirt and ran her fingers over his ripped abs. She had to lift his shirt to see his bare skin. Sage's body was like a work of art. She loved everything about it, from the hard muscles to the soft creases where his arms met his chest. Now she held his shirt above his ribs and kissed her way across his stomach, then pressed her cheek to his skin.

"God, I love being close to you," she whispered.

He touched the line of her jaw the way he often did, and that intimate touch made her long to be even closer, to touch every inch of him. She reached for him, but before she made contact, he lowered his mouth to hers and kissed her slowly and deeply. She couldn't have held back the moan that escaped her lungs if her life depended on it. Sage drew passion from deep within her every time they touched, and she'd given up fighting it.

"We should go inside," she managed.

"Better be careful inviting strange men into your room," he warned.

"If you're a strange man, I'll take my chances." She took his hand and led him to the bed.

Sage took a step backward.

"What's wrong?"

"I just had an idea. I'll be right back." In two steps, he was out the door.

Kate looked around the room, wondering what could have struck him so urgently. She sniffed under her arms. *Nope. I don't stink.* She glanced in the mirror and ran her fingers through her hair. *Not bad.* Before she could worry too much, Sage was ascending the steps two at a time. Kate opened the screen door and found him carrying his mattress over his head.

"What on earth are you doing?" She laughed as he carried it inside and set it on the floor in the screened-in area. Then he took the mattress from her bed and placed it beside it. The two mattresses took up all but a six-inch border around the room.

"Perfect."

"Aww. I like having to sleep close to you."

Sage slid his arms around her waist and kissed her. "That's not for sleeping."

Chapter Twenty

THE NEXT AFTERNOON, Sage and Javier painted side by side. Javier's eyebrows were drawn tightly together as his brush moved carefully along the concrete. He glanced at Sage every few minutes, his hopeful eyes seeking approval.

"You are very talented, Javier."

A smile spread across Javier's cheeks. He reached up to scratch an itch, and the ends of the paintbrush skimmed the fringe of his hair, leaving a bright yellow streak. Sage lifted his eyebrows, and Javier laughed and went back to work on the mural. He was painting the shirt of the little boy at the water's edge. Sage had been thinking of how much Kate adored Javier when he'd likened the image to him.

Oscar came out of the school with a small radio and turned it on. The music made a nice backdrop for the students as they painted. Sage walked behind them as they worked in groups of ten, rotating a new group in every forty-five minutes, thanks to Kate's organizational skills. Seeing the mural come to life gave Sage a feeling of fulfillment and pride. He'd watched the kids working side by side in the blazing heat for days, and he wondered what would happen if he ever tried to coordinate such an effort in the city. Sure, he might find a handful of students who would take part, but here, each student eagerly awaited their turn, magnifying the difference between having everything at one's fingertips and taking it for granted and having so little that the extras are cherished.

He glanced inside the classroom, where the next group of students were finishing their studies. The deal he'd struck with the students was that if they completed their work, they'd be allowed to paint. He'd never seen kids work so diligently.

Luce came down the dirt road and waved to Sage. He waved back as he went to greet her.

"Do you mind if I take a few pictures?" Luce asked.

"I thought you and Kate were working with Caleb today." Sage glanced at the road, but Kate was nowhere in sight. Things between them couldn't have been better, and Sage had never been happier in a relationship. *A relationship.* He reflected on the thought, thinking about Jack and Savannah, and Dex and Ellie, and how his brothers' lives had seemed full before they fell in love, but now they seemed revived with a different type of contentment. *Like me with Kate.* He loved that each day brought them closer together and hated that as each day passed, it brought him closer to leaving.

"We wrapped up early. Kate wanted to go into town and call Raymond." She pulled out her cell phone and waved it. "Do you mind?"

"No. Go ahead. The kids are doing a great job, aren't they?"

Luce snapped a few photos of the kids painting. "It looks great. Can I get one of you and the kids?"

Sage looked down at his white tank top and tan

cargo shorts, both streaked with colorful paint. "Sure. Why not? Hey, guys, do you mind if we take a picture together?"

Javier's eyes grew wide. "For the American papers?"

"No, for Miss Luce." *American papers?* The excitement in Javier's eyes brought another thought to Sage. He shot a glance at Luce, who smiled knowingly. She turned away under the guise of taking a picture of Oscar and a group of children standing at the other end of the building.

When she turned back, she took a few pictures of Javier and Sage. "Smile like you're a movie star," she said to Javier.

His eyes widened, and his lips spread into a smile as he reached for Sage's hand. After she took the picture, he said, "Miss Luce, will you put these in the American papers? Please?"

"I'm not sure what will happen to these pictures, Javier." Luce patted his head. "But I'll make sure that Miss Kate has enough copies for everyone."

The children gathered for more photos, moving in close at Luce's direction.

"Smile," she directed. "Beautiful. Now let's get a few with you lined up in front of the mural." The kids ran to the wall, stopping short of the wet paint. "That's perfect," Luce said.

"Will we see our picture on the computer?" a tall teenage boy asked. "Will Miss Kate show us?"

Sage realized that this was Luce's plan. She must have known how the children would react. And how much it would mean to them to see their photos in a newspaper. She probably also knew that seeing the light in Javier's eyes would be difficult for Kate to walk away from.

"You're a sneak," he whispered to her.

"Maybe a little."

"Just do me one favor. Do not release anything until you talk to Kate. This is her show, not yours and not mine. She calls the shots." When she didn't answer, he narrowed his eyes. "Deal?"

"Fine." Luce gave him a playful shove toward the kids.

Sage gathered the rest of the children from inside the school. They stood proud and smiling in front of the mural. Their bright smiles contrasted sharply with their dark skin, and their eyes danced with excitement. Sage stood behind them, thinking of how much Kate would enjoy seeing them and wishing she were there.

Luce took several pictures, and the children did exactly as she asked, moving closer together and then moving the shorter children to the front of the group, the taller ones in back. By the time Luce was done, Sage was tired of the whole process and itching to get back to painting. The children thanked Luce, and it struck him how polite and well behaved they were. In fact, they had been polite and respectful since day one—another marked difference between home and Belize. He watched one of the older girls put her arm around her younger sister and walk her back into the school building, and he felt a pang of longing to talk to his own siblings.

Three hours later, each of the children had taken their turn painting, and the mural was taking shape. Between Sage's long hours of painting and the children's efforts, the jungle had come to life. Lush foliage in various shades of greens and browns filled the left side of the mural. Giant leaves arched over tall grasses, and colorful flowers added depth and vividness to the forest. Javier had painted the upper half of the little boy beautifully, even if the tail of his T-shirt was painted with long streaks that hung below the boy's knees on the right side, as if the shirt were shredded. A seven-year-old girl had taken her brush to the shorts the little boy wore, which hung unevenly above his knees. She smiled proudly after she finished, her tongue poking out of the gap where she'd lost her two front baby teeth. Sage didn't have it in him to even the edges.

He cleaned up the supplies, eyeing one of the canvases. He'd been sketching the area that led to the undiscovered beach where Kate had taken him, and he was dying to bring it to life on the canvas. It evoked warm feelings for him because of the time they'd spent there, and he hoped to bring that feeling of love to the artwork. *Love. Love?* Sage removed the canvas from the box and set it against the wall, remembering walking hand in hand with Kate along the clay path. *Yes. Definitely love.* He smiled, his pulse kicking up a notch.

"The kids did an amazing job."

He spun around at the sound of Kate's voice, still reeling from the realization of his feelings. Kate wore a loose pink tank top and cutoff jeans shorts. He'd seen her in almost the exact same style of clothing for days on end, and still, she had never looked so beautiful. He wrapped his arms around her and kissed her luscious lips.

"I missed you." He nuzzled against her.

"Me too, you. I can't believe how much you guys got done and how different it feels to walk up to the building now. Oh my God, Sage. I can't believe I almost robbed the kids of this experience."

They stood hand in hand and admired the mural.

"Look at that mop of dark hair. That has to be Javier, right?"

She looked up at him with a warm smile and a soft gaze. A wave of love—sure and precious—swept through him. "Yeah" was all he could manage.

"I tried to reach Raymond earlier, but he wasn't around. I sent him an email asking if he'd be open to hosting more than just celebrities here. Even if I'm not going to be here, at least Caleb wouldn't have to deal with them." She smiled up at him and ran her finger down the center of his chest. "No offense, but it would be nice to have more regular people around here, too."

Sage nodded, reeling with the realization that what he felt for Kate was undeniably *love*. Everything tumbled together at once: the idea of the nonprofit, his love for Kate, the feeling of finally knowing how he could do something more meaningful with his life. Emotions soared through him—fear, elation, desire, worry—rendering his muscles tight. He needed to get ahold of himself and find his footing.

"I...um..."

"Are you okay?" Kate's voice was filled with concern.

"Yeah. I...uh...I forgot. I need to Skype my brother." *And maybe my father. Father? Holy hell. Yes.* He wanted his father's input on the nonprofit. "I'll catch up with you right after I'm back."

SAGE STOOD OUTSIDE the Internet café, taking deep breaths and blowing them out slowly, trying to settle his nerves. He felt like he'd sucked down five cups of coffee. His body whirred with excitement, and fear prickled his limbs. He had no fucking idea why he was scared, except that his father had that effect on him. Opening a company was vastly different from being an artist, and he knew his father wouldn't be thrilled. He had no idea why he felt compelled to talk to him about it. What was he looking for? Approval? Shit no. He knew it wasn't that. His father was a smart man, and he might have insight that Sage hadn't thought about, and even if some of that was negative, in case it was also valid, Sage respected his father and wanted to hear it.

When he finally went inside, the gods must have been shining down on him because the Internet connection was solid. At least for now. He emailed Dex with the subject line *Skype NOW?* Then he signed on to Skype and waited for Dex's call. As a business owner, Dex would be able to fill him in on the basic areas he should be thinking about. He wiped his sweaty palms on his shorts while he waited for the call to come through.

Dex's call came through a few minutes later.

"Dude!" Dex said with a grin that lit up his face. Dex's long bangs partially covered his eyes. He ran his hand through his hair, and it fell right back into place. At twenty-six, Dex was a self-made millionaire. He'd developed his first PC game at eighteen, and after graduating college, he'd developed another, which had sold millions and allowed him to start his gaming company, Thrive Entertainment. He'd since expanded his focus, and he and his girlfriend, Ellie, were developing educational software under a government grant.

"Hey, Dex. Before we talk, can you get Dad on the line? I wanted to talk to him, too, but I know he doesn't check email often."

"Yeah, hold on."

He watched Dex call his father and listened to him telling him to get on Skype. A minute later, Dex ended the call. "Okay, he'll be on in a minute."

Sage clicked the link to invite his father into the group Skype.

"Thanks, man. How are you? How's Ellie?"

"She's great. How are you down there in the heat? Miss the AC yet?" Dex asked.

"Nah. It's not bad. I'm working on a mural with the local kids, and watching them is really cool. Now I understand why Mom taught art on and off when we were growing up. The pride in their eyes is worth every drop of sweat."

"That's how Ellie feels about teaching. She's always talking about how the younger kids are so much less entitled than the middle schoolers. They still get excited over the little things that older kids think are stupid." Dex leaned closer to the monitor. "The *now* in your message seemed urgent. Is something wrong?"

"No. Nothing's wrong. I just needed to pick your brain. You know how I've always felt like something is missing in my life? Like nothing I do is meaningful enough to...I don't know. To matter."

"Yeah." Dex nodded. "That's why you went there, to see what other humanitarian efforts were all about."

"Right. Well, I'm seeing a girl here. Kate. And, Dex, man, I really like her." *Love her. I love her.*

"That's great, right? Or does this mean you're moving there and you want me to talk you out of it?" Dex narrowed his dark eyes. "Tell me what you need. I'll do it."

His father's call connected, and his image appeared on the screen.

"Hey, Dad," Sage said.

"Hi, son. You all right?" The four-star general in his father was ever present, even all those miles away. He was authority personified, from his squared-off shoulders to his tightly pressed, thin lips and dark, narrow stare—and he made Sage's heart slam against his ribs.

"Yeah, fine. I really wanted to pick your brain about business. Here's the deal. First, Dex, I definitely *do not* need you to talk me out of seeing Kate. She's the best thing that's ever happened to me, but that's not why I called. She runs the program in Punta Palacia for AIA. The village is a very remote, very small community, and the homes have no water and no electricity." He should have thought out how to explain this before rambling. "They need fresh-water wells, and while the government has money for them, they're a village of only a few hundred, and resources are tight. So the government isn't making them a priority."

"Do you need us to contribute funding for the wells?" his father asked.

"Of course not. I haven't done my research yet, but I'm thinking about starting a company. A nonprofit. One that uses the arts to support the building of wells in newly developing nations."

"I don't get it," Dex interrupted. "How will you use art to do that?"

"Hear me out. I've got all these contacts in the arts community. My stuff sells for obscene amounts of money. If we start an effort where artists donate high-end pieces of their work to the effort and we have an annual charity auction, we could raise a boatload of money each year, and that money could go right to the building of wells." The more he talked about it, the more solidly the idea took shape.

"You've got to think about overhead, paying staff," Dex said.

"Right. That's why I wanted to talk to you. I'll have to call my accountant and have her figure out all the financial details. But, Dex, off the top of your head, what else do I need to think about?"

Dex ran his hand through his hair again. "There's a lot to it, Sage, and nonprofits are totally different from my business. But in general, all the basics need to be covered. Liability and health insurance, tax issues, general administration, and overhead, which includes your office space, staffing, utilities, and I'd imagine that with what you're talking about doing, you'll have a ton of international stuff. I know nothing about that."

193

"Okay. And of course my attorney will need to work with the accountant to make sure it's a viable business model, but I think if we focus on just the effort of bringing wells, and not spreading ourselves too thin, we could reduce the amount of illness and provide a better way of life for people in remote villages." There was so much for him to consider that it seemed like an uphill battle, but the more he talked about it, the more certain he became that he wanted to do it. It was far more appealing than going back to a life that would never be fulfilling.

"The kids here get up before dawn. They go to the river and haul water for their families and gather sticks in the jungle for the stoves. Hell, by the time the sun comes up, they've done more than half the kids in New York do all day—and then they go through their school day and do it all again in the evening. This could change lives, and I want to be part of that."

"Have you thought about donating to one of the nonprofits that already does that type of work?" His father sat with his shoulders back and his chin angled down and set a serious gaze on Sage. "I'm sure there are plenty of them willing to take the funding."

"Yeah, I have. But you know I want to do more. Cutting a check every month doesn't do it for me. I've done that, and it still leaves me feeling empty." Excitement escalated his voice. "And now that I've seen firsthand the issues that bringing in celebrities can cause—even though they donate a shitload of money—I definitely want to bring solutions without creating a spectacle of the communities." And he didn't want Kate having to deal with people like Penelope and Clayton—if she decided to join the effort.

His father nodded but didn't respond.

"You'll have to get a great PR rep," Dex said.

"So you don't think I'm crazy?" Sage held his

breath, waiting for his father to say something. Anything.

Sage saw his brother's eyes dart in the direction of his father's image, and he knew he was holding his breath, too. His father had that effect on them.

"Have you thought about what happens if you're not successful?" His father ran his large hand along his jaw and rubbed his chin.

"This is all just a concept right now," Sage explained. "I haven't ironed anything out yet, but I'm not talking about giving up what I do for a living, just cutting back on it a little. And traveling more." *And being with Kate.* "If I try and fail, then I lose some capital, but I can always fall right back into my old life." The thought of it turned his stomach.

"You know nothing about that world, Sage. You've gone to Belize and found something that you feel good about, but it's a bit of a whim, don't you think?" His father lowered his chin and gave him the *be serious* stare that he knew too well from his childhood.

"You've always told me to be the best I could be. I'm not doing that locked in New York feeling like I'm drowning in deadlines and...money." Sage had never confronted his father about his beliefs, and now he felt as though he was standing up not only for what he wanted, but for Kate and for the people they could help. He took a deep breath, feeling the truth of his words. "Yes, this is fast. But I've found more here in two weeks than I've found anywhere else in twenty-eight years. And yeah, Dad, it's a hell of a risk, and you can say it's based on a whim. I don't even know if I'll do this or not, but I feel something doing this type of work that I don't feel back home, and I need to pay attention to that."

His father nodded, a slow, serious nod. Sage's mind screamed, *That's enough. Shut up.* But something visceral, and unstoppable, pulled the next words from his tongue.

"You fought for your country, Dad. I want to fight for those who can't fight for themselves." Sage felt deflated by his father's silent glare and proud of his ability to stand up to him at the same time, leaving him floundering somewhere in the middle, waiting for a thread of appreciation or pride to show in his father's eyes. His father didn't flinch. The firm line of his jaw didn't soften. *Shit.*

"I think it's a great idea," Dex said, before their father had time to chime in. "You've been looking for something like this for a while."

"Thanks, Dex."

His father nodded. One curt nod that sent a memory of hurt through Sage. How many times had he seen that curt nod? The nod that translated to, *You know what I think of this.* Yeah, Sage knew, but he was no longer a kid. He was a man, and he wasn't going to cower to his father's beliefs any longer.

Sage glanced behind him in the empty café and was relieved to see Makei standing at the entrance, his back to Sage, giving him at least a modicum of privacy.

"Son. This woman Kate. How does she figure into this...endeavor?" his father said.

In his heart Sage knew a man existed beyond the stern one who raised him. His parents had been married forever, and not once had Sage ever seen his father's eyes stray or heard his father rue any part of their relationship. He was a hard, bullheaded man, but he was a good man, and even if Sage didn't like his harsh style, he respected him, and that respect drove him toward the truth.

"I'm not gonna lie to you, Dad. I like her a lot." *Just fucking say it.* "Actually, I'm in love with her. I'm not thinking about taking on this business because of her, but if I do it, I hope she'll be a part of it."

His father lifted his chin and looked at Sage down the bridge of his nose.

"It scares the shit out of me, but..." Sage shook his head, then met his father's stare. "This is the way it is." Sage's chest tightened as he waited for his father to say something. Anything.

"Love." It wasn't a question. It wasn't a confirmation, and his father's expression didn't change when he said it.

It was a statement, and one that Sage didn't understand. He anticipated hearing a hundred reasons why he shouldn't be thinking about love after such a short amount of time of knowing a woman, and along with each one came a pull of a muscle, a twist in his gut.

"Son, when I fell in love with your mother, I was more scared about losing her than loving her."

His father's sincere tone caught Sage off guard.

His father's eyes softened as he continued. "Love is a funny thing, Sage. You've seen what happened with Jack, and you've watched Dex and Ellie find each other again. If there's one thing I've learned about love, it's that when the person you love appears in your life, you can't fight it. No matter how much that person frustrates you or pleases you, you are unable to walk away. Your heart draws you back." He rubbed his hand down his face.

The way his father spoke of love softened Sage's feelings toward him—even after the uncomfortable discussion that had taken place only seconds before.

"That's true, Sage. It's the most powerless and the most fulfilling feeling all wrapped up in one," Dex added.

"Thank God. I thought I was losing my mind." Sage sat back and let out a loud breath. "It scares the shit out of me. I mean, I haven't known Kate that long, and when I'm not with her, I'm thinking about her. When I'm with her..." *I can't get enough of her.* He rubbed the back of his neck, trying to figure out how to describe all the things he loved about who Kate was, and there was too much to tell. Instead he decided to explain it by way of what they knew about him. "She lives her life in the way I've always dreamed of living mine."

"You live a pretty good life." Dex shot a glance at his father.

"I know. I'm blessed. We all are. We do well for ourselves, but come on. Living in New York has hardly been my dream. My dream has always been to do more for others while continuing to work with my art. You gotta know that." He was waiting for his father's diatribe. It had to be killing him, holding back the fighting words about making a living and always bettering himself.

"Since you were a boy, you wanted to live in the forest," his father began. "There were times when I thought you and Jack might never come out of those damn woods." Then he smiled, and it was such a rare occurrence to see, that a lump rose in Sage's throat. "It's not surprising that you'd find a woman who has similar interests. And as far as fear goes, son, falling in love is scary as hell. It's like taking off your gun and walking into a battle unarmed."

Funny. That's kind of how Sage felt about confronting his father. He wasn't giving Sage his blessing about opening the nonprofit, but Sage hadn't asked for it—or needed it. He'd come to his father and Dex for information, or so he'd thought. He hadn't come to his father for his approval—at least not on a conscious level—but what his father was giving him was a glimpse of the loving man he'd always believed existed. And that was so much more valuable than his blessing over a business could ever be.

His father continued. "The person you love will know all of your secrets. She'll see your vulnerabilities, and if you've chosen well, she won't use those against you, but she'll use them to help you be the best man you can be."

And there it was. *The best man you can be.* He'd heard it a million times, so why, in this context, did it make tears press at his eyes?

Chapter Twenty-One

MOONLIGHT STREAMED DOWN upon the benches where Kate had first addressed Sage and the others. She remembered the way her heart had leaped in her chest the first time Sage sauntered through the narrow path like a breath of fresh air—only he seemed to steal the oxygen from her lungs. She'd barely been able to think straight with him looking at her, and now, as they sat beside each other with Luce and Caleb, she felt like that night was two years ago rather than a little less than two weeks ago. Her stomach still fluttered when she saw Sage, but there was a difference between butterflies fluttering when she *knew* he was going to kiss her and she anticipated how thrilling the kiss would be and the tornado that had whirled in her stomach when she wondered if he'd even notice her. She much preferred the butterflies that were currently nesting in her belly.

"Y'all mind if we join you?" Clayton carried his guitar in one hand and held Cassidy's hand with the other.

Kate noticed that Clayton's belligerence had tamed

since Sage had a talk with him. He no longer leered at her as if she were a piece of meat. She watched him wiping off the bench for Cassidy to sit down, and part of her hoped that he had just become more interested in Cassidy and that relationship was changing him. She looked away, knowing better than to think a tiger could change its stripes that dramatically. She'd seen celebrities become so close on these trips that anyone would think they were running away together to get married when they left Belize, only to find out that after the trip they weren't even noted as being a couple. The whole celebrity bed swap thing baffled her—and made her proud of the gentleman Sage was. She could only imagine how enticing it might be for a guy to bed a different beautiful woman every week.

"My PR guy said they're sending a local photog out for the meeting tomorrow. Cassidy and I will definitely be there." Clayton patted Cassidy's thigh. Cassidy smiled up at him. Her dark, spiral curls framed her face, and she wiggled beside him, flirtatiously blinking her eyes.

Even after almost two weeks, Kate didn't know what to make of Cassidy. She acted like a prima donna most of the time, but at other times Kate saw flashes of a very young girl, surely younger than herself. She knew from the application that Cassidy was the same age she was, but when she wiggled and flashed that innocent smile, she seemed eighteen instead of twenty-six.

Kate smiled at Sage. "You're coming too, right?"

"I'm all set. I'll be there."

Sage set a serious stare on Clayton, and Kate wasn't sure if she should feel bad for Clayton, since he was clearly making an effort not to be that sleazy guy anymore. At least not in their presence. When Sage took her hand, she decided she didn't care how she *should* feel. She liked his protective nature. He growled when predators came too close and stayed quietly nearby keeping them at bay.

Sage shifted his gaze to Caleb. "Caleb, I almost forgot to tell you that Kurt said you could Skype with him this weekend. Let me know what works and we'll set it up."

Caleb rose to his feet, pulling at the seam of his pants pocket. "Really? You're not pulling my leg?"

Sage laughed. "Really. He's just a regular guy."

"To you, maybe. But to me he's one of the most amazing thriller writers I've ever read." Caleb paced. "I can't believe it. Kurt Remington is going to talk to me. Thank you, Sage."

"Sure, no problem."

"That's really nice of you," Kate said. She'd been working with Caleb for almost two years and she'd never seen him spend so much time with the group. Sage had not only found out what he was doing for all those hours after he disappeared every afternoon, but he'd also totally hooked him up. His thoughtfulness was immense. It was just one of the things she loved about him.

"What good is knowing people if you can't exploit them?" He laughed as he pulled her closer.

"Do people do that to you? I mean, you're a well-known artist, so you must have people wanting to meet you all the time." Kate wondered about his life in New York, and she was looking forward to seeing him in his element. She wondered if he would act differently there. She couldn't imagine he'd change just because of his environment. At least she hoped not.

"Not many people want to track down an artist," Sage explained. "I mean, at galleries, sure, they talk to me, but I'm not the same kind of celebrity as Clayton or Cassidy. They're known by sight. I'm known for what I create. It's a whole different ballgame."

Clayton strummed his guitar, and within minutes he was belting out one of his country songs. Cassidy and Luce swayed to the music, and Sage's foot tapped to the beat. Kate moved her leg to the beat, enjoying the camaraderie of the group. He began another song, and between the country music, the friendliness of the group—which surprised her, given how things had been when everyone arrived—and the beer they were drinking, she wished the night could go on forever.

"What's your life like in New York?" she asked.

Sage furrowed his brows. "Not like this." He took a sip of beer, then set the bottle by his feet. He put his arm around her and pulled her close again. "Do you want to know the truth?"

"Preferably." She steeled herself for whatever he might reveal, though she couldn't imagine why he'd ask if she wanted to know the *truth*. What was so bad that he felt he had to ask that?

Sage rested his cheek against Kate's, facing away from the others. "I spend a lot of time in New York wondering what I can do to get the hell away from it."

The raspiness of Sage's voice in her ear sent a shudder through her.

"Is that true?" she asked.

"One hundred percent. I always thought it was because I wanted to get outside, closer to nature. Now I realize that my heart must have known you were waiting for me."

He kissed her neck, and Kate swooned. "That's a great line." *Why is my voice shaking?*

Sage drew back and looked her in the eye. "It's not a line. It's fate."

Fate?

Clayton broke into "Who Loves Who More" by Thompson Square.

Luce pulled Kate to her feet. "Come on. I only have two more nights. Dance with me."

Oh God. Sage only has two more nights. Kate felt her cheeks flush, but two seconds later Cassidy was dancing with them, and Sage had a lusty look in his eyes that made her want to dance even sexier. She didn't try to fight the urge; she let her hips sway and her chest shimmy.

Cassidy dragged Caleb to his feet. He moved like a robot with stage fright, but the smile in his eyes reflected the fun he was having.

In the next breath, Sage was at Kate's side, dancing with practiced ease, and boy could he move his sexy body. Kate wanted to dance like one of those women who could run their hands up and down a man's body while shimmying down to the floor, leaving the man drooling for more, but she knew she'd fall right on her ass.

"Now, that's what I'm talking about," Cassidy said, dragging her hand seductively down Sage's arm.

Kate fought a scowl as jealousy wrapped its prickly tentacles around her heart and squeezed.

Sage leaned closer to Kate, and she breathed a sigh of relief.

"I think Caleb's got some pretty fine moves." Sage tossed Caleb a nod of approval and turned his back to Cassidy.

Caleb's cheeks flushed, but Kate was glad to see that he didn't stop dancing.

Sage put his hands on Kate's hips and pressed himself against her; then he slowed to a romantic sway that went completely against the beat of the music, and she couldn't have cared less. In Sage's arms, beneath the beautiful night sky, she was the happiest that she could ever remember. For the next few hours, she allowed herself to set aside the worries of AIA and the community, the stress of public relations, and the appropriateness—or lack thereof—of the volunteers, and enjoy everything Sage had to give.

Chapter Twenty-Two

THE NEXT MORNING, Sage got up before Kate and left quietly. He showered and dressed at his cabin and then went for a walk, cell phone in hand. The sun had yet to creep to the tops of the trees, but the air was already sticky with humidity. Dirt billowed around his feet as he walked. The dryness reminded him of how little it had rained in the past ten days and made him think of the villagers' need for wells again. *Damn government.* He clutched his cell phone in his fist as he rounded the bend in the road, out of sight from the cabins. He preferred Skype so he could see the people he was speaking with, but getting anyone to Skype before the sun came up was not realistic. Besides, he'd paid for international cell phone coverage. Why not use it? The first call he made was to his brother Jack.

"Dude, really? It's five thirty in the morning," Jack's gravelly whisper complained.

"Yeah, I know. Sorry. I need a favor."

"Aren't you in Belize?" Jack sounded more alert now.

Sage heard Jack push himself from the bed and

waited until he heard the bedroom door close before speaking again. "I hope I didn't wake Savannah."

"I'm in a different room now. She'll sleep. What's up? You okay?"

Jack was nine years older than Sage, and although he'd been away at college and then married and in the military for all of Sage's teen years, he'd come home to visit as often as he could and had made a point of keeping in touch with Sage and their other siblings. He'd always been protective and interested, asking about Sage's grades, his girlfriends, his hobbies—that was, until Jack's wife, Linda, died in an accident that Jack blamed himself for. The two years that followed were painful for the entire family, as Jack disappeared from their lives and found salvage in the Colorado Mountains. Until he met his fiancée, Savannah, and found love—and his way back to his family—once again. Since then, Jack had gone back to being the brother Sage knew and loved, and now Sage had no hesitation calling him at the ass crack of dawn for a favor. His only reservation was not talking to Kate about it first, but the idea had fallen into place in bits and pieces throughout the afternoon after talking to his father and Dex. And by the time Kate had fallen asleep last night, it had formed into a full-blown concept. He wanted information and he wanted it now.

"Yeah, I'm fine. Do you still keep in touch with your engineering buddy from school? What's his name?"

"Craig. Yeah, why?" Jack yawned.

"He's part of AMC Utilities, right?"

"I think so. Where's this going, Sage? Cut to the chase. I went to bed about two hours ago."

"My girlfriend, Kate, works for AIA, the nonprofit, and she's been working to get wells brought in, but with a community of only a few hundred, the government is withholding funding." Sage ran his hand through his hair and sighed.

"I heard you were in love."

Sage smiled, despite wanting to get answers. "Mom or Dex?" he asked with a laugh. The Remington grapevine moved fast.

"Siena, actually. She texted me last night. It's true?"

Sage stopped pacing and stretched his muscles. *Siena?* "Yeah, it's true. Struck by the cupid. Hit in the heart and all that shit. Knocked the wind right out of me." *And I love it.*

"Yeah, that's how it happens." Jack laughed. "Wanna tell me about her?"

"She's smart and strong willed. Reminds me of Mom a little, the way she is with helping people, like you know she'd do anything to help someone, but don't do something disrespectful because she'll just as soon tell you what you did wrong."

"Hot?"

"Jack..."

"Total dog but a sweet girl? That's cool."

"No, you ass. She's the prettiest girl I've ever seen. Really. I look at her and I swear I'm like a high school kid with a hard-on." The sun rose to the tips of the trees. Sage wiped a bead of sweat from the back of his neck. It was going to be a scorcher.

"Good because I'd hate to have to tell you that my fiancée is hotter than your girlfriend. I'm sure she is, but I'd hate to rub it in your face."

"Ha-ha." Sage missed seeing Jack, and just hearing his voice made him feel closer. "Listen, I need you to call Craig, if you don't mind, and give him the info on where I am and ask him what it might cost to put in wells, or a community well."

"Sure. No problem. What should I do with the info? Call you back? Email?"

"Actually, can you text? Internet is spotty, but this

line seems to be working great."

"I hate texting, but sure. When are you coming home?"

"Sunday. Thanks, Jack. You're a lifesaver."

"Siena was bummed that she didn't get to Skype with you."

"Tell her to text me. I haven't been carrying my phone, but I will."

"You don't want me to do that. Spend time with Kate while you can. Just call Siena when you can so she doesn't feel left out." Jack yawned loudly.

"On that note, I'll let you get back to sleep. Love you, Jack. Thanks a lot."

Sage ended the call and left a message for his attorney asking what it would take to set up a nonprofit whose focus would be selling high-end art to fund the installation of wells in developing nations. He followed that call up with a call to his accountant, asking the same thing and requesting that she research the financial viability of such an organization. Maybe...just maybe, with his connections and Kate's experience, and the experience of a few hired experts, they could bring this thing to fruition. Kate would never have to worry about her work being for naught again, Sage could fulfill his desire to do something more meaningful while continuing to sculpt and paint. Surely the company would need capital at first, and he'd be able to put the insane amount of money he made to good use. Such an endeavor would also give him and Kate a chance at a future together, where they could nurture the values and dreams they both held close to their hearts.

No matter how much he wanted to stay until Kate had to leave, he had a show coming up the weekend after he returned and he needed to be there. He hadn't been kidding when he'd told Kate that he spent much of his time trying to figure out how to get the hell out of New York, and as he thought of how hamstrung he was by the upcoming show, it pissed him off. He wouldn't cancel. Canceling shows was the kiss of death for an artist, and this show was featuring artistic families. He and his mother would be featured together. He had to be there.

But after the show.

Maybe then he and Kate would have more time together.

Goddamn show. He didn't want to leave Kate. Not for an hour. Not for a day. Not for...ever.

The thought pushed him closer to the edge of solidifying the decision that would be both wonderfully freeing and dangerously risky. Kate was worth it.

KATE WAS ON her way to the mess hall when she finally spotted Sage walking down the main road. Waking up to an empty bed was a sore reminder that Sage would be leaving in a few days. Sometimes he got up early to draw or paint, so she wasn't alarmed when he wasn't there, but when she hadn't seen him at the school or in his cabin, she'd begun to wonder where he'd gone.

"There you are." He looked handsome and sporty in his loose white T-shirt and shorts. His arms and legs were golden brown, his muscles even more defined than they'd been when he'd arrived. The heat tended to lessen everyone's appetite. He could have walked right out of *Men's Journal.*

He kissed her good morning. "Sorry I left so early, but I didn't want to wake you."

"Everything okay?" She eyed the phone in his hand.

He shoved his phone in his pocket. "Yeah, I called Jack, and I had to return a few calls."

"I hate that you're leaving so soon."

"Me too, but you leave the week after me and you're coming to New York to see me after that, right? You didn't change your mind?" He held both her hands in his, his eyes full of hope.

"Yeah."

"Uh-oh. That wasn't a, *Yeah!* What's wrong?"

"Leaving is hard, and without knowing about the wells, I feel like I'm leaving things undone." She fanned her face. "Wow, it's hot today."

"Yeah, that it is." He gathered her hair and held it up off her neck. "Better?"

"Yes." She smiled up at him. "Thank you."

"I'm really proud of you, Kate. No matter what happens, I'm sure the people here know how hard you've worked on their behalf."

"Thanks. I know they do, but if we don't get the wells, then it doesn't really matter how hard I worked."

"It always matters. If you ask my father, he'll tell you that the only thing that matters is how hard you work."

His eyes shifted away from her then, and she followed his gaze as it trailed Clayton and Cassidy walking around the side of the cabins.

"They seem like they've changed, huh?" Kate shook her head.

"I don't know what to make of that guy."

"See? Even you don't trust celebrities," she teased.

"No. I don't really trust *him*, but I don't lump all celebs together." He took her face in his hands and rooted her to the ground with his serious gaze. "I know one thing, though, Kate. I'm falling hard for you."

I can't breathe.

He searched her eyes, and she knew she needed to respond, but words evaded her. She swallowed to keep air moving to her lungs.

He narrowed his eyes. "Did I say the wrong thing?

Too fast?" He released her cheeks, and she grabbed his hands and brought them back to her face.

She pressed his palms to her cheeks and breathed deeply. She opened her mouth, but no words came. She swallowed again and managed, "So am I."

He let out a loud breath and looked up at the sky clenching his jaw. "Jesus, woman. You just about gave me a heart attack."

"I'm falling hard too. Really hard. It's just...Our relationship is so unexpected."

He lowered his forehead to hers. *God, I love that.*

"I wanted to extend my trip and stay until you had to leave, but I have to get ready for a show the weekend after I'm home. I totally forgot about it until this morning." She heard the disappointment in his voice and felt it reverberate in her clenched stomach.

"We have another night. That's better than not having it," she said in an effort to keep herself from falling apart. How would she get along without him?

"What's your plan for today?"

"I'm helping Caleb make the rounds at the clinic; then I'm going into the village for the meeting. I want to be there early."

"I'm going to finish the mural today with the kids and then I'll get cleaned up and come over."

The mural. "I can't wait to see it. At least that's one thing that'll be complete before I leave. And it made the kids so happy to work with you. I'm really glad you pushed for it."

"I'm really glad you were okay with us doing it."

They walked over to the mess hall and found Luce reading a romance novel. She waved the book when they came in. "Living vicariously. Grab some food and save me from falling for some hunky hero I'll never meet."

Kate slid onto a chair with a plate of eggs and a cup

of coffee. "I can't believe you guys are leaving me. I'm gonna miss you so much."

"Me too." Luce set down her book. "Come see me when you're home and we'll hang out for a week before they ship you off again."

Kate watched Sage crossing the room toward them, and the idea of shipping out again didn't seem as exciting as it had before she'd met him. In fact, it felt downright awful.

Luce looked from Kate to Sage and leaned across the table. "Your whole world changed in two weeks, you lucky dog."

"I feel lucky, but I'm also a little scared."

Sage slid his hand across Kate's shoulder as he walked behind her. She eyed Luce, hoping she wouldn't ask about what she'd just said in front of Sage. Luce caught her glance and drew her brows together.

"Did I miss all the hunky hero talk?" He set a plate of eggs and Johnnycakes on the table and sat down beside Kate.

"We had only just begun." Luce smiled at Kate as she pulled out her phone. "Check out these great pics." She slid the phone to Kate.

Kate scrolled through the photos of Sage and the children in front of the mural. "They look so happy. And look at Sage, the proud teacher. I love these. Can you send me copies?"

"Good idea. I want copies too," Sage said. "We don't have any pictures together." He dug his phone from his pocket and handed it to Luce. "Do the honors?" He slid his chair closer to Kate and they smiled for several pictures.

"Okay, smooch shot," Luce said.

Kate happily obliged, pressing her lips to Sage's— not expecting him to deepen the kiss in front of Luce and in the middle of the mess hall. When he pulled back, her cheeks were hot and he had a smartass grin plastered on his face.

"Sorry. Had to do it."

She pushed him and caught a glimpse of Sylvia standing in the kitchen, puckering her lips in Kate's direction. "Oh my God." She laughed, but inside she cringed.

"Stop worrying about your reputation," Luce said. "I can see your little brain working. *What will they think of me now?*" She waved her hand in front of her face. "You know what they'll say? *About damn time.*"

Luce handed Sage his phone back and he scrolled through the pictures with Kate. "Thanks, Luce. I love these."

"Send them to me," Kate said.

"You know, I don't even have your cell phone number. Or your email." He leaned back in his chair and narrowed his eyes. "I'm beginning to think that maybe this really is a fling for you. No ties to bind us."

"Yeah, right, and that's why I want to come see you in New York."

He handed her his phone. "Can you put your info in there for me? Just in case you don't show up, so I can track you down and drag you back with me?"

"You're going to see him in New York? That's awesome. We can all get together." Luce finished her coffee.

Sage ate quickly and rose to his feet. "I've gotta get to the school. We're starting early so I can make it to the meeting this afternoon." He kissed Kate. "Make sure Luce tells you what she wants to do with those pictures."

Kate looked at Luce. "The pictures?"

"Thanks a lot, Sage."

"You PR people are sneaky. I'm not taking any chances that Kate's left in the dark with your wicked scheme. Kate, good luck. I'll see you there."

She watched Sage leave; then Kate locked eyes with Luce. "Spill it."

"Right after you do. What are you scared of?"

Kate dropped her eyes. "Everything. I think I like him way too much." She lowered her voice to a whisper. "Am I in one of those fake relationships because we're here?"

Luce rolled her eyes. "You really won't just let yourself trust, will you? You're so jaded by the celebs that you can't see straight. Repeat after me." Luce held Kate's hand. "I, Kate Paletto."

"I, Kate Paletto."

"Will not listen to my head. I am not a celeb chaser, and Sage is not a typical celeb."

Kate pulled her hand from Luce's. "Okay, I get it." She bit the insides of her cheeks to keep from smiling. "Thanks for the reality check."

"My pleasure. Now look at these pics. Let's focus on something important." She shoved her phone over to Kate again. "See how excited the kids are? They wanted to know if their pictures were going to be in an American newspaper, so I thought..."

"You thought, let's hype the mural and see what happens." *Of course you did.*

"Why not, Kate? You are leaving money on the table. Hell, you're leaving money in the pockets of people who don't need it, and you're doing it out of what? Pride?"

Kate clenched her teeth. She hated when Luce was right, and the more she'd thought about the things Luce had said to her, the more she saw the logic behind it. "So you think that by writing articles about the mural, you're going to get donations? How does that work exactly?"

"I swear AIA should hire me." Luce pushed her

curls from her face. "We go from the perspective of the kids. The pride they take in what they're doing for the community, and we do a full story on Punta Palacia. The village, the community, the town, and what AIA does for them. We paint the real picture, one they cannot ignore. Can you imagine children from the States fetching water before dawn or sleeping in hammocks?"

Kate shook her head. "If we do this, doesn't it just reiterate what I hate?"

"I've said it before...You know I love you, but how can you hate the very thing these people need? They need money. They need resources. Your fight is that you don't get the right kind of volunteers, but that's because AIA is marketing this area to celebrities. Punta Palacia is small, so a diva refusing to help has a little less of an impact than in a larger village where every extra hand is needed. So AIA is doing what works for their business plan. They're appealing to volunteers other than celebs for larger villages, where the need for bodies is greater. It's all how they spin the marketing."

"What the hell? You knew all of this and you didn't think you should sit me down and pound it into my head?"

"Have you ever argued with yourself? Especially about this subject? I don't know how Sage hasn't already walked away from that particular fight. The man is offering to pour money down Punta Palacia's throat by doing nothing more than what he loves, and you keep shutting him down. That's love for you. He is in deep."

Kate smiled. "You think so?" She knew so. She heard it in every word he spoke and felt it in his touch. Even the way he looked at her, like she was the most beautiful and the most important, person in the world, reeked of his love for her. And she was sure her love for him was just as evident.

Luce pretended to bang her forehead on the table. "For an intelligent woman, you sure are an idiot. Focus, Kate. I'm leaving soon, so if you really want to turn things around, you have a lot of lobbying to do, and be sure you want to, because once these wheels starts turning, they don't stop easily."

"I can't make those types of decisions. That's up to Raymond and his bosses. There's a lot of red tape with things like this. Procedures, guidelines. Luce, this seems like such an easy premise. Market it here or market it there, and how the villages benefit depends on what type of volunteers AIA brings in. How could I have been so blind?"

"You're not blind. You're trusting. AIA must need a place for problem celebrities. God knows celebrities are more than happy to throw money at their problems to make them go away, and this is a good cause. So they donate half a million dollars, flash a few pictures, and voilà. They're instantly the apple of the public's eye again. It's a win-win situation. Except for you, and for the programs that need more attention."

"I know you're teasing, but it makes me wonder. I mean I've begged for real volunteers for two years. And Raymond always blows me off." Kate rose to her feet. "I gotta get over to the clinic."

"I'm coming with you. Clayton and Cassidy are sleeping in." She made air quote signs with her fingers when she said *sleeping in.*

They cleared their places, and Kate waved to Sylvia as they left.

Sylvia blew her a kiss, making Kate's cheeks flush again.

"I've given five years to AIA. You'd think that my suggestions would at least be respected by now." She was getting angrier by the minute. "You know, I'm not just pissed about what this might mean in the grand scheme of things, but look at me. Oh my God. What kind of person am I? I thought I was helping the community by wanting labor, physical beings here to help, and the whole time I could have changed my thinking and come up with programs that would bring in more funding for their needs."

Kate stopped at the Internet café on the way to the clinic and sent an email to Raymond spelling out the things she and Luce talked about.

SAGE FOUND OSCAR in the school's small stockroom organizing his supplies. Wooden shelves lined the wall to the right, neatly organized with tools, buckets, and other supplies.

"Good morning." A friendly smile softened Oscar's eyes.

"Hi, Oscar. Would you like some help before I start painting for the day?"

"No, thank you. The painting is making the children very happy." He nodded, then glanced behind Sage.

Sage turned at a tug on his shorts. "Javier. Hey, buddy. What's up?"

"Can I paint today?"

"Of course you can." Sage laughed and crouched down to look him in the eye.

Javier looked down, his smile fading. "I'm having trouble with my lessons."

Sage drew his brows together. "Did you work with your teacher?"

He nodded, his hair flopping over his eyes.

"Did you try your hardest? I mean really try? Not rush through so you could paint?"

Javier drew his brows together and nodded.

"And did you ask your teacher for help?" Sage glanced at Oscar, who shrugged.

He nodded emphatically, his mouth pressed into a serious line.

"Hard work is important, Javier. If you tried your best, that's all we can ask for." He rumpled his hair. "I'll make you a deal. You can paint, but you have to continue to work your hardest to learn what your teacher has to teach you. Okay?"

Javier wrapped his arms around Sage's legs. "Thank you, Mr. Sage. Thank you!" Javier ran back to the classroom.

Sage watched him scamper away and turned his attention back to Oscar. "Oscar, do you mind if I keep a canvas in here after I start working on it? I'm going to ship them back to New York when I leave, but I don't want to take a chance of anything happening to them."

"No problem. I'll make room this afternoon. The kids will miss you when you're gone."

"Yeah. I'm gonna miss them, too." He would miss everything about Belize, from the horridly hot weather to the children's beaming smiles and Oscar's steadfast dedication. "I'll miss you, too, Oscar."

Oscar nodded, his cheeks flushing. "Kate too. She will miss you the most."

Sage patted him on the back. "Leaving Kate will be the hardest thing I've ever done. I'm counting on you to keep an eye on her."

Oscar pulled his shoulders back and gave a firm nod. "You can count on me."

Sage set to work on the mural. He'd left the bigger elements for the children—the sand, the forest, the animals—and had added finite details as the mural progressed. This morning he fleshed out the tree trunk, adding depth and slim cracks in the bark and rounding out a full umbrella of green leaves that stretched across the length of the building. The first group of children came out the door, and one of the teenage boys *whooped.*

"Look! Look!" he called to the others.

A collective gasp pulled Sage from the ladder where he was working. The sight of the children's joyful faces, their eyes dancing with happiness as they pointed to the wall, filled a hole that he'd been carrying within him for a long time. *This is what my life has been missing.* He climbed from the ladder and set down his paintbrush.

"Don't just stand there. Pick up your brushes and let's bring this mural to life," he said with a sweep of his hands. The children gathered around the paint, crouching on their haunches as they dipped their brushes and ran to the wall, where they set to work with intent eyes and careful hands.

A little girl, probably around nine or ten, pulled his arm and led him over to where a large green drip from the leaf she'd been painting was making a slow crawl south toward the ground. It dripped right through the petal of a red flower. She pressed her lips into a frown.

"I'm sorry," she said softly with just a touch of a Creole accent.

Sage patted her on the shoulder. "This is perfect."

The little girl looked from him to the wall and back again, her eyebrows knitted together. The boy next to her stopped painting to peek at what was going on.

"Let me show you something. May I?" Sage nodded at her paintbrush. She shoved it toward him. He carefully outlined a green leaf that bent from the stem of the plant she'd been painting and covered the drip. "See? It needed another leaf and that was the perfect spot. There are no mistakes in art. When something drips, it's okay. We just create something new from it."

The little girl beamed up at him.

Sage handed her back the paintbrush. "Go ahead. It's your leaf. You get to paint it."

For the next few hours, the children took turns painting, and Sage helped them learn about smooth strokes and shading, but mostly, he focused on the children having fun. He realized how much he'd been missing out on by working endless hours and focusing so intently on his art when there was so much more he could be doing for others. Sage was beginning to wonder *how* he would go back to the life he led now that he had experienced being a part of something so much bigger and more important, and he knew he never could. He was going to make the nonprofit work one way or another.

Chapter Twenty-Three

KATE, LUCE, AND Caleb made plans for a little surprise celebration for Sage in honor of finishing the mural. Caleb would take care of most of the details and let the parents and children know, and they hoped a handful would be able to show up on such short notice. With Sage and Luce leaving on Sunday, they planned to hold the party on Saturday morning. By the time they finished making plans and handling the rounds at the clinic, the afternoon sun was blazing hot, and when Kate and Luce reached the outskirts of the village, Kate's shirt was drenched. She had been thinking about their earlier conversation all afternoon, and she saw more clearly how she'd been standing in the way of funding, but she also began to wonder if she was working with the wrong organization. Would her requests have been taken seriously elsewhere?

"Luce, I feel like a total idiot. I'm a bright woman. How can I not have seen the benefit that went along with the annoying...obnoxious...self-righteous celebs?"

Luce fanned her face. "Sometimes we're blinded by our desire to do the right thing. You grew up believing that money was the root of all evil or some shit like that."

"Not the root of all evil, just overrated. Sort of unnecessary."

"Right, well, I'm sure your parents are lovely people, but that's really fucked up. Look around you. How did they get the Internet? How did the old logging cabins get renovated? How did they get water and electricity at the cabins? It all costs money."

An unfamiliar, much-too-new for the area truck rumbled down the road behind them, and Kate's stomach clenched. *The government reps.* They stepped to the side to let it pass and moved backward to try to avoid the clouds of dust left in its wake. They fanned the air in front of them and walked along the grass to keep from sucking in the dust.

"I know that, but I took it all on face value. When Raymond said we were getting all the funding we could and to make it work, that's what I did. I made it work, and I never minded that. I was resentful that I didn't have more interested volunteers, but I didn't mind the work I was doing. You know, this makes me want to step back from it all—or go full force to fix it. Have you ever felt that way? Like you want to run away and curse a blue streak all at once?"

"Only every day of my career."

People of all ages gathered in groups in the road and in the yards of their small huts, talking among themselves. Most of the men were still out at the fields, and while many children were at school, there were several young girls who regularly stayed to help their mothers with the cooking and cleaning, as well as toddlers, too young for school. Kate waved to an elderly gentleman sitting in a chair by his front door. He nodded and waved back.

The truck that had passed them was parked to the

side, and two men dressed in short-sleeved, button-down shirts were traipsing through the grass, holding enormous maps. Their faces were serious as they studied the area, pointing to different parts of the land. Panic prickled Kate's nerves. *What if this is our only chance? What if they deny us and they won't consider it again for a year or two? Then I've failed the community.* She had an urge to throw her hands up in the air and say, *Wait! I made a huge mistake. We can raise the money for the well. I know we can. Give me six months and then come back.* She also had an urge to turn and run back to the cabins, to find Sage and apologize for being so damn stubborn until she had no words left.

"What do you think? Should we go badger them?" Kate asked.

Luce shrugged. "I know about American PR, but Belize PR might be very different. What have you done in the past?"

"Emailed. About a hundred times over the last two years." Kate had sent so many emails lobbying on behalf of the villagers that she was sure whoever read the emails rolled their eyes when they saw them in their Inbox. "You know, standing here, watching them survey the land like they hold all the cards..."

"Which they do."

"Yeah, I know. But watching them pisses me off. Build the damn well. It's that simple. See the need. Find a way. Fill the need."

"And that's exactly what makes you so good at your job."

Kate spun around at the sound of Sage's voice. "Sage." She looked down at her sweat-soaked clothes.

"What's a little sweat between friends?" He pulled her close and kissed her quickly. "Hey, Luce, how's it going?"

"We can't really tell. One of those guys is the

engineer, we assume. We just got here, but they arrived only minutes before us."

"That's not really what I meant." Sage nodded toward Kate.

"She told me about the press for the mural, if that's what you mean," Kate said. "Sage, I feel like such an idiot. What Luce said makes sense. I think she's right, and I have been very, very wrong for a long time. You must think I'm an idiot for not using every possible avenue to gain attention and funding."

"I don't think that at all. In fact, you changed my thinking, which is a good thing. My first inclination was to paint and ship those canvases back to the States, remember? Then sell them and give the income to the community. But after listening to your reasoning, which I have to admit, at first seemed slightly on the conservative side, you made me realize there's a better way to do this."

"I don't follow," Kate said.

He pulled a fistful of rolled-up papers from his back pocket and flattened them against his thigh. "This is what it costs to put a single well for each family here." He pointed to a figure. "And this is what it costs to install a community well." He pointed to another figure. "Obviously, the community well is the more cost-effective route, and that's what the Belize government will be looking at. The way it works is that water is pumped from the ground into large tanks and gravity takes over from there. Each house has one water spigot, which I believe engineers call *the pipe*."

Kate listened with awe. He'd spent the morning painting. How on earth did he dig up this information, and where was he going with it?

"I know about community wells, but where did *you* get all this?" She pointed to the papers.

"I called Jack. He studied engineering and he went

to school with a guy who does this for a living. He pulled a favor. Basically, this is what we need to get the well." He pointed to the community-well figure. "The problem is, it doesn't cost that much more to put in a community well that serves three times as many people in a larger community, and that's what your engineers are going to squawk about. In their budget-conscious minds, why give water to a few hundred people when for a few bucks more they can give it to a thousand?"

"So we're back to square one?" Kate sighed, feeling defeated and beyond frustrated. She wiped her brow with her arm.

"No. That's what I was getting at next. Luce, you got me thinking the other day about PR and what it can do for a place like this. On the one hand, the wrong public relations will turn this village into a spectacle and a nightmare. These people have happy lives, or they seem to, and while they need better amenities, they don't necessarily need the fanfare that comes along with it. So, I had a few ideas. The first of which is my favorite." He shoved the papers back into his pocket.

"It's no secret that I feel a little strangled in New York, and I feel gluttonous with my income and all that I have. I came here to figure out a way to pay my good fortune forward. The one thing my art has done for me is given me the ability to earn a living doing something I love. It's just the location I don't love. I don't hate New York. I just wish I had more time in rural areas with grass and trees and not so much stress. And that's where this trip has made a difference. I'm well connected in the arts community, so why not open a nonprofit to fund villages like Punta Palacia through the arts? I'm not talking about bringing in celebrities. I don't think that's the right tactic for something like this. I envision keeping the close-knit, private villages as just that. Private. Without the disturbances of celebs and cameras. I envision the funding handled in the States, and then when the wells are installed, no press. Or if anything, a local photog taking a few candid shots without any fanfare or even recognition of who is there when they're onsite, so the focus is where it should be. Installing the wells, or running a program." He looked around. "By the way, where are Clayton and Cassidy?"

Kate and Luce exchanged a curious glance. Kate had been so involved in her own thoughts and what Sage was saying that she hadn't noticed that they didn't show up.

"No idea," Kate answered.

"Hm. We'll find them later, I guess. Anyway, I think we can market the idea to artists who create tangible art instead of actors and actresses, see who we can get to donate one piece per year and then hold an annual auction."

Luce nodded. "Brilliant."

"An annual auction? How can that possibly bring in enough money to help any community?" Kate watched Luce and Sage exchange a look that clearly said she had no idea what she was talking about.

"With the right artists donating their work, we could be talking a total of a few million, Kate. Some pieces go for the mid-six-figure range. If we do this right, with an annual auction and high-end work, we can help many communities," Sage answered.

Kate blinked several times, thinking she misheard him. "How much?"

"Millions. It's brilliant." Luce pulled out her phone and typed something in.

"I want in," Luce said. "I mean, part time, just to help you create a strategy and spread the word."

"Sure," he answered. "I figured you'd also know

some key PR players in the nonprofit world."

"In?" Kate asked. Why did she feel like she was lost? She was never lost.

"She wants to be part of the effort," Sage explained. "What do you think, Kate? Does it sound like something that might work?"

"I...Yeah. I'm floored." She shook her head. "That must cost a lot of money to start up, and it probably takes a lot of time, and I can't imagine the—"

Sage touched her arm, and when she looked into his eyes, she immediately felt calmer. She loved that about him.

"There are costs associated with setting up the actual nonprofit, but it's not an enormous sum of money. It takes a few weeks for each part of the process, probably ninety days on the outside, quicker if the attorneys pull strings. Then it's whatever we make of it. We can decide on what we'll fund and focus on those areas, such as wells. There will be some major expenses. I have an accountant who can handle the finances and ensure we're meeting all nonprofit requirements. We'll need someone to handle the administration of the business, and it'll mean researching villages, traveling, so there's a big time commitment, and the administrative expenses will need to be recouped by the sales at some rate—the accountant will handle all of that. It won't be an easy effort, but it would be a meaningful one."

I want to do that. She imagined the elation of the residents if she came into Punta Palacia with the news that they were bringing in a company to drill a community well. She eyed the two gentlemen and their big maps as they crossed the thick grass and walked into the jungle a few feet from where they stood. *It would be so great not to rely on people like them for a community's needs to be met.* Adrenaline soared through her.

"Do you really think that's all possible?" She bit her lower lip, trying to keep herself from getting too excited.

"Nothing in life comes with guarantees. If we fail, we fail. If we don't try, villages are at the mercy of people like them." He nodded to where the men had disappeared into the forest. "There'll be headaches and red tape, and according to Craig, there are all sorts of hoops to jump through to gain approval, but I'm confident that with the right people on board we can make a go of it."

We? "You keep saying we."

Sage held her gaze, and when he spoke, his voice was dead serious. "Kate, I don't know where we're headed as a couple, but this idea was born because of you, and regardless of where we end up, I was hoping that you'd want to be part of it."

Where we'll end up? "I..."

"I feel like I'm witnessing a major moment here. I think I'll wait over there." Luce walked away, and Kate looked up at Sage with a million questions.

Where are we heading? She had to concentrate on what he was offering first. What did it all mean? Where would she work? What resources would she have? She couldn't formulate the questions. He took her hand in his, and her mind fell right back to wondering where they were heading.

"You look like I scared the shit out of you, and I'm sure I did. This is a lot to process, and it's a huge idea taking shape, Kate. An idea that could bring the kind of resources that you want for villages like this one. It would bring fresh drinking water, alleviating the need for the kids to haul buckets before dawn and come to school exhausted." He stepped closer and his gaze softened.

"I want to be with you, Kate, but that doesn't mean that you *have* to be involved with the nonprofit, or that I have to open it. This is like the missing piece of my life. I have so much, and I can use what I have to help others. That would make me happy, but nothing would make me happier than being with you. Now, next week, ten years from now."

Kate swallowed hard. *Me too!*

"I'm not asking you to run off and marry me. I'm saying that I want this relationship. I want to see where it goes—separate from the nonprofit. I also want the nonprofit. It's a good idea. It's a meaningful endeavor, and it would mean the world to me if you wanted to be involved with it, but if you don't want to be, that's okay. I just need to know if you want *us*."

"I want us. I want to see where we go." *More than anything in this entire world, I want to be with you.*

Sage's lips curved into a smile.

"And I want to be involved with what you're planning, but I don't know anything about running a business."

"We'll hire experts who will guide us, and you do know about running a business. You keep schedules, budgets, oversee volunteers. You might not be well versed in the fundraising end of things, but you don't have to be. You can learn that. I can learn that. The PR person we hire will do that and tell us what we need to know. The most important thing is that you want to see where we go. As long as there's an *us*, anything else is doable."

"You're so confident. Aren't you scared?" *I'm scared shitless.*

"I'm more scared of not being with you than starting a business."

God, I love you. She clenched her lips together to trap the thought. "I...Oh God, Sage."

He smiled down at her. "I know."

And she knew he did.

"We're falling for each other and it's all so fast it feels crazy."

Yes! She managed a nod.

He brushed her bangs from her forehead. "It's all gonna be fine. I have faith in what I feel, Kate, and I can feel how much you care about me. I'm not worried."

"I do care about you. What if the business fails? I don't have a home, an income..."

"Kate."

"Would I work remotely? From my parents' house? Travel when I have to? How would I see you?" Kate was used to having her finger on every aspect of her life and keeping it all under control. In the span of ten minutes, Sage had managed to cast her organized life into the wind. Her stomach churned and her nerves tingled.

He must have read the worry in her eyes, or in her trembling limbs, because he settled his hands on her shoulders and said, "Breathe, Kate."

She nodded, taking one deep breath after another.

"We'll figure it all out. I know my artwork will sell at an auction, and I have friends who will want to take part in the effort. It's exciting. Risky as hell. But the worst that happens is that we try and we don't hit our mark, and then we regroup and figure out another way."

"What if...? What if *we* don't make it? Then I'll have given up..." She looked around at the place she'd called home for the past two years. The location she was getting ready to leave without any knowledge of where she would be going next. What was she really giving up? Her autonomy? She didn't love the idea of autonomy like she used to. She shifted her gaze back to him. She loved Sage.

"Well, first of all, I wouldn't try something this

serious if I didn't think we'd make it. And second of all, I've never been in love before." He searched her eyes as he drew in a breath.

Love!

"So I don't have much to compare what I'm feeling to, other than to know that it's way bigger than *like*, and it's scary as shit. But when I'm with you, I feel whole. I love the person you are. I love your heart, which I swear is bigger than anyone else's in the world. I love how you stand up for what you believe in, with me and for others. Kate, you're everything I could ever want. You're strong, and smart, and generous, and you're sweet, and delicious." He kissed her. "There's no better feeling in the world than what I feel when I'm with you."

You love my heart. She pressed her hand to his chest, feeling his heart beating just as fast as hers. "I love your heart too, Sage."

Luce's footsteps pulled her attention back to where they were. Several women stood with their hands clasped before them. Some covered their mouths, while others nodded with a dreamy look in their eyes. Kate felt her cheeks flush.

Sage took a respectful step back.

"Hey, lovebirds, here they come." Luce nodded toward the two men walking through the thick grass toward the group.

"You can do this, Kate. I have faith in you," Sage said.

Pull it together. Focus. How am I supposed to focus after everything Sage just said? Kate took a deep breath and pulled her shoulders back as the men approached. This was her chance.

The taller of the two gentlemen addressed them with a thick Creole accent.

"I am Ivan Dawson, from the Ministry of Rural

Development's office, and this is Paolo Hernandez, a developmental engineer. We are considering proceeding with the implementation of a community well."

There was a collective gasp, then a low murmur among the residents.

"Considering proceeding?" Kate asked. *That's not a rejection. Yes!* She shot a glance at Sage and Luce, and when a smile stretched across her lips, she was unable to rein it in.

Mr. Dawson nodded. "Yes, we are taking it under consideration."

Kate held her hand out. "I'm Kate Paletto. I'm with Artists for International Aid. Thank you. That is great news. Is there anything we can do to help?"

Mr. Dawson shook her hand and narrowed his eyes. "Kate Paletto?"

"Yes."

He shifted his eyes to Mr. Hernandez, then back to Kate. "You have been very persistent in your efforts to secure this well."

Kate held his gaze, but the weak tone when she answered reflected her silent internal cringe. "Yes, sir."

He nodded. "You're hard to ignore."

Sage cleared his throat and took a step closer to Kate, standing behind her and settling his hand on her shoulder.

"If you had not been so persistent, we might not be considering this location." Mr. Dawson turned and looked over the community again. "Your efforts have not gone unnoticed, Ms. Paletto. I will be writing a letter of commendation to the director of your organization."

Kate blinked several times, trying to mask her shock. "Thank you, sir. I'm...Thank you. What happens next for the people of Punta Palacia?"

"Mr. Hernandez will put in his recommendation, run the necessary tests, and we'll have a final decision within the next thirty days. Assuming the recommendation is accepted, we will begin implementation of the well within sixty days."

Another collective gasp rose from the residents and grew to a din of excitement. They spoke Creole too quickly for Kate to decipher exactly what was being said, but from the looks on their faces, she knew they were thankful for the hope they had just received.

"Thank you." It was all she could do to refrain from jumping into the man's arms and hugging him. "This means the world to everyone here. If the recommendation is accepted, you'll be changing the lives of all of these people. But you already know that. I can't thank you enough. And, Mr. Hernandez, thank you for coming out today. If I can do anything to help, please let me know." Kate's excitement gave her a bad case of motormouth. Sage squeezed her shoulder, and it was enough to pull her back down to earth.

"We'll be in touch," Mr. Dawson said.

They watched the men climb into their truck and drive back toward town. Once the truck was out of sight, Kate let out a loud breath. "Oh my God. I think we did it."

Before she had taken two steps, Adela embraced her. Her mother, Indira, was on her heels, pulling Kate against her plump bosom.

"Thank you," Indira said.

"It's a miracle," Adela said to the other women. She eyed Kate, and Kate knew she had slowed her speech, instead of rattling off her excitement in Creole, so she would understand.

They passed Kate from one resident to the next, and for the next ten minutes Kate was embraced by everyone in the crowd. Some whispered a quick prayer; others expressed their gratitude. Tears pressed at Kate's eyes over what her hard work had accomplished and at the thankfulness of the people.

As they walked away from the village and headed back toward town, the magnitude of what she'd accomplished coalesced with Sage professing his love for her and sharing his thoughts about the nonprofit. Until now, graduating college and committing to AIA topped Kate's *Things I'm Proud Of* list. They didn't compare to knowing her determination and hard work helped Punta Palacia be considered for a community well. As she walked hand in hand with Sage, she realized that she had completely misjudged him from day one, and she knew that one day she'd be adding *Building a Future with Sage* to that list, too.

Chapter Twenty-Four

SAGE HAD TWO things on his mind as he came around the side of the cabins. Celebrating Kate's achievement with her and finding Clayton and Cassidy. They'd made a promise to Kate and hadn't thought enough of her to follow through. The fact that she didn't end up needing their support didn't matter. A promise was a promise, and he'd be damned if he let Clayton dismiss Kate in that way.

He found them loading their luggage into an all-terrain vehicle. Clayton was dressed in a pair of distressed jeans and a white button-down shirt. Cassidy wore a very tight, short red dress.

"Hey, Sage, we're taking off," Clayton said, as if he hadn't just blown off Kate.

"Taking off?" Sage eyed Cassidy as she applied a fresh coat of red lipstick.

"Yeah, my agent called. I've got a gig lined up Monday, and he wants me well rested. Can't be jet-lagged when I'm performing."

"Clayton, did you forget about the meeting in the village today?" Sage was getting a clear understanding of what Kate had been dealing with for two years.

"Nah. Didn't forget. I canceled the photog after I got the call. No worries. It was all taken care of." He turned to Cassidy. "Come on, Cass. We'd better go if we're gonna make our flight." He reached out a hand to Sage. "Great to hang out with you, man. We'll have to catch up sometime in the Big Apple."

Sage stared at his hand. "Did it occur to you that maybe Kate was counting on your support at that meeting? You knew how important it was to her."

"Dude, the press didn't come. What does it matter? I wasn't about to go stand in the heat for something I don't give a damn about." Cassidy slid into the backseat, and Clayton closed the door behind her and walked around the car to the other side.

Sage clenched his fists, wanting to slam Clayton's disrespectful ass against the car and show him just how much Kate mattered and just how much he should care about the people of Punta Palacia. He narrowed his eyes. "I thought your little act the other night was too good to be true."

"The songs? Hell." He nodded toward the car. "Cassidy gets hot when I sing to her." He shrugged.

"You don't give a shit that you let Kate down." *I'll make you give a shit.* He closed the gap between them, his muscles twitching as he restrained himself from pounding the shit out of him, trying to ignore the devil on his shoulder that was making him see himself in Clayton for dismissing Kate when he'd been lost in his drawing—and that troublesome nag fueled his anger.

Clayton laughed. "Dude, it's not like I slept with her. Hell, even if I had, what would it matter?"

Sage grabbed him by the collar and slammed him against the car.

"Jesus." Clayton's eyes narrowed, filling with anger. "Haven't you ever let anyone down before? It's a fucking way of life for me, man. I let everyone down. Nothing personal about Kate."

Sage stared into Clayton's cold eyes, breathing loud and hard. *Haven't you ever let anyone down before? It's a fucking way of life for me, man.* It would be so easy to finish this. To take revenge for him letting Kate down and for the comment he'd made about her. But the rage that boiled in Sage's blood turned on him. Sage realized that he, too, had let Kate down. The night he'd been lost in his art, he'd done exactly what Clayton and Cassidy were doing. He'd chosen something else instead of keeping his promise. He'd let her down. He released Clayton and stepped back. Clayton stumbled a few steps before righting himself and turning angry eyes on Sage.

"What the hell? Priorities, man. What do *I* get for my efforts? That's what it's all about."

Sage took a halfhearted step in his direction, his muscles burning, sweat beading on his arms.

Clayton scrambled into the car and slammed the door. The car kicked up dirt as it sped away.

Goddamn it. What type of hypocrite am I? Kate might have forgiven him, and she might have said that she'd help him through the next time he forgot, but what the hell did that say about him? Or about what he felt for her?

The next time? What the hell? Sage had seen the hurt in Kate's eyes the morning he'd gone to apologize, and though she'd been too sidetracked this afternoon to say much about Clayton and Cassidy not showing up, he knew that somewhere in that beautiful head of hers she was linking their absence with what he'd done to her, even if she didn't realize it.

Well, hell. He had no right to give Clayton shit if he didn't give himself hell for doing the same thing. He'd excused himself for being oblivious to the time and to

Kate waiting to see him. *Excused himself!* It made him sick to think that he was that type of man. A man like Clayton, who put himself before others. Kate was too good of a person to have to deal with a man who got too sidetracked to care enough to be there for her when he said he would. *I need to fix this.*

I'm not sure I can.

I've been this way my whole life.

Kate's words resonated with him. *See the need. Find a way. Fill the need.* Sage's cell phone vibrated with a text from Jack. He had to prove to himself that he could change. Good intentions went only so far.

Sage dialed Jack's number. "Jack, it's me."

"I just texted you. Did you get the stuff Craig sent?"

"Yeah, thanks for that. Actually, Craig was more than helpful. I really appreciate you calling him for me."

"Sure. That's what family's for. Why do you sound like you want to kill me?"

"I've just got some shit going on. Listen, I need some more help, and this time I'm kind of at a loss. I have no idea who to turn to."

"What's up?" Jack's voice turned serious. Sage pictured him standing with his legs planted hip distance apart, his eyes narrowed and dark, his biceps clenching in that nervous way they did.

"You know how I kinda tune everyone out when I'm working?"

Jack laughed. "Shit. That's the understatement of the year. You've done that since you were little. I remember coming home for Christmas when you were five or six. You were so lost in your finger paints, I asked Mom if you'd gone deaf. You had me worried."

"Yeah, well, nothing has changed, and it's not a good thing. I gotta figure out how to fix that."

"Kate giving you shit?" Jack asked.

"No. I'm giving myself shit. I was thinking that I

might talk to a therapist or something to get some ideas. Didn't you talk to a therapist after Linda died?"

Sage cringed. "I'm sorry. I didn't mean to blurt that out."

"That's okay. The only one who really got through to me was Mom, if you can believe that. Well, and Savannah, but it was Mom's advice that hit home." Jack sighed. "So you want to conquer your *other world*. I wondered if—or should I say when—this would become an issue."

"You make me sound like a fucking alien."

"You kind of are. But then again, aren't all artists?" Jack laughed.

"So lay it on the line, Jack. What's wrong with me? I always wrote it off as just who I am."

"No shit. We all did."

"I've lost girlfriends over it for years. I've heard it all. I'm self-absorbed, selfish; I don't care about them." He sighed. "The thing is, I've tried to change, but when I'm working, I'm really focused, and now I *need* to change. Kate deserves more than some lame excuse about my inability to pull myself out of my work."

"You know, I thought I had tried to change before I met Savannah, too. Bro, do you really think you've tried to change?" Jack's words held a sarcastic note that took him by surprise and annoyed him.

"Of course. No one wants to be told they suck as a boyfriend."

"There is that, yes. Here's the thing, and don't get pissed at me for saying it. I'm not sure you really tried to change. Changing something you've been doing your whole life isn't something someone can make you do. You have to want to change."

Sage rolled his eyes. "I did try to change. Do you think I like having to grovel?" *It fucking sucks.*

"No, I don't think you like it. I think you just liked

what you were doing more than you liked who was waiting for you."

"Well, that doesn't take a rocket scientist."

"I told you not to get pissed. It'd be easier for me to hang up than spend my time walking you through this shit."

"I'm sorry. I'm just frustrated." He stood and paced, his shoulder muscles tight, pressing the phone tightly against his ear. "I don't want to be the guy who makes excuses. I don't want to look into Kate's trusting eyes and know I made her feel unimportant. Isn't there anything that you can tell me that will help?"

Jack's voice grew serious...and cold. "You'll figure it out."

"That's it? I'll figure it out? What the hell, Jack?" *I'm screwed*. He looked toward the path that led to Kate's hut. *Kate's screwed*.

"You've already done more than you ever have in the way of trying. You recognize the issue. You picked up the phone and called me. You'll figure this out. It just has to mean enough to you for you to do so."

"That doesn't help. Do you have a therapist's number or a book I can read that might help?"

"This change has to come from within. Listen, I gotta go meet Savannah, and I hate to cut you off, but, dude, trust me. Nothing I say will make you change. You gotta want it more than you want your next breath. If your gut doesn't ache over it, it ain't gonna happen." Jack paused for a second.

Sage stared at his cell phone, wondering what the hell he was supposed to do next.

"We cool?" Jack asked.

"Yeah." He didn't know if he should thank Jack or yell at him. *This change has to come from within. No shit.* "Love ya, man. I'll see you when I get back."

"Love you too. And, Sage, you know if I can pull my

head out of my ass, you can."

He sure as hell hoped so. Sage ended the call, whipped off his shirt, and threw his phone on his bed. Then he walked back outside to torture himself with sit-ups and push-ups. *See the need. Find a way. Fill the need.* Sage saw the need to fix his inability to come out of the depths of his work. Now it was time to square this shit away.

KATE PACED THE floor of her small room. Excitement and fear competed within her, sending the butterflies in her stomach into a wrestling match. She'd thought a cold shower would ease her nerves, but even after she was freshly showered and dressed in a pair of khaki shorts and a blue cotton tank top, her insides were still caught up in a whirlwind. She flopped onto the bed, then sprang to her feet and paced again. She'd been playing her conversation with Sage over and over in her mind. She loved being with him. Adored him! But Kate was used to knowing where she was headed, what the future held, even if for only two years at a time. For the first time in her life she felt stuck. What would it mean to be involved with a company with Sage? How could they see how their relationship was going to work if she was living with her parents? She couldn't get an apartment—what if they didn't work out and her only option was to go back into AIA or a similar organization? She couldn't be committed to a twelve-month lease.

A month-to-month lease?

She contemplated the option. *In New York?* How would she afford it? Would she be a volunteer? Would she earn an income? She had so many unanswered questions, and the only thing she was sure of was that she wanted to be with Sage. But she didn't want to assume she'd live with him. Hell, she didn't even know if she'd want to live with him.

She glanced at their mattresses in the screened-in area.

I want to live with him.

It was crazy. How could she want that after two weeks? What would her parents think? *Oh my God. What will they think if I leave AIA? How can I leave AIA?* There were too many loose ends, and what if Sage was just blowing smoke? *He's not a* blow smoke *type of guy. He gets shit done.*

What if working together is too stressful? It occurred to her that maybe he didn't mean they'd work together. He was an artist. So would she and the other employees travel and she'd see him when she wasn't traveling? *Ugh!* There were too many unanswered questions. This was all too much. She couldn't plan a single thing without knowing the answers, but she didn't want to push Sage, either.

I'm not asking you to run off and marry me. I'm saying that I want this relationship. I want to see where it goes. What does that mean? She was right back to not knowing how they could have a relationship without being in the same city. Could she get a temporary job in someplace like New York? What would she do? Work in a soup kitchen? Work for another nonprofit? The idea of living in New York made her nervous. She needed air.

Kate opened the screened door and stepped outside, taking a long, deep breath.

"Feeling confined?" Sage came up the path with a handful of freshly picked flowers and floppy green leaves in one hand and a bag in the other.

She ran down the steps to him and jumped into his arms. He caught her between his forearms, and she lowered her lips to his. *Better. So much better.* She drew back, feeling like new air had been breathed into her lungs. Calmer air. "Sorry."

"I'm not." He kissed her again. "Will I get one of those kisses every time we get a semi-approval for a well? Because if the answer's yes, the business model just got put into overdrive."

She slid from his arms back down to the ground. "I just needed that."

"I figured you were here mulling things over and driving yourself crazy."

"Really? You figured that?" *How could you possibly know?*

He arched a brow. "You're the most organized person I know. The stuff I said today must have sent your brain into a tizzy. There are no lists, no places for checkmarks, no organization of any kind."

"Okay, so maybe you know me a little."

He pressed his hips to hers. "A little?"

"Maybe a lot. But there are things you don't know about me. Maybe I'm okay with not knowing what comes next." *And maybe pigs really do fly.*

"Uh-huh." He held out the flowers. "I was proud of you today."

"Thank you. They're beautiful." They went upstairs into her room, and she filled a glass with water and set the flowers in them. She nibbled on her lower lip. She couldn't ask him about everything *now*. He'd feel rushed, pushed, overwhelmed. *I'm going to lose my mind.*

"Okay, where do you want me?" He looked around the room.

"What do you mean?"

Sage stood with a bag in his hand and a smile on his face. "We should talk. Do you want to go grab a beer and talk at the mess hall? Sit outside? If we stay in here, I'm not gonna talk. I can tell you that right now. You look too sexy with your eyebrows all pushed together and your eyes darting all over the room like you can't figure out what to focus on." He put his hands on her hips. "It makes me want to..." He kissed her.

Kiss me again. That makes me feel so much better.

"Love the nervousness out of you." He kissed her again.

Oh God, yes.

His hand traveled down her hip and squeezed. Kate's body melted against him as he deepened the kiss.

He pressed his cheek to hers and whispered, "I want to touch you until you can't remember what you were worried about."

"Yes," she said in one long, heavy breath. That was the one thing she was sure of. All the questions about the job and her living arrangements could wait.

He pulled back, and Kate forced her eyes open. She reached for him, and he took a step backward.

"Sorry," he said in a low, sexy voice that made her want to climb him like a tree and devour him. He reached for the door. "We have work to do."

Kate watched him walk out the door and stifled her frustration. She forced her rubbery legs to follow him out the door, where she found him sitting on the step, the bag he was carrying set beside him and a satisfied smirk on his face.

"Was that your evil plan? Get me all revved up and then leave me wanting more?" She plopped down beside him.

"Nope. My evil plan was to rev you up so you'd stop worrying. The wanting more part was just a bonus." He put his hand on her thigh, and it burned right through her shorts to her skin.

She lifted his wrist between her thumb and forefinger and moved it from her leg to his. "Let's not tempt fate. I can't be held responsible for how my body reacts to you."

He grabbed her cheeks and kissed her hard. "God, I love you."

Love! I think my whole body just went numb.

He held her stare, as if he couldn't believe he'd said it either.

Sage looked down at his hands. "I can't help it." He lifted his gaze to hers. "I do."

Oh God, yes! Me too! I love you too! She could hardly hear past the adrenaline rushing through her. This was different from *I love your heart*. This was bigger—so much bigger. Kate wanted to memorize his face, the mixture of love and worry in his beautiful dark eyes, the way he rubbed his hands together, unsure, nervous. She wanted to remember the way the humidity mixed with the jungle plants, and Sage's masculine, earthy smell sent a shiver through her. And as she said, *I love you, too*, she wanted to remember the look in his eyes.

"I love you, too, Sage." His face lit up, and she could feel love coming off of him in waves. *That's the look I'll always remember. The look that says I'm everything to you.*

He took her hands in his. "Do you know the song 'Brave' by Sara Bareilles?"

"'Brave'? No, I...uh...uh." *'Brave'?*

"I think of the song every time I see you. The song is about being brave enough to say what you mean. Kate, you're here without any family to lean on, without a best friend to help you through the hard times and celebrate the great times. You take care of so many people, and you set aside your needs to do it. You're the epitome of brave."

"You think I'm brave?" *Brave? That's...so big. Huge. As huge as I love you.*

"Incredibly brave. You're an inspiration." His brows drew slightly together as his eyes searched hers.

"We've come together so fast, and I wasn't sure if I'd scare you off by telling you how I felt, but then I thought of that song, and I thought of you, and I realized that I had to be brave. I *wanted* to be brave. I wanted you to know how I felt. I love you, Kate, right through to my soul."

"You didn't scare me off. You reeled me right in." She wanted to jump up and down and scream, *He loves me! Sage Remington loves me!*

He pressed his lips to hers. A long, slow, breath-stealing kiss, and Kate knew she'd never forget a single second of that evening.

Sage picked up the bag he'd been carrying. "I brought you a few things."

Kate trapped her lower lip in between her teeth, trying to rein in her excitement. "You love me *and* you brought me presents? Quick, check my pulse." She held her wrist out toward him. "Am I still alive? Where could you have gotten me anything?"

He laughed. "Don't get too excited. They're not that great. I ordered them when I ordered the supplies for the mural."

"But that was before we even got together." *You liked me enough then to get me presents?* She knew the answer, because she had felt the connection then, too.

"Yeah, and it feels like a year ago." He took a leather day planner from the bag and handed it to her. "I know you love your clipboards, but this way you have something that's dated, with places for your notes, resources, whatever you need."

Kate ran her fingers over the distressed leather. She flipped it over to the front and nearly cried when she saw her name in the upper-right corner. "This is...Sage. This is beautiful."

"I'm glad you like it." He dug into the bag and pulled out a stack of multicolored sticky notes. "To feed your addiction."

She laughed. "You really do pay attention to detail." She threw her arms around his neck and hugged him. "I figured those notes would make you think I was a little bit of a freak."

He pulled her in close and whispered, "I can't wait to meet the freak in you."

Goose bumps rose on her arms. *I don't have a freak in me. Do I?* She hadn't been with a man that she trusted enough to want to explore any freakiness that might be lurking inside her. One look at the desire in Sage's eyes and heat rushed through her. She trusted Sage, and she wanted him—God, how she wanted him. *Brave.* She took his hand and allowed her desire for him to lead them inside.

"But I wanted to..." He watched her turn on the radio. "Talk about the nonprofit."

"So did I, but..." She turned out the light.

"And our plans so you weren't anxious..." Sage's voice trailed off.

Brave, brave, brave. Be brave. "Let's lessen my anxiety without words, and talk later." With her heart slamming against her ribs, she closed her eyes, falling into the beat of the sensual tune. Her hips found the rhythm, and her shoulders followed.

"Oh, baby," Sage said in a low, sexy voice.

He pulled her to him, and she opened her eyes. Her cheeks heated, and she trapped her lower lip between her teeth to steel herself against her mounting embarrassment. She fought the urge to let him take over and shook her head slowly, hoping she looked seductive, her long hair brushing against her cheeks. She backed away from Sage, swinging her hips while wagging her finger from side to side.

"No, no, naughty boy."

His eyes narrowed, and the edges of his lips curved

up in a devilish, hungry grin. Knowing she was turning him on boosted her confidence. She turned her back and lifted her shirt up on one side, then the other; then she turned to face him, repeating the tease, as if she were a practiced erotic dancer, which surprised and aroused her. She moved around him, grinding her hips in to his, her palms flat against his chest as she shimmied down his body, inciting a titillating moan from Sage. She slid a tank strap off her shoulder and moved closer to him, rubbing her shoulder against his chest; then she lowered the other strap and let her shirt drop below her breasts.

"Kate," Sage whispered hungrily.

Kate glanced down. Her shirt was stuck around her ribs. *I'm the worst dirty dancer ever!* Sage's eyes roamed from her face to her breasts, where they lingered. She hooked her thumbs into the sides of her shirt, rocked her hips, and wiggled out of the shirt as if it were a skirt; then she swung it on her finger and tossed it at him. He grabbed it and took a step closer to her just as the song changed to "Walking on Air" by Katy Perry. *Shit!* Kate was determined to keep Sage's interest. She closed her eyes again and found her groove, moving her hips and shoulders. Her head lolled from side to side. She moved faster to keep up with the chorus, unable to stop the smile from stretching across her lips. After the chorus, the beat slowed, and she hooked her thumbs in her shorts and shimmied out of them, tossing them at Sage. Wearing nothing but her pink lacy panties, she snagged a scarf from the window and looped it around Sage's neck, using the two sides to pull his hard body against her.

"Mm." He lowered his mouth to hers and grinded his hips against hers. Kate released the scarf and slid her hands beneath his shirt. She shimmied down his body and pushed his shirt up, kissing his hot skin on the way back up. With one hand, Sage reached behind him and pulled his shirt off, sending the silky scarf sailing down beside them. Kate ran her fingers lightly along his sides, feeling his muscles jump beneath her touch. She bit her lower lip again—it had worked before to take her out of her own head and calm her nerves, and luckily, it worked again. The beat of the music slowed, and with one hard tug, she opened the button of Sage's jeans. He was breathing so hard, spurring her on. She slid his zipper down, then wrapped her arm around the back of his neck and pulled his mouth to hers. All of her embarrassment and her lingering nervousness worked itself out through that kiss. She licked along the curve of his lower lip, then took his lip between her teeth and drew back slowly. She was rewarded with a wanton moan.

"Jesus, Kate, you're driving me nuts."

He reached for her again, and she shook her head. Then she slid her hand beneath his briefs and wrapped her hand around his hard length. He reached for her again. She caught his hand midair and drew his fingers to her mouth. She rolled her tongue around his index and second fingers, then drew them out slowly, pulling a needy moan from his lips. She shimmied back down his body, tugging his pants along with her. Sage was quick to help, and within seconds he'd divested himself of every stitch of clothing. With her hand on his waist, she danced around him as if he were a dancer's pole. And oh what a glorious pole he was!

She came around to his front and found his eyes closed and his lips parted, making it easier for her to continue being brave. She kissed her way across his muscular hips to the dip at the top of his thigh. Then she dragged her tongue from base to tip and felt him shudder. His hands tangled in her hair—gently—adding no pressure, no direction. Just feeling her as she took him in her mouth and loved every blessed inch of him. He fisted his hands, tightening his grip on her hair, but still refrained from guiding her in any way. Hell if she wasn't already wet. Her seduction had worked on both of them. She kissed her way back up his body and felt his hands slide down her hips. He met her in a warm, delectable kiss as he slid his hand beneath her panties and teased her.

"God, Kate, I feel like I'm gonna explode." He kissed her again, and she couldn't think past her need for him. She pushed him playfully toward the mattresses. His eyes darkened, and when she pointed to the mattress, he went down willingly. She drew her panties down, her body trembling with need.

Jesus. Every inch of his body was taut, ready. He reached up for her, and she straddled him, burying him deep inside her, before lowering her mouth to his. In one swift move, Sage wrapped his powerful arms around her and swept her body beneath him with a sexy, guttural sound that was all male, completely indiscernible, and utterly captivating. He drove into her, pressing his whiskered cheeks against her face, and *oh God,* did she love the scratchy roughness of his whiskers and the virility of his body, the way he took control. Between the soft kisses he pressed to her earlobe and the hardness of his hips against hers, she nearly came apart.

"You're the sexiest woman I've ever known."

His breath was hot on her neck as he held her tight and moved slowly inside her, electrifying every nerve in her body. She felt the pull of an orgasm teasing her, tugging her toward the edge.

"Sage." One fast whisper was all she could manage before her fingernails dug into his back, her eyes slammed shut, and her head fell back as he carried her over the crest of a toe-curling, mind-numbing climax.

He was right there with her, meeting her thrust for thrust, carrying them both through a feverish release.

Kate closed her eyes as he came to rest on top of her.

It didn't matter if she knew what they were doing the next day, the next month, or the next year, as long as they were together.

Chapter Twenty-Five

SAGE LISTENED TO the night sounds echoing in the forest and watched shadows dance across the cabin as he lay with Kate on their mattresses. She'd completely blown him away. He'd been only half kidding about seeing her freaky side. Every time he thought he had her figured out, she revealed another part of herself. Whether it was the way she loved him, the way she kept the volunteers and the project organized, or her determination in advocating for the wells, she was always being more than he anticipated.

Kate's stomach growled, and she covered her belly with her hand.

He kissed her temple. "Wanna shower and go grab some food? Have a drink under the moonlight with Luce before she leaves?"

"You don't mind?"

"Mind? What am I? Six? I'm not competing for attention. I like Luce, and she's your friend. It's important for you to spend time with her." It dawned on him that she might want time alone with Luce, and as he'd watched Kate move seductively around him earlier, inspiration had hit him like a brick. He'd tucked it away until now, but he was itching to get his hands on that canvas. "Would you rather spend some girl time with her?"

"That's okay. I don't want to miss time with you."

"Kate, I have all night with you. You don't get much time with her, and we're both leaving in two days. Let's get cleaned up, grab a bite and a beer, and then I'll go paint while you two talk about how great of a lover I am."

She smiled up at him, and he couldn't imagine ever loving a person more than he loved Kate.

"A little overly confident?" she teased.

"Maybe. Would you rather I said you could talk about how much I suck in bed?"

She smacked his stomach.

"Right. That was my take on it. Always spin things positive." He pulled her up to her feet and hugged her close. She looked up at him again. He was always getting lost in her beautiful blue eyes. One kiss that lasted a minute too long, the right touch, and they'd be right back on that mattress.

"I love you, Kate Paletto."

"And I love you, Sage Remington."

An hour later, after they shared a shower and dressed, they went to the mess hall, where the kitchen was already closed for the night. Kate and Sage raided the refrigerator and ate standing in the kitchen like a couple of teenagers, filling their stomachs with fresh fruit and warm Johnnycakes with butter. It was just after eight o'clock, and Sage thought about the painting he was going to begin. A familiar adrenaline rush snaked its way through his body, and he reminded himself not to fuck up tonight. Not to get lost in his artwork and leave Kate hanging. She smiled at him as she ate the last bite of her Johnnycake.

"You've got that look in your eye," she said.

"What look?"

"That *I wanna go draw something look.*" She took a sip of her beer.

"I didn't realize I had a look."

Kate leaned against the refrigerator, and Sage moved in front of her, spreading her legs apart with his knees, then pressing his body against hers. "I thought maybe it was a different look."

"No. This is a definite *I want to paint* look. You have a few looks that I've noticed. You have the lusty, *I want to devour you* look, which melts my heart every time I see it."

"Careful giving away all your secrets." He leaned down and kissed her neck.

"Then there's your *get any closer to Kate and I'll rip your head off* look."

"I do not have that look."

"No, of course you don't." She rolled her eyes. "Maybe we'll just call it the *hands off my woman* look."

"Okay, maybe. I'll give you that one."

"And then there's the intense, *totally in-the-zone* artist look. I even like that one."

Sage felt his smile falter. "I'm working on that one."

"It's adorable. I've never known anyone who really zoned out like that."

He took a step backward and ran his hand through his hair. "It's not adorable. It sucks. It's disrespectful, and I'm gonna fix it."

"What's gotten into you?" Kate touched his arm, and he twisted away. "Sage?"

"Before Clayton left this afternoon, I went to give him hell about letting you down. I don't like people not keeping their promises, especially to you." He rubbed the back of his neck.

"It was fine. We didn't even need him."

"I know you didn't need him, but that's not the point. And it's not fine. I picked him up and slammed him against the car. I was pissed, and then I realized that I'm no better than him. And then...Shit, this is hard to admit. I realized that I was so angry with him *because* I saw my own actions in what he did. I didn't blow you off that night because I didn't think you were important. I blew you off because I was lost in drawing. If you take it apart, it all boils down to the same thing."

"Sage, that's not true."

He crossed his arms over his chest, tension settling onto his shoulders and back like a heavy cape. "You can't do that, Kate. You can't say it's okay. I need to be held accountable when I do something like that."

She pulled her brows together and shook her head. "It's not that big of a deal. I understand."

"Well, I don't, and I'm gonna fix it." He folded her into his arms and kissed the top of her head. "I never want to hurt you. I know in relationships that happens to some degree anyway, when couples disagree, or whatever, but I don't want you making excuses for me. I want to be the best man I can be for you. And you deserve a man who will put your needs ahead of his own." He pulled back and looked into her eyes. "I want to be that man, Kate, so you can't say it's okay. Deal?"

"But..."

He shook his head. "No buts. I want to be the guy you can count on. Always. I want to be the person that you can call and I'll know why you're calling before you say a word. I want you to know that and take it for granted, and you can't if you're busy making up excuses about why I was late, or didn't show up, or worked until three in the morning."

Kate sighed and bit her lower lip. She dropped her eyes.

"Hey, please look at me. I'm serious."

She met his gaze and nodded. "What you just said, about me calling you and you knowing what I'd want. You remembered what I'd said about having someone who could do that. That was like the second day after we met."

"I can do this, Kate."

"Sage, you already are that person. While we were standing here, I was thinking about if you'd stay out all night painting or if you'd come back to me. You knew."

"No. I knew what I was feeling bad about. It was just coincidence that you were thinking the same thing." He brought her hand to his lips and kissed the back of it. "But I will be that person, and I'll be more. You'll see, Kate. I've never told a woman I loved her before, and I take that seriously. I can't give you my heart unless my heart is worthy of all of you."

"You are more than worthy of me, Sage. So you get a little lost in your work." She shrugged, but he saw a shadow in her eyes.

"That look you have right now? I'll never be the cause of it again. Come on. Let's find Luce. We're getting a little deep, and if I can't carry you up the stairs to your hut and make sweet love to you to get rid of that hint of worry in your eyes, then at least I can deliver you to a girlfriend who is better prepared to tell you all the reasons why you can't put up with a forgetful artist."

THEY FOUND LUCE sitting at the small table in her cabin, surrounded by handwritten notes scrawled on notebook paper. She looked up as they said hello through the screened door. Her hair hung straight down her back, still wet from a shower.

"I knew you'd find your way here eventually," she said. "Come on in."

Luce waved to the bed. "Sit down. I want to show

you guys something."

Kate sat on the bed, and Sage hovered over the table, scanning the loose papers. "You've been busy."

"Hell yes. Like a dog with a bone." She gathered the papers in a pile and reached for Kate's beer. She took a long drink. "Oh, that is so good on a hot night. Thank you." She handed the bottle back to Kate. "Sage, I've been thinking about your idea, and I made a few phone calls. Do you know Shea Steele?"

Luce had a spark in her eye that Kate hadn't seen more than a few times since she'd known her.

"No," Sage answered.

"She's one of the best internationally connected nonprofit PR reps around. Whatever she touches turns to gold. She splits her time between Colorado and New York. Anyway, I hope you don't mind, but I asked her take on your concept, and she had some great ideas about how to package and market it. She said she knows companies that'll want to invest if you want to go that route, and she rattled off at least fifteen artists she thinks will want to take part. You might want to give her a call when you get home." Luce shuffled through the papers and spread three of them out across the table. She tapped one repeatedly, her eyes darting from Sage and Kate.

"I also did some research on different nonprofits that started and failed that had to do with the arts. I haven't come up with any that were trying to do what you're thinking of doing, but I did take note of a few so that you could review what didn't work for them."

"Thanks, Luce. This is great information." Sage picked up the papers and scanned them, then handed them to Kate.

"So, this is totally real. I mean, we're really moving forward with this?" Kate already knew it was real, but sitting there with the two of them and seeing that Luce had taken the initiative to research and think so much about the idea was confirmation. The serious look on their faces was proof of their commitment.

"Unless my attorney comes up with a reason not to or my accountant says it's going to be a total money sucker with no potential benefit—which we both know isn't going to happen—then yeah. I think so. I mean, once I took the idea further and went on a fact-finding mission about wells, I realized how much good we could do for people."

"You're doing this because of me." Kate's eyes shifted between Sage and Luce.

Sage sighed. He ran his hand through his hair and rubbed his hand over the tattoo on the back of his neck.

Kate scrutinized the look in his eyes and quickly named it. "You've got another look. The *shit, I've been caught* look."

"Kate, the things you said sparked the idea, so in that sense my fact-finding mission began because of you, yes. But if you think I'm doing this as a way to keep my girlfriend around, or as some kind of crazy gift or whim, you're wrong. This is going to take serious dedication, a lot of travel, and at the beginning, a moderate amount of capital. I've got my guys looking into the ins and outs of it all now and we'll see what they turn up." He took a long drink of beer and then set his bottle on the table.

"I'm dying in New York. I'm working day and night because what else is there to do? Go to bars? Socialize with the rich and famous? I told you, I'm spending half my time wondering how to get the hell out of there and the other half buried in my work. I have so much that it turns my stomach to think about it." He paced the floor.

Luce tucked her feet beneath her chair, giving him barely enough room to pass.

"I came here looking for answers, Kate. I found the

answer. I love what I do, and it earns me an obscene living. Tossing money into an envelope addressed to charities doesn't feel good. *Doing* something for others feels good. Making a difference, meeting the Javiers, Oscars, and Sylvias of the world and helping them get the resources they need to remain healthy or to make their lives better, that's what matters. Reaching out to the people who value their families and their simple lifestyles instead of their high-powered lunches and their fleet of vehicles, that's what matters."

"Wow. You two really are made for each other," Luce said.

"In everyone's eyes, I have everything. A great town house in Greenwich Village, enough money to buy anything I want, and a studio big enough that I could live in it. But I was empty, Kate. Depleted of all that mattered except my family, and thank God for them. Then I came here, and I met you." He sat down beside her. "I saw the needs of the people here, and it opened my eyes. You opened my eyes. And then I fell in love with you and—"

"Love? Love! Whoa, Nelly. Back up." Luce slapped her palms on the table, her eyes locked on Kate.

"You knew that. You told me he loved me before he did." Kate covered her mouth and mumbled "Crap" behind her hand.

Sage laughed. "I'm that transparent?"

"Like a kid chasing an ice cream cone," Luce said with a smile.

"Go on, please. You fell in love with me, and?" *Say it again. You fell in love with me. I'll never get sick of hearing it.*

"Then I fell in love with you and you were what was missing, Kate. And along with you came your generous heart and your desire to help others. Your industriousness and your determination and your drive. I'd be killing you slowly to ask you to come to New York and drown in the concrete jungle with me. When you love someone, you want to help them be the best person they can be. Kate, I want to help you realize your dreams, not stifle them, and if that means you stay with AIA or another nonprofit, then that's what you'll do, and I'll travel to wherever you are as often as I can. But if we can build a nonprofit together, travel together, use our connections and wealth to help others, then that's even better."

Oh my God. This is real. This is very, very real. She reached for his hand, needing to be sure of him. He was so confident about everything, even without knowing every detail or if they'd succeed. She stole strength from his touch.

"Okay," she said softly.

He continued talking as if she hadn't spoken. "You've helped me find the missing puzzle piece. I needed to have a connection to the outdoors. That much I've known since I was old enough to walk, but what I couldn't figure out was how to quell the nagging feeling that I needed to be doing more. I needed to be giving more, and I needed to still do my art because it's part of me. Without it I might go insane."

Luce's chin rested on her palm. She had a dreamy look in her eyes. "I think I just fell in love with you."

"Hey," Kate snapped. "Get your sights off my man."

Sage shifted his eyes to Luce.

She touched his cheek to draw his attention back to her. "Okay. I get it. It wasn't *because* of me, but I helped you find your way. That's good. I like that."

Sage drew his brows together. "Yeah?"

"Yeah. I *really* want to do this."

He leaned his forehead against hers. "Oh, thank God," he whispered. "I thought you had reconsidered from earlier."

Luce sighed. "This is better than a romance novel. Just don't sweep her off her feet and take her on my bed."

"Luce!" Kate laughed.

"Sorry for the diatribe," Sage said. "I've kind of had a lot going on in my head lately. It feels good to get it out."

"Belize does weird things to people. When you get back to New York, you'll wonder who you were for the past few weeks." Luce reached for Kate's beer again and took a drink.

Sage rose to his feet. "I'm a changed man, all right, but it has more to do with Kate than Belize. I'm gonna leave you women alone to talk about romance novels, or the nonprofit, or everything I've just said." He kissed Kate's cheek. "I promise you I'll come by tonight." He turned to Luce. "You're incredible, Luce. Thanks for all you did. I think we've got a winning team. We'll connect on all of this once I'm back in New York. Until then, I've got painting to do and a woman to woo."

Kate watched him leave, and as soon as he was out the door, she scooted closer to Luce and leaned forward, whispering conspiratorially, "My badass alpha hunk has a soft side, and I'm totally, completely, one hundred percent head over heels for him." She flopped back on the mattress with her arms out to her sides.

"As if I couldn't tell?" Luce finished Kate's beer. "Does this mean I'll be seeing more of you in New York?"

Kate sat up. "I have no idea." She laughed. "I have no clue. Not a single detail that I can hang on to or plan around, other than the way I feel about him. He bought me sticky notes."

Luce laughed. "Ooooh. Romantic."

Kate pushed her knee. "It was romantic. He ordered them from the States two days after he met me. Before we'd even kissed. And a leather day planner. Personalized."

"Well, forget the romance novel hero. They usually sweep the heroine off to Paris and buy them diamonds."

"I wouldn't last a day as a heroine, but he's definitely my hero."

Chapter Twenty-Six

THE SCHOOL WAS silent, save for the sound of Sage's breathing and the gentle tapping of his paintbrush against the pallet. The lighting in the classroom wasn't ideal, but the alternative of painting by moonlight, although more relaxing, wasn't a suitable option for the images that Sage had in mind. His arm moved in even, steady strokes. The scene in his mind was as vivid as if it were currently taking place before him. He envisioned Kate, wearing a short, colorful dress that hung loosely on her lithe frame, surrounded by rich hues of greens, browns, yellows, reds, and oranges. He imagined her breaking through a wild patch of verdant plants, the undiscovered beach falling away behind her. The water, a few shades lighter than her eyes, and the translucent sky keeping watch over her.

Sage's shoulders rounded forward as he focused on defining the lines of her brows, slightly arched up at the edges of her eyes, thinly manicured, so delicate and lovely. It was her lips that gave him trouble. In his mind he saw them as perfectly bowed, the lower lip fuller than the top, slightly parted. But when he dug a little deeper, he felt the fullness of her upper lip against his, and he knew that when he painted, to truly capture the essence of Kate, he had to put the fullness he felt into the image, even if, at first glance, it might appear wrong to others. He chose the brushes carefully, focusing on the shading and the shadows where the corners of her lips came together.

When he reached her chin, he had to take a step back. *Her beautiful chin.* That sweet little dimple that softened her face when she was upset. He could imagine that dimple would lend youthfulness when she'd grow old and gray with wrinkles traveling across the loose skin of her cheeks. He wanted to be by her side when she looked in the mirror after decades had passed and know that they'd enjoyed a lifetime together. He set to work on her chin and the line of her jaw. Sweat beaded on his forehead. Without thought, he pulled his shirt off and tossed it on the floor beside him. Hours passed like minutes as he poured his passion for Kate into creating her likeness.

Kate. God, he loved her. Maybe he would keep this painting as a surprise for her. He could see their lives coming together. Envision a future with her. The thought drove him to check the time. *Almost midnight.* He wasn't going to let her down again. He set his paintbrush down and stepped back from the canvas. He breathed a little harder now knowing he needed to stop painting. He promised Kate. It would be so easy to pick up that paintbrush and work for another three hours, four even, until he was content with the rounding of her cheekbones and the cast of light on her perky nose. He reached for the paintbrush. *Maybe just a few more strokes. Just a little definition around the dimple.* He thought about the frustrating phone call with Jack. Change had to come from within. This he knew, but damn it, what he really needed was a person to take away his brushes and demand that he leave.

He painted a few more strokes, rounded out the curve of her chin. Jack's voice rang through his mind. *I think you just liked what you were doing more than you liked who was waiting for you.* His hand stopped midstroke.

He set the brush down and stepped back again—every nerve in his body pulled him toward the canvas. Images of the lush forest that he longed to paint appeared in his mind like movie clips, mixing with the fear that if he lost the connection—lost this moment of inspiration—he'd forget the finite details that would make this painting come to life. His hands fisted, fighting against his heart, which willed him to clean up and walk out the door.

This moment. That's all they could be certain of. The future was a hope. A dream. He thought of Jack and Linda. Jack had never thought he'd lose her. He'd thought he'd see her after she returned from the store. He hadn't known she'd skid off the road and take her last breath while wrapped in his arms.

Sage's hands began to shake. He clenched his jaw against the memory of his brother's devastation. The empty look in Jack's eyes, his loss of will to carry on. Sage picked up his brushes and carried them to the sink, where he scrubbed them clean as if he were on autopilot. Thinking how, when he'd embraced his eldest brother after the accident, he'd felt the difference in him, the numbness that consumed him and settled around him like a cold winter's day.

After cleaning his supplies and work area, Sage carried the painting into Oscar's supply room and left a note for him. He grabbed his shirt from the floor and headed across the thick grass toward the cabins. He stopped in his own cabin. The missing mattress gave the room a deserted, lonely feel. He grabbed clothes for the morning, checked his cell phone for messages, and was surprised to notice he had a new text. He scrolled through a text from Rush. *Rush?* He clicked on it and read it quickly. *Sorry 4 saying that stuff in front of Kate. Didn't know u were in that deep. Happy 4 you 2.* Sage shook his head at how fast word traveled through his family.

He texted back. *No worries. Get 2gether when I'm back?*

Rush responded right away, which didn't surprise Sage. His brother loved his nightlife as much as he loved skiing. *Definitely.*

Sage typed a quick response. *K. Shutting off phone, not ignoring u.*

He turned off his phone and tossed it into his suitcase, then headed up to Kate's hut.

The lights were out when he arrived, and he found Kate sleeping in one of his T-shirts, sprawled across both pillows. He loved coming *home* to her, and the realization that he was leaving in a few days weighed heavily on him. If only he could stay with her in Belize, or bring her back to New York with him, but neither was feasible. This was one of those times his father's words would come in handy. *Man up, son. Do what you have to do.* He brushed his teeth, washed his face, and then stripped down to his boxers and, careful not to wake her, lay beside her, understanding exactly what Jack had meant—*I think you just liked what you were doing more than you liked who was waiting for you*—and knowing there was nothing he couldn't accomplish where Kate was concerned.

She turned on her side and cuddled against him. He wrapped his arm around her waist and she sighed, a contented sigh.

"You're here," she said sleepily.

"Always."

Chapter Twenty-Seven

IT DIDN'T MATTER that they'd made love for an hour, or that Caleb had come by to steal Sage away at exactly the agreed upon time so Kate could head over to the school with Luce for the surprise party. It didn't matter that Sage's favorite bird—a toucan—had appeared right outside their screened-in porch that morning, like a sign that everything was going to be okay, or that now, as she walked toward the school with Luce, her friend held her close and said all the right things to make her feel better. *It's only a few days. You'll see him soon. He's gonna miss you just as much. You'll be so busy here that the time will go quickly.* None of it made a difference, because Kate had spent the predawn hours fighting the heartbreak of Sage's impending departure.

"Do you want me to figure out a way to stay?" Luce asked as they arrived at the school.

"No. I want him to stay, and he can't. I appreciate you asking. I really do. I just feel so...not like myself." Several of the children ran toward them, speaking so fast that it took all of Kate's energy to put on a smile and focus enough to catch the meaning of their native tongue. She bent to speak to a little girl with pigtails.

"Yes, honey. Mr. Sage will be here very soon."

Sylvia had made fry jacks—deep-fried pieces of dough with honey drizzled on them—Johnnycakes, eggs, rice, and beans, and they were all laid out on a long table, each covered to keep the bugs away. She looked beautiful in a blue dress and a wide-brimmed hat.

"Your man will be here soon?" Sylvia asked Kate.

My man. Great. Here come the tears. Don't cry. Don't cry.

Luce patted her on the back and whispered, "This is so not like you."

Kate needed the reminder. She couldn't fall apart in front of the kids, and really, she couldn't afford to fall apart at all. She swallowed her sadness and forced a smile. "Yes, he'll be here very soon. This looks wonderful, Sylvia. Thank you for working so hard."

"My pleasure. He is a very nice man," she said with her thick accent. "The children will miss him." She winked at Kate. "You will miss him. Not to worry. I will keep your stomach full. That will help."

Kate didn't think she could eat a thing. "Thank you."

Javier tugged at Kate's shorts. "Miss Kate, here they come!"

Luce gathered the children in a group and stood with them while Kate gathered the mingling parents; then she met Sage's eyes and drank in his every step. She raked her eyes down his unshaven, incredibly sexy cheeks to the smile on his lips. A smile that she already missed even though it was ten feet in front of her. Muscles rippled across his shoulders and down his arms. His tank top clung to the muscled panes of his stomach, and by the time she drew her eyes back up, he was standing right in front of her.

"Someone's been sneaky." His voice was seductively smooth.

"How could we not celebrate for you and the kids?"

When he touched her hip, then kissed her cheek, she closed her eyes for a second, fighting the urge to wrap her arms around his neck and kiss him again...and again. The cheering of the children pulled her back to reality and allowed her not to embarrass herself.

"Come on. They're excited." She took his hand and they joined the others. The parents spoke Creole among themselves, and Kate noticed that as they thanked Sage one by one, they spoke slowly and carefully.

Sage embraced each of them, and he made a point of telling each parent something complimentary about their child or children. In two weeks he'd come to recognize their strengths and weaknesses. It was just one of the things Kate loved about him.

"You doing any better?" Luce brushed Kate's hair from her shoulder.

"Yeah. Sorry I was such a wimp earlier." She watched Sage pick up Javier and hug him, and the sadness was slowly replaced by a feeling of gratitude. In two weeks, he'd given these kids so much. She couldn't spend today wallowing in self-pity. This was a day to celebrate all he had done, and they both had a full agenda. This party was a gift, too. An hour to come together with the community and thank everyone for what they'd done.

"Come on. I have something I want to show you." Luce took her hand and walked her toward the school.

Kate smiled at Sage as they passed. He and a group of children were digging into the fry jacks and laughing.

Luce stopped walking beside the mural. "I want you to take two seconds and look around you. I

273

remember you telling me that when you first arrived there were about ten kids in the school on any given day."

She remembered. The school had felt lonely and cold.

"You did this, Kate. You are the one who talked with the parents and stressed the importance of education. You're the one who brought this community together on this level, something that may never have happened otherwise."

Kate felt herself smile.

"Now look at the mural. Turn around."

Kate did. The mural was gorgeous, and it made the building feel alive and happy.

"You might not have painted it, but you allowed it to happen and you facilitated it. Those kids jumping all over Sage? You helped them in so many ways. Please don't ever think that what you do doesn't matter. Your efforts have been vital to this community. And they'll be vital to many more."

"Oh, Luce." The tears she'd been holding back sprang free as she wrapped her arms around Luce's neck. "When I move to New York, you better not get sick of me."

"Who are you kidding? It'll be fun to watch a real-life romance right before my eyes." Luce smiled as she turned Kate by the shoulders toward Sage.

"Hi," Sage said.

"Hi."

"I can't believe you did this." Sage glanced at the kids running around the schoolyard. "I'm so proud to have been part of this community, even if for only two weeks."

"I didn't do all of it. Caleb and Luce helped, and Sylvia cooked. Everyone helped." She glanced at the kids. "I don't think they'll ever forget you, and with that beautiful mural, well, we might have to make a trip back in a year to touch up spots as the paint wears off from the rain and stuff." She'd been thinking about coming back to see everyone, and that seemed like a perfect excuse.

Sage draped his arm over her shoulder. "Baby, we can come back anytime your little heart desires. Besides, how romantic would it be to come back in a year and revisit your hut?" He leaned in close and whispered, "It is the first place we ever made love."

Kate felt heat creep up her cheeks. She shot a look at Luce, who, thankfully, was busy talking to Sylvia.

He used his index finger to draw her face back to his. "Hey, my job as your partner, your lover, and who knows what else one day, is to encourage your dreams and help you fulfill them, and I intend to do just that. We're going to spend our lives making a difference."

Kate was hung up on *who knows what else one day*.

"You've done that for me, Kate. I never knew how to fill the empty places in my life, and you took me by surprise and led the way." He ran his finger down her cheek. "I know how sad you were this morning. I felt it, too. I can't change the time we'll be apart, but I can promise you that once we're back in each other's arms, it'll take a crowbar to pry me away from you again."

Sage took a step toward her, and she caught sight of Sylvia and Luce behind him. She laughed as Sage embraced her.

"Are my hugs funny?" he asked.

"No, but that is." She pointed behind him at Luce and Sylvia puckering and making kissing noises.

Sage blew them each a kiss as a little girl came and grabbed Sage's hand, then dragged him toward a group of older kids by the mural.

He called over his shoulder to Kate, "Stop wondering what else we'll be one day. You'll know when it happens."

"You think you know me," she called with a hint of sarcasm. *You couldn't be more right.* She watched him with the kids and knew she was the luckiest girl on the planet.

AFTER THE PARTY, while Kate and Luce went into the village to take a few photographs, Sage and Caleb went into town to Skype Kurt. Caleb pushed his hands into the pockets of his shorts, then pulled them out for the fourth time in as many minutes.

"Nervous?" Sage had to remind himself that Kurt was Caleb's idol. He should be used to seeing people's reactions to his siblings. Men ogled Siena everywhere she went and women fawned over Rush. Apparently, Olympic skiers were like winter gods, no matter how snarky they were. But Kurt was a writer, not a public figure, and he certainly wasn't the kind of guy who sought out publicity. Like Sage, he tended to keep to himself. While Sage spent his free time in his studio, Kurt spent his in his writing room. Granted, his writing room was one to be envied. It had a view of the mountains on three sides and warm, inviting furniture that would make the most edgy person want to hunker down with a good book. In contrast, Sage's studio probably felt cold and empty to anyone but him. The large open loft had concrete walls and a concrete floor riddled with random splats of paint, various piles of metal, and lumps of clay. The last thing Sage wanted to worry about was ruining the floors when he was sculpting or painting.

Caleb shoved his hands in his pockets again. "Yeah. I'm nervous. Wouldn't you be? What if you met Vincent van Gogh?"

"Sure, considering he's dead." Sage didn't want to embarrass Caleb, but he did want to thank him. "Hey, thanks for all you did for the party. That was really nice of you. I appreciate your efforts."

Caleb looked down at the road. "It was nothing."

"No, it was something, and it meant a lot to me. And to Kate." He draped an arm over Caleb's shoulder and felt his body stiffen. "Listen, if you ever need anything, when you're here or after your assignment, you can come to me. Anytime." He had become fond of Caleb, and he wanted Caleb to know that his friendship was real and that he could count on him.

"Thanks."

Sage dropped his arm as they neared the café. "Really, man. Let's be sure to exchange contact information. I'll never be more than an email or a text away. And I mean that. I want to read that book of yours when it's done."

Sage waved to Makei when they entered the café. "Hi, Makei. How are you today?"

A smile spread slowly across Makei's face. He pushed himself from the stool where he sat at the counter. He wore a colorful cotton shirt that fit him better than the ones Sage had seen him in previously, giving him a more youthful look. Sage realized that he probably wasn't much older than Jack, though he moved like an old man.

"Good, thank you," Makei said. "Internet?"

"Yes, please, and two of your incredible papaya smoothies, please." Sage and Caleb sat at the bar while Makei plodded to the other side of the counter.

"Where is Kate today?" Makei asked. He set the computer monitor on the counter, then set the keyboard before Sage. His long, thin fingers trailed the edge of the counter as he moved around it to make the smoothies.

"She went into the village." Sage logged onto the computer and tried three times before finally securing a connection. He hoped that the connection would hold, for Caleb's sake. "Caleb, how much longer are you staying in Punta Palacia?"

Caleb tugged at the neck of his T-shirt. He bent his neck to the right, then to the left, as if he were stretching before a boxing round. Considering his pencil-thin neck was nowhere near the collar, Sage attributed his erratic movement to nerves.

"I'm not sure. I'm scheduled to be here another six months because of some timing and reassignment issue, but I might want to stay longer if they'll let me."

Sage made a mental note that Caleb wasn't aware that they might close the location.

Makei handed them each a smoothie. They thanked him, and he went to a table and folded his hands in his lap and gazed toward the front door.

Before clicking Kurt's name on the Skype address book, Sage turned to Caleb. "Listen, Kurt's just like you and me, okay? Probably more like you than me. He's a good guy. He's quiet. He probably won't make much conversation, but that's just the way he is. You'll need to ask him whatever it is you want to know, and don't be scared off by his silence."

Caleb nodded quickly.

"Sure you're ready?"

"Yeah. I'm sure."

Sage clicked Kurt's number, and they watched the Skype icon spin. Kurt's perfectly coiffed image appeared on the screen, and excitement filled Caleb's eyes, as if he were a kid seeing Santa for the first time. Santa in a neatly pressed polo shirt sitting in front of a wall of windows.

"You must be Caleb," Kurt said in an even, friendly voice.

"Yes. Thank you for taking the time to talk to me." Caleb's hands shook. Sage watched him slide them beneath his thighs.

"Sure. Sage tells me you're writing a book. Tell me about it."

Listening to Kurt as a writer rather than his brother was strange. Kurt had always been the watcher in the family. He took in his surroundings, and if Sage tried hard enough, he thought he could see his brother taking mental notes that he might use in one of his thrillers. Kurt didn't start conversations. He was the guy who nodded, threw in a word here or there, but preferred to be pretty much invisible. A bystander. Sage enjoyed seeing this less-introverted side of him.

"It's a thriller based here in Belize. Villagers are being killed and no one can figure out why..."

Sage listened to the description of the dark thriller Caleb was writing, and he couldn't reconcile the image of quiet, introverted Caleb writing about a killer running loose in the jungle murdering villagers. Then again, he'd never been able to reconcile Kurt's personality and his writing thrillers either. As he listened to his brother talk about story arcs, believable killings, and which gruesome details will lure in readers and which might turn them off, Sage wondered if there was some secret genetic trait that thriller writers had. Maybe they were quiet because in their minds they were always plotting the perfect murder.

With that thought, he wandered outside. The blazing sun beat down on his face as he lowered himself onto a bench in front of the café. He thought about the visceral pull he'd felt last night to continue painting and how strong that urge had been, how all consuming, and how real the fear of losing his inspiration had felt. But he'd done it. He'd taken the first step toward a change in his zoning out, and though he had no idea if he'd be able to fight the urge to continue painting every time he promised to be somewhere, it was a start. Jack had been right. It wasn't that Sage had been unable to change. He'd simply not been motivated enough to *really* try. He realized that Jack's disappearing into the mountains of Colorado had lasted so long for the same reason. He hadn't found a reason not to—until he'd met Savannah.

If Sage hadn't felt so confined in New York, if he hadn't needed to escape, if he hadn't heard about AIA, he'd never have met Kate. And if he hadn't met Kate, he'd still be floundering in a sea of indecision about how he could make his life more meaningful. He wouldn't know the feeling of loving someone so completely. Yes, he decided. Fate definitely had a hand in *their* lives. How could it not? And how could he leave her tomorrow?

Caleb came outside twenty minutes later with a bounce in his step. "That was amazing. Your brother is amazing. Thank you, Sage. I can't tell you how much that meant to me."

Sage pushed the thought of leaving from his mind. "Yeah?"

"Oh my God. I'm so pumped about writing. I can't even begin to tell you how great it was to talk to someone who totally gets disappearing into the world of writing." Caleb walked with renewed confidence, his head held up high, his shoulders back, and his eyes full of life.

"That's awesome." *Disappearing into the world of writing.* Maybe he and Kurt weren't so different after all. He wanted to disappear into Kate for the next twenty-four hours.

"He told me about a writer's conference he's going to be speaking at. I can't go, but wow. I can only imagine how great that would be. Your brother is so cool. You're so lucky."

Sage did feel lucky, but not for the reasons Caleb

might have thought. His brothers and sister were a constant source of support—even when they gave one another shit. He wondered what it must be like for Kate not to have a sibling to lean on. That was something he couldn't fix, but he would make sure that he was there for her. Unconditionally.

Chapter Twenty-Eight

KATE AND LUCE took their time walking back to the compound. They'd taken loads of photographs with the residents, and Kate had a hard time keeping the sadness about leaving at bay. With Luce and Sage leaving so soon, she wanted to spend as much time with both of them as she could.

"So, I'm really doing this. Do you think I'm making a huge mistake?" Kate asked.

"With Sage?" Luce wore her hair pulled tightly back in a clip, but the humidity had taken hold of the strands around her face, leaving them frizzy and wayward.

"No. My heart tells me we're right together."

"Totally. I told you when we first arrived that he was Mr. Chill, but what I didn't tell you was that he was also a guy who took action on things that mattered. Once I saw your reaction to him, I didn't want you to feel like I was trying to sell you on him." She flipped her hair over her shoulder. "You know, let things progress naturally and all that crap. But he's known for not being a press seeker and for volunteering at soup kitchens and things like that. I know his PR rep, and he never lets her publicize any of the good deeds he does. You gotta know that if I thought he wasn't your type of guy, I'd have told you right away." Luce wrapped her arm in Kate's. "So tell me, a mistake with what? What's bugging you?"

"Thanks for not telling me all that before. I'd have probably gone all googly-eyed over him."

"*Probably gone all?*" Luce teased.

"Shut up." She knew she'd gone googly-eyed over him when they'd met, but she thought she'd covered it well at first. "Anyway, I don't know. He's ready to start a whole company based on what I do. Am I crazy to consider taking part in it? I know nothing about running a company, and the more I think about it all, the more scared I get. I mean, at least with AIA I know where I'm heading. My trips are planned, my work is defined, and there are no unanswered risks. Well, except health-wise, you know." She sighed.

"And with Sage you have nothing concrete."

"Right. But with AIA, I don't have Sage."

"That's not true. He told you last night that you could basically do whatever you wanted. Work for AIA or another place, and he'd travel to see you as often as he could. Don't make this into an exclusive decision, Kate. The question isn't do you work with Sage and have a relationship with him or do you not. The question is—assuming you want a relationship with Sage, which you just said you did—where will you be happiest working? Sage sounds like a given no matter what you decide. At least as long as you want him to be."

She sighed. "The one thing I'm certain about is that I want Sage. My entire heart and soul is full of him. And I'd be happiest working with him, doing what he's going to try to do. It's perfect. By the way, he came over last night. He didn't zone out and forget." *Just tell me to stop worrying and to run off into the sunset with him. I wish he wasn't leaving. I wish I didn't have to feel prepared all the time. I wish...I wish I could be with him right this second.*

"Of course he did." Luce stopped by the path to Undiscovered.

"I still have no idea how he was able to pull himself out of that weird zone he falls into, but I'm glad he did. He tries so hard to do the right thing."

"The question is, how hurt will you be the fifteen times he forgets?"

"You're a buzzkill when you want to be. I thought you were pro-Sage." Kate eyed the road to the school. "Do you mind if we go see the mural?"

Luce linked her arm in Kate's. "Where you go, I go. I'm very pro-Sage, by the way. Especially after hearing him pour his heart out last night. I just know you. You're a planner, and he's a follow-his-gut guy. Not that that's a bad thing. At least you know he'll never come up with some convoluted plan to manipulate you. The guy wears his emotions on his sleeve."

Kate remembered his bulging veins and the look of anger in his eyes when he'd held Clayton against the tree, and how shocked she'd been when she'd first seen that side of him. Then, after hearing that he'd acted to protect her, she'd experienced a whole different type of shock. She was flattered, and intrigued, and floored to know that his feelings for her were growing as quickly as hers were for him.

The mural came into focus, and Kate stopped cold. "Look at that. Amazing, right?" Seeing the finished mural again brought as much sadness as it did excitement. It was just another sign that he would soon be leaving.

"The man's a master at his craft."

He's a master at everything he does.

"You think you'll be okay when he forgets to show up for dinner? Really?"

"I think if he were purposely avoiding me, I'd be mad," Kate admitted. "But he said I can't accept excuses and that I have to hold him accountable if he forgets me. I think that's admirable. I mean, how many guys would say that? He's good, Luce. He's right for me. I feel it in my bones. But we do need to figure out the details. Where will I live? What will I actually do? When can we see each other if I'm living with my parents? He tried to talk to me last night about it all, but I sort of seduced him instead."

"Seduced him? You go, girl." Luce followed Kate across the lawn to the school. They stood in the shade of a large tree, admiring the mural. "Sometimes I think it would be hard to be you, but right now, seeing that fulfilled look of love in your eyes, knowing you've been living with a glorious beach a few minutes from your perfect, secluded, elevated hut, I wish I were you."

Kate drew in a deep breath. "Why'd you say it would be hard to be me?"

"Because while I have to be a planner for my work because my clients are used to being babysat, if I had a guy like Sage swoop me off my feet and offer me my dream job and all the love I could ever dream of, I wouldn't care if I never planned another damn thing in my life. It must be hard to live in your head and to need every aspect of your life planned out." Luce turned back toward the road. "Come on. I'm broiling."

On the way back toward the main road, Kate thought of how quickly she'd fallen for Sage and how standoffish she'd tried to be when she'd seen him on the bus on the way there. How every time she looked at him her pulse raced, and how when she was with him, knowing every detail of where she was headed took a backseat.

"Am I worrying too much?"

Luce shrugged. "How the hell should I know? I could never live like you do. I would go nuts moving every few years. I like traveling, but I also like having a home base, you know? Someplace that when I return, I think, *Thank God I'm home*."

"He's not asking me to marry him and settle down. He asked me to see how the relationship goes and to work with him. What if working together is a mistake? I keep wondering about that." She played with romantic images in her mind of reading and hanging out in the studio with Sage as he worked and traveling to villages where they could actually help the residents, but in the next breath she worried about working that closely together. She'd watched her parents work and travel together her whole life, and while they seemed happy, she wasn't oblivious to the eye rolls and bouts of agitation between them.

"You need to have a talk with him. I didn't get the impression that he was going to do much with the nonprofit besides supporting the artistic side. He's not exactly a major negotiator or a businessman. You heard him say he would have experts to do all that. He's a smart man, and he loves you." At the edge of the road, where the main road met the lane leading to the school, Luce took a deep breath. "I do love it here in short doses. At home I'd be staring at skyscrapers and smelling garbage." She laughed.

"If the business doesn't work out, there are plenty of options for me to return to. But..."

Luce looked at her expectantly.

"I really want to be with Sage. I love him, Luce." She sighed dreamily. "He's so..."

"Hot?"

She laughed. "Yeah, but..."

"Thoughtful? Rich? Sexy? A good lover? Strong? Protective? Take your pick. You can stop me anytime."

"He's so...good. He's genuinely caring, Luce. I can feel how good of a person he is, and the rest is like icing on the cake." *And what a delicious cake he is. What am I gonna do when he leaves?*

SAGE HAD WORKED on the canvas through the afternoon while Kate and Luce were in the village. She couldn't get back soon enough. He wanted time with her—every second he could get before he had to leave. He'd been waiting for her to bring up the details of the nonprofit and, really, the details of their futures and what they both wanted. He had wanted to bring it up a hundred times. He was anxious as hell about leaving her, and every time he walked into her hut, the sight of her sticky notes and day planner full of must-do items were reminders of the organization that Kate depended on in her life. He wanted to give her that comfort even if he wasn't one hundred percent sure of all of the details himself.

He found Kate in her hut, working her way through one of her lists. Before opening the screened door, he drank her in for a minute. It would be more than a week before he saw her again, and though he was trying to be strong around her, every time he saw her, he was struck with a feeling of longing for the days he'd miss.

"How's it going?"

"Great. I'm just going over the things I need to wrap up before I leave here. I can hardly believe how soon I leave." She looked up at him with sadness in her eyes. "And I really can't believe you leave tomorrow."

"Yeah, we should talk about that." He settled his hand on her shoulder, and her smile faltered. He'd gotten so used to waking up beside her every morning, having coffee together, and meeting up again in the afternoon that he couldn't imagine how he would make it through a week of not seeing her.

"Want to spend our last afternoon together at the beach?" he asked. The memory of making love to Kate at the beach sent a bolt of heat searing through him. He cleared his throat to bring his focus back to her.

Kate rose to her feet. "Sure."

"Where are you going?"

"To get my bathing suit on."

"Damn."

She laughed. "I didn't say I'd keep it on."

An hour later, they were lying on the hot sandy beach. Sage's hands moved slowly across Kate's back, basting her with suntan lotion and loving the feel of her while he memorized the curves of her body.

"Do I really have to leave tomorrow?" He wished like hell he didn't have a show coming up. He'd love nothing more than to stay until Kate had to leave, then return home together. He set the lotion aside and took her hand as she sat up and moved closer to him.

"I know. I keep wondering the same thing."

"It's gonna suck being away from you," he admitted.

"I know. I'm so used to you that I know when you leave I'll be looking for you every time I go into the school or when I walk by your cabin." She lowered her eyes. "And when I go to bed at night. I'm not sure I know how to sleep alone anymore."

"Where do we go from here, Kate?" He watched her take a deep breath and blow it out slowly, wondering if she was as nervous as he was.

"I leave a week after you, and I'll go to my parents. Then..."

"How long would you like to be with them before

visiting me?" *A day? Two? A week?* He wondered if she could hear the desperation he felt.

She nibbled on her lower lip. "I don't know. A few days, maybe?"

He breathed a sigh of relief. "Have you given any thought to how much time you want to spend with me?"

"I've only thought about it every second of every day."

Her cheeks flushed, and he pulled her to his chest and folded her in his arms. "Me too."

"How long do you want me to visit?"

"Forever and a day."

She smiled. "No, really?"

"Really." He'd thought about it over and over, and he couldn't put a limit on their time together. He was already having heart palpitations about leaving her. Why would he want to go through that again in a few weeks?

"You want me to...stay?"

"More than anything. Until you get sick of me."

"Really? Oh my God, I want that too. I didn't want to have to leave you again. Would you mind meeting my parents?"

"Your parents, your friends, your elementary school teachers. I'll meet anyone you want me to, and I want you to meet my family, even if I'm worried about them scaring you off."

She laughed. "I'm trying to be okay with not knowing where we're headed and not having firm plans in place for myself career-wise, but I'm afraid I'm not doing a very good job of it. I'm scared to death about where to turn. I mean, you have this idea, but there's nothing tangible yet, and I don't want to be a freeloader when I visit."

"Freeloader? You're kidding, right?"

"No. I'm not."

The seriousness in her voice shouldn't have taken him by surprise, but it did.

"I've always had a job, a focus, and I can't just go stay with you and hang out all day. I wouldn't know what to do with myself."

"Kate." He pulled her onto his lap and drew her legs around his waist. "Let's talk about the nonprofit. It's a big talk. I'm gonna hold you tight so neither of us can dodge the conversation." He wrapped his arms around her waist. "I got an email from my lawyer and my accountant, and they both think it's a viable business to pursue. I want to do it, but I want to be very clear about what I'd actually do. I'm not a businessman. I'm an artist. I'll trust my attorney, my accountant, and whoever we hire to run the business to take care of that side of things. If you agree to be part of it, and I hope you will, then you'd define what you want to do and we'll work around it. Assuming we're a couple— and that's what I want more than anything else. I hope you know that."

"I do."

"Good. God, Kate, you've become everything to me." He ran his hand down her shoulder. "Sorry. I got sidetracked. Anyway, if you travel, I travel. I want to be part of it all, but I'm not a director. I'm the guy who makes the stuff that brings in funding. And you're the woman who figures out who to help and makes it happen with the communities, I think—unless you feel differently."

"Are you kidding? It would be a dream come true. But can you just take off and travel for whatever amount of time it takes? I mean, the coordination with local officials will take time, and then the actual implementation of wells or other programs, that'll take time, too."

"This is what I want to do, and I want to do it with you. I'll make it happen. This whole thing has made me really rethink my life. I live in the Village because it's convenient, but I hate it. *God, do I hate it.* I mean, in small doses it's great, but being here with you, actually spending time with someone who values the same things I do and who enjoys the outdoors as much as I do, it's been incredible. I feel like we're totally in sync, and I'm one hundred percent on board with all of this."

KATE COULDN'T REMEMBER ever wanting anything so badly in her life. The hope in Sage's eyes tugged at her heart. She was as scared as she'd ever been, but knowing she'd be with Sage made it worth the risk.

"Okay. Yes! Let's do it!" *Oh my God.*

He wrapped his arms around her and kissed her lips, her neck, her cheeks. "I'm so happy," he said between kisses. "I can't wait."

"Me either." Her entire body trembled. A good trembling, one that she relished. A tremble of hope. She'd still have to deal with telling her parents and telling Raymond. *Oh God, Raymond. AIA.*

"What's that look?" Sage cocked his head.

"What am I gonna tell Raymond?"

"I usually go with the truth," Sage suggested.

"Oh, yeah. *Hey, Raymond, I'm going to start another nonprofit to help newly developing nations?*" She rolled her eyes.

"I think so, yes. Kate, you never know when the two organizations can work together. If you think about it, there might be times we want to align ourselves with one of their missions. We're not doing anything wrong. We're doing something good."

She rested her head on his shoulder and breathed him in. "You're always so sure of things."

"I'm sure of this, and I'm sure of being with you."

"Me too."

"Kate, if you need something to do, to focus on when you come to New York, we should spend some time outlining the organization. The areas you're particularly interested in helping, your thoughts on travel, everything. I want to flesh this out as much as we need to for you to feel comfortable."

Kate climbed off his lap and sat beside him. "Does it bother you that I like to have things planned out?"

He laughed. "If it bothered me, we wouldn't be having this conversation. I never would have ended up in your bed the first time we made love, and I would never do this." Sage pulled her to him and kissed her deeply.

"God, I'm gonna miss that," she said in one long breath.

"Me too." He stood and held out a hand to help her up. "I hate that I'm going to have to spend a week without you before you come home."

Home. She loved the sound of that.

"What if your family doesn't like me?"

"What if yours doesn't like me?" He arched a brow.

"Stupid, right?" She sighed.

"We're both good people. What's not to like? Come on. Let's take a walk and we can talk about everything we need to figure out so that you're comfortable."

They walked along the shore, their feet kicking up little waves in the warm water.

"Caleb doesn't know anything about the possibility of AIA pulling out. Do you think you should mention it?" Sage asked.

"Not yet. I need to talk to Raymond about everything. I hope they don't pull out of here, and I think if I talk with him about Luce's ideas, it might help, too." A breeze kicked up off the water, and she turned her face toward it. "Mm. This is so romantic. You know it's not always like this. When I was in Albania, it was so cold that we had to deal with frozen pipes."

"Did you enjoy it as much as you enjoyed it here?"

"Yeah, I did. To me it's not about how beautiful the place is. Every place is beautiful. It's about the work I'm doing and how much it helps the people there. When I was in Albania, I was working with a local company to help them learn more efficient business practices. That's what the need was, so that's what I did."

"Did you work with kids there, too?" He guided them into the warm water.

"Each of us had a project outside of our volunteer work. Mine was an environmental club for the kids. I taught them about recycling, and we did a big project at the end of my assignment where we cleaned up a local park and took a bunch of pictures. It was really fun."

Sage turned to face her, squinting from the sun. The right side of his lips lifted in a smile. "Do you think you can stand living someplace for a few months out of the year and traveling for projects instead of living in a remote location for two years straight?"

She dug her toes into the sandy ocean floor. "I'm sure I can." *I can do anything as long as I'm helping others and spending time with you.*

"I need you to promise me that if you need anything, or you feel confined, you'll let me know. I don't want you to ever feel restricted." His tone turned serious.

"Okay."

"I'm serious, Kate. I've been thinking about this, and this is a big change for both of us. I'm also thinking that if you love living with me"—he pulled her close—"which I'm sure you will, then maybe we'll move out of the city and find someplace that's more suited to us. Maybe get a few acres somewhere, a small house with a studio for my work and whatever you want for yourself."

She took a deep breath. "You're thinking really far ahead. I'm worried about coming to New York and finding out that you loved me here but in New York I'm not quite as appealing to you."

His eyes darkened. "You're really worried about that?"

She shrugged. "It's romantic here. It's like a vacation for you. Your real life is far, far away, but what happens when your schedules and deadlines come into play? What if...there...you see me differently?"

He clenched his jaw, and Kate held her breath. *Shit. Shit. Shit. Why did I say that?*

"You know, I could see you anywhere. Here, New York, Pennsylvania, Paris. None of it would be different. Kate, I see you." He closed the gap between them and her stomach fluttered at the feel of his chest against her.

"I am in love with you, Kate. Who you are, the person you are, that doesn't change because of where we are."

"I...But..."

"What?" He brushed a strand of hair from where it had swept against her cheek.

God, I love you.

"Tell me."

"I'm just scared. I want to be with you more than I want to take my next breath, and I want to be part of the work you described, but I'm not anything special, and you're going back to a world where you are so well-known, and—" *Oh my God. I didn't even know I was this scared.*

He folded her in his arms and held her. "Babe, I am who you see. I am the man you know. You think I'm special because you love me. And I love that, but back in New York, it's my art that is special to everyone else, not me. And that doesn't affect who I am as a person." He drew back and looked deeply into her eyes. "We can be scared together, because I worry you might not find me as interesting when you have a sea of men to choose from."

"Yeah, right." She laughed under her breath.

"See how silly? That's why you shouldn't worry about me not wanting to be with you. It took me twenty-eight years to find you. I'm not letting go that easily. Let's not worry about the *what-ifs* and focus on the *what-we-wants*. Tell me what you envision for this endeavor of ours."

"Me? Isn't this your baby?"

"Nope. It's ours. So tell me what you're thinking. You have the experience. I just have dreams."

Ours. How on earth did I get so lucky? "Well, I think clean water is the main thing we should focus on because of health issues, but if we're working on wells, then maybe we can also bring in a project for the local children at the same time. Like I did with the kids here. And if we're on location for the installation of the wells, then we can cater the kids' programs to be no longer than that amount of time."

They turned and walked back down the beach.

"I like your idea about a program for kids. What about timing? Would you be okay traveling for, I don't know, one month out of every three?"

"Yeah. I think so. I'm sure you need time to work, too, and that would give us four times each year when we can make a difference. A big difference." Walking with Sage had taken the edge off her nerves. Just talking about what she might or might not want to do made her feel more comfortable with the whole concept of the nonprofit. Then again, Sage put her at ease with everything he did. Kate smiled at how he'd taken her needs into consideration first, instead of working around his own schedule, which brought her mind to New York again. "Sage?"

"Yeah?"

"Tell me what you're like when you're not here. What's your life like in New York?"

He looked down at her and smiled. "My life in New York." He sighed, as if he were about to tell a long story. "I get up and usually work out, maybe go for a run; then I work in my studio for a while. If I have a show, of course I go there. Sometimes I have to meet with clients who are commissioning work. I visit their homes or offices. I usually work several evenings each week, sometimes well past midnight if I'm in the middle of a project. I try to catch up with Dex for a drink every few weeks, whenever we're both around." He shrugged. "It's not very exciting. Every once in a while my mom sets up a dinner or lunch and we all try to get together for it."

She was quiet while she processed his answer. Working well past midnight several nights each week? How would that work? Would they ever see each other?

"Now, do you want to hear what my life will be like when we live together?"

"Sure." She was trying to figure out how she would fit into his life, and she hated how withdrawn she sounded because of it.

"I'll probably do everything pretty much the same, except I hope we'll have breakfast together, maybe take a walk some evenings." He stopped walking and placed his hands on her hips. "Dinner together is a must, to be sure that I'm not just your booty call. Oh, and I'll get my studio time in well before midnight. Just in case you want that booty call."

She laughed. "You're such a fool."

He swooped her into his powerful arms and ran into the water. "What am I?"

She wrapped her arms around his neck and rested her forehead on his. "You're the sexiest and sweetest man I've ever known, and I want to have breakfast and dinners with you. I want you at my beck and call for late-night booty action. And I want to meet your brother for drinks."

"And?"

And what? She couldn't think of anything else. She shook her head.

He swung his arms, readying to throw her in. She clung to him.

"And what?" she said through a laugh. Kate couldn't think of one thing to say that would stop him from throwing her into the water, so instead she lowered her mouth to his and took him in a deep, greedy kiss. His strong arms came around her, repositioning her legs around his waist. With the setting sun on her back and the heat of Sage pressed against her chest, a calm radiated through her. Even if she didn't know what would happen in a day, a month, or a year, she wanted every blessed second she could have with Sage. He laid her on the towels beneath the tree and kissed her until she could barely think.

"A week is too long," he said, before grazing her shoulder with his lips as he untied her bikini top and slipped it from her body.

His hand, sure and strong, traveled down her ribs, sending a full-body shiver through Kate. He looked down at her, his eyes dark, hungry, and so full of love that she had to wrap her hand around the back of his neck and pull him into another kiss to keep from falling apart, knowing that tomorrow at this time, he'd be gone. His hand slid down her hip, hooking on the bottom of her suit. She lifted her hips, and he drew the tiny swatch of fabric down, then slid out of his bathing trunks and settled himself above her.

Leaning on his forearms, his mouth an inch from her lips, he pressed his cheek to hers and whispered, "Don't worry over the silly things. Love me and let me love you. I will always be here for you, and I'll never let you down."

Oh God. "I know you won't." Tears pressed at her eyes as he slid into her and they became one. She loved him so much, everything about him, and as she wrapped her arms around his body and closed her eyes, the love swelled so big she thought her heart might burst. She opened her eyes as his forehead met hers.

"I'm so in love with you, Kate."

She opened her mouth to respond as he moved slowly, deeply, filling her completely. She had to catch her breath. The words were lost in their love. She felt a tear slip down the side of her face; then the pad of his thumb wiped it away.

He stopped moving. "Am I hurting you?"

She shook her head, still overwhelmed by emotions that felt thick and tangible. "No. I just love you."

He nuzzled against her neck and held her tightly. And as their bodies moved in sync and the sun fell from the sky, Sage settled his lips over Kate's and loved her right up over the edge, until she had to tear her lips from his to gasp a breath. She met each of his powerful thrusts with a lift of her hips, feeling her heart open and devour him. She had to have more of him, and she grasped at his back, his hips, anywhere she could find purchase, until he was breathing hard, sucking in air between clenched teeth, and the night air carried his name from her lungs. Sage was right there with her, filling her with his love and carrying them through his powerful release. His body shuddered as he came to rest. Their hearts thundered as if they were trying to break through their chests and join together as one.

"Don't forget me when we're apart," she whispered, though she knew he never would.

"We'll never be apart. I'm leaving my heart right here with you."

Chapter Twenty-Nine

KATE AWOKE SUNDAY morning nestled between Sage's arm and his chest, where her body melded perfectly to his. She didn't dare move. Sage was leaving in just a few hours, and some tiny part of her thought that if she didn't move, if he didn't wake, then maybe he wouldn't really have to leave. She lay with her eyes closed, breathing in the scent of him, willing her body to remember the feel of his leg beneath hers, the way his muscles twitched under her weight. She listened to the cadence of his breathing. It was even, comforting, and peaceful, unlike his ragged breathing when they'd made love the night before, first at the beach and then in her room. *A week isn't that long.* It felt like a lifetime.

He drew in a long breath, causing his chest to rise, taking her cheek along with it. Kate held her breath, hoping he'd stay asleep a little longer. Once he was awake, they had a million things to do before he left, and she just wanted to forget. She glanced at the table by her bed, littered with sticky notes. For the first time ever, she hated the sight of them, the stupid little reminders telling her all the things that meant Sage was definitely leaving. *Clean the cabin. Wash the sheets. Prepare for the next volunteer.*

The next volunteer.

She couldn't even reconcile Sage as a volunteer. He was so much more. Who was she kidding? He was everything.

He stirred, wrapping his arm around her and pulling her close, then kissing the top of her head before even opening his eyes. Kate sighed. *God, I'll miss you.*

"If I don't open my eyes, can we pretend I don't have to leave?" he asked.

Kate couldn't manage anything but a sad moan.

"Come here, babe." He pulled her over him and opened his eyes. "God, you're beautiful."

He kissed her, and a lump formed in Kate's throat. How could this be possible? She'd gone two years without seeing her parents. She'd left her few friends from college behind without a care in the world. Even Luce, whom she'd seen only a handful of times over the past two years, but whom she adored, didn't cause her to cry when she left. And in two short weeks she'd fallen so completely in love with Sage that she could barely think past the pain of him leaving.

"Hey," he whispered, brushing her hair away from her face. Sage pulled her close and held her while tears streaked her cheeks and tumbled onto his chest. "It's only a week. It'll be over before we know it, and then we'll be waking up like this again."

She nodded. "Technic...technically, it's a few days longer. I leave...I leave in a week, but I have to see my parents for a few days first." *God, I hate this.* She wouldn't feel right not visiting her parents first, even if she'd rather be with Sage. Of course, then she'd never want to leave him.

"We can get through a few days longer. We can do

anything as long as we know we'll be back together soon."

She knew he was right, but it hurt just the same. Kate didn't know how long she lay there, but she was thankful that Sage didn't rush her or make her feel silly for missing him before he was even gone.

They showered and dressed in silence. Sage moved carefully around her, touching her arm as she walked past him, pulling her close when tears rose to the surface. By the time they left her room, he had tearstains on the chest of his white T-shirt. He wore the same tan cargo pants he'd worn when he'd first arrived, and Kate felt a pang of longing to rewind time. They'd packed his bags the evening before, and while Kate spent time helping Luce pack, Sage had gone to wrap his canvases so they were ready to ship home. *Home.* Something miraculous had happened over the past twenty-four hours. Sage's home had become her home in her mind. She couldn't pinpoint exactly when or how the transition had taken place, but she was relieved to feel the comfort instead of the nagging anxiety that had prickled her nerves over the past few weeks.

They were picking up Sage's bags from his cabin when Luce came out of hers wearing a light cotton skirt and a tank top. Her blond hair lay straight and shiny, freshly combed and ready for the city once again. She wore makeup for the first time in two weeks, a sure sign of returning to her real life.

"Go see Luce," Sage said. "I just realized that I forgot something back at your place. I'll catch up in a minute."

Kate nodded, still unable to pull herself together, and she watched him hurry off.

"Thinking about hiding him in your cabin for the next week?" Luce called.

Kate sighed. "I wish."

"You'll see him in a week. It's not that long." Luce threw her arm around Kate. "You gonna be okay?"

"I have to be." *Even if I'm not.* "It's stupid, right? He's only been here two weeks, and I'm acting like we've been together for years."

"It's not stupid. You're in that honeymoon stage. You know, moon-eyed lovers, hot for each other every second, can't wait to be in each other's arms."

Kate couldn't even dispute her words with a joke. They were true.

The car ambled onto the property, and Kate's eyes welled with tears again, damn it. "Oh my God, I'm gonna miss you." Kate wrapped her arms around Luce's neck.

"Me too. I had so much fun, despite Penelope's tantrums."

"Me too."

"Come see me in New York. Promise?"

"It looks like I'm going to be living there, so..." Kate said.

"Living? As in for good?" Luce arched a brow.

Kate smiled, wiping the remaining tears from the corners of her eyes. "I think so. He asked me to stay and, Luce, I can't imagine ever leaving him again."

"Oh, Kate!" She threw her arms around Kate and squealed. "This is so great! We can see each other more often. I'll be there to help you with your nonprofit, and you'll love Shea." She grabbed her bags and they headed for the car.

"I'm excited. Nervous, but more excited than scared. I wish I was leaving with you guys." She spotted Sage coming down the path from her cabin. She felt a smile stretch across her cheeks as he came to her side and pulled her close again.

"You okay?" he asked.

"Yeah."

"She's gonna bawl her eyes out when we leave, but it's for me, Sage, so don't go thinking it's all for you," Luce teased.

Kate wrapped her arms around his waist and rested her head on his chest again.

"She'll miss us both," he said.

After putting the luggage in the car, Kate hugged Luce again, glad to hear Luce sniffling as they embraced. *Misery loves company.*

"We'll see each other soon," Luce said as she drew back. "I didn't get to say goodbye to Caleb. Will you tell him goodbye for me?"

"Wait!" Javier's voice called their attention back toward the cabins, where he was dashing across the thick grass toward them with Caleb in tow. "Mr. Sage!" He jumped into Sage's arms with a paper in hand and wrapped his arms around his neck. "I'm going to miss you."

Sage wrapped his strong arms around him. His hand cupped the back of his head and held Javier close. "Hey there, buddy. I'm gonna miss you, too. You'll take good care of Miss Kate for me, won't you?"

Javier nodded emphatically.

Kate couldn't hold back another rush of tears at seeing Sage and Javier together. She wiped them away with the crook of her arm, wondering how in the hell she'd ever put the pieces of her heart back together.

"I made you something." Javier handed Sage the paper. Sage scanned it quickly and then glanced at Kate with a soft smile. She leaned in close to take a look, causing more tears to fall.

Javier pointed at the drawing. "That's you, that's Miss Kate, and that's me. See me? I drew the eyes just how you showed me."

"May I keep this, Javier?" Sage asked. "You're such

an amazing artist. One day I'll be able to show people this and say, *I knew Javier before he became famous.*"

Javier's eyes bloomed wide. "Famous?"

"If you try hard enough, there's no telling how famous you can become." Sage winked at Kate.

She felt the time they had together slipping away as Luce climbed into the car. Sage set Javier down and patted his head. "Thank you, Javier. Promise me you'll study hard at your lessons and that you'll always be kind, because you're about the nicest kid I know."

"I promise." Javier pulled at his blue T-shirt, and his eyes dropped to the ground. In the next second, he threw himself against Sage's legs and clamped his arms around them. "I love you, Mr. Sage."

That's exactly what Kate wanted to do.

Sage picked him up again and hugged him tightly, then kissed his cheek. "I love you too, Javier. I think I'd better say goodbye to Miss Kate now. You know how girls are."

Javier giggled and nodded as if he understood the tease. Kate knew he'd go along with anything Sage wanted, just as she would. He had that effect on people.

Sage reached for Caleb first. "Caleb, keep writing. I want to read your story when you're done. And keep in touch. When you leave here, we'll bring you out to New York and you can meet Kurt in person."

Caleb held a hand out for Sage to shake it, and Sage pulled him into a hug. "We hug in my family, so get used to it."

Kate saw Caleb stiffen, but the happiness in his eyes told Kate how much that hug, and the offer, meant to him. Sage released him and turned to her, and her eyes welled again. She couldn't remember a time she'd cried so much. He held her tightly against himself again.

"You're trembling," he whispered.

She nodded.

"Oh, babe. I'm sorry. I wish I could stay right here with you. We'll talk on the phone every night. Okay?" She heard his voice crack and pulled back to look into his eyes. Seeing his damp eyes only made her cry more. "It'll cost a fortune," she said.

"I've already taken care of it. I arranged for an international plan on your cell phone. Texting, too, so you can call or text me anytime you want. It's done."

"But...how?"

"Let's just say that Luce sounds a lot like you when she wants to. Don't get mad at her. I held her at knifepoint." He smiled.

She glanced at Luce, who held her palms up in the air. "You should change your password. Remember when your phone broke while we were in Belize City the last time I visited, and you told me when the new one came that you listed *undiscovered* as your password?"

Thank God I did. "I can't believe you remembered. Thank you, Luce." She held on to Sage's waist. "I...I love you."

He placed his hands on her cheeks the way she loved. His brows drew together. "I love you, and when you come to New York, we'll be together every day. Don't worry about a thing. We'll figure out all the details, and our life together will be wonderful."

She nodded, knowing he meant every word he'd said and trusting that he was right. He lowered his lips to hers and took her in a long, greedy kiss—a kiss that told of how much he'd miss her and how much he loved her. It stole her breath and her anxiety along with it, as always. When he drew back and rested his forehead against hers, she closed her eyes, once again memorizing the feel of him.

"Keep your phone with you. I'll call you when I get

to New York."

"Okay," she whispered. They held hands until he was in the car, and then she climbed right in on his lap and hugged him again, kissing his lips, his cheeks, then his lips again. "Sorry. I just..."

"Love me," he said, then kissed her back again. "Now go or we'll miss our flight."

She lifted her brows. "There's an idea."

Caleb reached for her hand, surprising them both. She took it thankfully. She needed something to ground her once Sage and Luce pulled away.

"I love you, Kate," he said before closing the door. He blew her a kiss through the window, and she didn't even try to stop the next rush of tears.

"Do you need a hug?"

She looked at Caleb through blurry eyes, knowing how hard it must have been for him to ask, and seeing the worry lines on his forehead. The last thing he wanted was for Kate to fall into his arms, but it was the only thing she could do to keep from falling to her knees and throwing a tantrum like a two-year-old.

Caleb stood rigid, his arms hanging at his sides as she cried on his shoulder. Javier's hand patted her lower back, and Kate tried her damnedest to stop crying for his sake, but after a few minutes she gave up even trying. Eventually, Caleb lifted a hand to her back and mimicked the way Javier patted her. It made her laugh—*thank God*. It was all she could do to pull away.

She stared at the clouds of dust billowing over the road where the tires had just traveled. He was gone, and she had a whole day of work ahead of her.

"You okay?" Caleb asked.

"Yeah. Thank you. I'm gonna go back to my room for a minute, but I'll catch up with you right after." She knelt beside Javier. "We're gonna be just fine, Javier. I'm glad you came to say goodbye to Sage."

"I'm sorry you're sad. But my aunt said when people go away they're still in our hearts."

Kate thought about Javier's mom. If Javier could survive losing his mother, she could survive a week without Sage. She'd have to.

"I think your aunt is a very smart woman."

Her room felt lonely. Empty. Cold. She glanced at the mattress on the floor in the screened-in room. Sage had returned his mattress to his cabin the evening before, and now, as a lump formed in her throat, she noticed something beneath the covers. She drew them back and felt the goddamn tears return. She picked up the familiar linen bag, wondering how he could have gotten her the one thing she'd missed most. *The one thing I thought I missed most.* Now she knew that Sage was that one thing, and nothing else would ever come close. She withdrew the Starburst journal from its delicate wrapping and ran her fingers over the soft leather, then untied the thin leather strap and unwound it from around the journal. It was filled with recycled artist paper of varying colors and thicknesses. She lifted it to her nose and breathed in the leathery smell, then opened to the first page to write in it. A handwritten note, loopy and slanted to the right, was scrawled across the page.

Kate, my love,

You said this was the one thing you missed most while in Belize. When I ordered it for you, I remember wondering what it might feel like to be missed by you. Now I know, and knowing you love me is what will carry me through this next week. I hope you feel my love for you with as much certainty as I feel yours. I adore everything about you and cannot wait until you're in my arms again. I've taken the liberty of creating a list for when you leave Belize.

1. *Visit parents*
2. *Move in with Sage*
3. *Help people all over the world (with Sage by your side)*
4. *Live happily ever after*

I love you, babe, and always will.

—Your real-life, alpha brawn, hunky hero, Sage

Kate pressed the notebook to her chest, then dug her phone out from beneath the papers on the table and texted Sage.

Thank U 4 giving me the only list I'll ever need.

His response came moments later. *Thank U 4 giving me the only love I'll ever need.*

Chapter Thirty

LUCE WAS RIGHT. Sage had been back in New York for almost a week and he still felt different. The city noise was too loud, the thick, greasy smell made him sick to his stomach, and his town house felt empty without Kate by his side. He spoke to Kate every morning and again every evening, most days with a text—or ten—in between, and he still missed her so much he ached for her as if she were a phantom limb. He had to make it through only a few more days, and after she visited her parents, she'd be there with him. *A few more days. I can do that.* He'd been staying up most nights working in his studio and feeling like a walking zombie. It was better than lying in bed thinking about Kate until he hurt so badly he could barely move.

He'd gone to bed at three in the morning, and now it was nine and he was sitting in his attorney's office, wishing he had another cup of coffee. Or five.

"You look like hell." Marshall Taybor was a fiftysomething attorney with hair more gray than black, piercing dark eyes, and thick eyebrows that rivaled Eugene Levy.

"Yeah, well, I'm a little tired." *And lonely, which I've never been before, and it sucks.*

Marshall cocked his head to the side and narrowed his eyes. "Tell me it's not drugs, or drinking, or any of that shit."

"You've been my attorney for four years. Has that ever been an issue?"

"No, but you never know. Better men than you have fallen prey to the powder or the bottle and lost just about everything they had." Marshall leaned back in his leather chair and crossed his arms. He played racquetball every morning at five, which he never failed to remind his clients, and even in his suit coat, his muscles and lean physique were evident.

Sage sighed. "It's not that, Marshall. Can we get going here?"

"In a hurry? Sure. Okay, here's what I've got." Marshall pushed a stack of papers across the desk to Sage.

Sage felt Marshall's eyes scrutinizing his every move as he looked over the papers.

"It's all there. Once you elect a board of directors and officers, we can prepare the articles of incorporation, adopt bylaws, and file the necessary tax paperwork, the whole deal." Marshall leaned across the desk. "Wanna tell me about all of this? Why invest time and energy into starting something like this when you can just write a check to a company that already deals with charities in those areas?"

"Because it's what I want to do." Sage glanced up from the papers in time to see him raise his hands.

"What does that mean? You know there's a lot of administration that goes into this, right? You'll have to file annual reports. Someone's got to run the damn thing. If you're really thinking about international work, then I assume there's travel. Isn't that going to impact your work? Your life?"

Sage set the papers down on the desk. "I know all of that, Marshall. Have you ever felt like you wanted to do more? To give more? To be involved in helping others have a better life?"

"That's what the checkbook's for."

Sage laughed. "Yeah, I guess for most people it is."

"I thought you were just blowing smoke when you told me last year that you needed something more in your life."

Sage remembered the meeting well. He and Marshall had been discussing investments, and Sage had asked him what other people in his financial position did to give back. "Yeah, I remember you telling me to find a good woman and let someone else worry about the rest of the world." He took the paperwork and rose to his feet. "Now I've found both. A good woman and a way to give back." He shook Marshall's hand.

"That explains the bags under your eyes. You could have said that instead of letting me worry."

"Letting you worry is so much more fun." Sage opened the door to leave. "Thanks for everything, Marshall."

"Get back to me when you're ready. We'll get it all set up. And, Sage?"

"Yeah?"

"For what it's worth, the world needs more people like you."

"I'm not doing anything you couldn't do," Sage said.

Marshall sat back down in his chair and picked up his pen. "No, but you're giving up what half the world wouldn't. Your time and, at least at the beginning, a hell of a chunk of money."

Sage left his office confident about his decision. He pulled out his phone and texted Kate. *What should we call this little company of ours?*

KATE'S NERVES WERE strung so tight, she felt as though she might snap at any moment. She'd been on Skype with Raymond for the past twenty minutes. AIA was not pulling out of Punta Palacia. The spotty Internet connection had caused her to misunderstand what he'd been saying. AIA was having funding issues, and because of that, they needed to keep the celebrity volunteer program alive. Celebrities donated large amounts of money, which Kate knew some did for the sole purpose of gaining media attention, and hearing it again from Raymond had turned her stomach. Raymond had also spent the last ten minutes telling her all of the reasons that quitting AIA was a mistake.

"Raymond, you know how I feel about all of this. We've talked about it for two years. I think I'm ready for a change."

"But you can work with another site. You can run an area with real volunteers, not celebrities. Kate, you've worked with us for almost five years. You're one of our best volunteers."

She heard the sincerity in his voice, and it brought a wave of guilt.

"We haven't committed to your next location yet. I'll let you pick where you go," Raymond pleaded.

She could think of a million places where she'd like to go. Where she could do some good. A lot of good. But she couldn't think of a single one that was worth not being with Sage.

"Kate, how can you give up a known thing for something that isn't even a company yet? What if this guy blows it off? You've known him for two weeks. That's not very long. You know how these things go. You know how being away from the real world can change your perspective. How do you even know you'll be compatible when you're back in your real-life situations?"

Jesus. How could he know exactly where her fears were founded? Sage had put those fears to rest, but what if...

"What do your parents think?"

She was calling her parents after talking with him. She'd been trying to figure out how to tell them. She wanted all of her ducks in a row. She'd wanted to say she'd already handled things with AIA and was firm in her decision.

The text came in from Sage as she contemplated Raymond's words.

What should we call this little company of ours?

"Kate?"

She lifted her eyes back to the monitor.

"How about if I promise you'll be done with celebrities forever. I'll never send you back to that location. No more. I'll even put it in writing."

How many times had she asked for that over the past two years? Five? Ten?

Another text from Sage came through.

I'm thinking Hydration Through Creation (HTC). Picked up legal docs. We're almost there. Miss U.

Kate clenched the phone so tightly her knuckles turned white as two things became perfectly clear to her.

"Kate?"

She looked at Raymond again. She'd trusted him for the past five years. She'd spent two years begging him to make the very changes that he was now offering. *Two years* of being told he was doing all he could. Two years of him rationalizing why celebrities were needed there in the first place. *Two fucking years.* She dropped her eyes to the phone again. She'd known Sage for two weeks. *Fourteen days.* And in those fourteen days she'd never had to ask for a thing, and he'd given her so much more in those fourteen days than Raymond ever could. It didn't take a threat of her leaving for Sage to see the need right before his eyes, and he didn't need a threat as the impetus to do the right thing. He did the right thing because of who he was, led by his generous heart. The heart she'd fallen madly, deeply, passionately in love with. The heart of the man she knew she could trust beyond a shadow of a doubt.

Raymond's eyes were filled with worry. His mustache twitched nervously.

"Raymond, you've been really good to me for the most part, but I'm sorry. This is going to be my last assignment with AIA. I've made up my mind." She ended the call with Raymond, adrenaline sending her to her feet and spinning around toward Makei. He lifted his eyes to her from where he sat at the bar, and she felt a smile spread across her cheeks.

"I love him, Makei. Sage, the man I brought in to use the Internet. I love him. I do. I love who he is. I love what his vision is for his life. I'm doing this. I'm not going to stand in my own way anymore. I'm not gonna worry about lists, and *what-ifs*. I'm gonna take the chance and see what happens!" She hugged him, and he stood rigid in the same way Caleb had. "I'm sorry," she said as she pulled away.

Makei raised his eyebrows. "This is news to you?"

She laughed. "Well, kind of."

He shook his head and patted his hand over his heart. "Kate, I saw this love in you the first time you brought him in."

"You...You did?" She thought about the first day they'd come to the café. The way Sage had pulled her in front of the monitor to talk to his mother and the zing of electricity—and annoyance—she'd felt. She reached up and rubbed the back of her neck where he'd held her. She connected the dots of their love in her mind. Each heated glance, every time she pulled away, the way he'd looked at her on the bus during the ride from Belize City. There were too many moments to count. Yes, she believed Makei had seen her love for him early on. She'd just been too blind to see it. It wasn't on her list.

"You did," she said as she walked out the door.

She texted Sage. *U should have been on my list!*

As she walked back toward the compound, Sage texted back, *Should I worry that u've had 2 many beers?*

She laughed as she responded. *If u were on my list those first few days, I would have known not 2 waste them. Never mind. Silly stuff. I love the name. I love u.*

Chapter Thirty-One

HYDRATION THROUGH CREATION. The name had come to him as he left Marshall's office earlier in the afternoon. Sage had placed a call to Shea Steele, the public relations specialist that Luce had recommended, and they'd scheduled a time to meet the following week. The pieces were falling nicely into place, and for the first time in a few years, Sage didn't feel like he was stuck on the wrong path. This is what he needed, a way to give back. A way to make a difference. *And Kate.*

Christ. He hadn't even known he wanted a relationship, much less to be with a woman every second of the day. His feelings for Kate had taken him completely by surprise. Now he stood before the canvas that had arrived a few days after he'd come home and he drank in the image of Kate in the loose-fitting dress. In the nights since it had arrived, he'd completed painting the jungle around her, where their love had come to life. Last night, he'd finished painting the beach behind her. Remembering their lovemaking in the warm sun made him miss her even more.

His phone rang, startling him from his thoughts.

Siena.

"What's my baby sister doing up so late? Don't models need their beauty sleep?"

"Ha-ha. I was out with my friend Willow and remembered that you'd texted earlier about holding your phone at the gallery, so I thought I'd call. I knew you'd be up."

He had decided to give Siena his phone at the show so that he wouldn't miss any messages from Kate. If he was in an interview or talking with potential buyers, Siena would make sure he got Kate's message when he was done, and of all his siblings, Siena was the one who lived and breathed with her phone in hand. If anyone would understand the importance of watching for Kate's calls or texts, Siena would. Sage laughed.

"How did you know I'd be up?"

"Oh my God. Look at Dex and Jack. When they were first with Ellie and Savannah, it was like they never slept. I'm convinced that once you fall in love, your entire mind revolves around the other person. Night and day."

"Is that jealousy I hear?"

"No way. I'm too much of a control freak to let anyone take up my thoughts like that. Anyway, I'm glad you're back. I can't wait to see you. I'm happy to hold your phone, but if you're busy, what exactly am I supposed to say if she calls and there's a problem with her travel arrangements or something? Should I interrupt you? I figured we should clear the details before the show."

Sage hadn't thought that part through. "Hopefully, there won't be any issues, but if there are...flag me down if I'm talking to a buyer and I'll excuse myself if I can, but if I'm in an interview, just tell her you'll get the message to me. Does that work?"

"Sure. Do you care if I talk to her? Mom got to meet

her."

"Now, *that* is jealousy." He laughed, knowing how much Siena hated to be left out of anything having to do with family gossip.

"Shut up. If you love this girl, I should check her out, right?"

"Whatever. Sure. Talk all you want. You'll love her." *Just like I do.*

"When do we get to meet her?"

Sage looked at the painting again, wishing he was looking at the real live Kate instead. "Well, she's leaving Belize tomorrow to go see her parents for a few days. Then she'll come here. It probably won't be before Monday or Tuesday, but I'll make sure you guys get to meet her."

"I can't wait! And I'm excited to see you tomorrow, too. I'll be there early so we can coordinate."

Sage realized that Siena's organization skills rivaled Kate's, and he imagined they'd become fast friends. *Maybe even share sticky notes.*

Siena continued. "I think everyone's gonna be there, except maybe Kurt. He wasn't sure."

One of the things Sage loved most about his family was that when one of them had an event, the others tried to support them. Before he'd left for Belize, they'd held a surprise party to celebrate the release of one of Dex's record-breaking PC games, and his entire family had been there despite their busy schedules.

"That's great. I can't wait to see you, too, and thanks for helping with my phone."

Sage ended the call and stood before the painting of Kate. He could almost feel her hands as they broke through the jungle, pushing the leaves to the side, one leg up, midstride, the other gracefully stretched behind her. Her short dress barely covered her sexy thighs. It had taken him forever to get her beautiful blue eyes just right, and as he scrutinized his painting, he realized he'd nailed her lips perfectly. He'd captured the slim corners and the gentle, alluring fullness in the center. He thought of her first smile each morning when they'd woken up together and the way it seemed to say, *Oh good. You're still here.* He loved the way she sighed right after the smile formed, and then snuggled against him. He loved that moment of surety, when her cheeks relaxed and her muscles melted against him. God, he missed her. He checked the time. It was past midnight in Belize. She'd be fast asleep; he was sure of it. He imagined that she had all of her lists lined up and ready for the next morning when she was supposed to leave for the airport. He smiled thinking of the colorful sticky notes along her wall, her sink, and even on her mirror. He was going to be tied up all afternoon and evening at the show tomorrow. He had to hear her voice again—even though they'd already said good night a few hours earlier. *Just a quick call.*

"Hi."

Her sweet, groggy voice brought a smile to his lips. "God, I miss you."

"I miss you, too. I just went to bed about twenty minutes ago."

He heard movement, as if she was sitting up. "Why so late?"

"Just making sure I didn't forget anything. I also wanted to rearrange a list I had for tomorrow."

He smiled. "I love that about you."

"My neurosis?"

Hearing her smile warmed him all over. "Your organization. I just wanted to hear your voice again. I'm gonna be at the show all day tomorrow, so..."

"I know you are, and like I said earlier, you're gonna do great. I wish I could be there." She yawned, and Sage knew he should let her sleep.

"I won't keep you up. I love you, Kate. Can you text me when you get to your parents' house so I don't worry?"

"I'd rather talk to you than sleep anyway. Yes, I'll text, but you said earlier that you probably won't be checking your phone while you're at the show."

"I know, but I made arrangements with Siena. She's going to hold my phone and pass your messages to me. Otherwise I'll worry all afternoon." He was so excited about the painting that he debated telling her about it. She hadn't seen him painting it when he was in Belize and he'd decided to surprise her with it. Now that it was done and the likeness was so striking, he was going to take it to the show with him tomorrow. He liked the idea of feeling as though she were nearby. He wouldn't offer it for sale, of course, but he certainly could show her off to the world before hanging it above his fireplace so it would be ready when she came to see him.

"Okay. I'll be sure to text you. Oh, and I forgot to tell you. There was a scheduling issue and Caleb will be taking over my position for a while."

"He's a pretty quiet guy. Is he okay with that?"

"He's actually really excited. I think it will be good for him. It seems like there's a lot more to Caleb than he lets on, and I think you brought him out of his shell a little."

Sage was happy for Caleb, but he had more pressing questions in his mind. "I'm glad. Babe, I don't want to pressure you, but have you spoken to your parents? Do you know when you might come here?" He paced the floor, his nerves getting the better of him.

She yawned again. "Two or three days. I'll nail it down once I'm with them."

Two or three more days. Why did that seem like a lifetime? And why did Kate seem so nonchalant about it when he felt like he wanted to fight tooth and nail to get her here sooner? He knew he was overreacting. What was a few days, after all?

"Okay. I can't wait to see you."

"They're so happy that you and I have the same visions about helping others. They're really excited to meet you. I told them we'd try and come back the following weekend, if you don't mind."

"Anything you want. We can take a train down or we can fly; whatever you want. Get some sleep, babe, and enjoy your parents." He looked around his concrete-walled studio, which used to provide the perfect escape. Now it felt cold. Empty. Lonely. Kate couldn't arrive soon enough.

Chapter Thirty-Two

THE GALLERY WAS packed and had been since ten o'clock that morning. Joanie Remington was as relaxed as ever, in a flowing cotton skirt and a black, long-sleeved blouse. She stood before one of her sculptures, answering questions comfortably before a television camera. She had an easy nature about her, and she was immensely talented. As Sage watched her handle the interview as if she'd been doing them her whole life, when in reality, she'd spent very little time in the public's eye where her art was concerned, he was filled with pride. Between talking with patrons, taking pictures for the press, and handling interviews with the media, Sage hadn't had a minute to breathe. He was happy to stand off to the side for a minute, giving his mother the limelight.

"She's been planning for this for weeks, you know."

Sage pulled his shoulders back and stood up straighter at the sound of his father's voice, a reaction he'd had for as many years as he could remember. James Remington wore a dark suit and a starched, white button-down shirt, looking formal and important. His father always looked formal and important. Commanding. Sage glanced down at his dark slacks and loose linen shirt. It always took him a moment to look beyond the sharp edges of his father's personality, which made him bristle, and remember that beneath that harsh exterior was a loving man, even if he showed it differently than others might.

"I'm really glad we're getting to do this show together. In all the years I've been doing this, this is my first show with Mom."

"I think you're forgetting one." His father's eyes remained trained on his mother. "Your mother was exhibiting in the Mason Gallery when you were just a boy—seven or eight, maybe. You had been shadowing her in her studio for years by then. She took you and your artwork right along with her." He turned to face Sage and lifted his brows. "She was very proud of you. We both were."

Sage felt a pang in his heart as he tucked away the rare compliment. "I do remember that. I was never more proud as a kid than that afternoon." Sage was dying to get outside in the cool October afternoon, away from the stifling crowd, but based on the current state of affairs, it didn't appear he'd be getting a break anytime soon. He checked his watch. It was almost three. He should have heard from Kate by now.

"Have you seen Siena?" He scanned the crowd for his sister.

"She and Dex went to grab a bite. They should be back any minute. Jack and Savannah are here. They're in the room with that painting you brought back of Kate."

Sage's muscles tensed. This was the first time his father had mentioned Kate since Sage had come home. He waited for his father to say something about the painting. About the nonprofit. Hell, he waited for him to even acknowledge that he'd wanted to make a change in his life.

"I think I'll go find them."

It was his father's firm hand on his arm that stopped him from walking away. Sage looked down at the hand of the man who had raised him. He'd never once lifted a hand to any of his children. Sage was rooted to the floor.

"Stay."

One word. *A command.* Sage took a deep breath and clasped his hands in front of him to keep from removing his father's hand and making a scene. He clenched his jaw and focused on his mother as she wrapped up her interview.

"This business of yours. The well business. Please tell me your motivation behind it." His father released Sage's arm, but continued to stare straight ahead.

Suddenly Sage was eighteen again, trying to find the words to convince his father that he wasn't cut out for the military, which is where James Remington would have liked at least one of his children to end up. Jack had eventually become a Special Forces officer, but only after first going to a college of his choice, disappointing his father by refusing to even consider West Point. His father hadn't pushed Sage or his other siblings toward the military the way he'd pushed Jack, but the implication was understood. Sage had always been artistic, and his penchant for coloring outside the lines made him a bad candidate for anything regimented. The military would have been a grave mistake, and somewhere in his father's broad chest, Sage believed there was a heart that understood that.

He wasn't eighteen anymore, and as he turned to face his father, a new and different feeling came over him. He and Kate were about to take a significant step toward a future, and he had to stand up to his father and take a stance that would define him in his father's eyes as the confident, intelligent man he was. The gallery, however, was probably not the place for such a discussion to take place.

"Dad, let's go talk outside."

His father drew his brows together, then shot a look at his mother, who was heading their way with a warm smile on her lips. Her eyes darted from Sage to his father, and the edges of her smile drew down. Her eyebrows knitted together as she cast a stern, questioning gaze toward his father. Sage looked down, his gut clenching. All he wanted to do was find Siena and make sure Kate's flight had arrived safely, and now he was stuck dealing with whatever bullshit discussion his father felt was critical at that very second.

The sooner he got this over with, the better, and it was obvious that he wasn't going to be able to escape his father's scrutiny. *The hell with it.* He planted his legs and flexed his muscles, readying himself for the conversation. "Hydration Through Creation. HTC. That's what we're calling it."

"Why, exactly, are you doing it?"

His father held his stare.

Sage felt as though he were facing an opponent. He moved in close and spoke in a harsh whisper. "I don't want to do this here, but if you must...All this shit is great, Dad, but I want to do more. I want to make a difference in people's lives in a meaningful way. I want to experience the harshness of the world and then help to fix it." The words tumbled from his lips fast and heavy. He felt his mother's hand on his arm but could not tear his eyes from his father's. "We're not so different, Dad. Maybe our personalities are different. Hell, we're miles apart in that department, but you want me to be a good man. I want to be a good man in every way I can. Your definition of a good man is strong, responsible, and dedicated. That's what I am. Just not in the same realm of what you deem important."

His father opened his mouth to speak, and Sage cut him off, unable to turn off the anger that expanded his chest with heavy breaths.

"I'm everything you taught me to be, but my focus isn't politics. It's people. You've taught me to stand up for what I believe in. That's what I'm doing."

"Sage," his mother said.

Sage felt his nostrils flare, his jaw clench. He could not pry his attention from the man who was staring at him with an equally angry look.

"Sage," his mother said in a harsher whisper.

"One second," he snapped. "Go ahead, Dad. Get it out. Right here, right now. In front of all these people." When his father didn't answer, Sage did the unthinkable. He grabbed his father's arm and pulled him toward the room where the painting of Kate hung on the wall. *Emergence.* That's the name he'd given the painting. *An awakening.* Kate had awakened him in so many ways, from the love she inspired to helping him navigate the confusing depths of his life. He felt his father resist, and he held tight. He pulled his shoulders back and lifted his eyes to the painting.

"And I'm doing it with her."

His father shifted his eyes from the painting to Sage's hand on his arm. He peeled his fingers off of his suit coat, his eyes shifting to the crowd. No one seemed to be paying attention to the two of them.

"Son, I suggest that you take a deep breath now."

"You sugg—" Sage ran his hand through his hair.

"I didn't ask about the company to argue with you, but to tell you that I had a long talk with Jack about it." He looked across the room and nodded to Jack and Savannah.

How had he missed his six-foot-four brother and Savannah's long, fiery hair? *Jesus. Why the hell did you talk to them about this?*

"You're right, Sage. What you said to me when you were in Belize, and what Jack said to me about the person you are, it all hit home. I fought for our country. That wasn't my decision in the beginning. It was expected of me." He narrowed his eyes in Jack's direction again. "Jack had me take a good, hard look at you and your life. There isn't much difference between us, son. Not in the ways that matter."

Sage was breathing so hard he could barely comprehend what his father had said. He shot a look at Jack, arms crossed, powerful legs planted hip distance apart in his typical watchful pose. He lifted his chin toward Sage.

You did this for me.

Jack and his father had just repaired their own relationship after two difficult years, and now he'd gone to bat for Sage. Just as Jack had stood up for Sage, Sage was standing up for himself and Kate.

"Sage, I am not a risk taker the way you are."

His father spoke in a calm, even tone—so different from the gruff, judgmental tone Sage had expected—and it rattled his nerves.

"Are you kidding? You risked your life." Sage shook his head, still reeling with confusion.

"Yes. But I did it because it was expected of me. And then it was the man I had become. You're changing your whole life. Risking everything. Income, stability, your health. You're doing it out of the goodness of your heart, and you're ready to come up against me to do it. You're stronger, braver, than I could ever be."

Suddenly, Sage felt as if the air had been sucked from his lungs. *Strong? Brave?* His father's eyes softened; his thick brows relaxed.

330

"I could not be more proud of you, son."

Sage sucked in a breath. "You..." He'd waited his whole life for his father to appreciate him for who he was. Twenty-eight years of holding his breath when his father walked into a room came at him all at once. He felt something slide across his lower back to his waist. *A hand.*

You're proud of me.

"I've always been proud of you. Of the boy you were, so thoughtful and generous, and of the man you've become."

Always.

Sage was knocked completely off-kilter. He couldn't pull his thoughts together enough to focus. His eyes darted from his father to the picture of Kate. *Kate. Oh God, Kate. Did you get home okay?* He caught a glimpse of Jack moving toward him. The hand on his waist slipped away and his eyes drew back to the painting. *God, I miss you.*

His mother's voice sifted through the air. "Honey?"

His father's eyes shifted to the left.

"Mr. Remington?" A young blond reporter held a microphone at her waist, expectation in her blue eyes.

Sage tried to lift his lips into a smile but could not muster the mask. A lump had lodged itself in his throat.

"We'd like to interview you about this painting. *Emergence?* Do you have time?"

Emergence. *The painting of Kate. Kate. Shit. I need to find Siena. Get my phone. No. I need to leave. I need to find Kate.*

He cleared his throat to loosen the lump and find his voice. "Give...give me a minute. Please."

She nodded and stepped away.

Sage searched for the right words to say to his father. *I've waited my whole life...You finally see me for me. What the fuck took you so long?* When nothing felt right, he opened his arms and embraced him. Feeling his father's broad chest, the safety of his strong arms, the way, when he patted his back, it felt different. Prideful. *No. It doesn't feel different. It's felt that way all along. I was just too stubborn to see it.* The right words came to him then, and he drew back from his father's arms to look into his dark eyes.

He was the same man he'd always been, and now his father somehow looked different. Softer. Kinder. "Thank you, Dad."

His father nodded. A simple movement of his head, nothing more. He didn't offer a word. He didn't have to. He'd already given Sage the gift he'd waited for his whole life.

"You okay?"

He turned at Siena's voice. "Thank God. Gimme my phone." The curt tone was out before he could check it.

"Jeez." She dug it out of her purse.

Jack put a hand on Sage's shoulder. "That's some painting, Sage."

When he said, "Thanks, Jack," he was saying it for all Jack had done for him, and when Jack squeezed his shoulder, he knew he understood.

"That's what family's for," Jack said with a nod.

Sage checked his phone. No text from Kate. "I gotta get outta here." He didn't have a plan. He had Kate's parents' address and Kate's phone number, and that was enough. All Sage knew was that he'd waited long enough. This show was important—but not as important as Kate.

"You can't leave," Siena said in a fast whisper. "They're waiting to interview you. My friend Jordan is right there waiting for you." She pointed to the blond reporter.

Sage shot a glance at his father, whose arm rested across his mother's shoulder in a rare display of public affection. Was it that rare, or had he just paid more attention to the harsher side of him? The blond reporter approached his mother, and Sage pushed the thought aside. He saw Rush and Kurt come into the room and waved to them.

"I gotta call Kate. Have her interview Mom or Rush. Everyone loves Rush. Hell, have her interview Kurt. They're all newsworthy. Kate's plane should have landed almost two hours ago. I can't stay. I need to catch a train." *A train? Yes. A train.* What was he doing standing around in a gallery when he could be with Kate and her parents?

"There he is. I told you we'd find him." Dex and Ellie came into the room holding hands.

"Hi, Dex, Ellie. I'm sorry to run, but..." Sage looked around the room at his family, there to support him and his mother, and all he could do was think about seeing Kate. "I'm taking off."

"What? Why?" Dex looked handsome in his jeans and button-down shirt. He held tightly to Ellie's hand, which made Sage miss Kate even more.

"I can't wait another two or three days. I want to see—"

Dex and Ellie stepped to the side of the entrance. It took a second for Sage to realize that he wasn't dreaming. Kate stood in the doorway in a long-sleeved navy blue dress that stopped midthigh, her eyebrows knitted together, blinking repeatedly.

Tears stung Sage's eyes as the breath left his lungs. "Kate."

Jack reached for Kate's suitcases, which Sage hadn't noticed her holding. Kate nibbled on her lower lip, her cheeks flushed, her eyes damp. In two steps she was in his arms.

"Oh my God, I've missed you," he whispered against her cheek. In the next breath, his mouth was on hers in a deep, loving kiss. All of the emotion of the last week constricted his chest. He could barely breathe. She was there. Finally right there with him. He had to look into her eyes.

"You're here."

"I couldn't wait." Her body shook as she clung to him.

"You feel so good." He kissed her again, mildly aware of the people gathering around them, the flashes of the cameras, the murmurs of wonder. He didn't care how much of a spectacle they made. His world was finally righting itself again—maybe for the first time ever.

When they drew apart again, they were both breathing heavily, smiling like they'd just won the lottery. Sage wrapped his arm around her waist and held on tight.

"You're so damn beautiful. What about your parents?"

"They're coming for the weekend. I didn't want to wait to see you, so..." She shrugged, looking so damn adorable that Sage had to kiss her again.

Kate glanced around the room and quickly dropped her eyes. Sage realized that a crowd had formed around them: His family members stood close, strangers behind them, reporters taking pictures, scribbling on notepads.

He spoke to no one in particular. "This is my girlfriend, Kate."

Jordan, the blond reporter, spoke above the din of the crowd. "She's the focus of *Emergence*?"

"She *is* emergence," Sage replied.

Kate shifted her eyes to the painting and gasped. She shot a look at Sage. "When...?"

"In Belize, and I finished it here. It's going right in our living room." *Our living room.*

"Mr. Remington, can you answer a few questions now?" Jordan approached him.

Sage took Kate's hand and nodded proudly. "Now there's nothing I can't do."

"COME WITH US." Siena put her arm around Kate and guided her away from the crowd that had enveloped Sage after he was interviewed by Jordan and two other reporters.

Savannah held Kate's other arm, and Ellie flanked Savannah's other side. Both Siena and Savannah were several inches taller than Kate, and she felt vulnerable between them. She didn't want to leave Sage, but as they dragged her away, she looked over her shoulder and realized that it would be forever before he was free again. *Oh God. Will they give me hell for crashing Sage's opening?* She couldn't help it. After Sage had called the evening before, she had to see him. She just couldn't wait a few more days. She'd phoned her parents, who apparently held love in as high regard as helping others, which she'd never realized, and then she'd changed her flight arrangements. One look at the warm, excited smiles on the women's faces told her there was no way in hell they would give her a hard time about anything. They kept glancing at one another like they couldn't wait to hear juicy gossip. Kate didn't even know how to gossip. *Do I? Oh my God. I'm the gossip. They want the details about me and Sage.* For some reason that made her feel better, included. Now, as they brought her into a room in the back of the gallery and sat her on a couch between Savannah and Ellie, with Siena standing before them, arms crossed, her hand on her chin, Kate's stomach sank. *Oh, God, she's looking at me like she hates me already. I totally misjudged the situation.*

"So, Sage had no clue that you were coming?" Siena

asked.

"No." *Shit.*

"And you came straight from Belize?" Siena narrowed her eyes at Kate.

She nodded.

"Did you see his face?" Ellie put her hand over Kate's and squeezed. "I've never seen Sage that happy."

"You've got big ones," Siena said as she crouched before Kate and put her hand on her knee. "I mean, that's a long way, and what if...? I don't know. Anything could have gone wrong."

"Oh my God, Siena! Buzzkill much?" Savannah glared at her. She tossed her long auburn hair over her shoulder and draped her arm over Kate's shoulder. "Don't listen to her. It was incredibly romantic."

Siena hates me. She really hates me.

"Buzzkill? Oh my God. No, I'm so sorry, Kate." Siena's eyes softened, and the similarities between her and Sage came to life. The sincere smile, the light when it reached her eyes. "I love what you did, but I don't know if I'd ever have the guts to do it. I mean. Wow. When he kissed you, it took *my* breath away."

Kate breathed a sigh of relief. "I had to come here." Her eyes shifted to each of them, and she realized that her worries were unfounded. She might not have many female friends, but she knew the hungry-for-details look women got in their eyes, and she recognized it in theirs. "I know this is fast, and I know that you don't know me, but..."

Savannah pulled her close. "But we will. You're part of the family now. Sage said you're moving in."

Kate felt her cheeks flush. "That's the plan. I'm a little nervous. I mean, I've never spent time in the city, and I don't want to mess up his life, and I'm not a freeloader. I'm really not."

"Kate, would you stop? We're not judging you. If

you weren't a good person, Sage wouldn't have fallen in love with you." Siena looked at Savannah and Ellie. "Right?"

"No way. Sage sees right through people," Savannah added.

"X-ray vision." Ellie laughed. "And don't worry about messing up his life. Remington men are about the strongest men on earth."

"Hey, Braden men are pretty damn strong, too," Savannah said, flipping her hair over her shoulder.

"Yeah, so I've heard," Ellie said. "But I have yet to meet them."

"Who are the Braden men?" Kate asked.

The others exchanged a glance. "Sorry, you have a lot to catch up on," Siena explained. "Savannah's last name is Braden, and she's got five amazingly handsome, incredibly sweet brothers. And there's no doubt that the Bradens are strong. But they're a different type of strong, having grown up on a ranch. Hell, Rex is about the manliest cowboy I've ever met." Siena sighed.

"But Jade, Rex's significant other, would kick any girl's ass if she went near him, so let's not go down that road," Savannah added.

Siena continued. "Anyway, Sage is so different from my other brothers. He's always been more serious, more contemplative about life. I'm glad he found someone who believes in the same things he does. He told us all about Hydration Through Creation. He's really excited about it, and about you, Kate. We all are. We're happy for you."

"You are?" Relief swept through her.

"Yes! Until Savannah and Ellie came along, it was just me and my brothers. Do you have any idea what it's like to grow up with all those boys in the house?" Siena rolled her eyes.

"I do," Savannah said. "I love my brothers, but there's nothing like having sisters. I mean, I have sisters-in-law, and Siena and Ellie, who, well..." Savannah looked from one to the other. She leaned in close to Kate and whispered, "I have a secret that I'm trying really hard not to blurt out."

The excitement in Savannah's green eyes was contagious. "A secret?" *A secret!* It had been ages since she'd shared secrets with a friend. Hell, it had been ages since she'd had friends. The warmth of Savannah, Siena, and Ellie enveloped her, and her anxiety fell away. Kate felt like she was at a slumber party that she never wanted to leave.

"Savannah! Did you and Jack finally set a date?" Siena jumped to her feet.

"I can't say. I promised I wouldn't say anything until he told your mom."

"His mom already knows."

They all turned toward Joanie Remington's voice. "You're having a hen party with our newest hen and no one invited me?" Sage's mother flashed a smile at Savannah. "Jack just told me, and I couldn't be happier."

Savannah rose and embraced her. "Me too. I'm so excited, and I wanted to tell you right after we set the date, but he wanted to tell you in person."

"I'm glad he did, but now..." Joanie put her arm around Siena, and Ellie pulled Kate to her feet and draped an arm over her shoulder as Joanie and the others huddled together. "We need to plan a bridal shower!"

Kate loved the warmth that passed between Siena and Savannah with nothing more than a glance, and the way Siena reached for Ellie's hand when her mother mentioned the bridal shower. She'd never been part of such a close group of women before, and as Joanie reached for Kate's hand, she had to swallow past her longing to remain a part of it.

"Kate." Her voice was tender as she patted Kate's hand. "Sage has told me so much about you. I knew that first time we Skyped, when I saw that gleam in my son's eyes as he pulled you close and introduced us, that his heart had opened up to you. I hope we can spend time getting to know each other."

Don't cry. Don't cry. Now she knew why Sage was such a good man. How could he not be, surrounded by this type of love? "I...I look forward to it." *More than you could ever know.*

Chapter Thirty-Three

SAGE HAD DREAMED of this moment since he'd returned from Belize. He unlocked the door to his town house and threw the door open; then he turned to Kate, and he had to take a moment to catch his breath. He couldn't believe she was there beside him, looking up at him through her thick lashes, a nervous smile on her lips.

"Welcome home."

"Home."

He nodded. "Home. Our home." With his hand on the small of her back, she walked inside. Sage carried in her bags and set them by the front door. He watched her eyes rove from the overstuffed blue sofa, covered with colorful, unmatched pillows, to the leather recliner and the stack of books beside it. *I should have put those away.*

Kate took a step forward and ran her hand along the cherrywood railing that led up to the second level, where the kitchen was tucked out of sight. A dining room table filled the balcony area that overlooked the living room. She reached for Sage's hand and walked with him toward the fireplace, running her eyes over the plants set atop the built-in bookshelves to its left. She followed the foliage down the edges of the shelves.

"I realized after I got home that I should probably trim those back. They're kinda jungle-ish, aren't they?"

"I love them." She picked up a frame from the mantel and sucked in a breath.

"It's one of the pictures Luce took at breakfast, remember?"

She nodded and ran her fingers over their smiling faces. "You've already had it printed and framed."

"All of them. There are some upstairs, blown up larger, and a few in the bedroom."

"Oh, Sage. I love that you did that." She wrapped her arms around his waist and pressed her cheek against him.

She felt so good against him. *God, I missed you.* "The painting of you will go right above the fireplace—that is, if you don't mind."

She looked around the living room again, and her eyes caught on the glass doors that led to the garden in his backyard; then they lifted to the glass panels that spanned the back of the room and arced over the far end of the living room, giving it a greenhouse feel.

"Sage," she said in one long breath as she walked toward the doors. "Oh my gosh."

He picked up a remote control from a sofa table by the wall and pressed a button. The garden illuminated from the ground up, and Kate gasped another breath. "You must spend hours out there."

"I always thought I would, but I never made the time." He wrapped his arms around her from behind and kissed the side of her neck. "But I will now."

She turned in to him, and he lowered his mouth to hers and kissed her until he couldn't remember a time when she hadn't been in his arms. When they drew

342

apart, she was looking at him with all the love and all the desire that swelled within him. Jack's words whispered to him: *You just liked what you were doing more than you liked who was waiting for you*, and Sage knew, without a doubt, that with Kate in his life, he'd make the time to do all the things he always thought he would but had never done. Loving her like she'd never been loved before was on the top of his list.

The End

Please enjoy a preview of the next
Love in Bloom novel

Flames of
LOVE

The Remingtons, Book Three

Love in Bloom Series

Melissa Foster

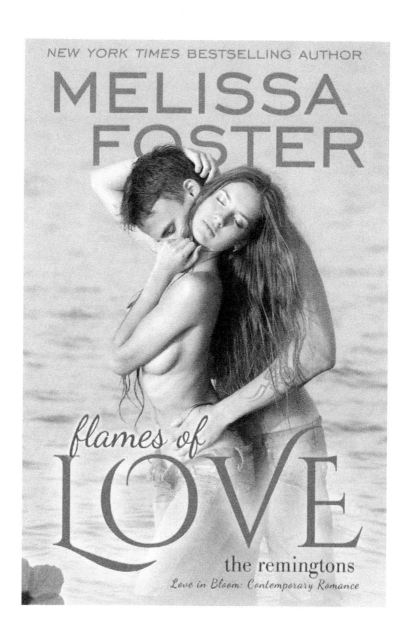

NEW YORK TIMES BESTSELLING AUTHOR

MELISSA FOSTER

flames of LOVE

the remingtons

Love in Bloom: Contemporary Romance

Chapter One

SIX INCHES OF fresh snow covered the roads. Even with the windshield wipers set to high, Cash Ryder could barely see a few feet in front of the all-terrain vehicle he'd borrowed from his buddy Tommy. The roads appeared empty, but he knew that in a storm like this one, there could be fifty cars just outside his limited range of visibility. It was as if New York had been swallowed by snow, and Cash wondered how many accidents the local fire department would have to deal with. As a firefighter, he'd seen it all, from overconfident teens skidding into trees to truckers unable to stop their massive rigs from rumbling over the tops of cars that had collided on black ice. Cash was headed to his eldest brother Duke's house, just outside of New York City, and the storm had come out of nowhere. He needed a break from the city. Hell, he needed a break from life. Visiting his brother for the evening had seemed like the perfect escape. He hadn't seen him for a few months, and the last time they'd been together, Cash's emotions had been raw. He'd laid into Duke—and everyone else who was in his path—

347

with a venomous rage that even he hadn't known he possessed. Luckily, Duke wasn't a grudge holder. He understood that even the most prepared person could be knocked sideways on occasion, and Cash knew that Duke would always be there for him.

He gritted his teeth as memories of the tragic day that completely fucked with his mind played through his head like a bad rerun. His pulse sped up, chased by full-body chills. Sweat beaded his brow despite the cold. *Shit. I couldn't get to the guy.* He tried to comfort himself with the last, and most difficult, reminder the therapist his chief had told him to speak with had given him. The one she felt was the most important—and the one that he could barely stomach. *It wasn't my fault.*

Skid marks across the fresh snow pulled him from the painful thoughts. Not just skid marks, but thick trails, as if a car had skidded sideways. He eased up on the gas and craned his neck, squinting into the storm. *Shit. Definitely recent. Definitely over the edge of the mountain.* He pulled onto the shoulder, cursing under his breath, and pulled his woolen cap over his head, zipped his parka, and slid his hands into his thick gloves. He pulled out his cell phone and reported the accident to 911. Then he grabbed the emergency bag that contained a first-aid kit, a glass-breaking tool, and other rescue items he never left home without and headed into the storm.

SIENA REMINGTON'S TEETH chattered as she struggled against the airbag pressed against her chest. *Okay. Okay. Calm down.* Wasn't that the key to surviving? Remaining calm? Her heart slammed against her ribs, which ached from the impact of the accident. She tried to get her bearings, but all she could see was white. The car leaned to the right, and she had no way of knowing if she was on the edge of a precipice or on solid ground. She hadn't seen anyone on the roads, and she'd skidded off the pavement ten minutes ago. She hadn't even told her friend Willow that she'd left the city and was on her way. *Oh God.* Her cell phone rang. She scanned the floor. *Goddamn phone.* She hadn't even reached for it when it rang as she was driving. She'd glanced at it—for a second, maybe two—and then *wham!* Her car was skidding off the road toward the edge of the mountain. Now the frigging phone was nowhere in sight. *And I'm going to die out here in bumfuck New York. Shit. Shit. Shit.*

"Hey, you all right in there?"

A man's deep voice broke through her worry. "Yes! Help me. Please!" *Oh, thank God.* "Hurry. Please hurry." She grabbed her hat from her pocket and pulled it down low over her head, debating braving the conditions and getting out of her car. She couldn't remember ever being so cold.

A gloved hand cleared the snow from her window; then a set of eyes pressed close, one hand shielding them as the window fogged from his breath. Siena gasped a breath before realizing that any sane person would be covered up in this weather. Her heartbeat picked up as she stared at the mask that covered everything but a swatch of skin around serious, dark eyes. *Sexy dark eyes, filled with serious concern. Jesus, what am I thinking?*

"Please help me." She struggled with her seat belt.

"Are you hurt? Injured in any way?"

Siena moved her legs and arms. "No. I don't think so."

"Good. Your car is sideways." His voice was muffled behind the mask and the window. "It's stable, but when I open this door, it could jostle it into a slide, so I want to get you out as fast as possible. Can you get out of your seat belt?"

She pulled at the buckle. "Yes. Yes, I think I can." *Oh God. Please get me out. Sideways?* "A slide? Like I could slide off the mountain?" Tears pressed at her eyes.

He looked away, then back through the window. "I don't think so. You're on a pretty flat spot. Got the seat belt off?"

"Yes. Wait. You don't *think* so? What if the car slides? Am I near a big drop? Jesus, I don't want to die."

His eyes narrowed. "Calm down," he commanded.

Siena clenched her chattering teeth.

"I'm a firefighter. I can get you out, but you have to remain calm. Can you do that?"

She nodded. *A firefighter. Thank God. Hurry. Hurry.*

He didn't seem to struggle with the door. He opened it slowly, and his powerful arm circled her shoulder. "I've got you. Now slide your legs over and out of the car. You sure you're not injured?"

She felt safer just knowing she wasn't alone, but as she stepped from the car onto the steep incline, she slipped and reached for the first thing she could hang on to—him. She clung to the man's thick parka as he pulled her away from the car, his arms circling her. Her legs began to shake. Or maybe they'd been shaking the whole time and she just hadn't realized it.

"You're okay. I've got you." His voice soothed her.

He did have her. His body was so big, it practically consumed her. She opened her mouth to speak, but her jaw was shaking too much to form any words. She nodded again, looking down to keep the snow from her eyes.

"I've gotta get you up there." He pointed to the road. "The emergency crew should be here soon, but I want to get you into my truck and warm."

It was snowing so hard she could barely make out the road at the top of the hill. Her cute Burberry coat did nothing to warm her from the cold that was quickly settling into her bones. His masculine scent permeated her fear as he pressed his body against her, and the combination of being safe in his arms and his warm, earthy scent comforted her. She climbed up the bank, still within his grasp. Every time she lost her footing, he held her up.

"You've got it. That's it."

She clung to his encouragement like a lifeline.

"That's it. Take your time. I'm right here."

Back on the road, she focused on the headlights from his vehicle. *Safe. I'm safe.*

"Let's get you into the truck."

The tracks from her car were almost completely buried beneath fresh snow. If he hadn't come along, she would probably still be down there.

"Th-thank...you," she managed. He'd spoken with such care, so different from the men she socialized with. They'd never brave a blizzard to rescue her. She was sick of those kinds of men. They treated her like she was stupid and easy just because she was pretty. She wanted to be loved and cherished, romanced, not taken out to dinner with the expectation of sex. She didn't want to be wined and dined with diamonds on every finger. She wanted a man who would look at her the way her brothers looked at their girlfriends and fiancées. Her brothers would go to the ends of the earth to rescue her or their girlfriends, no matter what the risk. *Romance. Yes, that's what I want.* How much more romantic could things get than being rescued by a mysterious stranger in the middle of a snowstorm? She allowed herself to fantasize about it for a moment, giving herself something to focus on besides the fact that she'd just slid fifty feet down an embankment and had nearly frozen to death. As if the accident might have almost been worth it. As if fate had a hand in it.

The man settled Siena into the passenger seat, and

she saw his eyes darken, growing more serious. Then he climbed into the driver's seat, sighed, and cranked the heat.

She took off her thin leather gloves and put her bare hands in front of the heater. "Ahh. That's so much better." Her shaking calmed to a mild tremble. "Thank you for helping me."

He shifted his eyes to hers. "I have to go back for my bag. I called 911, so the emergency crew should be here soon. Stay here, okay?" He climbed from the truck, leaving Siena to nod after him.

Now that she was out of danger, reality came rushing back to her. She was supposed to be at her friend Willow's parents' house over an hour ago. *Damn it.* She needed to call Willow. She waited for her rescuer to return, thankful for the warmth. Twenty minutes later, she wondered what was taking him so long. She could probably climb down and get her phone herself instead of making him do everything for her and, she realized, she also needed to retrieve her purse. She wasn't hurt, and now that she knew she wasn't going to die, she wasn't as frightened. Siena put her gloves back on and trudged through the thick snow to the edge of the road, shivering and regretting her decision. She peered over the edge of the mountain but didn't see the guy anywhere.

"I told you to wait in the truck." His stern voice came from nowhere. "Visibility is near zero. If a car comes by, you could be killed."

She strained to see him through the falling snow.

"I'm right here." He climbed up over the edge of the road with a bag strapped to his back. "Don't you get how dangerous these conditions are?" He grabbed her arm and dragged her back toward the truck.

Too fucking sexy, even without being able to see his face, and a big-ass chip on his shoulder. Fantasy dead.

Moving on. Except her heart wasn't moving on. It hammered against her chest.

Siena pulled her arm from his grasp. "I have to get my purse."

"I'll get it."

"I need my phone."

He opened the truck door and shoved her in, then pinned her to the seat with his dark, sexy stare. "Use mine."

She looked down at his thick gloves, one on her thigh, one on her arm, keeping her from leaving the truck. A flash of fear shot through her. She didn't know him, and she was no match for his strength. What if he wasn't a firefighter at all? She took a deep breath. If he wasn't there to help, why had he left her alone in the truck? Wouldn't he have taken her off to some kind of rape-and-pillage shack in the woods somewhere?

I'm being stupid. Of course he's here to help.

She pushed aside the thoughts and followed her gut instinct. Something in his eyes made her feel he was trustworthy, although she definitely wasn't used to being told what to do. Siena was one of New York's top fashion models. Men lavished her with gifts and went to great lengths to get her attention. She didn't even like being lavished by the wealthy suitors who pursued her, but she definitely preferred that to the attitude-ridden rescuer before her. She dropped her eyes to his broad shoulders, square as the day was long, and she could almost hear the hot-man-on-the-premises warning bells go off in her head.

There's one hell of a body beneath that parka. She trembled again, but she couldn't tell if it was from the cold or the thought.

She narrowed her eyes, scrutinizing his goddamn sexy eyes again. *Look away. Just look away.*

His eyebrows drew together and scanned her face

as intently as she had been scrutinizing his. The concern she'd seen earlier had vanished, replaced with something harder. Colder.

"What's your name?" His voice was gruff.

She tugged off her hat, challenging him with a hard stare. "Siena Remington." *That's right.* The *Siena Remington.* Her snooty thought was wasted. By the look in his eyes, it was clear that he had no idea who Siena Remington was.

"Well, Siena Remington, I'm Cash Ryder. Didn't it occur to you to put chains on your tires? Or maybe to skip your evening drive altogether?" He pulled his hat off, sending his dirty-blond hair tumbling down over his forehead. It brushed his lashes, softening his look as he raked his eyes down her trembling body.

Her heartbeat sped up again. He needed a trim and a shave, and she wished he'd put his hat back on. It was a lot easier matching his attitude when she didn't know for sure how hot he was.

"Or maybe you couldn't wait to show off your new designer jacket?" He smirked.

She pulled her hat back on, anger brewing in her belly. "It's a rental car." No way did she just almost die miles from home and then get rescued by a guy who looked like Chris Hemsworth and had a chip on his shoulder as big as Alec Baldwin.

"Why are *you* out in this mess?" She was shivering inside the truck and he was solid as a rock outside, snow piling up on his shoulders. *Of course he is. All that anger in his blood must keep him warm.*

He narrowed his eyes again. "Visiting my brother." He shook his head. "Didn't you think twice when you saw the snow?"

"I didn't know it was going to be this bad. It wasn't this bad in the city." She slid from the truck to her feet and stood in front of him. Jesus, he was tall. And so damn close to her that she could feel his thighs pressing against hers.

He shot her a look. "Where are you going?"

"Walking."

He grabbed her arm. "Oh no, you're not. I didn't just save your ass to have you die of hypothermia or get run over by a car." He wrapped a powerful arm around her waist and lifted her back into the truck. "Close"—he locked eyes with her—"the door."

"No."

"Do you *want* to die in the cold?"

She pressed her lips together. "I'm not going to be the damsel in distress for some cocky firefighter to brag about rescuing." She wiped the snow from her jeans where it had blown in through the open door. Damn, it was cold. And he was so damn hot, and such an ass, that she wanted to kiss him and smack him in equal measure.

He leaned in to the truck, his face an inch from hers. His eyes darkened to nearly black, and a grin spread across his lips.

Siena could barely breathe. She tried to blink away the heat that rolled off him in waves.

"I'm shutting the door," he said in a seductive tone, as if he'd said, *I can't wait to lick every inch of you.*

Her whole body shuddered, and she wished her teeth would stop chattering, though she had a feeling it was nerves more than the cold causing it. "I'll...call..." *Shit. Who can I call?* "One of my brothers to get me."

"I already called 911, but I guess they're overwhelmed with calls tonight." He pressed his gorgeous mouth into a tight line, then leaned in close again. "You would make someone else come out in these conditions and risk their life when I'm already here, wouldn't you?"

Yes! No! Shit, how did you make me sound so selfish?

She slammed her back against the seat and stared straight ahead, steeling herself for what was sure to be the ride from hell back to her apartment.

(End of Sneak Peek)
To continue reading, be sure to pick up the next
LOVE IN BLOOM release:

FLAMES OF LOVE, *The Remingtons*, Book Three
Love in Bloom series, Book Twelve

LOVE IN BLOOM
is a contemporary romance series
featuring several close-knit families
Check online retailers for availability

SNOW SISTERS

Sisters in Love
Sisters in Bloom
Sisters in White

THE BRADENS

Lovers at Heart
Destined for Love
Friendship on Fire
Sea of Love
Bursting with Love
Hearts at Play

THE REMINGTONS

Game of Love
Stroke of Love
Flames of Love
Slope of Love
Read, Write, Love

MORE BRADENS COMING SOON

Taken by Love
Fated for Love
Romancing my Love
Flirting with Love
Dreaming of Love
Crashing into Love

Acknowledgments

Thank you to my fans and friends who continue to support and inspire my writing. I enjoy writing as much as you enjoy reading, so please keep your emails and social media messages coming. I appreciate hearing from you.

A special thank you to Russell Blake for giving me Punta Palacia, the name of Sage and Kate's fictional world, and to Monica Hulke Abraham for taking part in a Facebook outreach contest and coming up with the perfect name for Sage's company, Hydration Through Creation. Many thanks to Rebecca Lipman for sharing her Peace Corps experience with me. I have taken many creative liberties in the story with regard to AIA, and those changes are not a reflection of misunderstanding but rather creative need.

The support of the members of Team Pay-It-Forward, the blogging community, Kathleen Shoop, and my sisters-at-heart, the volunteers of the World Literary Café, is endless. Thank you all. It's great to be in the trenches with such warm and supportive friends.

My editorial team never fails to amaze me. Tremendous gratitude goes to Kristen Weber, Penina Lopez, Jenna Bagnini, Juliette Hill, and Marlene Engel. Enormous gratitude goes to my cover designer, Natasha Brown, and my formatter, Clare Ayala, for their endless patience and expertise.

This has been a tremendously busy year for me and my family, and I could not focus on my writing if not for their support and understanding. Thanks, guys. I love you more than chocolate (even though I'll fight you for the Snickers bar every time). You own my heart and I adore you.

Melissa Foster is a *New York Times* and *USA Today* bestselling and award-winning author. Her books have been recommended by *USA Today's* book blog, *Hagerstown* magazine, *The Patriot*, and several other print venues. She is the founder of the Women's Nest, a social and support community for women, and the World Literary Café. When she's not writing, Melissa helps authors navigate the publishing industry through her author training programs on Fostering Success. Melissa also hosts Aspiring Authors contests for children, and has painted and donated several murals to the Hospital for Sick Children in Washington, DC.

Visit Melissa on her website or chat with her on The Women's Nest or social media. Melissa enjoys discussing her books with book clubs and reader groups and welcomes an invitation to your event.

Melissa's books are available through most online retailers.

www.MelissaFoster.com

CPSIA information can be obtained
at www.ICGtesting.com
Printed in the USA
BVOW08s1210080617
486315BV00001BA/15/P